DON'T TURN YOUR BACK II

INTERVIEW WITH A DEMON

James E. Stodghill Jr.

Copyright © 2023 **StodghillWorks**

All rights reserved. No part of this publication may be reproduced, distributed, or transmitted in any form or by any means, including photocopying, recording, or other electronic or mechanical methods, without the prior written permission of the publisher, except in the case of brief quotations embodied in critical reviews and certain other noncommercial uses permitted by copyright law. For permission requests, write to the publisher, addressed "Attention: Book Rights and Permission," at the address below.

Published in the United States of America

ISBN 978-1-959173-74-8 (SC)

StodghillWorks
1443 Kings Point Way SW,
Conyers, GA 30094
stodghillworks@aol.com

Order Information and Rights Permission:

Quantity sales. Special discounts might be available on quantity purchases by corporations, associations, and others. For details, contact the publisher at the address above.

For Book Rights Adaptation and other Rights Permission. Call us at toll-free 1-678-358-3565 or send us an email at stodghillworks@aol.com.

Dedication

This book is dedicated to my wonderful wife, Marie Stodghill, and our marriage. She is my precious gift from God. God Himself gave me the companion that I had been praying for, and that He had prepared especially for me for this season in my life.

When we were married, we acknowledged Jesus as the center of our marriage and as the bond that holds us together. His love for us and our love for each other causes our relationship to be stable and secure. I love her as Jesus loves the church.

Through the power of the Holy Spirit we will always be faithful to God and each other and we will fulfill over destiny in Christ Jesus.

Acknowledgments

I am tremendously grateful to Mr. Calvin Pender and Mr. Edward Moon for their friendship and encouragement. Their enjoyment of book one, "Don't Turn Your Back," and their expectation of this book, the sequel, was highly motivational. They read and reviewed the first draft of this book. They are both my number one fan.

I also want to acknowledge my sister in the Lord, Pastor Portia Minter. She also enjoyed book one. Without knowing it, she inspired the focus on demons in this book. Because she represents my target audience, Christians, I wanted to fictionally portray the reality of demons in a more visible way. In the book of Luke, demons recognized and spoke with Jesus. In my book, I wanted Rev. Zackery to see and to speak to demons and thereby suggest to the readers how they should learn to deal with their demons. I don't know who said it first, but there is a cliché that says: "Don't let the devil ride with you, cause he might want to drive."

I used to think that was true. Now I know better. There is no might about it. If you let him ride, he will, most definitely, without a doubt, try to drive.

Additionally, I want to thank my wife, Marie, for being a constant motivating force in my life, for telling me daily how proud she is of me, for taking such good care of me that I am in need of nothing, and for supporting me in every aspect of the creation of this manuscript.

Finally, and most importantly, I want to acknowledge Jesus. One of the main focuses of His ministry was shining a light on the presence of demons and casting them out. Just as it says in Ephesians 6:12:

For we wrestle not against flesh and blood, but against principalities, against powers, against the rulers of the darkness of this world, against spiritual wickedness in high places.

Therefore, my goal is to remind the reader that demons, demonic forces, and the devil are still active and must be recognized and fought.

Contents

Chapter 1	The Safe Is Not Safe	1
Chapter 2	The Goodbyes	3
Chapter 3	The Battle for the Book	17
Chapter 4	The Managers Meeting	27
Chapter 5	Demons in The House	30
Chapter 6	Ditched	35
Chapter 7	The Interview Begins	37
Chapter 8	Home Sweet Home	45
Chapter 9	The Strategy Revealed	54
Chapter 10	The Awakening	59
Chapter 11	Bad Billy	66
Chapter 12	Cooling Off in Jail	74
Chapter 13	The Reunion	78
Chapter 14	The Setup	101
Chapter 15	The Release	103
Chapter 16	Taken Hostage	106
Chapter 17	Salvation at a Cost	119
Chapter 18	The Vision	138
Chapter 19	Faceoff	143
Chapter 20	Billy Returns	148

Chapter 21	The Break in	157
Chapter 22	The Big Barn	159
Chapter 23	The Fish of Gold	169
Chapter 24	A New Ally	181
Chapter 25	The Betrayal	186
Chapter 26	The Body Count	192
Chapter 27	Body Guard	195
Chapter 28	Hang-em High	207
Chapter 29	Final Preparations	215
Chapter 30	Bubbles	221
Chapter 31	What Do I Do	223
Chapter 32	The Unforeseen	225
Chapter 33	One Last Time	231
Chapter 34	Caught in the Act	234
Chapter 35	Keep a Low Profile	240
Chapter 36	Spotted	244
Chapter 37	The Ambush	248
Chapter 38	The Ceremony	253
Chapter 39	The Burning	276
Chapter 40	The Introduction	281
Chapter 41	The Surprise	291

CHAPTER 1
THE SAFE IS NOT SAFE

Four people stood on the South River Bridge in the sights of binoculars. Someone was watching as a small safe was dropped over the side into the waters below. The binoculars followed the group as they left the bridge and got into a car at the edge of the bridge. When the car had pulled off, the sights of the binoculars returned to the spot in the river where the safe had gone into the water.

There in the wooded area above the bridge, a man lowered the binoculars. He was a slim man, almost six feet tall, with black hair, blue eyes, and a beard. He turned to his left, looked down the road, and raised the binoculars again. There in his sights was a woman jogging toward the bridge. He estimated she was about five feet tall. Her blond ponytail bouncing in the air behind her petite fine body, tightly covered by a pink and black spandex running suit. His heart rate began to soar. His breathing became heavy. He felt along his belt until he touched the handle of his hunting knife. He reached down. At his feet, he picked up a roll of duct tape. He was late. He should have been in position by now.

"Let's go, Billy boy," he whispered to himself.

He hurried down the hill through the trees, to intercept the unsuspecting jogger. When he got to the bottom of the hill, he hid behind his designated tree and waited.

'She should have gotten here by now,' he thought. He peeped out from behind the tree and looked down the road. She was not there. He turned around and leaned out. There she was going over the bridge. He leaned back against the tree and closed his eyes. Before long, his heart rate and breathing were back to normal. He stuck the duct tape into his jacket pocket and made his way down the bank to the edge of the water under the bridge. He had to find this thing that had kept him from his prey. He stripped down to his underwear, and quickly jumped into the water. The water was freezing so he swam as fast as he could to the spot where he thought the safe was. He went under. The water was not that deep because there had not been any rain in several weeks. When he came up, he had the safe. He side-stroked to the bank. Before long he was fully dressed, walking to his car that was hidden in the trees next to the road.

Chapter 2
The Goodbyes

(Saturday morning, 9:00 am)

The four silent soldiers got out of the car and walked to Reverend Zackery's brother's house. They all felt they had been in a long, hard-fought battle. Pam felt an ever-increasing strength that she had never felt before. Her sorrow over the death of her aunt was fading too fast. She could feel her facial muscles tightening and her sight was becoming more piercing. She began noticing everything as her focus went rapidly from one item to the next.

Dave, on the other hand, was beginning to become overwhelmed by all that was waiting for him, that he had to deal with, in the days ahead. He knew his manager, Mr. Monroe, was going to be very upset about him being days late for the conference. He didn't know if he was going to have a job. He didn't know if he would find his wife in bed with the insurance man when he got home. He didn't know if he wanted to stay married, if he still loved her, or if he ever loved her. He didn't even know if he was going to be able to stop himself from getting a gun and killing the insurance man.

Jason was still angry. He wanted Tamera to die. Her eternal prison cell was not enough punishment for him. In his mind, he kept seeing his grandmother's burned body. It was as if there were weights on his eyebrows. As he walked into the house, he tried to force a smile on his face, but he couldn't. Reverend Zackery, holding open the door, patted him on his back as he walked by.

"Go on in the kitchen and have a seat. We can eat while we talk. There's a few things we need to talk about before y'all leave," Reverend Zackery said. They all sat at the table. "The grits are in the crock pot. They should be ready. It won't take but a few minutes to do the bacon and eggs." Rev. Zackery walked to the China cabinet, reached into his coat pocket, pulled out his long barrowed pistol and placed it on top of the cabinet.

"What happened to the brains?" Dave asked as he watched Rev. Zackery place the pistol on top of the cabinet. "I'm going to need some extra brains to deal with what I've got to deal with when I get home, even if they are pig brains. A pig could think better than me, right now."

"Yeah, I got you covered, Dave. Don't worry. Everything will work out. You're not the same man that you were. God allowed you to go through this to show you some things."

"He showed me some things, all right." Dave covered his eyes as he thought about his wife and the insurance man in bed. "I just wish I could stop seeing it."

"Would you rather be in the dark," Rev Zackery interrupted. "Think about it, now you know the truth. The truth is the light. Now you can see clearly and now you can make wise decisions. Let the love of God lead you. God took you through all this, but it wasn't just so you can see that your wife was cheating on you. He wanted you to see yourself and He wanted you to see Him. He's with you now. Just trust Him."

"Ok reverend, "Dave said. "Are those brains ready yet?"

"Everything's done." Reverend Zackery was about to put Dave's plate down on the table, then he stopped. "Let's pray." Everyone closed their eyes but Pam. "Lord, bless this food and all of us who are eating it. In Jesus name I pray. Amen"

Dave started eating as soon as the plate hit the table. Reverend Zackery put the other plates down and everyone at the table except Pam began to eat.

"Aren't you eating, Reverend Zackery?" Pam said as she stopped her fork filled with eggs at her lips. Her eyes looked over his facial features.

"No. I have decided to fast. I need to hear from the lord." Reverend Zackery paused. "The food is safe to eat, Pam."

Everyone looked at Pam who was staring sternly at Reverend Zackery. Pam shook her head to snap herself out of her trance. "I'm sorry Reverend Zackery." Pam normal expression came back. "I have been feeling so funny ever since we left the bridge. I can't explain it. It's just weird." She began to eat.

"That's why I'm fasting. I know that I need to pray for each of you and myself. We all have been though a lot, but we still got a lot to deal with. Dave has already talked about his issues. Pam, you're changing emotionally and it's probably the results of your twin sister. I noticed that her powers were reduced when you used yours. Maybe now that she is incapacitated, you are getting all of her powers. If so, you will have to learn how to control it. I will have to pray hard over that. Finally, Jason."

"You don't have to pray for me. I'm good," Jason snapped.

Everyone in the room was shocked by the amount of anger that had been in his face.

"Yes, that's right son. You're good," Reverend Zackery said. "However, everybody needs prayer, so I'll include you in my prayers, too."

"Whatever," Jason murmured. "I just want to get this funeral over with."

"I'm glad you mentioned the funeral. There's something you need to know," Rev. Zackery said excitedly.

"What's that reverend," said looking up at Rev. Zackery.

"Your grandmother came to see me about a month ago." As Reverend Zackery began to tell them what happened, he began to visualize what happen that night.

It is now a month before. Rev. Zackery was sitting in his recliner when he heard a knock at the door.

Rev. Zackery pulled his pistol from the desk drawer and walked cautiously toward the door. "Who is it?"

"It's Ma'amie Scott, reverend. I'm alone. You won't need the pistol."

Rev. Zackery opened the door slightly wondering how she knew he had his pistol. "My needs, my pistol, my decision, what can I do for you?"

"May I come in? I want to make funeral arrangements."

"Funeral arrangements?" Rev. Zackery ask suspiciously. "Who is the funeral for?" He opened the door and let her in.

She walked to the sofa. "It's for me."

"You!" Rev. Zackery scouted. "Why would **you** want **me** to make funeral arrangements for **you**. You are not a believer and I have never seen you at my church, and you're the root lady."

"So, you know who I am?"

"Everybody in Tipton knows Miss Ma'amie or at least has heard a story about something you have done." Rev. Zackery frowned, walked to his desk, and laid his pistol down. "So, what are you really up to?"

"Look Rev. Zackery, a few weeks ago, I found out that I'm going to die real soon. So, I started reading the bible again." She paused to see his reaction. "Yes, my mama used to read the bible to me when I was a little girl. She died when I was little, but I remember her funeral and what the preacher said."

"What did the preacher say?" Rev. Zackery was still frowning.

"He said I'd see her again, in heaven."

"Yeah, if she was a believer, she is in heaven, but you, on the other hand, are headed in the opposite direction. So, if you see her again, it will only be because your mama didn't make it to heaven, cause hell is where you're going."

"Well, I was reading in the bible where Jesus died for all my sins. It said all I had to do was repent, confess, and believe, then I would be saved, and I would go to heaven."

"Yeah, I know that's what it says, but it also says you must be born again, and only the pure in heart shall see God." Rev. Zackery stopped. He walked up to her and put his face close to hers. "While you are here, don't touch nothing, and don't take nothing out of this house."

"Well can I at least sit down?"

"No! You came here to put roots on me, didn't you?"

"Why would you think something like that?"

"Cause, you're a root lady. That's what root lady's do. Cause I'm taking your customers and cause I'm putting you out of business."

"On the contrary, you're the reason I have as much business as I do," Ma'amie was getting angry. "Most of my customers are members of your church."

"You're a liar, just like your father, the devil," Rev. Zackery folded his arms. "Just last week, one of my deacons, Paul Crowder came to me and repented for going to see you. He said he was never going back."

"Well, I hate to bust your little sanctified bubble, but he came back day before yesterday. You see about two weeks ago, he paid me to put roots on his mother-in-law. Then when she got sick, he probably felt guilty, and that's when he came to see you. Well, day before yesterday he came back to see me. He paid me again. This time it was to take the roots off her. So, you see reverend, you're good for my business and I'm good for yours."

"So, you do admit that you put roots on his mother-in-law," Rev. Zackery said pointing his finger in her face.

"I didn't put nothing on her. He put them on her."

"Well, you gave him the roots," Reverend Zackery said throwing up both his hands.

"I gave him a bag of powered Ex-lax, and told him to sprinkle a little in her food for three days. I didn't know that the fool was going to pour the whole bag in her mashed potatoes and gravy. That woman was crapping non-stop all the next day. She stayed on the bathroom so much that he had to go outside to pee. Finally, Paul couldn't take the smell any longer, so he came back."

"So, what did you do, then?" Rev. Zackery smiled while shaking his head.

"I gave him a very small bag of crushed up Pepto Bismoth tablets. I heard that his mother-in-law did leave, but it wasn't because of me. It was because she thought he was trying to poison her." Ma'amie paused. "So, you tell me Rev. Zackery, on a sin scale from one to ten, how big was what I did. Does that make me evil?"

"You may not be actually doing it, but you make those people believe that you're practicing witchcraft. That is evil," Rev. Zackery said as he began to pace back and forth. "However, it's not quite as evil as I thought it was."

"If I had not been available, your little deacon would have found a real root lady. You're criticizing me, you need to be criticizing your sermons. I'm just trying to make a living," Ma'amie said as she was about to sit down. She stopped before she sat and looked at Rev. Zackery.

"Go on. Sit," Rev. Zackery said.

"Thank you." Ma'amie sat down and pulled her arms out of her coat. As her coat opened, exposing a pretty, wool, form fitting dress, he could see the cleavage of her breasts. It had a very low V-neck.

"Let me take your coat," Rev. Zackery said as he reached down. Placing one hand on the back of the sofa, she raised up off her coat, grabbed the collar with the other, pulled it from beneath her, and placed it on Rev. Zackery hand. As she did, her breasts were only two feet away from his face. Rev. Zackery froze for three seconds as he looked at her breast.

"Are you going to take my coat?"

"Yes," Rev. Zackery said snapping out of his trance. "That is a very pretty dress." He looked her over from head to toe. Her skin was prettier than the dress. He could tell he was breathing heavily as he laid the coat over a nearby chair. He walked over to his desk and picked up a pad and a pen. "Now, you say that you want to make funeral arrangements."

"Yeah, I'm not expecting a lot a people. Most of my customers will be ashamed to come, especially since they're your church members. I have a few relatives, my grandson, a daughter-in-law, and a niece. If they all come, I want them to have good memories of my funeral. It will be their last memory of me, so I have prepared a program. It's in my coat pocket."

Reverend Zackery saw a sheet of paper sticking out of her pocket. He got it and began to read. "Procession, scripture, prayer, comments (three minutes), musical selection, eulogy, recessional; it looks good," Rev. Zackery said surprisingly. "Except you have **ten** people making comments. That's thirty minutes right there and that's if they keep it to three minutes. You know, they never talk less than five to ten minutes. That's too many people."

"I'm sure they will not speak more than three minute, most of them less."

Reverend Zackery frowned, "How can you be so sure?"

"Cause I wrote down exactly what I want them to say. I told them not to change a single word." Ma'amie paused. "The last speaker may speak for more than five minutes, I haven't talked to him yet."

"The last person." Reverend Zackery looked at the last name on the list. "That's me. What in? Who in?"

"I wrote some comments on the back of that paper, that I would like you to consider saying."

"You must be out of root infested mind, if you think I'm gonna let you dictate to me what to say about you." Reverend Zackery began shaking his head. "Who are the rest of these people on your comments list?"

"Well, they are customers who owe me for services. They may or may not show up. However, I told them that if they didn't, I would come back and haunt them."

"I thought you repented," Reverend Zackery snapped.

"I did that before I repented."

"You say you repented." Rev. Zackery said doubtfully. "Have you accepted Jesus as your personal savour."

"That's the other reason I'm here. I want you to lead me to salvation."

"I knew you were up to no good," Reverend Zackery said as he picked up her coat and handed it to her. "You don't care anything about Jesus. You just want to get out of going to hell."

Ma'amie took the coat and threw it on the sofa. "Hell no, I don't want to go to hell," she screamed. "And yes, I want to see my mama again." Tears began to fall from her eyes. "If God hadn't taken her away from me when I was a little child, maybe I wouldn't have ended up this way," she sobbed. "I don't have nobody. My daughter-in-law hates me. She wouldn't let my only grandson have a relationship with me when he was growing up. The only persons that ever cared about me was my son, who is dead now, and my little Pam." Ma'amie stood there with her head down, taking heavy breaths. With each breath, more tears poured from her eyes.

Reverend Zackery's anger turned to compassion, as he bit his lips and tried to blink away the tears forming in his eyes.

Ma'amie looked over at his desk. She quickly walked over to it. Rev. Zackery's gun was lying on it next to his bible. As she reached down Rev. Zackery began to back toward his front door. To his surprise, Ma'amie picked up his bible, opened it, and began to flip pages. When she found what she had been looking for she spoke. "Here in Matthew 11:28, Jesus says, 'Come unto me, all ye that labour and are heavy laden and I will give you rest." Ma'amie flips some more page. "Then here in Revelation 3:20, Jesus says: 'Behold, I stand at the door, and knock: if any man hear my voice, and open the door, I will come in to him, and will sup with him, and he with me."

"You can't trick me," Rev. Zackery said waving his finger in front of his face. "You practice witchcraft."

"You act like witchcraft is the biggest sin in the world? When King Saul disobeyed God, the prophet Samuel told him that rebellion is as the sin of witchcraft. I guess you never rebelled against God." She took a step toward him. "Well, have you ever intentionally disobeyed God?"

Rev. Zackery didn't speak. He just nodded his head up and down.

"Well that was rebellion, which, according to the bible, is just as the sin of witchcraft."

"I see you have been reading your bible."

"I also read that 'all have sinned' and by faith in Jesus, 'His blood cleanses us from all sin.'"

Rev. Zackery began smiling and nodding as a tear fell from his right eye, "You are so right, Miss Ma'amie, there is room at the throne for all who want to come to Him. His love for us is so great that He reached way down and saved someone so undeserving as me. Surely, He can save you. It's not for me to decide if you are sincere or not. God looks at the heart. He knows. Please forgive me" He reached out his hands to her. "Let's pray the prayer of salvation."

Ma'amie walked to him and took hold of his hands.

"Bow your head, close your eyes, and repeat after me in prayer and believe these words with all your heart," Reverend Zackery said.

"I will."

They both bowed their head and closed their eyes. When Rev. Zackery was about to speak, a thought in his head told him to open his eyes. When he did, he saw her looking directly at him. "Close your eyes for the prayer."

"Okay," Ma'amie said closing her eyes again.

Rev. Zackery closed his eyes. "Repeat after me." He opened his eyes again to see if her eyes were closed. Again, she was looking right at his eyes. "I see you have a problem keeping your eyes closed."

"I think I read somewhere in the bible where it says to 'watch and pray'. Is that right?"

"Yes, Miss Ma'amie, I believe you're right. How about closing one eye."

"That'll work, reverend," Ma'amie said closing one eye.

"That's not the eye you use to put the evil eye on people, is it?"

"Sorry," Ma'amie said, switching eyes.

Rev. Zackery closed one of his eyes and said, "Now repeat after me. Dear God, first I want to thank you for all that you have done in my life."

"Dear God, first I want to thank you for all that you have done in my life," she repeated.

"Everything that has happened in my life has brought me to this precious moment of salvation."

"Everything that has happened in my life has brought me to this precious moment of salvation."

The images of the past dissolve and Rev. Zackery is back in his kitchen talking to his guests again.

"So, I led her in the prayer of salvation, the same way I did you Dave," Rev. Zackery said shaking his head and smiling. "Afterwards I hugged her and told her that heaven was rejoicing because she got saved. Then she asked, 'So I'll see my mama again?' I said 'Yes, you'll see her again.' She was so happy and so was I."

"That makes me feel so much better, Rev. Zackery. Thank you." Jason got up, went to the preacher, and hugged him tenderly for a long time.

"I want to know what comments she wrote for you to make at her funeral," Pam said happily.

"There's not going to be a funeral," Rev. Zackery paused. "It's going to be a home going celebration. And, you'll just have to wait till then to find out what she wrote."

"You're too cold, reverend," Pam said smiling.

"I know, but I'm glad you mentioned it, again. Is Saturday a good day? That hole in the church floor should be patched up by then for the service." Rev. Zackery paused. "Are you all gonna be able to come. Do you want to make comments?"

"Yeah," Dave said. "You can put me down for comments."

"Me too," Jason said.

Everyone looked at Pam who was looking intensely at her glass of orange juice. She was holding her hand about two inches from the glass. She looked up when she noticed that everyone was watching her.

Of course, I'll make comments," she said as raised her glass. "She was like a mother to me."

Everyone around her wondered if she had grabbed the glass or if the glass had moved into her hand. Rev. Zackery broke the silence.

"Good! Everything is settled."

"Reverend, those brains sure were good," Dave said leaning back and patting his stomach. "I guess I need to get moving. I've got to get to that conference to see if I still have a job. Then I've got to go home to see if I still have a wife. I'll see all of you Saturday."

"Don't you think you ought to call your wife? You know, a courtesy call, just to let her know you're," Rev. Zackery paused, "alive."

Dave looked at Pam and Jason and then down at the floor. "I didn't want to disturb her. She's been pretty busy as far as I could see."

"I'm not talking about just for her sake, I'm talking about for your sake, too. Now that you're saved, the Lord expects you to do what is right. You know the right thing to do is to call your wife."

"Yes, sir. I'll call her right now, if."

"If what?"

"If you lay holy hands on me," Dave said softly. "The Lord is going to have to help me with this conversation."

Rev. Zackery immediately walked over to Dave, placed his hand on Dave's forehead and said, "Help him, Lord. Please, help him."

"Amen to that!" Jason said shaking his head up and down.

"And help me, too, while you're at it because I wouldn't call her nothing but a few four and five letter words." Pam said turning her head away with a look of discuss.

"You can use the phone in the hall, for more privacy," Rev. Zackery said.

"No. I'll use that one on the wall." Dave walked across the room, picked up the receiver and started dialing. "If you are listening, maybe I won't lose control."

Everybody waited for Dave to speak in the phone. Then, finally he spoke.

"Hello Carol, this is Dave."

No one had to wonder what she was saying because her screams were so loud that Dave had to hold the receiver away from his ear.

"Where in the devil have you been? People have been calling here asking me where you are, and I had to tell them that I didn't have a damned clue. Why? Because my inconsiderate idiot of a husband didn't have the decency to call his wife. Are you at the conference now? I sure hope you are, because if you aren't, not even my daddy is going to be able to save your job."

"Carol!" Dave yelled trying unsuccessfully to get her to stop and get her to listen.

"You've got a lot of explaining to do when you get home buddy. And don't think you're going to get off the hook easy either."

"Carol!"

"You have made me the joke of the month!"

"Carol!"

"Why do you keep calling my name?" She stops finally.

Pam lowers her head, covers her frowning eyebrows and her eyes, and says silently, "That bitch."

Jason just sits there shaking his head from side to side.

Rev. Zackery walks over and hands Dave his bible.

Dave takes the bible and nods at Rev. Zackery.

"Carol, I've been through a lot in the last few days. I lost my phone. I was locked up in jail. My car burned up. And, someone I was close to, was killed in a fire."

"What are you talking..."

"Carol just listen!" Dave paused and she was silent. "I'm on my way to the conference or what's left of it. I'll call you tonight. Okay?"

There was a pause. "Are you okay? Are you hurt?" she asked less angrily.

"Just a few bruises."

"Okay! Call me. But make sure it's before nine. I've got to catch up on some of the sleep I lost worrying about you. Bye!" She hung up before getting a response.

"Bye," Dave said to the dial tone. Dave handed the bible back to a smiling Rev. Zackery. Jason started to clap his hands and everyone else joined in.

"I don't know how you did it?" Jason said holding up both hands.

"It must have been the Lord," Dave said.

"Yep. God gave you strength. I'm proud of you, son," Rev. Zackery said as he hugged Dave, tightly.

"Strength to punk out!" Pam said unapprovingly. Everyone looked at her.

"Well, I guess I'd better be going," Dave said. "May I use your bathroom before I go."

Rev. Zackery nodded.

"Yeah, I know how you feel. That conversation almost made me want to throw up, too," Pam smirked.

Dave stood. Then Jason and Pam stood.

"We're leaving too," Jason said. "I going to take Pam back to Atlanta, then I'm going home for a few days." Jason looked at Rev. Zackery. "I'll be back Friday to view the body and settle with the funeral home."

Pam and Jason hugged Rev. Zackery and he walked them to their rental car. Dave ran out, hugged Pam. As Pam was getting into the car, Dave whispered in Jason's ear.

"I have something for you." Dave put something in Jason's hand. It was a wooden cross with a leather neck strap. "I carved it for the communion table wood."

"Well Dave, I don't know what to say. No one has ever given be anything like this before," Jason said smiling. He looked it over carefully. He saw a color change in the wood at the bottom, so he pulled on it. The rounded tip of the came off revealing a very pointed end almost two inches long.

"Hey, the lug wrench I gave you came in handy, didn't it?"

"Yeah! It was a life saver." Jason put the leather strap over his head. "Thanks partner, I will wear it next to my heart. It will be something to remember you by." Jason and Dave hugged.

"I'll see you at the funeral."

"Okay, I'll see you then," Jason said smiling.

Dave then turned and hugged Rev. Zackery. "Thank you, sir."

"I'll be praying for you, Mr. Parker."

Rev. Zackery waved as both cars pulled away. He walked back into the house, closed the door, and looked up. "Lord, I need you, right now. I need to know what to do, what to say, what to pray. I need for you to speak to me, send me a word, show me the way that I should go. Please! Lord." He looked on the table and saw his bible. "Thy word is a light unto my path, and a lamp unto my feet." He picked up the bible, went to the dining room table and began to read.

Chapter 3
The Battle for the Book

(Saturday morning 11:30 am)

Jason and Pam rode in silence for ten minutes. Jason was feeling uneasy about Pam's character changes. Her eyes were scary, he thought. They never stopped moving. As he turned on the highway, he looked at her closely. Her facial expression appeared frozen. It wasn't hate, but there was a hint of anger. She was beginning to look like her sister, Tamera.

Jason broke the silence. "What's going on with you?"

"What do you mean?"

"I know you know what I mean. You are changing. You used to be sweet, now you're cold. You don't sound like yourself. You don't even look like you. You look like her," Jason said.

"So, I look scary."

"It's good to know that you can read my mind," Jason said. Then he thought something to see if she would read his mind and respond. 'You look scary, but I'm not scared.' He turned and looked at her and thought, 'I love you, but self-preservation is the first law of nature.'

"I love you, too." She forced a smile and laid her head back and closed her eyes. "I haven't felt sad about Auntie all day. I'm supposed to miss her and be sad about her death, but I feel numb. That really bothers me. I feel stronger. My mind is sharper. I can read some of your thoughts. That part doesn't bother me, but I loved Auntie all my life. She raised me. She taught me everything I know. I should still be crying. Instead, I feel numb."

Jason slowed the car, pulled over to the side of the road, and stopped. He looked at her and she looked at him. "Look, there is one thing I know. Your feelings don't mean nothing. Feelings can't be trusted. Feelings are not dependable. They change. They fool you. It's not about feelings, it's about will. It's about making a decision, and then doing it. If you decide that you want to do what is right, you might not feel like doing it. You do it regardless of how you feel. Gramma 'loved' you, you 'loved' her. I don't care what you feel. You know part of her is still with you. Her words and teachings are still a part of you." Jason paused. "Don't worry about how you feel. Just know."

"You're right Jason," she said looking and sounding like herself again. "And this is what I know. We should destroy that book."

"What book?"

"Dave found this witchcraft book in that well where you found me. It's still there. We need to go back to Auntie's and get that book and destroy it. I sense that the witches want to get it and do something bad."

"Wait a minute," Jason said placing his hand on his forehead. "There are more of them."

"There is a coven. I don't know how many witches there are, but there is a witchhead, a group that makes major decisions."

"How do you know this?"

"Auntie told me that when my mother found out that she was going to have twins the witchhead decided that the second child, me, should be killed. That's why she ran away and left me with Auntie, your grandmother. When the witchhead found out that my mother had hid me, they were going to make her tell them where I was. They cornered her on the roof of a tall building. However, to keep me safe she jumped."

"So, this witchhead killed your mother? They tried to kill you, and now they want the book." Jason took a deep breath. "Are you sure that's all you want to destroy?"

"Yes, Auntie said that Tamera could only sense me when I used my powers. She's in the river, so they won't be able to find me now. We'll just destroy the book, so they can't use it. Then I can leave all this behind me."

"They killed your mother and all you want to do is destroy their book?"

"You need to get anger management therapy," Pam said shaking her head. "Can we just destroy the book?"

"All right! Let's do it." Jason put the car in drive and pulled off.

"We'll need flashlights, so stop at the next service station."

It wasn't long before they saw a service station. When Jason got back into the car, he handed Pam the bag. She looked inside and asked, "Do you think you got enough flashlights?"

"Two big ones and two little ones," he responded smirking as he looked at Pam. "It is better to be safe than sorry. An ounce of prevention is worth a pound of cure. It's better to be an hour early than to be five minutes late."

"Okay, okay, I get the point, but what is the duct tape for?" she questioned pulling a large roll of duct tape out of the bag.

"I carry duct tape on all my dates."

"You're sick," she said shaking her head. "But it's good to have the old Jason back."

"I'm trying, but it's hard." He increased his speed to 60 miles per hour.

"You'll see a big rock in about ten minutes. Turn left at the next street"

Soon they passed the big rock and were traveling down the dirt road to Ma'amie's burned down house. They were both surprised to see a car parked in the yard.

"Slow down," Pam whispered. "Somebody is up there. I can see them walking through the burned wood. It must be them."

"You can see that far." Jason said straining to see. "Do you see guns? They might have guns. We better be really careful."

"They see us. There are three of them and neither one of them has pulled out a gun."

"Yet," Jason added.

"When you stop, keep the engine running just in case."

Dave stopped the car in the road blocking in their car which they had backed into the driveway. There were three men standing in the debris looking at them. The one in the middle was the biggest. He appeared to be six feet six, two hundred and fifty pounds. The other two were about six feet even. The one on the left, was husky, while the one on the right was more muscular and fix. Pam and Jason waited for them to move but they just stood still. Pam opened her door, got out, and looked over the car, while Jason sat with his foot on the brakes, the engine still in drive and running. He kept both hands on the steering wheel.

"What are you doing? You're on my property." Pam yelled. "I hope you haven't taken anything. Everything in there, belongs to me."

Three men looked at each other. They were all dressed in black jeans, and black hoodies. The one in the middle moved forward while the other two moved to the right and left respectively. Soon they were all on the ground about twenty feet apart moving toward the car.

"And who are you, Miss?" the one in the middle asked, as they all came to a stop.

"All you need to know is, I own this property, you are trespassing, so you need to get in your car and leave, right now," Pam said pointing to the black car.

The three men began moving forward. Pam motioned as if she was pulling a pistol from the back of her pants. Jason rolled his window down. They all looked at Jason who had taken his hands off the steering wheel. They could no longer see them. They stopped. Then the man in the middle spoke again but this time to the other two.

"Let's go," he said. Immediately, they walked toward, and got into the car.

Pam got back into the car with Jason, who slowly backed up far enough for them to get out of the driveway. As they passed by Jason and Pam, there was a prize fight stare down. Nobody showed any fear. Their car turned in front of Jason's and speeded down the gravel road away from the highway.

Pam and Jason waited for the car to get out of sight. Then she looked in the dash and got one of the flashlights they had bought earlier. "Let's go. We need to get the book quickly because they will be back." Pam ran to the area where the well was located jumping over and around a maze of burned debris. She was going down in the well before Jason got to the steps. Jason was moving slowly because he kept watching the road. After he felt that the car was gone, he carefully made his way toward Pam.

The crosshairs of a long-range rifle followed Jason as he made his way through the debris. When he stopped at the well, a finger began to squeeze the trigger. One of the men that had left in the black car was in a tree with a rifle pointed at Jason. He spoke to the men on the ground.

"I got the man in my sights. Take him out?"

"Yeah," said the man who had done all the talking with Pam.

Just before the man in the tree made his final squeeze, something appeared at the bottom of the rifle sights. He lowered the sights. He could see Pam's head and arm. She was holding up a book.

"They have it! They have the book!"

"Good. Kill both of them."

The man in the tree put the crosshairs on Pam's head. It seemed to him that she was looking directly at him. He was about to pull the trigger when she put the book in front of her head. Not wanting to damage the book, he raised the crosshairs to Jason's chest and squeezed the trigger. Jason went down. He looked back to where Pam had been. She had gone back down out of view.

"I got the man, but the woman went down under the floor."

"We'll take care of her. You stay there just in case she comes out before we get there." The two men on the ground ran to the car.

Back at Ma'amie's, Jason laid still in the rubble. "Was that a gunshot I heard?"

"Yeah," Pam said. "It was them. I saw something moving in a tree. Then I saw a reflection of the sunlight that you might get from a piece of glass like in the sights on a rifle. That's why I pulled your leg."

"You could have just said 'duck or get down'. You almost pulled my leg outta socket,"

"Sorry, there wasn't any time," Pam said. "You're still breathing ain't you?"

"Yes ma'am, for now. Is the shooter still in the tree?"

"I can't see anything. But there's one way to find out," she said as she slowly crawled out of the well keeping as low as she could.

"What are you going to do?" Jason waited for an answer but instead he heard a car coming down the road. "It's them."

"You stay here. I'm going to take the book and run into the woods. They will follow me, cause they want the book. I'll lose them in the woods, then I'll meet you back at the big rock in exactly one hour."

"Are you sure you can lose them?"

"I know these woods like the back of my hand. You just be there, at the big rock, on time," she said handing Jason the flashlight.

The black car slid to a stop as Pam stood up, took a step and jumped over debris, hit the ground, and ducked down below the foundation as a shot sounded from the trees in the distance. The two men jumped out of the car. One ran to one side of the debris and one to the other. At the same time, Pam ran full speed toward the woods. Another shot was fired. The bullet hit a tree near Pam as she entered the woods. Seconds later the two men entered the woods in different angles trying to close her in.

Jason stayed low. He waited a minute, made his way through the debris, and then ran to the black car. He hid behind the car. The shooter, still focusing his scope and attention on the woods, did not see Jason. Jason took the single edge razor blade out of his back pocket, slid it out of the cardboard. Then he cut off the value stems of the two tires on the side of the car closest to him, which was the passenger side. The tires quickly went flat. Jason crept to his car and got in. He started the engine. The car was pointed in the wrong direction. He had to turn around. He drove the car slowly into the driveway. Then he put the car in reverse and ever so slowly he moved back until he was back on the road. He wondered why he had not been seen. He was glad, until he looked down the road and saw the shooter come running around the curve in the road. Jason quickly put the car in drive a sped down the road. He watched in the rearview mirror as the shooter jump in the black car and started after him. The shooter didn't get far. He jumped out of the car and aimed the rifle. Jason kept his head low, but he never heard any shots fired. He got to the highway and turned right. He had to find a place to wait.

Pam was now running down an overgrown path which she knew would split into two paths about twenty yards further down. She could tell that one of the men was on the path behind her. She didn't know where the other one was, but she knew he would eventually have to come down the path too. Just before she reached the split in the paths she stopped. There was a big tree with a ditch beside it. She ducked down into the ditch behind the tree and waited. It wasn't long before one of the men came running by her. It was the one who had done the talking. The man stopped for a second when he reached the split, then he ran down the path to the right. That path was less overgrown. He wasn't gone very long before the second man came by. He stopped and was about to go to the right as well when Pam came out of the ditch and stood beside the tree. She had the book in one hand and a dead tree limb in the other. She threw the limb and hit the man in the back of the head. He quickly turned but as he did, he reached under his sweatshirt and pulled out a pistol. Pam seemed surprised to see that he had a gun. She ducked behind the tree. As he moved forward, she opened the book, grabbed several pages in one hand and the rest in the other. She held the book out, so he could see it as she peeped her head out.

"Throw your gun in those bushes or I'll tear this book to pieces," Pam said.

"And then what?" he said.

"Then you can come and get the book if you're bad enough to take it," Pam said as she began to pull the book apart.

"Okay! Don't tear it!" He tossed the pistol into the bushes. "Now put the book on the ground."

Pam stepped out into the path and tossed the book on the path behind her. She looked confidently at him and beckoned him to come with her finger. "Come and get it, big boy."

He did not hesitate. He charged forward as she stood frozen waiting. When he was within striking distance, he reached out with his left hand grabbing her left shoulder as he threw his right fist as hard as he could straight at her head. At the last second, she knocked his right arm to her right while moving her head to the left causing him to miss her. Simultaneously, she brought her open palm up striking his nose with the intention of driving his nose bone into his brain. However, at the last second, he turned his head. Her death blow failed. However, his nose was severely broken and bleeding profusely. He crumbled to the ground at her feet holding his face moaning in pain.

Pam was confused. She had planned to kill him in one blow. Now, she had to decide how she was going to finish him. She decided that she would snap his neck, however, when she was about to reach down and grab his head, she heard the other man running down the path. She kneed him hard in the chin, knocking him to the ground. She picked up the book and a small rock and hid behind the tree. When she heard the man stop to check his companion, she tossed the rock down the path behind her. The second man pulled out his pistol and moved forward. Pam was holding the book high above her head as she waited. She saw the pistol first as he moved past the tree. She brought the book down hard on his arm, knocking the gun to the ground. He reached for it, however, before he could get it, she kicked it into the ditch. He stepped away from her, reached into his back pocket and pulled out a very large pocketknife. He opened it carefully as if trying not to cut himself in the process. The silver blade was at least six inches long and almost two inches wide. It was almost blinding when it reflected the rays of the afternoon sun in her eyes.

Pam held the book out in front of her with her left hand and her right hand was open ready to grab his arm. He began swinging the knife at her quickly from left to right and back in one fluid motion as he stepped forward. Pam blocked his thrusts with the book as she moved back. Each time he slashed the thick leather cover of the book. He did this, three times. However, on the fourth time he swung the blade high causing her to raise the book in front of her face. Then he jabbed straight for her stomach. When she saw the blade coming, she tried to jump back but she was too late. The blade began to sink into her abdomen. She brought the book down and out against his bicep stopping the penetration. At the same time, she straightened her fingers and jabbed straight for his left eye. He ducked away but only after his eye was pushed deep into his eye socket. Pam spinned around 360 degrees holding the book with both hands. She slammed it against back of his head. He went down to his knees holding his eye. Pam looked down. The knife was dangling from her stomach. She pulled it out and raised it above the man at her feet. He raised his arm to block the blade from his head. Pam grabbed his wrist and stabbed the knife into his shoulder. Leaving the blade in his shoulder blade, she grabbed his wrist with both hands and twisted his arm behind his back forcing him down on his stomach. While continuing holding his wrist, she stepped over him and brought her knee down on his neck, pinning his face to the ground. She pulled the knife out of his shoulder and slid the blade over the ribs of his back until it was positioned between two ribs behind his heart.

"This book just cost you your life," Pam said. She raised her body over the knife and pushed. However, before she able to push the knife into his heart, something hit her in her back that knocked her forward causing her head to go back. As she fell forward, she saw her blood splatter on the side of the man's face. She dropped the knife, held her hands out in front of her as she hit the ground. She pushed and rolled away from the man. That's when she realized that she realized that she couldn't breathe. She knew why. She had been shot. The bullet had gone into her back, through chest and out just above her right breast. She crawled toward the ditch where the gun had gone, while the two men helped each other. The man who had done the talking picked up his knife, the book, and then the other man. They both watched as Pam collapsed and slid into the ditch. Then they slowly made their way back toward the road. It wasn't long before the man with the rifle met them.

"Give me a hand with Manny. He's hurt pretty bad," the biggest man said.

"What about the girl," his companion said slinging the rifle over his shoulder and sliding his head through the strap.

"You got her, Walt. She wasn't dead when we left, but it won't be long."

"The man, she was with, got away," he paused. "He cut the valve stems on two tires. I called Mike. He's bringing a tow truck."

"How did you let that happen?" He stopped.

"How did you let that little girl do this to both of you? She was going to kill you if I hadn't shot her when I did."

"That was no ordinary little girl. She had skills. She was fast," he said looking at all the blood coming from his other companion's face. "Mike better get here soon, Manny is losing a lot of blood."

"Are you sure we don't need to go back and check on the girl?" Walt said.

"Like I said, she's dead or dying in the woods now."

"Okay, Steve, it's your call. I hope this doesn't come back to bite us…" Walt was interrupted

Hey! She's as good as dead. Manny needs help, now! We got the book. Mission accomplished, even though it was costly."

"I better call for an ambulance. He doesn't look like he's going to make it."

"There's a first aid kit in the car. Let's get him there, first. Then, you can call while I stop the bleeding," Steve said as he watched the blood continue to flow from his nose. "Let's move!"

They each grabbed a wrist and pulled an arm around their neck. Then they both grabbed a leg. They lifted him up and began running back to their car.

Chapter 4
The Manager's Meeting

(Saturday afternoon 2:00 pm)

Dave walked into the conference room 3 as he had been directed by the hotel clerk. There in front of him was a long conference table. He could see the backs of all the department managers of the company. The director of operations, Mr. M. R. Monroe was standing in front of them, writing on a large erasable marker board on the wall. When he noticed Dave coming in, he faced Dave and froze. An angry frown fell down his face like a shadow. Everyone turned and watched in dread as Dave walked up to the end of the table where there was a vacant seat. No one knew what Mr. M. R. Monroe was going to do; they just knew it was going to be bad.

"I'm sorry about being late, Mr. Monroe. I've really been through..."

"You're sorry about being late," Mr. Monroe screamed, interrupting Dave's apology. "If you had gotten here ten minutes after our first meeting Tuesday morning, you would have been late," Mr. Monroe yelled as he walked down to the end of the table where Dave was now sitting. "But, here it is Saturday afternoon and nobody has heard a damned thing from you. You're not late." Mr. Monroe placed his hands on the table, leaned across the table and put his nose four inches from Dave's nose and screamed, "You're AWOL."

Dave looked cowardly down at the table.

"You are absent without leave. If you weren't married to Mr. Thompson's daughter I would fire you right here, right now. Who do you think are? Look at me when I'm talking to you."

Dave looked up. His expression had changed. There was rage in his eyes. He quickly reached out with his right hand, grabbed Mr. Monroe's red tie, and jerked it. Mr. Monroe's body was pulled onto the table. Dave stood up kicking his folding chair back and up into the air behind him. Then he grabbed the knot of Mr. M. R. Monroe's tie with his left hand and pulled the back tail of it so hard that Mr. Monroe began to choke. Fear gripped Mr. Monroe's heart because he could barely breathe. Dave slowly walked around the table. He backed up Mr. Monroe by his tie, and then slammed his back against the board on the wall.

"One thing is clear." Dave said angrily. "You don't know who you're talking to. You better ask somebody. I am not the one to be messed with. Somebody better tell him who I am," Dave said turning toward the shocked managers. Nobody spoke. Dave wrapped the back tail of the tie around his fist and pulled. This time he cut off Mr. Monroe's circulation. His face immediately began to lose its color.

"You're Dave," one manager said.

"David Parker," said another.

"He's Mr. Parker, sir."

"That's who I am, David Parker," Dave said loosening grip on the tie so that Mr. Monroe could finally breathe. One tear fell from each of Mr. Monroe's eyes. "If you ever get in my face screaming at me like that again, I'm going to poke both of your eyes out." Dave pushed Mr. Monroe's eyeballs into his sockets. "Do you understand me?" Dave removed his fingers.

Mr. Monroe still couldn't speak because the tie was still too tight, so he just nodded. Dave's rage began to dissipate. He released his grip on Mr. Monroe's tie and turned and faced the managers who were very relieved that the situation had ended. Mr. Monroe leaned back against the board as he pulled the tie from his neck and dropped it to the floor.

"I've been through so much stress recently," Dave said apologetically looking first at the managers then at Mr. Monroe. "Someone very close to me was murdered." Tears welled up in his eyes. "I didn't realize how much she meant ..." His voice broke and the tears began to flow. "To me. She was such a sweet," he couldn't stop crying as he broke down in sobs. "She was so sweet and kind to me," he sobbed, "and I treated her so badly. I never got the chance to say I'm sorry."

The managers gathered around him to console him, and then Mr. Monroe spoke.

"Dave, I want to apologize for my actions. They were totally inexcusable and unprofessional. Please, forgive me, it will never happen again. I apologize to the rest you too. I will try to communicate better in the future," Mr. Monroe said sincerely.

"I forgive you, Mr. Monroe. I hope you can forgive me."

"I can see that you have been though a lot. Why don't you take some time off? Call the office on Monday and let us know when you are ready to come back to work."

"Thank you sir, I will. I really need to get home to my wife," Dave said wiping his face with his hands.

The managers began to pat him on the back as he was leaving. One of them hit him in the middle of his back and something fell out of the back of his pants and hit the tile floor with a loud noise. They all looked down, and silently backed away from Dave and the object on the floor at his feet. It was the long-barreled pistol that Rev. Zackery had place on the cabinet. Dave quickly picked it up, moved his suit coat to the side and stuck it in the back of his pants again. He walked out leaving a room full of statues.

Chapter 5
Demons in The House

(Saturday afternoon, 5:00pm)

Rev. Zackery was sitting at the dining room table at his brother's house. He had his bible in his hand and his head bowed in prayer.

"Lord, I come before you with a heavy heart. I know that I'm supposed to have unwavering faith and total confidence in You. Now I don't doubt You. I know, You can do all things, and nothing is impossible for You. It's not You; it's me Lord that I doubt. In the past few days, You tested me and the devil tempted me. I failed the test, and I yielded to the temptation. I know how You are, Lord. If I fail one of Your tests, I'll have to take it again, and again, and again until I pass it. That tells me that this witch thing is not over. Speak to my heart, Lord," he paused and held the bible close to his heart.

Outside of the back, bedroom window, Billy was prying up a window with a crowbar. He pushed it up and the screws in the window lock were pulled out of the wood. He then opened the window and quietly climbed through. He walked to the door, slowly opened it, and peeped out. He could hear a man talking from a room at the end of the hall.

"What's that, Lord? The power is in My words. Speak My words. Hmmm. The power," Rev. Zackery whispered. "The power," he said louder, "to pass the test is in speaking Your words. Thank You, thank You, thank You, Jesus."

Billy watched from the hallway as the smiling man raised his bible in the air and walked into the kitchen. Billy tightened his grip on the crowbar as he followed the man. He was careful to keep out of his sight.

Rev. Zackery walked to the sink, laid the bible on the counter, and began to wash dishes from the morning meal. With the crowbar behind his leg, Billy moved quickly toward Rev. Zackery's back. However, before Billy could get halfway across the room, Rev. Zackery quickly turned around and faced him.

"I've been expecting you," Rev. Zackery said sternly.

"You've been expecting, me?" Billy asked, surprised.

"Not you, him" Rev. Zackery said angrily pointing at Billy's face.

Billy quickly looked behind him. Nobody was there. He looked back at Rev, Zackery, who had returned his attention to washing dishes.

"He knows who I'm talking to. Speak up demon, don't be scared." Rev. Zackery turned around with an even angrier expression. "Speak up," Rev. Zackery screamed.

Instantly, Billy's stiffened. His whole body froze except for his lips, eyes, and eyebrows. Then Billy heard words that he did not control come out of his mouth.

"You dare to challenge me?"

Billy's eyes widened and his eyes began to look all around as his mouth moved and words came out in a loud scary voice.

"Who do you think you are?" the voice said.

"Galatians 3:26, demon," Rev. Zackery said.

"What?"

"Don't act like you don't know the word, demon. Gallatians 3:26 'For ye are the children of God by faith in Jesus Christ.' I have faith in Jesus. You said, who do you think you are? Well that means I am a child of the most, high God."

"You are not a child of God because you are a sinner. 1John 3:8a," the demon snarled.

"Ahh, 1John 3:8a," Rev. Zackery said reaching for his bible.

"Evidently, **you** don't know the word. 1John 3:8a says 'He that committeth sin is of the devil.' So, guess what sinner man. You are the devil's child."

"That was the old me. 2Cor 5:17, 'Therefore if any man be in Christ, he is a new creature: old things are passed away; behold all things are become new.

"Look at your old wrinkled up face."

"I'm not ashamed of my face. Why are you hiding yours?" Rev. Zackery said.

"I'll show you my face," the demon said as his extra-large head covered Billy's. His skin color was still light gray and his fingers and fingernails were very long. His expression was mean and evil, with frowning eyebrows. "I'll also show you that there's nothing new about you. Let me remind you of who you really are." The demon's arm protruded out of Billy's body. It was hairy. He had long fingers and long fingernails. As the demon waved his arm in an arch, a scene appeared. Rev. Zackery recognized his old house and then he saw himself sitting on the sofa. "When you were saying your goodbyes to your little friends, you left out this part, didn't you?"

Ma'amie was repeating the prayer of salvation.

"And You said if I do this, I shall be saved," Ma'amie said.

"Thank You Lord. I am now saved." Rev. Zackery yelled in excitement.

"Thank You Lord. I am now saved!" Ma'amie repeated.

"Praise Him! Give Him the glory!" Rev Zackery shouted

"Thank You Lord! Hallelujah! I'm saved!" Ma'amie ran up the Rev. Zackery and hugged him tightly. Their embrace lasted for two whole minutes. However, in the last thirty seconds their smiles faded away and their heartrate and breathing began to increase.

"Aha! You felt her nipples harden on your chest, didn't you? That wasn't the only thing that was starting to get hard, was it?" the demon said.

"How can you show me this? Were you there?

"Let's just say, I know somebody, who knows somebody, who was there. They told me the whole story or should I say gave me the video."

Back in the scene, as Ma'amie and Rev. Zackery separate, their eyes lock. Then as they step back from each other, Rev. Zackery's eyes become glued to the cleavage of her breasts, and Ma'amie's eyes look at his crouch.

"Well," Rev. Zackery said looking away from her body, "I've got a busy day tomorrow, I will work on those arrangements, if you still want me to." Rev. grabbed her coat with one hand and her arm with the other and began leading her to the door.

"Yes, please make the arrangements," she says brushing her breast up against his arm as they walked.

When they reach the door, Rev. Zackery opens the door and holds out her coat. However, instead of taking it, she turns around, so he can hold it for her to put her arms in. He looks at her fine body. As he holds the coat for her, she slides both hands in and he raises the coat to her elbows, when suddenly he comes forward, pining the coat between them and pining her body and the side of her face against the wall. He lowers his face next to hers and begins to kiss her cheek, until he sees her tongue come out the corner of her mouth. He quickly moves back, spins her around, and moves forward again, kissing her passionately.

Back in the kitchen, Rev. Zackery looks angrily at the demon. "Hey, that's not what happened. I didn't do that. You're a dirty, stinking, freaking, lying demon."

"You call yourself a preacher. The word says, if you lust after a woman in your heart, it's just as if you committed adultery. You did lust after her, didn't you?" The demon put his nose up against Rev. Zackery's nose. "Didn't you?"

Rev. Zackery turned around and began washing another plate, "I was tempted but I did not yield."

The demon went back inside of Billy and Billy came out of his trace. He watched Rev. Zackery as he rinsed the plate. Billy slowly raised the crowbar over his head. He was just about to slam the crowbar against Rev. Zackery's head when Rev. Zackery saw the reflection of Billy in the plate. Without looking, Rev. Zackery swung the plate around with all of his might, striking Billy in his face. The crowbar fell from Billy's hand, as he collapsed at Rev. Zackery's feet.

"I got something for your demonic…" Rev. Zackery stopped. "Sorry Lord." Rev. Zackery got a roll of duct tape out of his cabinet drawer, and began wrapping Billy's legs, hands, and arms. Once he finished, he dragged him into the bedroom. Billy woke up as Rev. Zackery was getting his hat.

"What are you going to do with me?" Billy said as he laid on his back on the floor.

Rev. Zackery walked to the dresser, tore a piece of duct tape from the roll, and covered Billy's mouth. He took a pillow out of the pillowcase and replaced it with Billy's head. He taped the pillowcase around Bill's neck. "I'm going to do something to you that I have never thought about doing before. I'm going to exorcise your aaaa, sorry Lord, soul." Rev. Zackery walked out.

Chapter 6
Ditched

(Saturday, 6:30pm)

Jason had been waiting in the woods across to street from the big rock for hours. He had seen an ambulance come and go. Then a wrecker came and left with the black sedan. Still there was no sign of Pam. He decided that he would go back to the woods to see if something had happened. He wondered if she had failed to get away. "Why did I leave her?" he whispered. "Oh God, what have I done?" he said looking up.

He went to his car and drove back to the ruins of Ma'amie's old house. The shadows from the nearby hills had begun to cover the trees, so he grabbed the flashlight from the dashboard, and went into the woods. It wasn't long before he came to a path. He shined the flashlight close to the ground. He saw spots of mud in the path. "That's not mud," he said aloud, "it's blood."

He hurried down the path following the spots, until he passed the big tree. There he saw some large areas of blood. He knelt on his knees by the largest spot, and he began to cry. His tears began to flow, and he began to sob and moan, as he fell forward on face. "Oh God, you let them kill my grandmother, and now you let them kill Pam. I just have one thing to ask of you, just let me kill them. Please, God."

Jason began to breathe heavy breaths, as rage grew with each breath. Then he heard someone call his name. Holding his breath, pushing himself to his knees, listening intently he heard it again. It came from the ditch near the big tree. He grabbed the flashlight and pointed it in the direction of the tree. Then he saw it, Pam's foot. He rushed to her, slid down in the ditch next to her. She moaned when he tried to lift her. Her blood-soaked sweatshirt let him know that she had a chest wound. Still, he pulled her with him as he crawled out of the ditch.

"I forgot about the one with the rifle," Pam whispered and then began taking short quick breaths.

"I am so sorry Pam. I never should have left you," Jason said sliding his arms under her body.

"It's not your fault. I should have stuck to the plan."

"This is going to hurt, but I've got to get you to the hospital. Your lungs are filling up with blood. Stop talking," Jason said as he picked her up, placed her on his shoulder, and began running to the car."

Chapter 7
The Interview Begins

(Saturday night, 7:15 PM)

Rev. Zackery pushed the bedroom door with his foot until he could see the if the body he had left on the floor was still there. He walks into the room slowly. The pillowcase was still taped over the man's head, so he couldn't see Rev. Zackery walk toward him with a kitchen knife in one hand and his bible in the other.

"I see you're still here," Rev. Zackery smiled. "The man in the tombs, who had the legion of demons was able to break the chains that the people had put on him. Let's just see what you were able to with this duct tape." Rev. Zackery walked up to the man and knelt at his head. He laid his bible down beside him and pulled his shoulder. "Turn over real slow and let me see your hands. I just want to make sure that you and your demon buddies are still bound."

Rev. Zackery picked his bible up and put the knife to the man's throat as he began to roll over slowly. When he had turned completely over, Rev. Zackery was surprised. "You've been busy. You almost got your hands loose. I'll fix that," he said adding more duct tape to the man's hands. Then he turned him on his back again, removed the pillowcase from his head, and the duct tape from his mouth. "Who are you, son? Why do you want to kill me?"

"I ain't telling you a damned ..." the man's sentence was interrupted when Rev. Zackery slapped the man across the mouth with his bible.

"No cursing in this house! If you curse, I'm gonna bible slap you again. What is your name?" Rev. Zackery said raising the bible over the man's head.

"Billy," the man said licking the blood from his lip. Instantly, he began to stiffen.

"Well, Billy, do you know who I am?"

"Go ahead preacher. Do your damned bible thing again, Rev. Z", a different voice said.

"So, you're back," he said lowering his bible as he watched Billy's face change.

"So, you're back," the demon said mimicking Rev. Zackery. "I never left."

"The bible says that at the name of Jesus demons tremble." He paused, "Jesus, Jesus, Jesus."

"No, stop it. I'm trembling, I'm trembling." He paused. "If you're going to quote scripture, at least, quote it correctly. You are one sorry preacher. How in the devil do you think you can cast out demons?"

"I'm not going to cast you out, in the devil, I going to cast you out in the name of Jesus, demon."

"Come on then. Hit me with your best shot, Z. Bible slap me again."

"I probably shouldn't have hit Billy, you're the culprit here." Rev. Zackery looked up. "I'm sorry, Lord. Please forgive me."

"You didn't hit God in the mouth. That was Billy's lip you busted. Saying you're sorry to God is not going to 'unbust' Billy's lip. You're just an old, arrogant, violent, hypocrite."

"You know me too well, demon. What you don't know is, you saved Billy's life."

"What you talking bout, Lewis?" the demon said talking like Arnold in the TV show 'Different Strokes.'

"If you hadn't spoken up when you did, I would have stabbed little Billy boy in the throat, instead of slapping him with a plate. And I'll tell you something else, either you are going to come out of Billy or I'm going to tie a concrete block to Billy's legs and drop you and Billy into the river."

"What are you waiting on, Z? You don't have what it takes. Let's get the show on the road."

"You're too anxious. You're up to something and I'm not falling for it. Anyway, I got something for you while I was out." Rev. Zackery said as he walked out of the room. Seconds later he walked back in with a bag. "I can't have you laying on the floor. That's not very Christ like. Let me get the bed ready. You would rather be on the bed, wouldn't you?" Rev. Zackery said as he spread a sheet of black plastic over the bed. He also put an old blanket on top of the plastic. Rev. Zackery stood Billy up and then laid him on the bed. "How's that, demon. Are you comfortable? I want you to be comfortable cause I want you to go to sleep now. I need to talk to Billy."

"Now, why would you want to talk to Billy, when you can talk to me?"

"I want to tell Billy about Jesus. I want to give him a chance to be saved."

"If you knew what Billy did to this young girl, two months ago, and what he was planning to do, yesterday, you wouldn't be so worried about his salvation. You'd be wishing for his annihilation."

"Yeah? Maybe, I can get him to repent. Go to sleep, demon." Rev. Zackery laid the bible on Billy's chest and began to praise God. "Oh Lord, I praise Your Name. You are so holy and righteous. You are my…"

"You might be interested in knowing that Pam has been shot and that she is in critical condition in the hos…," the demon voice grew softer, and he went to sleep. His image faded, Billy's face reappeared and Billy woke up.

"What? Where is she?" Rev. Zackery said.

"Where is who?" It was Billy's voice again.

"You said Pam had been shot."

"I didn't say nothing. I don't know nobody named Pam. What are you going to do with me? Why am I on your bed like this?"

"Is that you Billy?"

"Yeah, I mean yes sir."

"Do you know, you got demons, son?"

"No sir. What are you going to do with me?"

"Do you know me?"

"No, sir."

"Why do you want to kill me?"

"I don't want to kill you."

"You were about to crush my skull in with a crowbar."

"I don't know what you're talking about. The last thing I remember was being in my garage. Then I woke up here on your floor.

"So, you've never seen me before?"

"Your face does looks familiar," he paused. "You look like the man I saw on the bridge, yesterday."

"You saw us on the bridge? What did you see?"

Billy's face stiffened, and his face contorted. "He doesn't remember anything. He doesn't know anything. He just does what I tell him to do."

"Why are you back?"

"I thought I heard you ask me about Pam?"

"You're a liar like your father, the devil. You don't know anything about Pam."

The demon emerged from Billy's body from the waist up and sat up on the bed. "Would you like to see Pam? Yeah, I know you would. Behold!" The demon waved his arm in a semi-circle and he and Rev. Zackery were in an ICU unit of a hospital, outside of the open door of the room where Pam was. They were invisible to everyone except themselves.

There, standing just inside the doorway, were two doctors talking. Rev. Zackery could see Pam lying in bed behind them. Pam was asleep, tubes in her chest and arms. One of the doctors wore blue scrubs. The other one had on black slacks and a white coat.

"I don't know why her lung didn't completely fill with blood," the doctor with blue scrubs said.

"The black guy that brought her in, taped her up real tight with duct tape. He probably saved her life," the other doctor said.

"He probably was the person that shot her in the first place."

"You think. Did you have the nurse call the police?"

"Yes. They will want to talk to him, so don't let him back in here till the police get here."

"All right, but what am I supposed to tell him. He's getting impatient."

"Just keep stalling. Is he still sitting out there in the hall?"

The doctor in blue looked back outside the door, "He's gone!"

"You check the ICU waiting room and the men's room. I'll call down to the front desk."

The two men left the room in opposite directions. Rev. Zackery was about to go into Pam's room, when the door of the ICU room next to Pam's opened and Jason's head emerged. Rev. Zackery could see a patient in the bed behind him. The patient seemed to be suffering from burns because her entire face was bandaged. Her singed hair and angry eyes were the only thing uncovered. Rev. Zackery could only see her eyes because she had raised her head in pain to see Jason better. As Jason watched the nurse at her station, waiting for the right opportunity, Rev. Zackery notice that the burn patient was getting out of bed. The patient unhooked the saline drip from the pole, laid the bag on the floor, picked up the pole, flipped it upside down, holding it like a club, and moved quietly and quickly toward Jason.

"Watch out," Rev. Zackery yelled. "Look behind you." No one heard him. Jason was watching the nurse who had just turned her back to put away a file. The patient was right behind Jason. She pulled the pole back so that she could hit him with all her strength. She began to bring the pole forward, her hands high above her head, the pole level to the floor. In two seconds, Jason was out the door and in Pam's room closing both doors behind him.

Rev. Zackery didn't realize it, but he had stopped breathing, his face was frozen with fright. As he stood there looking at the door, he took a deep breath and blew it out loudly. He turned quickly toward Pam's room and instantly he was inside. The demon was sitting in the chair next to the bed with his legs crossed and a big Cheshire cat smile on his face.

They both watched as Jason walked up to Pam's bed, lowered his mouth next to her ear and whispered, "Pam, can you hear me?" She said nothing. He grabbed her hand. "If you can hear me squeeze my hand." Rev. looked anxiously to see any movement of Pam's hand.

"Excuse me, sir. We need to ask you a few questions." Jason looked around and saw two police officers and the two doctors standing in the doorway."

"Okay," Jason said shaking his head up and down. "I have a lot to tell you."

"Would you step out of the room, please?"

Rev. Zackery followed them out of the room. He stopped at the doorway and listened

"What is your name sir, and what is your relationship to this patient?" the officer with the corporal strips said.

"My name is Jason Scott, corporal Lanier," Jason said reading his name tag. "My grandmother, Ms. Ma'amie Scott, was this lady's nanny since she was a baby."

"You're Miss Ma'amie's grandson?" They both looked worried. "Didn't Miss Ma'amie die in a fire, recently?" corporal Lanier asked.

"No! Somebody killed her. They broke into her house, tied with up, and set her house on fire. They burned her up alive," Jason was becoming angry and loud.

"Keep your voice down, sir!" the corporal said sternly. "What is the patient's name?"

"I would rather not say. Somebody has already tried to kill her once, if they find out she's alive they may try again."

"Sir, we are the police. If you refuse to co-operate, if you refuse to answer our questions, you can be charged with obstruction of justice, and arrested."

Sergeant Hilliard knows me. He was at the fire. He also knows of the patient. I would like to talk to him and let him decide whether or not to release her identity." Jason said looking the corporal in his eyes. "I have his card, let me give him a call. Then he can tell you what he wants you to do."

The two officers look at each other.

Suddenly a loud, constant, ringing sound came from inside Pam's room. It was the heart monitor. It indicated that Pam's heart had stopped beating. Rev. Zackery looked around. On the bed, sitting on top of Pam was the demon. He had one hand covering her mouth and the other pinching her nose suffocating her. Rev. Zackery ran over to the demon, pulled his hand away from her nose and began beating the demon with his bible.

"Code blue!" the doctor yelled as the team rolled the resuscitator into the room.

The vision disappeared and Rev. Zackery was back in the bedroom. Instead of beating the demon, he was beating Billy in the chest.

"You foul, evil demon, from the pits of hell. You used me so you could try to kill Pam," Rev. Zackery screamed." After each word he hit Billy in the chest. "She had better not be dead!" Rev. Zackery slammed the bible down on Billy's chest one last time.

The demon's face appeared over Billy's. "I hope you got all those pent-up emotions out of your systems," the demon said shaking his head. "Poor Billy is not going to last much longer at this rate."

Rev. Zackery almost out of breath, regained his composure. "Do you expect me to believe that what I just saw was real?"

"You believe what you want to believe. Why would I show you something that wasn't real? What do I have to gain by lying?"

"You are a liar and a deceiver. That's what you do. I'd be crazy to believe anything you show me," Rev. Zackery snarled.

"Look I was given orders to show you that. If it was up to me, I would ripe you apart, right now, and make you wish you were never born. I don't know why they are stopping me."

"Who's stopping you?" Rev. Zackery said.

"My superiors."

"You should have kept your mouth close, demon. You got the nerve to threaten me," Rev. Zackery said shaking his head. "I was going to cast you out let you go into the fish in the fishbowl over there, but now I'm going find me a roach and cast you into that. Then I'm going to burn you up."

The demon got quiet.

"Thank You, Jesus, for Your protection. Thank You Lord for binding this demon," Rev. Zackery yelled throwing his hands up. Then, suddenly he looked at the demon and asked, "What hospital was that?"

"Thomas Jefferson Memorial. Go ahead call. But you better ask if they have recently admitted any women with a gunshot to the chest."

Even though there was a phone on the nightstand by the bed, Rev. Zackery went to use the phone in the kitchen.

Chapter 8
Home Sweet Home

(Saturday night 8:10 PM)

Dave sat in his rental car, three houses down from his house, on the opposite side of the street. He had been there for at least an hour watching his bedroom window. He could see the light was on, but the blinds and the curtains were closed, so there was little chance that he would be able to see anyone. Still, he was hoping that he would, at least, see a shadow, or two. Seeing two shadows would pretty much confirm what he had seen in the crystal ball. After all that had happened, the memory of seeing his wife in the crystal ball was almost like a distant dream, well nightmare. He didn't know what he was going to find when he went into his house, he just knew that he didn't want to be the one to be surprised. He sat there wondering what he would do if he found the insurance man in his bed with Carol. He took Rev. Zackery's pistol out of the dash. He opened the chamber. There were six bullets. He got out of the car, stuck the pistol in the back of his pants, put on his coat, and started walking toward his house. He unlocked the front door and walked in. The entrance alarm sounded. He froze and listened. He didn't hear any footsteps, so he quickly walked to the alarm panel and entered the code. He waited and listened. No one was home. He reset the alarm for stay and walked up the stairs to the bedroom. Everything looked normal. The bed was neatly made, and the items on the dresser were organized the way Carol liked it. Dave fell across the bed stretching out his arm.

"There is no bed like your own," Dave whispered. "Thank You Lord." A grateful smile spread across his face as he closed his eyes and took a deep fulfilling breath. Before he could exhale, the peace he was feeling disappeared. The entrance alarm sounded again.

"Carol!" Dave said excitedly as he walked toward the stairs. His excitement died and he stopped when he heard a man's voice. They were coming up the steps.

"You know this is the last night that you will be able stay here. My husband will be back in two days."

"Well, that should give us two more nights," the man said. Dave knew it was the insurance man.

"No! It will take a day to get the scent of your love juices out of my bed. I will need to wash the sheets, the mattress pad, and then flip the mattress," Carol said laughing. "Oh yeah, I probably will need to shampoo the carpet as well." They walked into the room as Dave closed himself in the closet, leaving it cracked just enough for him to see them.

"I don't know how I'm going to explain the carpet burns."

"What carpet burns?"

"These," Carol said as she raised skirt and lowered her panties on one side exposing two marks on the cheek of her buttock. "You are so rough. You probably did that on purpose."

"Why would you have to explain anything to him." Chuck was angry. "You're not going to have sex with him anymore, are you?"

"Well, he is my husband," Carol said slyly turning her back to him and then looking back over her shoulder and winking at him.

"I thought you said you were going to leave him. You said you love me. You said we were going to be together."

"That was just sex talk. You don't make enough money to take care of me. But don't worry, we will still be able to spend time together, every now and then."

"You are a cold-hearted lying bitch. I'm leaving!"

"Are you sure?" Carol said. Without looking at him, Carol unzipped her skirt, let it drop to the floor, and bent over the bed.

Chuck walked up behind her and dropped his pants.

"Hmmmm Hmmm," Dave said clearing his throat as he walked out of the closet. They both looked to their right and froze when they saw what was in Dave's hand.

"Dave!" Carol yelled. When she yelled Chuck started to reach for his pants.

"Don't move!" Dave snarled as he pulled back the hammer of the pistol. There was a loud click.

"David Parker, stop this right now," Carol shouted with a trembling voice.

"You think you can just come into a man's home and have sex with his wife in his own bed," Dave's anger was rising, "and think you can get away with it?"

"You need to talk to your wife about that. She invited me over. She came on to me."

"You, prick." Carol snapped. "That's right, blame everything on me."

"You are to blame!" Dave screamed. "You let him come in here and put you in every position imaginable. You let him do things to you that you won't let me even think about doing. And, you did things to him, you have never done to me."

"Oh my God, you have a camera in here. You have been spying on me."

"Man, you are just going to have to shoot me, cause I'm going to put my pants on," Chuck said as he slowly began to move his hand down toward his pants.

The sound was as loud as thunder, as the bullet exploded from the pistol in Dave's hand. Still the explosion was overshadowed by Carol's scream that followed. Chuck grabbed his chest, closed his eyes, fell back, and hit the floor. Carol backed to the wall with her hands up.

"Please, Dave," Carol sobbed. "Don't kill me." She closed her eyes and waited for her bullet. Dave couldn't believe that the trigger on the pistol was so sensitive. He had barely touched it. He didn't intend to shoot. Yet now that there was a hole in the wall, and he had their undivided attention and obedience. He walked forward and stood there looking down at the insurance man. He thought about the scenes he had seen in the crystal ball, scenes of this man and his wife, in his bed. Before he knew it, he had pulled the hammer on the pistol back.

"No, no, please, don't," Chuck pleaded.

"Dave, please," Carol begged, realizing the Chuck had not been shot.

"Don't say another word, either one of you," Dave screamed as her lowered the pistol down to Chuck's head.

Outside the house, Dave's neighbors had heard the gunshot, and the scream. One of them had call 911. It wasn't long before the sound of police sirens could be heard in the distance. A crowd had gathered in the yard of Dave's next-door neighbor. They all pointed as two police cars pulled up. Four policemen got out. Two cops went to the back, one stood against the wall of the house next to the front door, and the other one went to talk to the people in the yard.

"Who called 911," the officer asked.

A lady, around eighty years old, raised her hand. Her name was Martha Cummings. She was Dave's next-door neighbor. She and her husband had been living there when Dave bought his house. She was completely grey, and her hair looked as if she had just left the salon.

"Over here officer!" she said as she walked toward him. "I knew there was going to be trouble when I saw Dave get out of that car over there," she said pointing to Dave's rental car, parked one house down from hers, which was next door to his. "That's not his car."

"Ma'am, the 911 operator said that you heard gunshots."

"I knew he was going to shoot somebody, cause when he got out of the car, he stuck a really big pistol in the back of his pants. Carol, his wife has been letting this man come over at night. He's been staying all night. Dave must have found out about it. Lord knows what's been going in there."

"You're saying he had a gun when he went in the house?"

"A really big pistol is a gun, isn't it? Are you writing this down, officer", she looked at his name tag, "Pender? You need to be taking notes."

"Okay, ma'am." The officer took out his pad and pen.

"Now, I'm Martha Cummings with an 'S.' I live next door to the scene of the crime. I saw Dave, I mean David Parker, my neighbor, go in the house, first. Then I saw Carol, his wife, and her male friend, whose been spending the night for about four nights now. At first, he, Carol's male friend that is, would leave real early in the morning, but the last two days, it was like they didn't even care if anybody saw them. They would leave together in the middle of the day."

"Ma'am, what about the shots."

"Oh yeah! Dave went in, then Carol and the man went in. That's when I heard the shots, and I heard the scream."

"How many shots did you hear?"

"I don't know. Two or three, I guess. He probably shot them and then shot himself, a murder suicide."

Their conversation was interrupted by the officer near the front door. "Hey Sarge, somebody's coming."

"You people, get back inside your houses!" Sargent Pender shouted as he moved quickly toward Dave's house. Nobody in the crowd moved. They all watched as the front door was thrown open and a man in a shirt and his underwear ran out the door. "Get down on the ground, now!"

"Don't shoot!" Chuck yelled, falling to his knees as Pender moved forward with his pistol ready to fire. Quickly Pender put the cuffs on Chuck and took him to the police car. Before he could open the door, he heard the upstairs window open. He looked back and saw a pistol sale through the air and land in the yard. It was followed by five bullets and a casing.

"I'm coming out," Dave yelled.

The officer at the front door was crouched down with pistol pointing inside the door. He watched as Dave walked slowly down the stairs with his hands up. He kept his gun trained on Dave as Dave walked out the door. Without being told, Dave laid face down in the grass and put his hands behind his back. Pender and the other officer came up to Dave. Pender put his knee on the back of Dave's neck and cuffed him while the other officer kept his gun aimed at Dave.

Officer Pender leaned down close to Dave's ear. "Are you David Parker?"

"Yes sir, I live here."

"Where is your wife, Mr. Parker?

"She's in the bedroom."

"Is she," Sargent Pender hesitated, "unharmed?"

"She is," Dave cleared his throat, "unharmed."

"Put him in our car. I'll go check on the wife," Sargent Pender said to the officer beside him.

Officer Pender immediate entered the house, his pistol pointing the way. He opened the back door letting the other two officers inside. "Check down here," he said to his comrades. They headed off in opposite directions. He walked to the bottom of the stairs and called out, "Mrs. Parker, where are you? This is the police. I'm coming up." There was no response. "Mrs. Parker, this is the police. Can you hear me." Still nothing. He started walking slowly up the stairs.

In the bedroom, Carol was standing in front of her dresser, holding a hairbrush in her right hand, looking at her flawless skin one last time. She closed her eyes and slapped the brush up against her right eye. The pain was greater than she had anticipated. There was a slight cut beneath her eye. She moaned as she fell forward against the dresser. Laying the brush on the dresser she carefully laid herself down on the floor and closed her eyes. She heard the policeman when he walked to the doorway of the room. She remained motionless.

"Steward! Call for an ambulance," he yelled to one of the officers on the floor below. Then he walked into the room. "Mrs. Parker? Can you hear me?" he called as he touched the vein on her throat to see if she had a pulse.

"No! Get away from me!" she screamed quickly rolling away from him to a sitting position, her back against the dresser, and her arms out in front of her face.

"Mrs. Parker, you're safe, now. I am a police officer."

"Oh, thank God!" She lowered her arms. "Did you get him? Dave. My husband, did you get him. He went crazy."

"Yes ma'am, we got him." Pender moved his head closer to her. "Did he, Mr. Parker, do this, to your face? Did he hit you."

"It was like he had gone insane. I tried to explain, and he just hit me," Carol said getting up and sitting on the bed.

"Mrs. Parker, I wouldn't move around too much. You could be injured. The paramedics are on the way. Let them check, first."

"Oh, yes, you're right. He's never hit me that hard before." She lightly touched her now swollen eye with two of her fingers. "I might need to get some x-rays taken."

"Mrs. Parker, do you feel like answering a few questions? You don't have to do it now, however, I've found that you remember more when the incident is fresh on your mind."

"Yeah sure, I can answer your questions. I'm coherent."

Pulling his pad from his back pocket and a pen from his shirt pocket he asked, "In your own words, just tell me as best you can what happened here, today. Not too fast please. I'll be taking notes."

"Are you ready?"

"Yes ma'am."

"Well, I had an appointment with my insurance salesman, and I, I needed some information from my records. So, we came here to get the information. Anyway, I came up here to find the information and that's when my husband came in. He had a gun. He made Charles, the insurance man, come up here to our bedroom. He made Charles pull off his pants. Then he told us to get on the bed. I think his plan was, to claim that he caught us making love and then he could say he killed us because he went crazy, insane. Anyway, I told him that I wasn't going to get on the bed. He got angrier, so he balled up his fist and hit me in my eye, knocking me to the floor. That's when Charles tried to get the gun. I heard Dave shoot the gun and I screamed. I must have fainted after that, because that's all I remember, until you got here. Is the insurance man all right?

"He's fine ma'am," Pender said looking up at her. "He wasn't shot." Officer Pender continued to write as he spoke. "And you said after he hit you in the eye with his fist, you heard a shot. Was it just one shot, ma'am?"

"Yeah, as far as I know"

"Is that everything, ma'am?"

"Yes, that's it."

"Okay, the paramedics will be here shortly." Pender turned to leave.

"Officer, Pender?"

"Yes ma'am?"

"Where is Chuck, I mean Charles, the insurance man."

"He's outside in the police car."

"You're not arresting him, are you? He didn't do anything. I will testify to that."

"No, we just needed to get a statement from him."

"Can I see him, now? I want to apologize to him all of this."

"Yes, of course." Pender walked to the edge of the bed. "Are these his pants?"

"Yeah."

"The paramedics just pulled up. I'll let him come in, after the paramedics check you out and after he puts on his pants."

"Okay, but please, make sure you tell him that I want to see him."

Pender shook his head 'yes' as the paramedics walked into the room.

Chapter 9
The Strategy Revealed

(Saturday night 11:15 PM)

Rev. Zackery hung up the phone. He had found out that there was a Jane Doe in intensive care who matched Pam's description. The nurse had asked if he would come down and identify her. Rev. Zackery worried that what the demon had shown him was true. He grabbed his hat, went to the door, opened it, and was just about to rush down to the hospital, when the thought 'I need to pray,' came to him. He shut the door quickly, sat down at the dining room table, removed his hat, and began to whisper a prayer.

"Lord, it has started, a full-scale attack, from the enemy, on all fronts. You warned me that it was going to happen. Now, I'm coming to You, again Lord. I'm depending on you to direct my steps. Tell me what to do, please. Everyone is depending on me." Rev. Zackery stopped and waited for the Lord to reveal His will to him. Ten minutes went by. Still, he waited. "How am I going to win this battle," he whispered, resting his forehead in his hand as his elbow and arm propped his head up on the table. Slowly he raised his head. "For we wrestle not against flesh and blood, but against principalities, against powers, against the rulers of the darkness in high places, against spiritual wickedness in high places," he said quoting the bible. "Thank you, Holy Spirit for bringing that to my remembrance." He paused. "Now what is the rest of that scripture? There's something that come before that 'for.' Aaah. Oh, yeah. 'Finally, my brethren, be strong in the Lord, and in the power in his might. Put on the whole armor of God, that ye may be able to stand against the wiles of the devil.' That's it! I need to put on my armor. I am already girted in the truth. I am the righteousness of God, so I have on my breastplate.

I guess my feet are shod with the gospel of peace. Now it says 'Above all' take my shield of faith, my helmet of salvation, and my sword of the Spirit, which is the word of God.

Now, is that all? No! It says, praying always, in the spirit." Rev. Zackery shook his head up and down. "My offensive weapons are the word of God, and prayer."

He thought he heard something coming from the bedroom. He strained to hear something, anything. Then, he heard it. A noise was coming from the bedroom. Rev. Zackery quietly moved toward the bedroom. He turned the doorknob slowly and cracked the door just enough to see the bed. Billy was standing beside the bed. He had removed the duct tape form his hands and he was bending over, unwinding the tape from his legs. Rev. Zackery walked to the cabinet where he had left his pistol. He reached on top, and it was not there. He then went to the hall closest where his brother kept his double barrowed shotgun. He checked to see if it was loaded. It was. Rev. Zackery took the shotgun and walked into the room. Billy looked up to see the two barrels pointing at his heart.

"Don't shoot! Please!" Billy pleaded.

"Get that duct tape off the dresser. Tape your legs up, again."

Billy took the tape and began to tape his legs together. "Keep going around until I tell you to stop." When Billy had wrapped the taped around his legs at least ten times, Rev. Zackery ordered him to wrap the tape around his right forearm all the way down to and including his hand. When this was done, Rev. Zackery leaned the shotgun against the wall and walked toward Billy. "Turn your back to me and give me the tape." Rev. Zackery taped his forearm to his stomach. He then rolled a desk chair up to Billy and sat him down in the chair.

"What are you going to do with me now?"

"Are you hungry?"

"Yeah, I'm starving."

"Well, let's get something to eat. We can talk while I fix the food. Hopefully, we can have a conversation without being interrupted."

"Okay," Billy said slowly not knowing what Rev. Zackery was referring to.

"Now, if I remember correctly, you were telling me what you saw me on the bridge."

"You threw a safe into the water, and …"

"And you got it out, and opened it, right?" Before Billy could answer, he started to stiffen, and his eyes began to roll to the back of his head. Rev. Zackery quickly put his bible on Billy's head and shouted, "In the name of Jesus, I command you demon, to release your power over Billy. Instantly, Billy was back.

"Yes, yes sir. I got it. I saw her. She was in the glass, but she was also in my head."

"Did she tell you to kill me?" Rev. Zackery pressed the bible hard against his head.

"Not so hard, please, I'll tell you what you want to know." Billy pushed Rev. Zackery's hand lightly with his free hand.

"Sorry!" Rev. Zackery removed the bible from Billy's forehead. "I guess we should introduce ourselves to each other. I'm Rev. Leroy Zackery and you are?"

"I'm Billy." There was a pause. "Burton."

"I can't say it's been a pleasure meeting you, but it has been interesting."

"I don't know what you are talking about."

"Billy, when you opened that safe and saw the crystal ball with the woman inside, I believe a spell was cast on you. The woman in the crystal is a very powerful witch. She sent you here to kill me. Can you remember what happened when you first saw the crystal."

"I opened the safe and removed the towel. That's when I saw it, the crystal ball, and the woman inside it. She looked at me. She was surprised to see me.

I don't know how, but I could hear her, not with my ears, but in my head. She screamed at me.

As Billy describes what happened the day before, the scene changes to Billy's work shed.

Billy is standing next to an old wooden table with a metal wedge and a sledgehammer lying next to the open safe. The black towel that had been covering the crystal is in his hand as he bends over and looks down at the woman moving inside the crystal ball.

"Get me out of here or I'll kill you."

Billy jumps back, looking around to see who had said those words. "Who said that?" Billy realized that he hadn't heard the words. It was like a thought but with a woman's voice. He walked back to the crystal. Holding it up close to his face, he was mesmerized as he watched her point to herself each time she said 'me.'

"It was me. I said it, me. If you get me out of here, I'll give you anything you want, money, sex, power, anything."

"How am I supposed to get you out of there?" Billy shouted putting the crystal on the table, grabbing his hammer, and raising it over his head. "You want me to bust it open."

"No! Wait!" she screamed.

Dropping the hammer at his feet, Billy held his head with both hands, to keep it from splitting apart from the painful blast of sound inside his head. "Find Jason. He trapped me in here. He'll know how to get me out."

"Who? What did you do to my head?" A few seconds later the pain subsided. "Find who?"

"His name is Jason. Come closer. I'll tell you what I want you to do."

The scene of the memory disappears. They are back in the bedroom.

"After that, the next thing I remember was waking up here, taped up, in this room, with you."

"So, you weren't sent here to kill me. You wanted to make me tell you how to get to Jason, then your plan is to take him to her, and then you'd kill me."

"Reverend, I don't know what you're talking about, I don't want to kill you."

"Son, the witch put you in some kind of trance," he shouted as he rolled Billy into the kitchen. "But you've got worse problems than that."

"What?"

"Demons, Billy boy. You got demons." Rev. Zackery pushed the rolling chair up to the table then leaning his face down in front of Billy's, he spoke, "You're tore up from the floor up." Then walking to the refrigerator, "Bacon, eggs, and toast okay with you?"

"Yes sir, that sounds real good."

Chapter 10
The Awakening

(Sunday morning 2:30 AM)

The ER nurse walked out of the burn patient's room and went back to her station. Immediately the burn patient got out of the bed, her pain being total disregarded and overruled by her rage and hate. She walked to the medical waste container and pulled out a used hypodermic needle. Sticking the needle into her morphine drip bag and sucking it full of morphine, she hurried to the door and opened it slowly. The nurse had her back to the door, so she quickly left her room and entered the adjacent room, Pam's room. She made sure the nurse had not seen her before she shut the door completely. Turning her hate filled eyes, and holding the needle like a dagger, her thumb on the plunger, she walked quietly up to and looked down at Pam who was in a drug induced sleep. Sibal pressed the needle to Pam's neck. It pushed the skin down until it penetrated. She could have shot Pam full of morphine at that moment, however, she wanted Pam to know who was going to kill her. Pulling the needle out, she sat on Pam's left arm and pinned the other one with her hand. Then with the hand that was holding the needle, she knocked several times on Pam's forehead until Pam's eyes opened. Sibal leaned down toward Pam's face.

"Officer Sibal, you're alive," Pam said softly and calmly. Then as she yawned, she said, "We thought you blew yourself up."

"Blew myself up! Somebody put that dynamite up there by the plunger. Who was it?"

"It was the righteous reverend," Pam giggled. "He saw that someone, you, had put dynamite all around his church so he cut the wires on all but one. Then, he threw that one back to where the lines were leading.

"Well, thank you very much. He'll be the first person I visit after I take care of you."

Sibal jabbed the needle completely into Pam's neck and waited for Pam to react. Pam only smiled.

"You didn't feel that? Are you paralyzed?"

"I felt it, but it didn't hurt, and guess what? You don't scare me. Anyway, don't you want to know what happened to your little friends?" Pam giggled again.

Sibal pulled the needle out and leaned back, "Okay, what happened to them?"

"You were wondering why they never came to see about you, weren't you?

"I said okay. What happened to them?"

"Well Tamera, my sister dear, we trapped her in the crystal ball and we threw her in the river."

"What? How did?"

"Tamera is history." Pam smiled with bright eyes and a satisfied look on her face. "We got rid of her for you."

"What do you mean for me?"

"Come on, Sibby, when you pushed the plunger to explode the dynamite, all of us were inside the church. You were trying to kill everybody, including Tamera. I figure, you wanted her out of the way so you could take her place. You want to be the HWIC."

"What?"

"The head witch in charge." Pam smiled again. "See, we did you a favor."

"What about Dutchman. What happened to him?"

"He wasn't your boyfriend, was he?"

"No! Where is he? Is he still alive?"

"Well, I'm happy to say he did not make it. Jason stabbed him in the neck with five number two pencils and then shot his kneecap off, and that was after he beat him in the ground. He's dead. The cause of death was blood loss. All his blood ran out of his neck into the dirt."

"That butthole killed Dutchman?"

"Yelp."

"You so high on drugs, you don't even know you'll be dead in two minutes," Sibal said as she moved the needle toward Pam's neck.

"We got rid of all your competition, why don't you just say thank you, and leave us alone?"

"Look at my face!" Sibal snarled as she pulled back some of the bandage on the burned side of her face.

"Good googalar moogalar! I'd rather be dead than to look like that," Pam giggled.

"Don't worry. I'm going to take care of that right now. I just wanted you to know it was me who put you out of your misery." Sibal held the needle out over Pam's neck so Pam could see her coming demise.

"The burned side is not that bad, but those scratches going down your face, now that's horrible. Oh, I remember now, I did that."

"That's right bitch, now die!"

"Wait a minute!" Pam frowned.

"For what?"

"Tell me this. Is there some kind of ceremony or election to become the new leader of the witches clan?"

"Okay, I'll grant you one last request, since as you say, you did me a favor. Normally, it passes down through the bloodline, from parent to child. If there are not any children, the strongest witch become the HWIC as you put it. However, this is only temporary, because once we find a virgin surrogate, which we already have, and she is impregnated with the demon seed, which will happen Tuesday, when the baby is born, she will become the leader. The baby is almost always a girl. The head council puts something in the virgin that kills 'y' chromosomes. When the baby is born, she must be raised and trained before she can take control. So, if I become the head witch, I would control the whole process. I could drag out the training process for years before I had to give up my position."

"So how do they determine who the strongest?"

"A fight to the death, either before or at the big ceremony."

"So, you're the strongest?"

"I think so, especially since you say Dutchman is dead, however, even if there are some stronger, most people don't want it bad enough to die for. I want it that bad."

"Yeah, you also want it bad enough to kill for."

"Yeah, that's right. You took care of your sister for me, now I'm going to take care of you."

"You wish."

"What do you mean?"

"Look at the door."

Sibal look at the door and saw the ER nurse standing there with her mouth open.

"What are you doing with that needle," the nurse shouted from the door. "Security, security!" she screamed, "Code Red."

Sibal was about to push the needle into Pam's neck when Pam's head raised. Pam bit into Sibal's hand. Sibal released Pam's arm, placed her hand on top of the one holding the needle, and pushed down with all her might. It was not quick enough. Pam hit Sibal's hands and slid her neck away from the needle. The needle was driven into the bed. Sibal jumped off Pam's other arm, pulling the needle out of the bed and was about to move in again, when Pam swung the nurse call button, hitting Sibal hard on the bridge of her nose.

Sibal dropped the needle, fell to both knees, and then toppled over to the floor holding her head.

Two security officers came up quickly and stood behind the nurse.

"Get that one on the floor. Put in the bed next door and handcuff her to the bed. I'm going to call the police. You can read my report later." The nurse went to her desk and picked up the phone. "Reverend, I don't know how you knew to call me, but you were right."

"It was the Lord, He spoke to me," Rev. Zackery said. "Is Miss Williamson okay?"

"Yes sir. She is now. Thank you for calling." She hung up the phone.

The two security officers came out of the room. One got a chair sat next to the door, the other one walked over to the nurse. "What was that all about?"

Holding up a plastic bag containing the needle, "Our burn patient was about to stick this into our gunshot patient's neck. And get this, some preacher called and told me to check on her. He said the Lord spoke to him. That woman would be dead now, if he hadn't called when he did. Can you believe that shhhh, stuff?"

"You're kidding, right?"

"I wish. I heard when that black guy told the police that someone might try to kill her. I guess he was right. Is he still out there in the waiting room?"

"No, the police took him in for questioning."

"I'd better call them right now and let them know that he was right," she said pressing the keys on her phone.

Miles away the phone rang at the police station. The corporal at the front desk answered and listened. "Okay, nurse Erwin, I'll let them know."

The officer left the desk and walked into the interrogation room where two policemen were questioning Jason. One was a detective and the other had brought Jason from the hospital. When the officer from the desk whispered in the detective's ear, he looked at Dave.

"What is it? Did something happen to Pam?"

"You were right. Someone, a patient, tried to kill her. But she was not harmed. She's fine."

"Look sir! I've only been here a few days. I came to visit my grandmother. I didn't know Pam was going to be at my grandmother's house. I knew my grandmother had raised her, but I just met her a few days ago. All I know is some people are trying to kill her. Since the day I got here, these people have made several attempts to kill her. These people are witches. They are the same ones who killed my grandmother."

"Witches?"

"They call themselves witches, the believe they are witches? You can call them whatever you want to call them, but they killed my grandmother, and they are trying to kill Pam." Jason paused for a breath. "That's all I know. Just call Sergeant Hilliard He was there at my grandmother's house the day she was killed."

"Okay, we'll call him. You can go. I'll have someone take you back to hospital. What will you do now?"

"When she's able, I'm going to take Pam home and then I'll come back for my grandmother's funeral."

"All right, just wait in the reception area, and someone will come and get you."

"Could you direct me to the restroom?"

"It's down that hall, take a left and you'll see the sign."

Jason followed the directions to the restroom. Once inside he called Rev. Zackery and told him what had happened from the moment they left his house until the present time, then he waited for Rev. Zackery to respond.

"It was Sibal," Rev. Zackery finally said.

"It was Sibal? What are you talking about, reverend?"

"The patient, in the room next to Pam's, is Sibal, the police officer who poured the gasoline on Ma'amie at her house."

"I thought you said she was dead. Anyway, how would you know that? It just happened."

"I called the hospital and told the nurse to check on Pam cause I saw Sibal in the room, holding a needle to Pam's throat." Rev. Zackery waited for a response but only heard a deep breath being exhaled. "I also saw you when you were hiding in Sibal's room before you sneaked into Pam's room. Sibal heard you talking to the police. That's how she knew it was Pam in the room next to hers. Jason, don't trust anyone, not even the police. Get Pam out of there as soon as possible."

"You'll have to tell me all about this later. I am really beat. I can't even comprehend what you're saying right now. I've got to get some rest."

"Why don't you come here? Me and Billy will go to the hospital and stay with Pam."

"Who is Billy?"

"It's a long story. I'll fill you in later. The door key will be under the flowerpot on the porch. I'll see you later this morning."

Jason went to the reception area and waited for a ride back to his car at the hospital.

Chapter 11
Bad Billy

(Sunday morning 4:10 AM)

Rev. Zackery and Billy walked out of the house. With a tight grip on Billy's arm, and with troubling concerns about the state of mind of his travel companion, Rev. Zackery led Billy to the car. He had to take him with him. He couldn't leave him with Jason. He couldn't just leave him tied and gagged in the crawl space under the house, or could he? Maybe he should.

"Look Billy, how are you feeling?" Rev. Zackery said turning Billy toward him.

"Fine."

"I need for you to be on your best behavior. You've got to keep those demons under control, cause I've got to go to the hospital to care for a friend. Can you do that?"

"Yes sir, I can do that."

"Okay, get in, and let's go. And you demons, don't make me act a fool on y'all," Rev. Zackery warned as he started the car.

"Reverend, when I black out, that's when the demons take control of me, right?"

"Yeah, that's right Billy. I believe they had control of you before you found the crystal. In fact, one of them told me that I wouldn't care about you if I knew what you had been planning to do yesterday, before you found the crystal." Rev. Zackery paused. "What were you planning to do, Billy?"

"It's very hard to talk about that, reverend," Billy said squirming in his seat. Beads of sweat began to form on his forehead. Then it happened. His voice changed. "Billy doesn't want to talk about it."

Rev. Zackery stomped on the brakes, threw the gearshift into park, and guided the car as it slid to a stop on the side of his driveway. Billy's head hit the dash, however, before he could rebound Rev. Zackery pushed Billy hard against the passenger window pinning him. Billy's head turned toward Rev. Zackery, but it wasn't Billy's head. It was a demon's head. This one was new. He was clean shaven, handsome, with an attractive smile.

"Did you really think that Billy could control us?" the demon said shaking his head, flashing that appealing smile. "You've got to be the dumbest preacher of all time. I thought Steven was dumb. Man, you got him beat."

"Steven, in the bible? Why are you calling Steven dumb?"

"He kept preaching to those Jews even though he knew they were getting angrier and more violent by the second. But, no, he didn't stop, he just kept on preaching, even when they were stoning him. That was dumbest thing I had ever seen, until now. You have seen what we can do. You know how powerful we are. You know that Billy boy has a weak mind. Still, you think he can control us. That's so dumb, it's pitiful. I'm really going to enjoy killing you. I think I'll torture you first." He smiled again.

"What's your name, smiley."

"My name?" The demon laughed. "Just call me Bob. It's short for boss of Billy. I give the orders in this body."

"In the name of Jesus, demon, I command you, Bob…"

"Command this," the demon shouted interrupting Rev. Zackery. Then using Billy's body, he knocked Rev. Zackery's arm away and lean his face up to Rev. Zackery's. "Who in hell do you think you are? You can't fight against me."

"I'm Rev. Leroy Zackery. If you didn't know, you shoulda asked one of your little demons. They know who I am. Anyway, you're the one who is going to hell not me. Before long you'll be roasting in the lake of fire, where there will be weeping and gnashing of teeth. They won't be calling you Bob then. They'll be calling you shish kabob"

"Oh, you got jokes. Ha, ha, ha. Before long I'm going to have you cursing your Jesus and bowing to me."

"Demon, you don't scare me. I knew you were going to try something."

"Is that right? Well Leroy, did you know that after I ate the food you prepared for Billy boy, he was going to take one of your forks and put it in his pocket so that at just the right time he could pull it out and stab you in your throat," the demon said while pulling the fork out of his pocket. He pushed Rev. Zackery against his door. As the demon brought the fork forward, Rev. Zackery grabbed his wrist with his right hand, stopping it.

"I can count, demon. I put two forks on the table, I took one fork off, and I washed one fork. Come on demon, I knew you had the fork. I was just waiting for you to make your move cause I wanted to see if Billy could resist your influence over him. You are the one, who is not too bright. They evidently didn't put you over the other demons because of your smarts. Hold on demon," Rev. Zackery tried to look through the demonic image covering Billy's face. "Billy are you in there. You can fight these demons. Just say the name of Jesus. Billy! Billy! Can you hear me." Rev. Zackery waited. Then he directed his comments to the demon. "Can he hear me?"

"Yeah Leroy, he can hear you, but he can only do what I let him do. Do you want me to let him speak to you? Hmmmmm. If you really want to hear him, ask me real nice like."

"Okay. Demon…"

"That's Mr. Demon."

"Mr. Demon, will you let Billy speak to me, please?"

"Sure Leroy, but you need to put your ear next to his chest, because he is very weak."

Rev. Zackery leaned forward, and he could hear a faint voice. It sounded like Billy's.

"I'm trying but he is too powerful," a voice that sounded like Billy's said.

"Don't worry Billy, they are not going to kill you. They need you. You are their host. They must protect you. Without you, they will have to find somewhere else to exist."

"That's right, Leroy, we need him, but we don't need you," the demon said pulling the fork back to stab Rev. Zackery in the neck. "Bye," the demon said as he smiled brightly, but his smile was short lived as Billy's body began to shake violently. The demon looked down and saw that Rev. Zackery was holding a taser to Billy's side. The fork fell from Billy's shaking hand and his body fell forward against the dash. The demon's head covering Billy's turned toward Rev. Zackery. The demon looked fearful. Before the demon and Billy's body could recover from the first shock, Rev. Zackery ran around the car and pulled Billy back into the house, tasering him every few seconds. When they reached the bedroom, Rev. Zackery tasered Billy continuously. until the demon yelled out.

"Stop it! You are killing Billy."

"I bind you demon, in the name of Jesus, I command you to go," Rev. Zackery tried to think of somewhere to send the demon, "into my brother's fish." Rev. Zackery stopped tasering Billy and watched as the demonic image completely disappeared from Billy's head. However, the goldfish in the fishbowl was racing around madly. It was continuously crashing into the walls of the bowl until it finally came up about a foot out of the bowl and landed on a magazine flapping like crazy. Rev. Zackery quickly picked up the magazine, dumped the fish back into the water, and placed the magazine on top of the bowl. Once again, the fish began racing around madly, in the bowl.

Twenty-five minutes later, Rev. Zackery was walking into the intensive care unit of the hospital. It looked exactly like the demon had shown him. He walked to the nurse's station and greeted the nurse. "Hi Miss, I'm here to see…"

"You must be Rev. Zackery. I recognize your voice. I'm the nurse you spoke with earlier. If you hadn't called when you did, your friend would probably be dead right now. Our burn patient had a bad reaction to her medication, at least that's what the doctor said, and she went into your friend's room. She just about to stick a needle in your friend's neck, but your friend woke up and fought her off until we could get there. That was a close one, and you said God told you to call me to check on her, because you saw someone in her room." The nurse stopped talking, finally.

"It a pleasure to meet you, nurse," Rev. Zackery looked at her name tag, "Carson. May I see Miss Williamson now."

"Yes sir! She's awake now. She asked for some food. She is alert. She gave us all the information we needed. You can go in. She's in that room, right there."

"Thank you." Rev. Zackery walk into the room and closed the door.

Pam was biting furiously into a piece of fried chicken. Without looking up and with a mouth full of chicken, she spoke.

"Hi Reverend!"

"Hi Pam, how are you doing? Are you in much pain?" he said pulling a reclining chair closer to the bed.

"Pain? Well Rev. Zackery, pain is just a combination of fear and a signal to the brain that something is not right."

"Okay, are you in much pain?" he asked again.

"I cut off the signal, and I have no fear, therefore there is no pain. The bleeding has stopped, and my body is repairing itself rapidly. I will be able to leave tomorrow."

"Why don't you let the doctors determine that, Pam?"

She stopped eating, turned her head toward Rev. Zackery, and starred sternly into his eyes. He starred back sternly into hers. This lasted for at least twenty seconds until Rev. Zackery looked away and spoke.

"I understand someone tried to kill you tonight."

"Yeah, it was Sibal, the cop who we thought had blown herself up. She's next door. I heard the nurse say that you called and told her to check on me. She said, you said, that the Lord said, that someone who in my room."

"Well, something like that."

"The nurse said that you saved my life, Rev. Zackery," Pam smiled.

"I saw you in a vision."

"A vision?"

"Yeah, it seems that we're not done with your sister, Tamera."

"What do you mean?"

"This man that I have duct tapped in my trunk, saw us when we dropped the safe in the river. He fished it out. Somehow Tamera sent him to my brother's house to kill me."

"Is she out of the crystal ball?"

"No, but still she was able to get inside his head."

"Well how did you know Sibal was in my room?" Pam pushed the food cart to the side.

"Billy, the man in my trunk, also has demons."

"Demons!"

"Yeah, powerful demons. One of them showed me when Sibal came in your room. That's why the nurse came in when she did, that's how I was able to save you."

"Rerevend! I hate to bust your bubble again. You didn't save me, you saved Sibal. If that nurse hadn't come in when she did, Sibal would be dead right now."

"Dead? How?" he asked.

"I thought about you, so I didn't kill her. You told me that I have to learn how to control these new powers that I have, so I thought about that, and I let her live."

"So, you could have killed her, even though she had you pent down on the bed with a needle to you neck," Rev. said unbelievingly.

"Ye-ah! I'm glad I didn't kill her, cause I found out that in two days there is going to be a big ceremony where all the witches will pick a new temporary leader." Pam smiled. "They're all going to be in one place at the same time, Rev. Zackery."

"What are you planning on doing, Pam?"

"They are not going to stop looking for me. You know that. They have tried to kill me two times in the last two days."

"I think you had a little to do with that. I thought you were going to go back home. What happened to that plan, Pam!" Rev. Zackery said shaking his head.

"What do you want me to do, keeping running till they finally succeed in killing me? Well, I'm not running, nowhere. I'm gone take care of this once and for all, right now." Pam stopped looking at Rev. Zackery and looked at the door. "Come in here," she yelled. The door slowly opened, and the nurse walked in. "Forget everything you just heard, go back to your station, and do your job." The nurse turned around and began to walk out. "Close the door." When the door was closed, Pam looked at Rev. Zackery again. She took a deep breath and blew out. "We could use your help."

"We?"

"Jason and me! Rev. Zackery, they are going to start the process over again. They are going to get a virgin girl like they did my mother, get her pregnant with some evil demon seed, and make her give birth to the next witch queen or whatever they call her. Can you just stand by and let them do that?"

Rev. Zackery laid back in his chair and looked up at the ceiling and began to contemplate his current situation. He began to pray.

"Lord, I'm here in the hospital with Pam, a wounded, but powerful, potential witch. There is Jason, a revenge crazed potential mass murderer at my brother's house, cause my house was blown up. They want me to help them stop an evil plan by killing who knows how many witches, people.

Then, there is Sibal, blood thirsty witch in the next room who would love another chance to blow me up. I've got Billy, a demon possessed potential killer, duct taped in my trunk. And I don't have a clue what is going on with Dave, who I promised to pray for. Well, first things first. Lord please bless Dave wherever he is right now."

CHAPTER 12
COOLING OFF IN JAIL

(Sunday morning 5:30 AM)

Dave was asleep on a bench in a holding cell in the city jail. It was a fairly large room with three benches and a commode in the middle of the room. There were two other prisoners in the room. They were both black men. They were sleeping on benches as well. Dave laid there on his back with his arm over his eyes to block out the bright lights overhead. His sleep was disturbed when he heard loud voices coming down the hall. He heard the cell door opened and then slam shut. He partially uncovered his eyes as three big Latino men walked up to the first bench. They gathered around the bench and one of them shook the black man and woke him up.

"What? What you want?" the man looked up and said.

"Esse, you on my bench. You need to move," the smallest Latino said.

The black guy looked at all three of the men standing around him and he slowly got up and moved away. The Latino who had spoken sat down in the middle of the bench. The other two moved toward the next bench where the other black man was. He was already awake. He got up before they reached his bench. The second Latino sat down. Then the last Latino walk over to Dave's bench and stood over Dave. Dave moved his arm down from covering his eyes to covering his nose and mouth.

"Hey! You on my bench," the last Latino man said.

Dave quickly sat up facing the largest and the third Latino. He didn't look him in his eyes. He sat there watching his hands as they balled into fists.

"Move, now!" he shouted.

Dave slowly stood up slowly facing the man. They were the same height. The anger in the man's eyes was overpowered by the rage in Dave's. They both just stood there.

"Make me move," Dave shouted just as loud.

Seeing his defiance, the other two Latinos came and stood next to the one in front of Dave. Dave looked from one to the other, then he took a deep breath and blew in out loudly. As he did, he glanced to his right and to his left and saw the two black men behind him.

"If Rev. Zackery was here, he would say something from the bible, like come let us reason together," Dave said shaking the frown from his face.

"Are you a preacher, esse?" the smallest Latino said.

Dave reached out and grabbed the arm of man in front of him and pulled him gently to the bench.

"Sit down, all three of you. I want to tell you a story." The three Latinos sat on the bench while the two blacks stood behind them. Dave looked each one in their eyes. He had their complete attention.

"Look guys, I don't want to hurt nobody, but I'm on the edge right now. It won't take much, and I just might lose it. See, I've been through a lot in the last few days. I picked up this girl when I was driving to a conference. I didn't know she was running from this man who was trying to kill her. I don't know how, but he caught up with us at this motel. He killed the motel clerk and almost killed me. He shot me in the leg. That's when I find out that this murderer is a witch. Anyway, we weren't supposed to, but we left the motel when the police went to catch the killer. They didn't catch him, but they did catch us. We were in the back of the police car and he, the killer, who must have seen us when the police put us in their car, he came after her. He crashed his car into the police car, killing the two policemen in the front seat. I hit my head against the cage between the front and back seats. See this scare in my head." Dave parted his head, so they could see. "Then the killer gets out of his crushed-up car and tried to kill us again, but the girl sets him on fire with a cigarette lighter and a can of hair spray. I think she killed him. Anyway, we leave there. She makes me take her to the house of this fortune teller, who is her aunt. And get this, the girl is white, but her aunt is a black lady. Well, the aunt has this crystal ball. I accidentally touch it while I'm thinking about my wife and then, all of a sudden, inside the crystal ball, I see my wife and our insurance man having sex, in my house, in my bed." Dave is getting louder and louder, angrier and angrier.

"Calm down, esse. You gone blow a gasket," the smallest Latino said holding up both hands.

"It was my wife, it was my insurance man, it was my bedroom, and it was my bed. I'm looking in the crystal ball at my wife is doing stuff with this man that I ain't even seen in porno movies."

"That would have made me crazy," one of the black men said.

"I was crazy. So, me and the fortune tellers grandson went to get some liquor. When we got back the house was completely engulfed in flames. Some more witches had come. They killed the fortune teller. They tied her to a chair and set her on fire. They burn her up and her whole house. At this point, I leave to go back home. I think it's all over. No. A witch follows me, shoots out my tire and I crash my car. So, I run to this church, and I meet this black preacher, Rev. Zackery. I'm at his house when the girl and the fortune teller's grandson find me, using the crystal ball. They are not there an hour when three witches come there. They blow-up the preacher's house and almost kill all of us. So, we ran in the church and fought them there. We killed two of them and trapped the head witch inside the crystal ball. We won." Dave pauses. "Then I come back home. I'm in my bedroom and my wife comes in with the insurance man, so I hide in the closet. When they begin to take off their clothes, I lose it. That's why I'm here."

"You had to do what you had to do," the biggest Latino said.

"Naw, you couldn't let them disrespect you like that," the black man said. The biggest Latino turned and gave him a high five. They all turn back to Dave. His expression had turn from anger to sinister.

"Yesterday, I almost pushed my thumbs through my boss' eye sockets, and today I almost shot the insurance man's penis off." Dave closes his eyes and drops his head. "Now, I've done what Rev. Zackery would have advised me to do. I have tried to reason with you. All I want to do is get some rest here in jail on this bench." He looks up at the three Latinos sitting on his bench. "So, I'm going to ask you just once, can I just lay down in peace?"

The three Latinos got up quickly. "Okay esse, please, lay down. We didn't know. You need your rest," the smallest one said.

"Here, you can lay you head on my sweater," the biggest one said taking off his sweater and placing it on the bench where Dave's head had been.

"Thank you, guys, I really appreciate this." Dave became very emotional and began to cry. They all hugged him, and Dave laid down. Before long he was asleep again.

Chapter 13
The Reunion

(Sunday morning 7:30 AM)

When Jason woke, it was just beginning to be light outside. He stretched on the sofa at Rev. Zackery's brother's house. He had gotten almost four hours of much needed sleep. He thought about calling the hospital to check on Pam and Rev. Zackery, but he decided that he would get something to eat first. He sat up on the sofa and was about to move when he heard something clicking. It was very erratic. It was coming from the room at the end of the hall. Jason quietly got up and walked in his socks down the hall to the door which was ajar. Through the crack in the door, he scanned as much of the room as possible until he saw what was making the noise. The fish in the fishbowl was jumping up out of the water hitting a magazine that covered the fishbowl. Jason watched the fish for a minute as it franticly moved inside the fishbowl, then he slowly pushed open the door. He scanned the room again. The clicking stopped. He looked at the fish. It was still. It was looking at him. He walked closer and put his head very close to the fishbowl. 'Take the magazine off the top of the fishbowl, and put your hand in the water,' he thought.

"You want me to take the magazine off, and put my hand in the water," he said to the fish. 'Yes,' he thought. He picked up the fishbowl and carried it into the kitchen and sat it on the counter. He opened the refrigerator, took out some eggs and cheese. Then he put some bread in the toaster. He looked at the fish. It was still looking at him.

"Are you hungry, little fish?" he asked politely as he turned on the electric burner on the stove. He made himself a cup of coffee. He made himself an egg and cheese sandwich. He sat at the kitchen table and began to eat, then he looked at the fish again. 'Put my hand in the fishbowl,' he thought. He took a bite of his sandwich. "You want me to put my hand in the fishbowl," he said to the fish. To his surprise the fish rocked it's body slowly up and down like it was saying 'yes.' Jason got up noticing that he had not turned off the burner and the frying pan was beginning to smoke. He quickly moved the pan.

'Put my hand on the burner,' he thought. He turned to toward the fish. It was still looking at him. "You want me to put my hand on that hot burner." The fish rocked up and down again. Jason moved his face up to the fishbowl, his eyes locked with the fishes. He picked up the bowl and walked to the stove. "Okay," he said as he put the fishbowl down on the hot burner. He grabbed the hot frying pan and quickly removed the magazine, replacing it with the hot frying pan. Jason went back to the table, sat down, and continued eating his sandwich as he watched the fish.

The fish swam around, jumped up, and hit the bottom of the hot frying pan. It stuck to it for a second and then fell back into the water, barely able to swim. Soon the water began to boil, and the fish stopped moving. It floated on its side to the top of the bubbling water.

"That was so good," Jason said cutting off the burner as he walked back to the bedroom where he had seen a TV. He wanted to see the morning news before he called the hospital. However, before he could sit down with his coffee, the phone rang.

"Hello," Jason said expecting to hear Rev. Zackery's voice.

"Jason! What are you doing there? You're supposed to be home by now."

"Hey Dave. We ran into a little trouble. Pam was shot."

"What? Who did it? Is she okay?" Dave asked.

"She'll be okay. We went by Gramma's to destroy that witch book that you found in the well. They, three witches, were there looking for it. They attacked us, and she was shot. Rev. Zackery is with her now. I'm sorry, how are you doing, Dave?"

"Pretty good comparatively speaking."

"No, really, how was the homecoming?"

"Well, I'm in jail. My wife is claiming I tried to kill her. Other than that, I got a some really, good, sleep last night. Best of all, no witches are trying to kill me."

"When are you getting out?" Jason asked.

"I don't want to get out. I haven't felt this safe in a week."

"Be for real, dude. Nobody likes being in jail."

"I am being real. I need to be locked up. I almost killed two people in less than eight hours. I don't even know what I'm capable of doing any more."

"When do you go before the judge?"

"Tomorrow, early Monday morning is what I'm hearing. They're giving me a cooling off period. I need it. I almost shot that insurance man testicles off."

"Just his testicles? You're nicer than me."

"All I'm saying is that I need to rest my mind."

"Don't get too comfortable?"

"What's up, Jason. I hear trouble in your voice."

"Those witches are planning to start the process of getting another head witch."

"What do I care about what they do. I never want to see or hear anything about witches ever again."

"Okay, but Pam and I are going to stop them." Jason waited for a reaction. There was a long pause.

"How are you going to do that?" Dave finally replied.

"We're going to kill them."

"Kill them! In legal terms, would this be considered premeditated murder in the first degree?" Dave asked sternly. "How many witches are we talking about?"

"I'm not sure. Maybe a few hundred."

"Do you know how crazy that sounds? You did just say that Pam had just been shot, didn't you? Please tell me that you are going to wait until Pam is well?" Dave begged.

"No! It's going down in two days. We're going to trap them in their meeting place when they gather for the big ceremony, and then we're going to burn them up, every last one of them. They're going to burn, just like my gramma did." Building rage could be heard in Jason's voice.

"Calm down Jason! You need to get yourself under control. How does Pam feel about this plan of yours?"

"It's not my plan, it's her plan. I was going to take her home and then go home myself. She was the one who wanted to go and destroy the book. The three witch dudes were already there looking for the book. She decided to confront them. She ordered them to leave her property. When they came after us, we split up, her decision. She was supposed to lose those guys in the woods, and then meet me at the big rock. But no, she decided to kill the two that followed her into the woods. That's how she got shot. Now, she wants to put an end to this whole mess, once and for all. She's going to do it with my help or without it. I'm going to help her. Plus, they killed my gramma. I want them dead. So, I'm gone kill as many of them as I can before they kill me."

"So, this is a suicide mission. You don't even expect to make it out alive. What about Rev. Zackery? What did he say? Is he in on this, too?"

"Rev. Zackery is doing what he does best, he's praying," Jason said shaking his head.

"Come on, you know we would probably be dead now if it wasn't for Rev. Zackery."

"Yeah, you're right. I'm sorry, he's a good man." Jason paused. "Look Dave, there's something else you're right about, I don't think Pam and I are going to be able to pull this thing off, and get out alive, without help. We need your help, Dave." There was a long silence. Then Jason heard another voice on the phone. Someone was speaking to Dave.

"I've got to go Jason, the jailer just told me to hang up. I've got to go back to the holding cell, now. Ask Rev. Zackery to say a prayer for me, please, bye."

"Okay, I…" The phone dial tone sounded, so Jason hung up. He walked to the TV, began searching for the news. He was still changing channels when he heard the door open.

"Jason," Rev. Zackery yelled.

"Hey, I'm back here in the bedroom. I hope you don't mind. I just wanted to watch the news." Jason walked out of the bedroom into the hall and then he stopped in surprise. "Pam! What are you doing out of the hospital?"

"She made the nurse release her," Rev. Zackery interjected.

"I'm well enough to handle the rest of the healing process by myself. We don't have any time to waste. The big day is Tuesday. We have a lot to do, and very little time to do it," Pam said as she slowly moved her injured shoulder back and forth.

"At least, let me look at it and change the bandages. It looks like it's starting to bleed again. Pam, you're moving too fast," Rev. Zackery pleaded.

"I said I can handle it."

"No Pam, it is bleeding, a lot," Jason warned.

Pam touched her back and then looked at her fingers. They were red with blood that had come through the bandage and the hospital gown that was tucked down in her jeans. She quickly walked to the kitchen, turned on the stove, put the tip of a butcher's knife on the burner of the stove, and walked over to the kitchen table. She pulled her arm out of the hospital gown, pulled off the bandage, and leaned face down across table. "Cauterize it."

"Do what?" Rev. Zackery said totally opposed to the thought of taking that red-hot knife and putting it on Pam's back. Before he could object further, Jason was pressing the knife to Pam's back. Jason held it there for two seconds, which seemed like minutes to Rev. Zackery.

"Have mercy, Jesus," Rev. Zackery grimaced.

The smell of burnt flesh filled the room as Pam lay silently over the table, every muscle in her body tense.

"Are you okay?" Jason whispered in her ear.

"No, but I will be when this pain stops. Did the bleeding stop?" she said in a strained voice.

"Yeah, you're good," Jason said. "Was that like a mind over matter thing?"

"I thought I would be able to block out the pain, but I was wrong. I felt every bit of it. It hurts like hell, whatever that means. I need to lay down."

"Take her to the bedroom next to where you were Jason. Too many demons have been in that other room."

"Demons?" Pam sighed. "I thought the demons were in the man in your truck. I didn't know you had them in your bedroom too."

"Oh, my goodness, I forgot about Billy again." Rev. Zackery moaned.

"Speaking about demons, I hope you didn't need that demon fish that you had in the fishbowl," Jason said.

"Why? What did you do to my brother's fish."

"I killed it!"

"Why, what did it do?"

"It tried to get me to put my hand in the fishbowl. Then it tried to make me put my hands on the burner on the stove. So, I put the fishbowl on the burner and boiled it."

"My brother told me to take care of that fish," Rev. Zackery said.

"Go get Billy and the rest of your demons out of your trunk, reverend," Pam said as she laid on the bed. Jason pulled up a chair and sat near Pam. Rev. Zackery went to get Billy.

"Do you believe all this demon stuff Rev. Zackery has been talking about. He's got this man duct taped to a tree limb in his trunk. When I saw him, the man was freaking out. Rev. Zackery has had him in his truck for who knows how long. When we left the hospital, we went out to his car and he opened his trunk, the man was about to pee on himself. Rev. Zackery pulled him out of the trunk, leaned him up against the car, unzipped his pant, and cut one of his arms free so he could pee. Then he taped him back up and put him back in the trunk. I tell you the man was terrified. That doesn't seem like the way Rev. Zackery would treat anybody," Pam said as she lay on her stomach, her face toward Jason.

"He told me he saw me when I was hiding in the room next to yours at the hospital. He said it was Sibal."

"Yeah, it was Sibal. Are you getting the same feeling that I am?" Pam whispered.

"He has the crystal ball."

"How else could he see what was happening."

They stopped talking when they heard two people come in the house, walk down the hall, and enter the room. Rev. Zackery had Billy by the arm, as he led Billy into the room. His hands were duct taped together behind his back and tape was covering his mouth. Pam sat up on the side of the bed.

"Pam, Jason, this is Billy; Billy, Pam and Jason," Rev. Zackery said as he pointed to each person as he spoke. "Billy is a little upset from being in my trunk."

"Mmmm mmmmm," Billy murmured.

"My cold trunk for so long," Rev. Zackery said and turn toward Billy. "Are you calm enough for me to take the tape off your mouth, now?"

"Mmmm mmmm," Billy murmured again moving his head up and down.

Rev. Zackery removed the tape, and then went into the other bedroom.

"Please, help me. This man has kidnaped me and is holding me here against my will. Please call the police. He says that I broke into his house and tried to kill him, but I don't remember anything, except waking up here taped up on his floor. Please, just call the police," Billy pleaded.

Rev. Zackery returned with a rolling chair, a new roll of duct tape, and a pair of scissors. He proceeded to put duct tape back over Billy's mouth. He taped Billy's ankles together. He then taped his arm to his body just above his elbows. He cut the tape binding his hands and sat him in the chair. Then he taped his arms to the arms of the chair, and finally he taped his body to the back of the chair. Pam and Jason looked at each other and then back at Rev. Zackery.

"I know you have some questions, but instead of answering a million questions, I'm just going to let you see for yourselves. Okay?" Rev. Zackery raised his eyebrows.

"Okay," Pam and Jason replied together.

Rev. Zackery bowed his head and began to pray. "Heavenly Father, I come to You, in the name of Jesus asking that you fill me with your Holy Spirit. Protect me from all demonic forces in Jesus' name I pray, amen." Rev. Zackery then turned toward Billy, "I want to speak to a demon. Demon come forward. By the power of the Lord God Almighty come forward." Rev. Zackery waited. Nothing happened. "We can do this the easy way, or we can do it the hard way." Rev. Zackery looked back at Pam and Jason. "Give me a second." He rushed out of the room and was back in a minute with his bible. He put it on Billy's head and shouted, "Demon come forth." Nothing happened. "Demon, I command you to reveal yourself." Nothing. Rev. Zackery hit Billy in his chest three times and yelled to the top of his voice. "Demon, I command you, in the name of Jesus, to reveal yourself."

This time something happened. A cloud-like image appeared over Billy's head. It grew to about twice the diameter of Billy's head and slowly came into focus. As it did, an angry expression appeared on it, and it spoke with a deep angry voice.

"You have my attention," the demon in Billy said.

"You have my attention as well," said another ominous voice coming from behind Rev. Zackery.

"And me, too, preacher."

Rev. Zackery froze as he could feel the demonic presents coming up behind him. He jumped around holding the bible up in front of his face just low enough for him to see over it clearly. He was shocked to see Pam's body and Jason's body with demon heads on them. He backed up to the door of the room.

"It's just one of you, and it's three of us. I think you're in big trouble, preacher," the head on Pam said as she and Jason walked toward him.

Rev. Zackery lowered the book. "That's the problem with you demons, you try to think too much. Your little pea size brains can't handle the pressure. Sit down!"

Pam and Jason with their demon heads stopped, backed up to the bed and sat down. Rev. Zackery walked past Billy hitting him in the chest with his bible as he passed. "You shut up." He walked up to Jason and hit him in the chest. "You shut up, too." Then he stood in front of the demon head on Pam. "Okay, since you want to talk. Tell me, what are you doing in Pam. What are you trying to get her to do? Speak up, now," Rev Zackery scream as he hit the demonic head with the bible.

"Okay preacher, you want to know. I'll tell you. I'm feeding her pride," the demon head stated reluctantly.

"Go on."

"She is beginning to think she can beat anybody and do anything she wants. She feels like she's smarter than anybody else. I'm going to feed her arrogance and her desire for power until she bites off more than she can chew. Then I'll have her, she will be killed, and her soul will the lost forever." There was a conceited grin on the demon's face.

"So, you're saying she is not saved."

"Saved? She won't be saved until she gets to heaven. You can preach to her and pray for her all you want. For as long as she lives in this body, I will always be pulling her down."

"You don't know what you're talking about demon. All anybody has to do is accept Jesus as their personal savior and they will receive salvation."

"You don't know what you're talking about, preacher. You think you're saved but you're not. You don't even believe. You don't have any faith. Look at Billy. You have kept him tied up for two days, beating him, and torturing him. And you've got the nerve to call yourself saved. You hypocrite," the demon yelled.

"You filthy, lying, deceiving, demon!" Rev. Zackery's nose was right up against the demon's nose, both faces frowning. Rev. Zackery moved back and slowly walk back and forth in front of the demon head, then he looked at the demon and spoke. "Has Pam been intentionally keeping anything from me? Don't lie!"

"She doesn't want you to know that she loves Dave."

"I already know that, demon."

"Well, she doesn't want you to know that she wants to have hot, passionate, no holds barred, low down dirty sex with Dave."

"I know that, too. Tell me something I don't know."

"She doesn't want you to know that she went to Sibal's hospital room that night after Sibal attacked her."

"Show me what happened."

"I can tell you what happened, but if you want to see, you'll have to get him to show you," the demon said pointing to Billy's demon head.

Rev. Zackery looked at the demon head on Billy's body. It was looking down. Rev. Zackery hit Pam in her chest. "You be quiet," he said as he walked up to Billy and stopped.

The demon's head on Billy's body looked up at Rev. Zackery. "What?"

"Don't be cute. It's not you. Show me what happened."

"What happened? Why are you asking me, I don't know what you're talking about?"

"Don't make me bible slap you!" Rev. Zackery said as he raised his bible across his body.

"Okay! Move back a little." The demon waved Billy's arm and a large image appeared.

It was Sibal's hospital room on the night before. Pam is standing next to Sibal bed. Sibal is in a drug induced sleep. Pam pinches Sibal's nose. Sibal awakes in fear. Pam releases her nose and covers Sibal's mouth with her hand and raises one finger to her lips. Sibal acknowledges Pam's hand signal for quiet. Pam removes her hand.

"I'll get right to the point, you can either agree to help me Tuesday at the ceremony or I'll kill you right now. Choose! Now!"

"I'll help you," Sibal responded quickly. "What do you want me to do?"

"You will get me into the celebration and introduce me as the rightful heir, as the coven leader. Tell them that I will take on any and all challengers. If anyone challenges me, I'll kill them."

"What do you know about being a witch?" Sibal argued.

"I know that anyone who goes against me will pay for it with their lives. I have all the power that my sister had. If she could run the coven, I can run it. If you support me, I'll reward you with a high position. On the other hand, if I even sense that you want to stab me in the back like you did my sister, I'll boil you in oil. I mean that literally."

"I swear, I will never betray you," she said and waited for a response. Pam just looked into her eyes. Then, she continued speaking. "Thank you for letting me live and giving me a chance to serve you. Are you going to get me out of here?" Sibal said pulling her arms against the straps holding her to the bed."

The demon waved his arm again.

"Does Jason know about this?" Rev. Zackery asks as the image fades into a mist.

"Why do you ask me questions you already know the answer to."

"I just like the sound of your voice. It's so, demonic," Rev. Zackery snickered.

"No! Of course not, Jason doesn't have a clue. He's being set up for a major setback, poor soul," the demon head said with a happy smile.

Rev. Zackery hit Billy in the chest with the bible. "Shut up," he said as he walked to over to Jason's demonic head. He hit Jason's chest with the bible. "Okay, it's your turn."

"It may be my turn, but the more that you learn, the hotter you're gonna burn, Leroy," the demon head said.

"So, let me guest, you're a poet, and you don't even know it," Rev. Zackery snapped.

"Well actually, it's said, when Lucifer was head, of the choir that fled, from heaven. I used to write songs, you know sing-a-longs, I don't think I'm wrong, I was seven."

"What are you doing in Jason?" Rev. Zackery said interrupting him.

"I'm not going to, say anything to you, about what I do, to this soul. You can beg you can plead, you can make Jason bleed, do whatever you need, till you're old, and gray, did I hear you say, you're already that way, Mr. preacher. Go ahead bible slap me, you think you can trap me, your words don't mean crap see, I'm unreachable."

"You're not unreachable, you're sickening. I know what you're doing. Jason wants revenge. Any fool can see that by the way he talks."

"Seeing and talking ain't knowing and walking, I know what he's thinking, and it's stinking."

"Keep it to yourself. You don't know didley," Rev. Zackery said disgustedly as he turned his back to the demon.

"I know that he, had a plan B. I know it was a something that she wants to see, cause if Pam could see, she wouldn't want to be, in close proximity, of the ceremony." There was a pause, then a different voice said. "He is willing to die and go to hell to see all the witches burn, all the witches."

Rev. Zackery turned around to see a different, frightening, face on Jason. To Rev Zackery it appeared to be the face of death.

"In the name of Jesus, demons go back, conceal yourselves," Rev. Zackery screamed.

Instantly, the demon heads disappeared. Pam and Jason were surprised to find Rev. Zackery standing much closer to them. Seeing their shock, Rev. Zackery turned and walked toward Billy.

"What just happened?" Pam whispered to Jason.

"How did he get over here," Jason whispered back worriedly.

"Looks like Billy is not the only one with demons," Pam whispered.

Rev. Zackery walked up to Billy, placed the bible on his head, and spoke. "In the name of Jesus, demon inside of Billy reveal yourself."

Instantly a mist appeared over Billy's head. The head of a man became clearer and clearer. It was the demon Gon. However, instead of looking mean, evil, with frowning eyebrows and horns, he looked well-groomed and pleasant, with no horns. He still had an extra-large head. His skin color was still light-grey and his fingers and fingernails were very long.

"Hi, my peoples. What's happening Pam? How they hanging Jason, my brother?" The demon said, his image covered down to Billy's waist now. The demon had on a white dress shirt, a blue tie, and a blue pull over sweater. His arms and hands moving expressively as he talked.

Pam and Jason did not respond. They were both amazed and amused.

"This is a new look for you," Rev. Zackery said.

"Z, you know I always try to look my best when we have company. Now, tell me, what's on your mind? What can I do for you, Rev. Z?"

Rev. Zackery was caught completely off guard by this new version of the demon. After taking a few seconds to compose himself, and instead of speaking in a commanding voice, he asked politely, "Would you show us Dave Parker, where he is right now, please?"

"Of, course Z. Oh, by the way," the demon said, turning and smiling toward Pam and Jason. "My name is D. Gon and I'm so glad to finally meet you. Rev. Z has thought so many wonderful thoughts about you two. He thinks so highly of you."

"Now, would be a good time for you to do what I asked you to do," Rev Zackery interrupted sternly.

The demon head turned from Rev. Zackery toward Pam and Jason again. "He can be so impatient sometimes, and you really don't want to see his violent side. He'll bible slap a bitch in a minute." The demon raised his arm toward Rev. Zackery. "Excuse me." Rev. Zackery moved across the room next to Pam and Jason. Then, the demon waved his arm in a big arch. As his arm moved the wall and doorway changed into a giant picture screen.

Dave was being placed in a two-person jail cell now. There was a bed on both sides of the room and a commode in the center of the back wall. The jailer was removing the handcuffs from Dave's wrists.

"You think you can come in my jail and start a riot, wife beater," the jailer yelled as he pushed Dave roughly into cell. "I know your wife. We went to high school together, we were friends. Carol is a wonderful woman, always has been." He locked the cell door. "You think I'm going to let you beat my friend and get away with it, not a chance. I'll be back in a few minutes with a little treat for you, wife beater."

Dave turned and Pam thought he was looking at her.

"Dave? Dave, can you see me? Can you hear me?" she stood up and yelled. Dave turned and sat on one of the beds. Pam looked at the demon. "Can he hear me?"

"Sorry Miss Pam, this is just like a TV," the demon said condescendingly. "Is your real hair color blond?"

"Show us the place where the witches are having their ceremony," Jason asked excitedly.

"What ceremony?"

"Don't play. There are going to be hundreds if not thousands of witches and demons there. I'm sure you know everything about it. Show me the building," Jason insisted, his anger showing.

The demon said nothing. He just stared angrily back at Jason.

"Show him, demon!" Rev. Zackery commanded.

The demon waved his arm over the jail scene, and it was replaced with a scene showing a large old empty building. Jason picked up a pen and a notepad from the nightstand by the bed and began to draw a diagram of the building.

"Okay let me see what it looks like if I'm standing in that door right there," Jason said pointing. The demon waved his hand again and he could see the building as if he were standing in the door he had asked about. Jason completed his diagram.

"Are you done, now," Pam asked Jason anxiously.

"Yeah, I got exactly what I needed."

"Okay, let me see Dave again, Mr. Gon."

"Finally, somebody with manners," the demon said waving his arm again. The scene was back at the jail cell

The jailer was unlocking the cell door. There was a big, tall, hillbilly looking man, in prison attire, standing next to him. The jailer opened the door and let him in.

"Don't kill him, just welcome him to the penal system. Be 'real' sweet. I'll have your cigarettes and I'll even throw in a joint or two when you get out of solitary," the jailer said locking the door. "He's a wife beater."

"I'll give him the royal treatment, boss," the hillbilly said as he sat down on the bed across from Dave. The sound of the jailer's footsteps faded in the distance.

"So, you beat your wife," the hillbilly said calmly.

"No, but I wish I had. I caught her and her boyfriend in our bedroom. I had already seen them doing stuff in my bed that I had only seen on porno films," Dave said as his anger began to show.

"What do you mean you saw? You had a camera in the bedroom?"

"Something like that. He treated her like a prostitute, and when he did everything he could think of, she suggested nastier things for him to do." Dave looked up at the hillbilly with such anger, that it made the hillbilly lean back. "I wanted to hit her at least one time. I had them, in the bedroom. I had my gun on him. His pants were down. I was about to pull the trigger." Dave stopped.

"So, what happened. Did you shoot him?"

"No."

"I would have shot his ball off. You are a strong man," the hillbilly said jumping to his feet and pacing back and forth flailing his arms. "If it had been me, I would have killed them both right there in the bed." He stopped and turned toward Dave. "How were you able to control yourself?"

Dave's voice became calm again. He raised his eyebrows to erase the anger from his face. "I thought about Rev. Zackery. He has been praying for me. He told me that Jesus died on the cross to pay for my sins, so God could forgive me. He said if I don't forgive others then, God won't forgive me. So, I thought about it. My wife and I haven't been married that long. I don't know what she's been though to make her the way she is. She's just a person like me. I've done some pretty bad stuff in my life." Dave paused and looked directly into the man's eyes. "So, I was standing there, and I should have been angry, but instead I felt sorry for her. I felt like consoling and hugging her and kissing her. I would have, except I knew where her lips had been."

"So how did you get in here?"

"He made a move. He went for his pants. The gun went off, and I shot a hole in the wall, she screamed, he ran out in his underwear, and somebody called the police. When the police came, she said I hit her and tried to kill him." Dave's head lowered down into his hands that were propped on his knees and began to cry. The hillbilly sat down beside him and put his hand on his back.

"Don't worry, buddy. You know what they say in church, weeping may last for a night, but you can dry your eyes in the morning."

The demon waved his arms and the scene disappeared. "That enough. I can't take no more. That was sickening," the demon said turning toward Rev. Zackery and raising his chin. "Go ahead bible slap me again."

"Rev. Zackery has been slapping you around, with his bible," Pam asked sympathetically.

"Yes ma'am, he may look nice, but he can be really mean, to be a preacher."

"Rev. Zackery," Jason said with a condescending look. "I'm so disappointed in you. Can he even feel it, when you hit Billy?"

"If I were to hit Billy with a plate, the demon wouldn't feel it, but when I hit Billy with my bible, Billy feels the bible and the demon feels a sword slicing and stabbing him. The word of God is a two-edged sword," Rev. Zackery said holding up his bible.

"He is always misinterpreting the scripture, he ain't no real preacher. He wasn't sent, he just went," the demon argued.

Rev. Zackery swung the bible around to hit the demon in the mouth. However, just before the bible hit the demon head, it disappeared. The bible landed on Billy's face knocking it back.

Pam and Jason looked at each other and then back at Rev. Zackery, who immediately turned, walked out of the room down the hall and into the bathroom. Once he was gone, Jason held out his diagram and spoke.

"Look, if what the demon showed us is true, we can block these exits and we will have all the witches trapped. We can kill them all in one big swoop." Jason had a sinister smile.

"How will we get out?"

"Oh! Yeah. I forgot about us," he smirked. "We need somebody outside one of these exits to let us out at just the right time."

"We need Dave."

"I don't think he wants to be involved."

"Not even if it means that we would be killed?" Pam asked.

"He said we should just leave and go home."

"You talked to him?"

"Yeah, he called here not long before you got here. He called from jail. That's why I believe, the building the demon showed us, was the real thing. All we need to know is, where this place is."

"I can get that information from Sibal," Pam said with a little frown on her face. "So, all we need now is Dave." They stopped talking when they heard Rev. Zackery walking down the hall.

Rev. Zackery walked into the room. He hit Billy on the top of the head with the bible and yelled, "Demon, in the name of Jesus, show me Dave, now!"

The demon appeared, but this time his expression was unlike anything Rev. Zackery had ever seen before. He looked as if his feeling had been hurt. He said nothing. He waved his arm and the jail cell reappeared.

The hillbilly still had his hand on Dave back when they both heard a shout.

"What in the hell is this?" The jailer was at the cell door. "You were supposed to kick his teeth in and you're in there making love to him." The hillbilly and Dave were both looking at the jailer like little children being scolded. "Are you going to do what I asked you to do or not?" the jailer said lowering his voice.

"Okay boss, I'll do it." The hillbilly stood up and moved to the cell door.

"I'll be back in fifteen minutes. You'd better take care of this by the time I get back. The charges got dropped. They are getting ready to release him."

"Okay boss, I'll take care of it," the hillbilly said as he watched the jailer walk away. Then he turned, walked back, and stood in front of Dave. "I'm sorry man, I know you been through a lot, but I'm still gonna have to rough you up a little bit."

"You're sorry!" Dave said loudly looking up.

"Yeah, I am, but sometimes you just gotta do what you gotta do."

"Hey, I understand." Dave stood up, rubbing the fingers of his left hand across his forehead. "You gotta do what you gotta do."

The hillbilly balled up his fist and was waiting for Dave to drop his hand from the front of his face.

"Don't drop your hand, go for his eyes," Pam shouted.

Just as Pam said, instead of dropping his hand, Dave's fingers shot forward hitting both of the hillbilly's eyes. The hillbilly raised his left arm covering his eyes and turned his left side toward Dave.

"Now hit him in the throat," Pam yelled.

Dave immediately threw a karate chop to his throat. The hillbilly went back on the bed, his head hitting hard against the wall and bounced forward. Dave grabbed the hillbilly's jumpsuit and pulled him forward. The hillbilly fell face down to the floor between the beds. One arm covering his eyes, the other arm protecting his throat.

"Stomp him," Pam screamed.

The image suddenly disappeared. The demon moaned as if in severe pain as Rev. Zackery pushed the bible into the chest of the demon. When the bible was halfway into the demon's chest, Rev. Zackery spoke.

"You can't fool me, demon. What you showed me is not what really happened. You're trying to deceive me. I have been pretty nice to up till now, cause you have been useful. However, if you try to deceive me again, I'm going to cast you out of Billy into the pit of hell where you will remain until the day of judgement. Do you understand me?"

"Yeah, you can try, ahhhhh," the demon moaned as Rev. Zackery pulled the bible across his chest like a sword. "Okay, what do you want me to do?"

"Go back to where you started making things up. I'm going to ask Dave when I talk to him, so you'd better not lie."

"Okay," the demon said waving his arm. A picture of the jail reappeared.

The hillbilly had his hand on Dave's back, when they both heard a shout.

"What the hell is this." The jailer was at the cell door. "You were suppose to kick his teeth in, and you're in there making love to him." The hillbilly and Dave were looking up at him like little children being scolded. "Are you going to do what I asked you to do or not?" the jailer said lowering his voice.

"Okay boss, I'll do it," the hillbilly said, walking toward the jailer.

"Do it now."

Dave stood up and backed away from the hillbilly. However, it wasn't far enough. The hillbilly threw a left jab to Dave's chest, followed by a right hook that glanced off the side of Dave's head. Dave ducked and lunged forward hitting the hillbilly in the chest with his shoulder. The hillbilly barely moved. Dave tried to pick him up and throw him to the floor, but he failed. The hillbilly clamped Dave's head and shoulder to his left side and began hitting Dave continuously in the stomach with his right fist, until Dave fell to his knees in front of the hillbilly. The hillbilly grabbed Dave by his hair and pulled his head up. His right fist aimed at Dave nose. Dave dropped both arms to his side and offered no resistance.

"Unzip my jumpsuit," the hillbilly ordered.

"Well, I guess I'll leave you two love bird alone." The jailer said, smiling as he turned and walked down the corridor.

"I said unzip my jumpsuit. Don't make me have to bust those pretty little lips, and don't try anything stupid."

Dave reached up and started pulling the zipper down exposing more and more hair. When the opening reached the hillbilly's waist there was a shout.

"That's enough. Stop it," Rev. Zackery shouted looking away.

"No! You said you wanted to see the real deal. Well, here it is, preacher," the demon snapped, refusing to stop the image. "I want to see this."

"In the name of Jesus, demons reveal yourselves", Rev. Zackery yelled.

Instantly, the demon heads appeared on Pam and Jason.

In the jail scene, where once there had been a confident smirk on the hillbilly's face before, however the smirk turned to concern as he noticed a change in Dave's expression. He pulled Dave's hair, tilting his head so he could see Dave's face more clearly. The fear he had seen just seconds before was gone. What he saw was not anger or rage. It wasn't even hate. It looked like pure evil. The hillbilly should have reacted then, but he didn't. When he saw a little smile appear on Dave's face, he knew it was too late. He could feel Dave's fingers digging into his testicles and then pulling them. The pain was so excruciating that the hillbilly couldn't even breathe. Dave pushed the hillbilly back against the cell door as he stood to his feet. Then the hillbilly inhaled, grabbed his groins and tried to scream but nothing came out. Dave laid him on his bed and watched as he laid there facing the wall holding his testicles moaning.

"That's enough demon," Rev. Zackery said hitting the demon on the top of the head. "In the name of Jesus, demons conceal yourselves."

The demon waved his arm and the scene disappeared. Then the demon heads disappeared revealing Pam's, Jason's, and Billy's faces. He looked straight ahead and mumbled something. Rev. Zackery pulled the duct tape from his mouth.

"I need to pee, please."

"Okay Billy, let me cut you loose? You have really been patient," Rev. Zackery said pushing Billy back into his bedroom. He picked up some scissors from the dresser to cut the duct tape. "You can go by yourself, can't you?"

"Yeah," Billy said surprised.

When the tape had been removed. Billy wobbled toward the bathroom. His joints and muscles were stiff and tight, respectively. He got to the bathroom door, however, instead of going in, he started running for the front door. Rev. Zackery, who had been watching, yelled out, "Stop him. Don't let him get out"

Pam and Jason looked up just in time to see him run pass their door. Pam jumped up to run after him, but Jason blocked her.

"Let him go! We don't need him anymore. Rev. Zackery is holding him against his will. Rev. Zackery has lost it. He has gone demon crazy. Maybe if Billy leaves, he'll come back to his senses. Pam pushed pass Jason, however she stopped at the doorway and watched as Billy opened the door and ran out.

"Why didn't you stop him?" Rev. yelled angrily. "Come on we've got to catch him."

"Let him go! What are you doing, reverend.? You keep him taped up. You beat him with your bible of all things. I hate to say it, but you are losing it." Jason explained.

"Yeah Rev. Zackery, what is the real deal between you and Billy," Pam added.

"I need Billy. We need Billy."

"We need him?" Jason questioned.

"We need him for what?" Pam asked angrily.

Rev. Zackery pointed to Billy. "He has the crystal. He has Tamera."

"Oh! I forgot all about that. How could I have forgotten about her?" Jason said more to himself that the others.

"This is a good thing," Pam exclaimed. "All we have to do is follow him and he'll lead us back to where he left the crystal."

"You're right, let's go!" Rev. Zackery said anxiously.

"I'll follow him. You two drive down to the highway. He's got to have a car hidden in the woods somewhere. I'll call you as soon as I know something.

Chapter 14
The Setup

(Sunday afternoon 1:30 PM)

"Well, this is highly unusual. She really shouldn't be moved with her burns," the ICU nurse said frantically.

"I beg your pardon. You have your paperwork. This is completely in order. What is not in order, is for you to give my patient Percocet without testing her for allergies," the doctor scolded.

"The police need to be notified. She tried to kill one of my patients last night."

"That's your fault. It was the Percocet that you gave her that cause her actions. Now, I am willing to overlook this error, however, if you choose to obstruct my patient from leaving this facility, I will advise my patient to sue the doctor, this hospital, and you, for malfeasance, and negligence. Do I make myself clear?"

"Yes doctor, perfectly. I apologize. Everything is in order," the nurse said as she looked over the papers quickly.

The orderly pusher the gurney down the hall and into the elevator. The doctor followed.

"Sibal, we thought you were dead," the doctor said.

"Not yet!"

"Are you going to be all right?"

"Find me somebody healthy, a young girl that's pretty. I need a face transplant, not tomorrow, today."

"Okay, I'll set it up for this evening if we can find somebody," the doctor said pulling out his phone.

"You'll either find somebody or I'll use your face." Sibal stared ominously into the doctor's eyes.

Using his phone while leaving the hospital, the doctor made the arrangements. Once outside, Sibal was put in a private ambulance.

"Okay, the arrangements are made," the doctor said calmly.

"You found somebody?"

"Actually, I know of two. You can choose the one you like."

"Excellent, now write down these instructions for Howard, cause after I'm done, I want you to give me a shot to stop this pain and put me to sleep. Okay?" Sibal moaned.

"Okay."

"Tell Howard that an intruder is going to try to take over our coven at the ceremony. Tell him I said to build a special stage for the ceremony. The stage needs to have a trap door just to the right of the person speaking at the podium. Under the trap door put several long, sharp spikes. Tell him to make it so that when I hit the release, not only will the trap door open, but it will cause the curtains in the front of the stage to fall off, so that everyone can see what happens when the intruder falls through the door on the spikes. You got that?" Sibal waited for a nod. "Okay, put me out."

Chapter 15
The Release

(Sunday afternoon 3:00 pm)

Dave was led into the courtroom by two deputies. The judge was already at the bench looking over the case reports. Without looking up the judge spoke.

"It looks like you have been a very disruptive guest in our facilites, Mr. Parker. You put one of our inmates in the infirmary and because of you I've had to discipline one of my officers." The judge looked up. Dave continued to look down at the floor. "It looks like you wife made some false statements to the police. Did you hit your wife, Mr. Parker?"

"No, Your Honor," Dave said still looking at the floor.

"Well, I'm dismissing the charges against you. However, I am granting a temporary restraining order that your wife has requested. For the next two weeks you should not be within fifty yards of you wife. Do you have any questions?"

"Yes, Your Honor. I need to get some clothes and personal items from the house. May I do that?"

"An officer will accompany you to the house to today when you leave here. You will be allowed to get only your personal belongings. Is there anything else?"

"Yes, Your Honor. I called my bank this morning and all of my accounts, the joint accounts, and even my personal account, have zero balances. All my credit cards have been cancelled. How do I get my money from my personal account back?"

"You'll need an attorney, Mr. Parker. Now, if there is nothing else, you are free to go."

"Thank you, Your Honor."

Twenty minutes later, Dave pulled up to the front of his house. The policeman was right behind him. The two men walked to the door. Before they could ring the bell, the door opened. It was Carol.

"What is he doing here," she screamed while blocking the door. "I have a restraining order against him."

"Yes ma'am," the officer replied. "However, the judge has allowed him this time to get his personal belonging. It will only take a few minutes. Please," the officer said while moving pass her.

They walked up the stairs to the bedroom. Carol followed. Dave opened a bag of large black garbage bags and pulled one out. He opened the top drawer where he kept his underwear neatly folded. However, they were not folded. Everything was jumbled up and there was wet red paint covering everything. Dave opened the next two drawers and paint covered those clothes, too. Dave quickly walked to the closet. When he opened the door, he found all of his clothes on the floor covered in red paint.

"All of this is ruined. You're not going to take any of this are you?" the policeman asked.

"It's evidence. You need to include this in your report," Dave said as he began stuffing his clothes into the bags.

"Evidence of what?" Carol yelled. "I didn't do that."

"Well, how do you explain this?" the policeman asked.

"I don't have to explain anything. He got his belongings. If that's all he wants, get him out of here."

"I'm ready," Dave said calmly.

They walked out of the house. The policeman walked Dave to his car.

"You can't be within fifty yards of her. If you do, we will have to arrest you."

"Don't worry officer." Dave got in his car and drove straight to the bank. He opened the black garbage bag and pulled out the sport coat on the top. Avoiding the still wet paint, he reached inside the coat pocket. His hand went down through the hole and he felt around the inside lining until he found it, the key to his safe deposit box. Minutes later he walked out of the bank with thirty, one-hundred-dollar bills in his pocket, and a brown paper bag in his hand. He sat down in the rental car and dumped the bag out on the passenger seat. There was his passport, an old watch his daddy gave him years ago, his high school class ring, and a faded picture of his first high school sweetheart, who dumped him for the star basketball player. One by one he put them all back in the bag until he got to the picture. He looked at the picture for a long time. Then he rolled the window down, threw the picture into the breeze, started the car, and headed to the only place where he felt someone cared about him. He headed back to Rev. Zackery's.

Chapter 16
Taken Hostage

(Sunday 6:15 PM)

Jason was in the woods. He had no idea where he was, much less where Billy was. He pulled his phone from his pocket and dialed.

"We're up here on the highway," he heard Pam say. "Where are you? Did Billy have a car?"

"I lost him."

"How did that happen?"

"He must have seen me."

"Well, you've got to keep looking. You can't let him get away. He has the crystal."

"Look! It's going to get dark soon. I need to get out of these woods."

"Rev. Zackery says follow the sunset, west. He says you should come to a dirt road. When you get to the road turn right, then you will be going north. That road goes to the highway. We'll meet you there."

"All right," Jason said disgustedly. He looked up and began walking in the direction of the sun. Then he heard it, a radio. It was coming from behind him. He carefully and quietly worked his way through the trees and bushes until he saw an opening. There in the opening was a car. Billy was sitting on the hood looking in his direction. He was wearing an Army field jacket.

"Come on out. Don't be scared."

Even though the person was looking down, Jason knew that it was Billy's body, however, it was not Billy's voice, and it was not Billy's head. The head was enlarged. The voice was similar to that of the demon that had showed them the building where the witches were going to be, however, it was deeper in pitch. Jason stood up and walked into the clearing.

"What do you want, Gon?" Jason said as he approached cautiously. The demon looked up. It was not Gon. This face was the face of an older man, maybe in his fifties. "Okay, you are not Gon. Who are you?"

"The name is Bailtron. I'm Gon's superior," the demon stated formally. "I have more authority and more power. I have been assigned to handle negotiations with you, specifically."

"Okay, Bailtron, what do you want?" Jason asked causiously.

"You know that she is going to double cross you. Don't you?"

"Who's going to double cross me?"

"Pam. All she wants is to get back with her sister. She's going to set her free. The woman who had your grandmother killed, is going to be set free. Pam is just going to let her go."

"That's not true. Pam's sister tried to kill Pam, several times."

"Well, why isn't she dead?"

"Everybody she sent failed. Pam was able to beat them. She even beat Tamera."

"No! You were the one who beat Tamera. You were the one who trapped her in the crystal. Think about it. You found Pam when she was in the well. She would have died. You found her in the woods. She would have bled to death. She would be dead several times over if it had not been for you." The demon raised his eyebrow and gave Jason a little smirk.

"So, what's your point, demon?"

"She is going to double cross you."

"How?"

"You think that you and Pam are going to trap all the witches in the building and burn them up, don't you? Well, suppose I told you that Pam is going to get Sibal to introduce her as the next leader of the witches."

"You're crazy, demon. Pam hates the witches just as much as I do. They killed my gramma, the woman who raised her."

"She never cared anything about your grandmother. But she does care about her own blood, her sister. Why do you think she stopped you from killing Tamela? She convinced you to throw her in the river. You could have killed her then. If Billy hadn't found her, Pam would have gone back to get her precious sister and you would have never known, at least not until you woke up one night with Tamela standing next to your bed."

"Pam would never do that to me," Jason said angrily.

"That's what the fox thought."

"What fox?"

"There was a fox and a snake at the river. They both wanted to get to the other side. However, the snake couldn't swim. The fox offered to let the snake ride on his back. When they got to the other side, the snake bit the fox. As the fox lay there dying, he asked the snake, 'why did you bit me?' The snake said, 'Didn't you know I was a snake?'," Bailtron paused. "I'll ask you the same question, don't you know that Pam is a witch?"

"And you are a demon. Why should I trust you?"

"If I help you kill them, guess who gets credit for all those lost souls? We both win. You hate those witches. You are going to kill them even if you have to kill yourself in the process."

"You got that right, demon. They are all going to die, even if means that I have to die."

"Well, you might be interested in knowing what Pam and Sibal are planning. Look at this." The demon waved his arm and the scene appeared next to the car. Remember when Pam and Sibal were in the hospital? This is something you don't know. The scene showed Pam in Sibal's hospital room.

"You introduce me as the rightful heir to lead the coven. I'll come in with the crystal in my hand. I'll hold it up, so everybody can see Tamela inside, then I'll call for a vote."

"No! That's not how it goes," Sibal interrupted. "You have to call for any challengers."

"Why would anyone have the nerve to challenge me?"

"I know you will have one challenger."

"Who?"

"Dr. Stample, Steve. He is powerful, and he will challenge you, because you are an outsider."

"Kill him!" Pam ordered.

"What?" Sibal shouted. "If you want to lead the coven, you have to prove yourself."

"Kill him, if you want to be my second in command." Pam looked deeply into Sibal's eyes. "Is that going to be a problem for you? You didn't have a problem trying to kill my sister."

"No! It won't be a problem." Sibal thought for a moment. "What about your friends?"

"You mean Rev. Zackery, Dave, and Jason?"

"Do you want me to kill them too?"

"Rev. Zackery is harmless, plus he's into demons now. Dave has gone back home. He's got more problems than he can handle, with his 'whorish' wife. I'm not worried about them. Jason, on the other hand, might be a problem. He is filled with hate. He wants to kill every witch in the coven, especially you."

"Let me kill him, please. I want to make him suffer," Sibal snarled.

"Don't bother him. Stay out of his way. If he becomes a problem, I'll kill him myself."

The demon waved his arm and the imagine disappeared.

"Sounds like you're in trouble. Sounds like your friend is not really your friend," the demon said. "And, it looks like you need my help."

"How can you help me?"

"If you give me permission, I can warn you when someone is trying to sneak up on you. I can tell you when to run and show you which way to go. I can keep you safe. Once you give me permission, all you have to do is call my name and I will come to your aid. It's as simple as that. What do you say?"

"I say I don't need your help, demon."

"Really? I'll tell you what, I'll give you the first request free. So, if you need me, call me. Until then, 'here's Billy'," the demon said in voice like a game show announcer.

The demon head disappeared, and Billy's was back. He looked shocked to see Jason at first, however, he quickly became amused, a big smile appeared on his face.

"This is better than I ever could have imagined," Billy said.

"Yeah! How so?" Jason smiled back.

"The lady in the glass ball sent me to Rev. Zackery's house so that I could make him tell me where you were. Now, here you are. My job is almost done." Billy slid off the hood and stood in front of the car. He reached both hands into his coat pockets. He pulled out a roll of duct tape and tossed it to Jason. Jason caught it with one hand. Billy pulled a pistol out of the other pocket. "Tape your legs together. I wouldn't want you to kick me. Ten times around ought to do it."

Jason, surprised to see the gun, bent over and did as Billy had said. He tore the tape and stood up straight again.

"Now wrap it around your wrist."

Jason did it.

"Now hold out your hands."

Billy came over, took the tape that was hanging down from Jason's wrist, and taped both wrists together and then both his hands.

"Now, hop over to the back seat and sit down."

Jason hopped over to the car.

"That woman in the crystal ball is a witch," Jason said as he sat down on the back seat. "She has gotten in your head. She is controlling you. You can break her control if you concentrate."

"She said that you knew how to get her out of the glass ball. She said she would give me whatever I wanted if I made you get her out. She's not controlling me. We have a deal."

"She not going to give you anything. Once she gets out, she's going to kill you. You can't trust …," Jason's words were cut off when Billy put a piece of duct tape across his mouth and another across his eyes.

"Lay down on the seat. If you move, I swear, I'll cut something off," Billy said as he pushed Jason down on the seat. Just at that moment the cell phone in Jason's pocket began to ring. Billy ignored it. He got in the front seat and began to drive.

A few miles away Rev. Zackery and Pam were coming down the highway.

"There's no answer." Pam said concerned that something was wrong.

"We'll just go to the place where he said he was and blow the horn. He'll hear us. We'll find him. Don't worry."

"Yeah, maybe his phone died," Pam said.

"There's the dirt road now."

They were almost at their turn when a car came out of the dirt road, turned on the highway, and speeded past them.

"Hey! That looked like Billy," Pam yelled.

"Did you see anyone else in the car?" Rev. Zackery asked.

"No, I didn't see anyone, but that doesn't mean he wasn't in there."

"Should we follow him or look for Jason?" Rev. Zackery asked.

"We need to follow him. We need to get Tamela."

"What if Jason is still in the woods," Rev. Zackery said looking suspiciously at Pam.

"If Jason is in the woods, he can take care of himself."

Rev. Zackery pulled into the dirt road and turned around. He quickly accelerated to sixty miles per hour, as he drove down the curving highway. They went past four roads before the highway straighten out. They could see for three or four miles and there were no cars on the highway.

"He couldn't have gotten that far ahead of us." Pam said. "He must have turned off on one of the roads we passed. Turn around!"

"Okay." Rev. Zackery slowed the car and turned around in the middle of the road. "I believe all those roads are dead end roads. Some are kinda long though."

"We'll just have to try them all. Did you see the tag number?"

"No! I didn't even see Billy," Rev. Zackery said. "I saw someone driving the car, but I'm not sure if it was Billy."

Two roads back down the highway, Billy was turning into a driveway of a small house with barn behind it. He stopped the car, opened the barn door, and then pulled the car into the barn. Once the barn door was closed, he pulled Jason out of the car, pulled the duct tape off his eyes, cut the duct tape from his legs and put the pistol in the middle of his back.

"Go over there and sit down in that chair by the table," Billy ordered.

Jason saw a chair in front of a wood table. On the table was something very familiar. It was the safe. As he got closer, he saw the top of the crystal. His heart began to beat rapidly. When he got to the chair, he could see a figure standing in the crystal. He bent over the table and saw Tamela's angry face looking up at him.

"Sit down," Billy shouted at Jason. Billy turned toward the crystal ball. "Okay lady, I got him here, now what?" Billy said as he took rope off a nearby shelf. Billy seemed to be listening to her, but Jason didn't hear anything. "Okay, now we torture him until he talks. Well, we are going to have to wait until tomorrow cause I'm tired, and sleepy." Billy paused. "I'm not listening to you. It's gonna have to wait until tomorrow. I'm not listening," Billy said loudly as he closed the top of the safe over the crystal. Billy got some rope and tied Jason to the chair. "That ought to hold you till tomorrow, nighty night." Billy was walking toward the door when he heard a high pitch sound. Jason could hear it, too. It was coming from the safe. It was faint at first, but it quickly became unbearably loud. Billy covered his ears with his hands. "Okay, just stop it. Stop screaming." The screaming stopped.

A few miles away Rev. Zackery and Pam had given up their search and were headed back to the house when Pam sat straight up in her seat.

"Turn around!" she shouted.

"What? You said it was no use looking anymore," Rev.Zackery said sadly.

"I sense her."

"Who?"

"My sister, Tamela."

"What about Jason?"

"Once we find the crystal, we can locate Jason." Pam was almost frantic. "Hurry up, before I lose this," she paused, "awareness."

Back in the barn, Billy walked over to the safe and opened it.

"What do you want?" he said dejectedly.

"Let me see him, again," the voice from inside the safe said. This time Jason could hear it.

Billy picked up the crystal and held it in front of Jason. Tamela and Jason looked into each other eyes.

"You put me in here, now you are going to get me out," she snarled.

"Now, why would I do something like that, honey?" Jason smiled.

"You're smiling right now, but you won't be smiling when I get through with you."

"You can't do anything to me."

"I can make Billy kill you, if you don't get me out of this crystal."

"Who do you think you're talking to. If I get you out, then you are going to make him kill me anyway, just like you had your flunkies kill my grandmother."

Billy pulled the crystal back and was about to put it back in the safe when she spoke again.

"His arms are not tied good enough. Nail his hands to the chair."

"All right! Then can I please get some sleep?" Billy begged.

"Yes. But we are going to get started early in the morning," she commanded.

Billy got a hammer and two long nails from a box on the floor. He held Jason's right hand and positioned the nail in the middle of the back of it. He raised the hammer. Jason closed his eyes and tightened all his muscles in anticipation of the pain, but nothing happened. He opened his eyes and Billy was still holding the hammer up.

"What are you waiting on? Do it!" Tamela screamed.

Billy raised the hammer higher and then began to bring it down.

"Bailtron," Jason shouted.

Billy froze, the hammer only inches away from the nail. Bailtron's demon head appeared over Billy's.

"You like to cut it pretty close, I see," Bailtron said as he put his head down close to the nail. Then he looked at Jason, their faces only three inches apart. "You rang. What can I do for you, Jason my boy? Are you ready to make a deal?"

"You said I had one free request." Jason said.

"Did I say that? You know for yourself, nothing in this life is free. However, I guess I did say that. What is your request?

"Make Billy release his grip on that nail," Jason said.

"Okay."

The nail being held by Billy's fingers, fell over and slid off Jason's hand to the floor.

"I never thought I'd ever say this but, thank you demon."

"Oh, it was Bailtron when you needed me, but now that I have got you out of your mess, it's demon. Well, your mama was a demon, and your grandmama, too."

"I'm sorry," Jason pleaded. "Thank you, Bailtron."

"Look, I really didn't mean that about your grandmother," Bailtron said apologetically. "Have you considered my offer? Are you ready to make a deal?"

"I have been pretty busy. Can I sleep on it and tell you in the morning?"

"Well, I'll give you till sun-up. Then I will need an answer. Remember, we want the same thing, all those witches dead. I'm the only one that can really help you."

"Okay, Bailtron."

"Get some rest. 'Here's Billy!'"

The demon head disappeared, and Billy brought the hammer down full force on his thumb and forefinger.

"Got to me more careful," Billy yelled, dropping the hammer and grabbing his hurt fingers.

Inside the crystal, Tamela stood in a state of shock, her mouth open, wondering what she had just seen. Her shock was interrupted when Billy quickly took the crystal off the table, threw it in the safe and closed the top. Billy made his way to the door, while rubbing his fingers. Billy cut off the light and walked out of the barn.

It took a few minutes, but Jason's eyes adjusted to the darkness, and he could see the image of the table. He hopped the chair over to the table. Now he could make out the image of the safe. In fact, he could see a faint light around the top coming from inside of it. He rocked the chair forward until he was on his toes. He fell back. He hopped the chair closer to the table, then he tried again. This time he rocked himself forward so hard that he hit the table with his chest as he had planned. Jason put his nose to the edge of the top of the safe and lifted it up. He tried to flip it open, but it came back down. He repositioned his nose and flipped harder. This time the top fell all the way back. Jason let the chair fall back to the sitting position. He could see her, and she could see him. They just stared at each other. The hate was overwhelming.

Pam and Rev. Zackery were parked on a dirt road off the highway. They had been there for ten minutes.

"Rev. Zackery! I sense her again. It's strong. We must be close," Pam said.

"Which way?"

"Back this way. It must be one of the houses we passed."

Rev. Zackery cranked up the car, turned around, and drove toward the last house they had passed.

Back in the barn, Tamela was the first to stop staring. She turned her back to Jason, she consciously changed the expression on her face from hate to an expression of humility and sincerity, then she spoke in an audible voice that Jason could hear clearly.

"You know, I didn't have anything to do with the death of your grandmother," she said turning around. Dutchman was not supposed to harm her, he was just supposed to kill Pam. I am not responsible for her death. It was Dutchman and those idiots he took with him."

"You know," Jason said shaking his head and calming himself, "you are so full of it. It stinks every time you open your mouth."

"I didn't tell him to do what he did!"

"Yeah, maybe not, but you did try to kill Pam, Rev. Zackery, and me, several times. Furthermore, if you ever get out of that crystal ball, you are going to keep trying to kill us and anybody else that gets in your way. My grandmother was in your way. You may not have told Dutchman to burn her up alive, but you wanted her dead," Jason paused to calm himself because he was beginning to get very angry again. "I hold you personally responsible. That will never change."

"Okay, your right. It was my responsibility, even though I didn't want it to happen. All I can say now, whether you believe it or not, I'm sorry about your grandmother. Now, it's true I have been trying to kill Pamela, and everybody who is trying to protect her; you, Rev. Zackery, and even your grandmother. I had to do what I did. You don't know Pamela! You don't have any idea what she has been doing. You know, I 'm a witch. Well, Pamela is also a witch. But unlike me, she is an evil witch who needs to be stopped."

"What has Pam been doing that's evil?" Jason asked anxiously.

"She has been violating our laws?"

"Your laws! You mean witch laws."

"Yes! Witch laws. You have laws don't you. Well, witches have laws, too. We have powers that you don't have. If a witch does things that draws attention to us, it puts all of us in danger. You 'normal' people hate everything that is different from yourselves, especially witches. If your people ever found out about our organization, they would hunt all of us down and kill all of us. You know I'm right," Tamela said pointing her finger at him.

"You all need to be killed. You killed my grandmother."

"My main responsibility is to protect the coven. Part of that responsibility is to make sure that all the witches obey the laws. If a witch breaks the law, then they must pay the consequences. In Pam's case, the penalty is death."

"You never said what she did. Tell me what she did that was so evil," Jason demanded.

"She killed her own mother. Her mother, our mother was one of us. She was a witch, too. Pamela, my sister, killed my mother!"

"She said the head council caught her mother on a rooftop and she jumped so that they couldn't force her to tell them where Pam was," Jason replied.

"Lies! All lies!" Tamela shouted. "Our mother was the leader of the witches. Pam and I were her successors. Pam, my mother, and I all lived together until me and Pam were about to turn twelve. At that time my mother was to choose who would become her successor so that the formal training could begin. Pam knew our mother was going to choose me, so she killed her."

"You're saying that Pam pushed her mother off the top of the building," Jason said incredulously.

"No! Pam poisoned her own mother and tried to blame me for it. The only thing that saved me was the confession of the person who gave Pam the poison."

Jason felt confused. He didn't know what to think. He laid his head back against the chair and within minutes he was asleep.

"Since you won't let me in your mind while you're awake, I'll get in while you're asleep," Tamela said, pressing her hands to each side of her head in concentration.

Chapter 17
Salvation at a Cost

(Sunday night 10:30 PM)

Rev. Zackery had just driven past a driveway when Pam shouted.

"Wait! I sense her again. I think this is it. Back up! Turn into that driveway and go about twenty feet or so. Turn off the lights."

Rev. Zackery could barely see, however, strangely Pam could, so Pam had to direct him. Once the car was parked, Pam reached up, turned the car's interior light switch to off, got out, and walked around to Rev. Zackery's window.

"Do you have any weapons," she asked.

"A lug wrench is in the trunk, and I think I have a screwdriver in the toolbox."

"Give me my purse."

He handed her the purse. She took a can of hairspray out and stuck it in her back pocket.

"Hairspray?"

"It's worked for me before," she said.

Rev. Zackery got the lug wrench and the screwdriver out of the trunk. He offered the lug wrench to Pam.

"I'm good," she said shaking her head, no.

"Here, at least take this," he said shoving the screwdriver in her other back pocket.

Rev. Zackery and Pam began walking quickly down a long dirt and gravel driveway toward the one-story house. They were trying to be as quiet as possible, however, the sound of their steps on the gravel seemed to echo in the dead silence of the night. They were about fifty feet from the house when a light in a room on the right side of the house came on. They stopped and moved into the ditch next to the driveway and waited. There were no trees along the driveway, just plowed fields. Another light came on in the middle room of the house. Then the front door opened. Two large figures appeared in the doorway, one human, one not. Pam and Rev. Zackery heard the human yell out. The human wanted to make sure that they heard him.

"Go see if there is anything out there, and if it is, tear a hole in their butt," Pam and Rev. Zackery heard a man's voice say to his companion. "Lady! go!" the man in the doorway yelled. Immediately, the large dog beside him charged. Pam pulled the screwdriver and the hairspray from her back pockets. She stabbed the screwdriver into the dirt at the top of the ditch. Then she pulled a cigarette lighter out of her front pocket and tested her flame thrower. The bright orange flame shot two feet from the can.

"I'll take care of the dog," Pam whispered.

Rev. Zackery quickly climbed out of the ditch, moved in front of Pam and yelled at the top of his voice. "Hey mister call your dog. We don't want to hurt her. We are looking for our friend. He was taken." The dog was moving straight for Rev. Zackery.

"Lady! come!" the man cried out.

The dog slid to a stop a few feet from Rev. Zackery, turned and hurried back to the house.

"Can you help us? Can we come up?" Rev. Zackery asked.

"Yeah, come on?"

"Go get the car, please," Rev. Zackery said as he walked toward the house.

Pam went back to the car and drove up to the house. By the time she reached the house, the man and Rev. Zackery were sitting on the porch talking. Pam walked on the porch looking for the dog. She was sitting next to Rev. Zackery with her head on his leg, being soothed by his gentle rubs.

"Mr. Carson, this is my friend Pam."

"Howdy, miss," he said reaching to shake her hand. "Rev. Zackery, told me that someone took your friend."

"Yes sir," Pam said sitting on the porch rail. "I'm sure he's somewhere close by."

"Well, there have been some strange things happening at the farmhouse two houses down the road. Last week I drove by there and I thought I heard a woman scream. I stopped my car and listened, but I didn't hear nothing else. But I just can't get that sound I heard out of my head. Then a couple of days ago I went by there around three in the morning, and there was this crazy looking blue green light coming out of his barn. If your friend was taken, my guess is he's there."

"We believe he's in trouble, sir. If we don't get to him soon, he may be murdered," Pam said.

"Go back down the road, the second driveway on the right. And, don't make a big commotion like you did when you came down my driveway."

"Thank you so much, Mr. Carson, and you too, Lady," Rev. Zackery said looking from the man to the dog. They got up to leave.

"Pastor, keep an eye out for me cause I'll be coming over there to your church to hear you preach."

"Please come and bring Lady with you. It will be good to see you both again."

"Y'all be real careful, now."

When they got in the car, Pam went to the driver's side. She quickly drove to the second driveway, turned off the cars headlights, and drove all the way to the house, stopping between the house and the barn. They quickly got out leaving the doors open.

"You check the house, and I'll check the barn," Pam ordered.

"No! We need to stay together. I'm coming with you."

"Fine," Pam snapped as she shined her flashlight on the padlocked barn door.

"I'll get it," Rev. Zackery said as he moved up and pried the latch off the door with his lug wench. When they opened the door, they saw Jason in the chair in front of the table where the light was coming from the safe. They walked closer and saw Tamela inside the crystal, and Tamela saw them.

"Jason," Pam whispered. He said nothing. She walked up to him and pushed his shoulder. "Jason." He still did not acknowledge her.

"Baby sister," Tamela said smiling.

"Hi," Pam said looking down at the figure in the crystal. Rev. Zackery came up quickly and flipped the top of the safe closed. "That was rude," Pam said frowning at Rev. Zackery.

"We need to stay focused." Rev. Zackery picked up the safe from the bottom since the lock was broken. He carried it to the car and put the safe in trunk. When he returned to the barn, Pam was still trying to revive Jason.

"What do you think is wrong with him?" she said.

"Looks like he's in a trance. My guess, it's Tamela's work. Let's get him in the car," Rev. Zackery said as he tilted the chair back. "Grab that side." Pam took hold of the chair, and they began to drag it toward the car. Once they got to the car they untied and laid him in the back seat. Jason slept through it all.

"Okay, let's go," Pam said opening the car door on the driver's side. She put her hands on the keys which were already in the ignition. Rev. Zackery just stood outside the car looking at the house.

"We need to find Billy first, he is more of a danger to us now."

"Somehow, I knew you'd say that. You and your precious Billy," Pam said disgustedly.

"Look, Billy knows all about your plans."

"So what? That idiot can't do anything," Pam said.

"What about the demon that takes control of Billy? You think you have powers. I believe Billy, when he under the influence of the demons, may have supernatural abilities. So, don't underestimate him. I know you think that you are tough, but don't mess around and get you butt whooped."

"By Billy!" Pam scoffed. "I'd beat him with one hand tied behind my back and with a blindfold on."

"Okay, killer, come on. Just make sure you keep your torch and the screwdriver ready." Rev. Zackery pried the back door open with the lug wrench and they walked into the kitchen.

"This should be real easy," Pam whispered. "I hear him snoring. He's upstairs."

"Praise the Lord."

They started up the stairs and were halfway when the snoring stopped. They froze and listened. There were no sound to be heard except the heavy breathing of Rev. Zackery.

"You're really out of shape Pastor."

"Your mama," Rev. Zackery said louder than intended.

"Pastor!"

"Be quiet, please." Rev. Zackery said putting one finger up to her lips. They both looked up the stair. They were just about to move when they heard something. It was whistling in the tune of "Mary Had a Little Lamb." After the whistling stopped, the song was sung, however, the words were different.

"The reverend had a little witch, little witch, little witch. Zackery had a little witch whose heart was black as coal. If he keeps listening to her lies, her denies, and alibis, and if her lies he justifies, he's going to lose his soul," the voice said from the darkness at the top of the stairs. "Rev. Zackery! You didn't really think you were going to sneak up on me, did you?"

"That's not Billy, it's the demon," Rev. Zackery said to Pam. Then turning toward the top of the stairs, he yelled out, "What are you afraid of, demon? Why are you hiding in the dark?"

"Reverend, you and your little witch are the ones who are sneaking around in the dark," he said turning on the light. There at the top of the stairs was Billy, with the demon's head. He was holding a sixteen-gauge, pump, shotgun. "What are you afraid of?" the demon said cocking the shotgun and aiming it at Rev. Zackery. The demon head disappeared, and Billy's returned.

"In the name of..." Rev. Zackery shouted as the shotgun blast cut his sentence short. Rev. Zackery fail back. Pam watched as Rev. Zackery tumbled down the stairs. Billy watched stoically as Rev. Zackery's body came to a stop and lay motionless in a very awkward position on the floor below. Billy cocked the gun again, aimed, and shot. Pam ducked down. He missed her completely. Pam jumped over the rail and dropped to the floor. By the time he had cocked the gun again, Pam was through the front door and out of the house. When Billy reached the front door, he saw Pam speeding in the car down the driveway, to the road. He then rushed to the barn as the car went out of sight.

When Pam reached the highway, she slowed only enough to make a sliding turn. The car fishtailed momentarily before she stomped the accelerator. She didn't slow down until she turned into the driveway of Rev. Zackery's brother's house. After she had unlocked and opened the door to the house, and turned on the porch light, she went back to the car, pulled Jason's limp body out by his arm, hoisted him over her shoulder, and carried him into the house, all the while not knowing that she was being watched.

Two men were in a car parked in the trees, across the road, about two hundred feet from the house. The man in the driver's seat was looking through binoculars, the other held a cellphone near his mouth below his bandaged nose.

"We found her," said the one with the cellphone. "What are our instructions."

"What do you think? Kill her!" the voice on the cell phone screamed.

"Yes ma'am," the man said.

"I was told you failed last time. Don't fail this time, cause if you do, you will regret it. It will be the last time you fail."

"Yes ma'am," he said ending the call.

The men got out of the car. The driver got a rifle out of the back seat. He propped the rifle on the hood of the car and took aim on the door.

"Just get her to come to the door and then get out of the way," the man with the rifle said.

The man with the bandaged face pulled a switchblade knife and spoke. "If I get close,

you won't have to do anything."

"Hey! You heard Sibal. We can't take any chances. If I get a shot, I'm taking it. Don't, get in the way."

"Look at my face, Walt. She did this to me. She's mine!"

"She beat your butt last time. What makes you think it will be any different, now. All she has to do is hit you in the nose."

"She's mine!" he snarled pressing his bandaged nose up against the face of the man holding the rifle. Then he pushed the tip of his knife into the neck of his co-conspirator and said, "Do you understand me?"

"You need to be careful who you threaten."

"She mine Walt, mine!"

"All right Manny, she's yours. Go!"

Manny ran across the road keeping the trees between him and the house. Once he got to the driveway, he walked down the center of the driveway. He walked up on the porch and knocked on the door. Pam had just put a wet cloth on Jason's head. The knock startled her. She went to the closest, got the shotgun, and walked cautiously to the door.

"Who is it?" she asked.

"My name is Emanuel Brown, ma'am. My car broke down a couple of miles down the road and my cell phone died on me. Can I use your phone to make a service call? I have roadside service. I don't need to come in. If you have a cell phone, I'll step off the porch and you can set the phone on a chair on the porch. I'll wait in the yard until you get back in the house, before I use it," he said as he walked to the edge of the porch.

"Come on in, Manny," she said smiling.

Manny froze with fright. He was just about to run when he heard a click. He turned his head slowly. He saw the shotgun barrel in the slightly ajar door. It was pointed at his stomach.

"You remember me," he said forgetting about his false scenario.

"I make it a point to remember everyone who tries to kill me. Still, the way I see it, you tried to kill me, I tried to kill you, so as of right now, we're even. Now, I'm giving you a choice. You can come in, talk with me, and see if we can make a deal, or you can die right where you're standing, and I'll make a deal with whoever is out there in the woods." She paused. "Oh yeah, you've got three seconds. One, two…"

"Okay, I'm coming in," Manny said as he walked toward the door.

"Turn around and walk backwards until you feel the barrel of the gun in your back," she said.

From the woods, Walt could see an image of someone peeping through the crack in the door. He was about to shoot when Manny turned and began backing toward the door. Now, the site of the rifle scope was trained on Manny's chest which was aligned with the opening in the door. "I warned you, Manny," Walt said as he squeezed the trigger.

The shot rang out. Manny was knocked against the door frame and the door. He fell across the threshold pushing the door halfway open. The bullet had passed through Manny chest, through the opening in the door just as Walt had planned. He wondered if he had hit his target. He moved the scope of the rifle down to Manny's body. He was motionless. Then he saw something that made him smile. He could see the barrel of the shotgun lying on Manny's arm.

"Gotsha," he said aloud. He watched and waited for several minutes. He lowered the rifle and ran across the road when something appeared in the doorway. He raised the rifle. Looking through the scope, he saw that it was a piece of paper hanging from door handle. The words on the paper read, "LET'S TALK."

Walt fired two times into the door and two into the wall beside it. The piece of paper fell to the floor. He chambered another round, scanned the doorway, the windows, and the entire front of the house through the scope. He saw no movement. He moved cautiously toward the house until he saw something move. He raised the sights of his rifle. There was another piece of paper on the door handle. It read, "I GUESS THAT'S A 'NO'". Someone moved pass the door and it closed partially. He fired three more times into the door. Then, he moved the scope back down to Manny's body. The shotgun barrel was gone. He ran across to the other side of the driveway and positioned himself for another shot. He attempted to chamber another bullet but his clip was empty. He dropped the empty clip to the ground and when he reached into his jacket pocket for another clip, he heard a voice behind him say "Out of bullets?"

Walt slowly turned around. Pam was standing three feet away, pointing the shotgun at his face. Walt tossed the rifle down to ground beside him wondering why he wasn't already dead.

"I saw how bad you beat my associates when you were in the woods. They said that you got lucky," Walt said as he slowly took off his jacket and tossed it to the side.

"They were the lucky ones. If you hadn't shot me in the back, your associates would have died that day."

"They both said that you have hand to hand combat skills. They said that you wanted to fight them, that you like fighting. Do you think you can take me?" Walt challenged. "Those guys were bigger than me, but they weren't as good as me." He backed up into the front yard of the house. Pam follow. As she passed his rifle and jacket, she lowered the double barrel shotgun and pointed them toward his knees.

"I'll make you a deal. If you answer me one question truthfully, I'll throw down this shotgun and give you a shot at my title."

"You got a deal," he couldn't help smiling. "What's the question?"

"Did Sibal send you?"

"How do you know Sibal?"

"Sibal and I fought before. That scratch down the side of her face, I did that. I actually messed up her whole face, however, she blew herself up and the burned off the scratches on the other side."

"Is that so? Well, news break, she has a new face now. She got a transplant."

"She stole somebody's face," Pam said shaking her head. "Look Walter! Sibal and I made a deal. If she sent you to kill me, then that means the deal is off. Wouldn't you say?"

"When did you make a deal with Sibal, if you don't mind me asking?" Walt asked.

"Both of us were in ICU, day before yesterday. We fought there, for a second time. I won again. I was going to kill her there, but I offered her a way to save her life." Pam paused. "Did she send you? If you lie, I'll blow your kneecap off right now."

"I thought we had a deal. I said I would answer your question if you would fight me."

"Did she send you?" Pam screamed.

"Yeah, Sibal sent me."

"To kill me?" she said softly.

"She sent us to stake out the house. When we saw you, Manny called her on his cell phone, and she told us to kill you."

"I've got one more question for you?" Pam asked, taking the shotgun shells from the weapon, and throwing them and the shotgun to the ground.

"Okay?"

"Why did you kill Many?" Pam asked. "You shot him to keep me from killing him."

"For what it's worth, when I shot you, it wasn't personal. I was just doing what I was paid to do," he said as he watched Pam toss the shotgun to the ground. He began to wonder if he could beat her. She seemed so confident.

"I could use someone, that does what he's paid to do, because I plan to take over the coven."

"Are you one of them?" Walt said surprised.

"Them? I'm Tamela's sister. You do know who Tamela is, don't you?"

"Tamela was the leader of the coven. She's dead now," Walt said.

"You said 'one of them.' Does that mean you are not in the coven?"

"I work for Sibal, so technically, I guess I am, however, I don't know much about the stuff they do in the coven. I'm just an employee."

Well, Tamera, my sister, tried to kill me, so I trapped her. She's in the house right now," Pam said pointing toward the house.

"If that's true, where have you been? Do you belong to another coven?"

"I was taken away at birth. I didn't even know about my lineage until a few weeks ago when my sister kept sending people to kill me." Pam paused. "I killed them all," she said staring deeply into his eyes to see if there was any fear. She saw none. "Then she came to kill me herself. I defeated her, too. Like I said, she's trapped in the house."

"You beat Tamela, the queen?"

"Yeah, but she's not the queen anymore. I am. So, I'll make you the same deal that I made Sibal."

"What's that?"

"If you introduce me to the coven at the ceremony, I will make you second in command."

"What about Sibal?"

"I'm going to kill her, and I think I'll do it in front of everybody at the ceremony. You see, you can tell her that you killed me, then when the ceremony starts, you and I will walk in. I will show everybody that Tamela is trapped in my crystal ball, and they will make me their leader, or queen or whatever they call it. What about it?"

"Sorry. I like your courage, and you are drop-dead gorgeous, but you are too stupid."

"Why do you think that?" Pam said surprised.

"You should have killed me when you had the chance. You never should have put your gun down. Sibal said to kill you or else. You've got to die."

"Or else what?"

"Or else she was going to have me, and Manny killed."

"Is Manny's cell phone in his pocket?"

"Yeah."

"Okay, this is what I want you to do." Pam paused. Positioning her feet in a fighting stance with her hands on her thighs, she leaned her head forward. "After I beat you in the ground, I'm going to send you and your dead friend Manny back to Sibal with this message. Tell Sibal that I will give her one more chance. Tell her to call me on Manny's cell phone."

"The only message I'm going to deliver is 'mission accomplished,'" Walt said as he danced forward in boxing mode. He threw two quick left jabs. Pam moved her head just enough for him to miss her. Then she shot her clawed hand forward hitting his forehead and tried to rake them down his face, however, when he ducked forward, he was caught with a powerful right hook that caused his body to spin completely around. Walt was surprised at how quick she was. He rubbed his nose which was bleeding from the cut made by her fingernail. Before he could move his hand, she kicked him so hard under his chin that both his feet flew up into the air as he fell back and hit the ground.

Pam did not notice the strange light coming from the bedroom behind her as she waited confidently for Walt to get back to his feet. As he stood in front of her, she could tell his confidence was gone.

"Last chance. Do you want to work for me, or do you want to get seriously hurt?"

"It's not over yet. Let's do this," Walt said as he quickly spun around and kicked her in her chest. The kick pulled part of the tape on her bandage loose. Pain shot through her whole body as she placed her hand over her bandages. "How is your chest wound?"

Pam was shocked that she didn't react quicker. His moves did not happen in slow motion as they had seemed before. Her powers were getting weaker.

Inside the house Jason was sitting on the side of the bed next to the safe he had opened. He and Tamela were staring at each other through the glow of the strange light. Tamela held her hands to the sides of her hear and yelled out.

"Tell me how you trapped me in here?"

"I didn't trap you. You trapped yourself," Jason said while in a trancelike state.

"Get me out of here?"

Outside, Pam had been circling to keep Walt off balance. However, he charged straight for her. She quickly dove toward his legs and rolled. He fell forward, hitting the ground, but rolling instinctively back to his feet. Within seconds, they both stood facing each other. He charged again. This time he moved more cautiously attempting to grab her arms. As he moved forward, she threw dirt in his eyes, temporarily blinding him. She grabbed his wrist, pushed his arm up, and hit him in the Adam's apple with her pointed knuckles. He jerked his arm away from her, pushed her in her chest, and ran, wiping the dirt from his eyes in the process.

Having put a little distance between them, he turned and charged again, this time yelling all the way. As he reached striking distance, she jabbed her fingernails toward his eye. He ducked under her hand and went for her legs. She moved to her left and spun around. She almost made him miss. His outstretched hand caught her sweatshirt and he slung her over him to the ground beside him. She tried to crawl away, but he would not release her shirt. When she kicked him in the top of his head, he caught her leg and begin to crawl on top of her. She growled and scratched furiously with both hands at the top of his head. Then he grabbed one of her hands and pulled himself further on top of her. She continued to growl and scratch with her other hand as fear began to overtake her. She clamped onto his ear, but before she could pull, he grabbed her other hand, pulled it down and crawled completely on top of her. He then sat on her stomach and force both of her hand above her shoulders. She continued to squirm.

"Give it up! It's over," he yelled.

She acted as if he hadn't heard him. She squirmed harder until he lifted his knee and press hard against her chest wound. She moaned in pain as she stopped squirming. He moved his knee off her chest and over her arm clamping it beneath his leg. Then he clamped her other arm with his other leg. Now, both of his hands were free as he sat on her chest.

"I can show you where Tamela your queen is. You can't free her without me," Pam pleaded.

"Tamera is dead as far as Sibal is concerned, and she wants to keep it that way," he said rubbing his ear and then looking at all the blood on his hand. He also touched his nose. It began to sting where she had scratched him. "You got my nose pretty good." He paused." Don't worry, I'm not going to mess up a pretty face like yours." He placed his hand on her neck, grabbed her jaw and straighten up her face, then he pulled a short knife from an ankle holster and put it to her neck. "You're something special. You would have made some man, maybe even me, a good woman. What a waste," he said shaking his head. "Your title is mine."

"You never answered my question," Pam whispered.

"What question?" Walt asked.

"Why did you kill Manny? Was it because you didn't want him to kill me?

"Manny broke my number one rule. He threatened to kill me. I don't do well with threats."

Just as he was about to drive his knife into her throat, he heard something coming behind him. Both he and Pam looked up. A car with its lights out was coming quickly toward them. Walt raised up one knee preparing to jump. However, before he could move, Pam clamped her arm around his other leg. The car hit Walt's back and slid to a halt. Then the car backed up exposing Pam lying on the ground holding his shoe. A person opened the car door, ran around to the front of the car where Pam was laying.

"Pam! Are you all right?"

"Dave! I can't believe it! It's you!" she yelled excitedly. She raised up, holding out her arms. They hugged warmly. "You saved my life again," she said kissing him continuously all over his face. He picked her up and began to carry her to the house.

"Did I hit you with the car? Did I hurt you?" Dave said worriedly.

"No! You saved me." Pam was really enjoying being in Dave's arms. "I missed you so much. I was so worried about you. Are you all right?" She thought about the jail scene the demon had showed them. "Being in jail is nothing to be ashamed of. What happens in jail stays in jail."

"Jail?"

"Yeah, Jason told us you were in jail."

"Oh yeah. It did get pretty hairy in there, but I survived."

"Hairy? Yeah, I heard it can get, 'pretty hairy'," Pam said as they passed Walt's motionless body, Pam looked down. "Is he dead?"

"I hope not but he was attacking you, so I had to do what I had to do."

"Put me down. We'd better check." Dave lowered her feet to the ground beside Walt's body. No sooner than she was standing next to him, she kicked him hard in the side. He moaned. "He's alive. Help me get him on the porch. We need to tie him up."

Pam got on one side while Dave got on the other, and they began to drag him toward the house. When they got to the steps, the light from the open door exposed the blood running down Walt's neck from his ear. Pam smiled at her hardy work.

"You did that to his face?" Dave said looking at the three marks down his face.

"I'm not through with him yet. There's some duct tape in Rev. Zackery's bedroom. I need to tape him up," Pam snarled. "He's the one who shot me in the back."

As they pulled the body up on the porch, Dave saw the other body lying in a pool of blood.

"Jason told me about that. How bodies many are there?" Dave said.

"The score is one to one," Pam said.

"The score? What do you mean?" Dave released Walt's arm and so did Pam. He dropped hard to the floor.

"They got Rev. Zackery," Pam said as she took Manny's cell phone from his back pocket.

"They killed him?" Dave said in shock.

"Yeah."

"No! How could God let that happen?" He began to walk in a small circle. Then he stopped. "What about Jason? Is he okay?"

"He's going to be okay. He's inside," she said as they walked over the dead body into the house. They walked down the hall. There was a strange light coming from the room where Jason had been sleeping. They ran down the hall and looked into the bedroom. What they saw, scared them to their core. Jason, a hammer in one hand, was standing over the crystal which was sitting on the nightstand. The other hand was behind his back. The cross, made from the communion table wood, the cross with the sharp end showing, was being held in that hand like a dagger. Inside the crystal, the source of the strange blue light, Tamela was holding out her arm toward Jason with her palm aimed at him.

Dave and Pam both screamed at the same time, "Dave! Don't do it."

Jason stopped for a second, turned his head back to see Pam and Dave moving toward him. He raised the hammer higher and quickly brought it down. Dave dove toward Jason pushing Jason into the wall. His arm came down toward the crystal, but he missed. The hammer crashed into the nightstand as Dave fell to the floor. Pam went for the crystal. With one hand, she snatched it from the nightstand with the other, she picked up the safe which had been lying on the floor. Jason pushed his face from the wall and raised the hammer up again, but the crystal was gone. Pam had it. She had put it in the safe which she held behind her as she backed out of the room. Jason moved toward her. His hate filled eyes scared her more than the hammer that he was holding over his head as he moved toward her.

"Jason!" she screamed. "Jason!"

The sound of the second loud scream penetrated the barrier of the trance, and Jason regained awareness of his surroundings.

"What! Why are you screaming?" he asked.

"Why are you coming at me with a hammer?"

Jason looked up at his hand and the hammer in amazement. "Good question. Why am I coming at you with a hammer?" he said lowering the hammer. "Did you step on my blue suede shoes again?"

"You ain't never had no blue suede shoes," she said with a little smile.

"Is he all right now?" Dave said from the floor.

Jason turned and saw Dave on the floor. "Dave!" he said excitedly as if it was his first time seeing him. "What are you doing down there?"

"Yeah, he's okay, now. I hope he remains that way after he finds out about, everything," Pam said concerned.

"We have some bad news," Dave said solemnly as he stood up.

"What is it?"

"Rev. Zackery is dead. Billy killed him," Pam said biting her lips.

Jason slowly backed to the bed, sat down, and lowered his head into his head. "It's all my fault."

"No! It's not your fault. We had already rescued you. Rev. Zackery wanted to get Billy, for some insane reason. He went in Billy's house, not to kill him, but to capture him and bring him back here. Billy heard us, and he started shooting. That's what happened. Rev. Zackery got himself killed. He almost got me killed, and you, too." Pam paused. "He was obsessed with those demons. His obsession got him killed," she screamed.

"Calm down, sweetie," Dave said as he walked up behind her putting his hand on her shoulder and turning her around from facing Jason to facing him.

"Yeah sweetie," Jason said standing up pulling her partly around toward him. "You're right, it wasn't my fault. It wasn't your fault either." He pulled her into his arms. "There was nothing that you could do. Thank you for saving me. Thank you!" he said looking angrily at Dave.

"Can I talk to you to you in the other room," Dave said to Jason.

"What is it that you don't want me to hear?" Pam asked.

"It's a man-to-man thing," Dave replied.

"I ain't going nowhere" Jason said. "Say what you want to say, right here in front of Pam."

"Okay, okay," Dave said. He thought for a moment turning to Pam. "It looks like both of us want you. I was going to suggest to Jason that we hold off on completing for your affection until after we finish doing this thing with the witches. That's it."

"You're married, unhappily I might add," Pam said looking confused at Dave.

"Not for long, I'm getting a divorce," Dave said.

"Compete? How can you compete with me? You crossed over to the other side. How was it?" Jason said to Dave waving his hand.

"What are you talking about?" Dave frowned.

"Nothing!" Pam said.

"Nothing? You would choose him over me, now?" Jason asked.

"Why not? You have so much hate in you that there's no room for anything else," she said turning to Jason. "All you can think about is killing my sister, Tamera."

"Yeah, that's true. Definitely! Killing your sister is on my bucket list, but you need to remember that I would be home right now if we hadn't stopped to get that book. I was helping you. When those witches shot you and left you in the woods to die, I was the one who found you. After that, when Sibal tried to take you out at the hospital, at least, I tried to protect you there, but the police took me to the police station for questioning. By now, you should know, they will never stop coming after you, that's why we came up with this plan to kill all of them. It's not just because I hate them, some of it, is to protect you, Dave, and me. You know this." He paused. "I care for you. We've been through too much, all of us. Maybe, after this is over, I'll be able to feel again, love again, and understand what I'm really feeling." He looked at Dave. "You're right Dave. We need to stay focused on the task at hand, then we can talk about feelings. Anyway, there's no guarantee that any of us will survive this."

"I hate to be a killjoy, but I just saw a car pull out of the woods," Dave said.

They all ran to the porch. Both men were gone.

CHAPTER 18
THE VISION

(Monday morning 6:00 AM)

He woke up with duct tape over his mouth. He tried to move his arms but couldn't. They too, were duct taped to his sides from his armpits to his elbows. He could bend his arms at the elbows, but his hands and fingers were each taped. They looked like duct tape mittens. His legs were also duct taped from his thighs to his ankles and there was something taped between his legs that prevented him from bending his knees. His shoulder, his right knee, and the back of his head were hurting terribly. He wanted to moan but fought it. He stayed as quiet as possible as he looked around the room. Next to the bed where he was lying, he could see the dawning light coming through the window. It revealed the dim images of strangely shaped furniture. As his eyes adjusted, he could tell that the shapes were clothes, boxes, and basically trash piled on top of the dresser, the drawers, and a chair next to the bed. There was a foul odor coming from the bed. It wasn't urine or fesses. It smelled like death, like a dead carcass had once laid where he now was. He began to itch, just thinking of the bugs that were probably crawling up his sleeves or his pants legs.

Rev. Zackery was alone in the room. He could only assume he was still at Billy's house. The last thing he remembered was jumping out of the line of fire of Billy's shotgun, and then falling down the steps. He wondered what had happened to Pam and Jason, what Billy had done to them.

"If I had only left without trying to get Billy," he whispered to himself. "This is just a test." He closed his eyes and began to pray. "Lord, I know that every test is a test of faith. You already know everything. You know where my faith is, and I know that You just want me to see for myself whether I have the faith necessary to deal with this situation. You want me to see if I trust You." He paused. "Lord, I trust you, but if there is an area of doubt anywhere in my mind, my spirit, or my soul, I ask you to give me the strength to believe. Give me wisdom to know what to do and what to say. Speak to me Lord, please." His whispers grew louder. "Give me what I stand in need of, and I will give you all the honor, all the glory, and all of the praise. In Jesus' name I pray. Amen." He opened his eyes and there in front of him was Billy with the demon head. Quickly the demon moved forward and covered Rev. Zackery's mouth with duct tape.

"Rev. Z. You're all duct taped up. Billy just wanted you to know that you reap what you sow, just like the good book says. He didn't put any plastic on the bed like you did for him, but he wanted me to tell you, if you need to use the bathroom, go right ahead. He doesn't care if you mess up the bed or your clothes for that matter, cause he's not going to clean it up. Nope, not Billy boy. Also, he doesn't have a bible to beat you with, so I had him put a phonebook on the foot of the bed," the demon said smiling. "Oh, and that prayer you just prayed, it got me right here," he said holding his hand over his heart. "I especially liked the part about every test is a test of faith. Wrong Z! This next test is a test to see if you have any balls. Are you going to be a man or squeal like a little punk?" He paused. "You're right about one thing, though. God does already know, and He does want you to see. But guess what Z? I already know, too, and I'll show you, right now. Take a look at your future."

The demon waved his arm and a scene appeared.

In the scene, Rev. Zackery could be seen standing in his pulpit. As the view panned around, the church hall could be seen from behind Rev. Zackery. The church was filled people. There was a casket on a new section of wood flooring in front of a new communion table. There, standing in the center aisle was Tamera. She was dressed in her black hooded robe, and she was pointing at Rev. Zackery.

"You have been weighted and found unworthy. You are not a true man of God. You are a liar and a deceiver. Your God has turned you over to my god for punishment. You stand condemned," Tamera cries out. "Bring him to me."

Two men force Rev. Zackery from the pulpit and stand him in the aisle in front of Tamera.

"Kneel at my feet," she commanded.

"I will not," Rev. Zackery yelled.

Pam nods and the two men holding Rev. Zackery's arms simultaneously kick the back of his knees and he goes down to the kneeling position.

"Your God has condemned you. Swear allegiance to me and you can live out the rest of your life in comfort and luxury, or you can watch your friends die and then be killed yourself." She pointed behind him. When he looked, he saw several men bring in two crosses from the back room of the church on the right side of the pulpit. Tied to the crosses were Jason and Dave. The men stood the crosses up in front of the communion table by dropping them into specially prepared holes. Then they pushed the casket back against the crosses.

"Swear allegiance to me!" she shouted.

"Never!"

Tamera nodded again, and the men began to pour gasoline over Jason, Dave, the communion table, and the casket.

"This is your last chance." Tamera said nodding.

One of the men opened the casket. Instantly, Pam sat up and was dashed in the face with gasoline. Another man walked up with a fiery torch.

"Rev. Zackery! Help us!" Pam screamed.

"Wait!" Rev. Zackery screamed. "I swear"

The demon waved his arm and the scene disappeared. Rev. Zackery was mumbling something from his tape covered mouth.

"Are you trying to tell me something, Z?" the demon asked.

Rev. Zackery raised his forearm and moved his tape covered hand, motioning for the demon to come closer, then moved his hand to his mouth.

"Now, reverend, you know Billy wouldn't want me to take that tape off your mouth. You might start praising the Lord up in here, up in here. Billy is sick and tired of your sermons, but don't take my word for it. Here's Billy," the demon said taking a step back.

The demon head dissolved leaving Billy's. There was an evil smile on Billy's face as he moved toward Rev. Zackery. He grabbed the phonebook as he approached.

Rev. Zackery opened his eyes and saw Billy walking toward him with a phone book held high in his hand. He realized that he had been dreaming. It had seemed so real, yet he knew that he had been asleep and that he had just awakened.

Billy jumped on the bed and sat on top of Rev. Zackery's stomach, pinning his arms down.

"Rev. Zackery? Now tell me. Why did you and your little hooligans break into my humble home, and take my prized possession, the little lady in the glass ball?" Billy said raising the phonebook over Rev. Zackery's face. "Why?" Billy said slamming the phone down on the side of Rev. Zackery's face. "Why?" He hit him again.

Rev. Zackery mumbled.

"I want it back and you are going to help me get it back. Do you understand me?" Billy said hitting him one last time."

Rev. Zackery began shaking his head 'yes' and mumbling loudly.

"Let's go and get it," Billy said as he got off the bed.

Rev. Zackery mumbled louder, waving his hands toward Billy. Rev. Zackery then brought both hands up to his mouth and mumbled.

"Well, if you think I'm gonna take that tape off your mouth, you're crazy." Billy said laughing out loud. "Come on, reverend, let's take a little ride back to your house. I'll drive, you can ride in the trunk."

Billy cut the tape from Rev. Zackery's legs and they started their journey to retrieve Billy's, Lady in the glass ball.

Chapter 19
Faceoff

(Monday morning 7:00AM)

Sibal was intently looking in the mirror at the places where the stitches were on her face. The color of the new skin was lighter, smoother, and prettier than her old skin. She was covering the old skin and the stitches with as much makeup as possible when her assistant, Howard, came in.

"Boss, Walt is here. He brought Manny. He's dead. Shot in the back."

"Okay, bring Walt in."

When Sibal saw Walt, her worse fears were realized. The three marks down his face told the story. Except for his nose, they did not cut the skin as hers had been, but it was definitely the mark of Pam.

"Why did you even bother to come back," Sibal snapped angrily, rubbing the stitches on her neck.

"I wanted you to know what happened, and she told me to deliver a message to you."

"Okay, what is the message?" her anger turned to worry.

"She said she was going to kill you in front of everybody at the ceremony, that is, unless you make a new deal with her." Walt waited nervously for a response.

"She wants to make a new deal, even though I tried to kill her."

"She said she knew you would try it," Walt said condescendingly. "She told me to tell you to call her on Manny's cell phone. She's willing to give you one last chance."

"Call Manny's number on your phone," Sibal ordered.

After dialing the number, Walt heard Pam's voice. "Hello Sibal."

"This is Walt, I told Sibal that you were willing to give her one last chance, like you told me to. She wants to talk to you."

"That was smart," Pam said. "I could use a smart man like you. Maybe you could be my bodyguard. Think about it?"

"Yes ma'am, I'll think very seriously about it. Here she is." Walt handed Sibal the phone.

"Was Walt telling the truth? Do you really understand why I did what I did?" Sibal asked.

"Yeah, absolutely. I know you Sibal. Power and strength are the only things you understand. You'll ponce, like a vicious wolf, at the slightest sign of weakness. I like that about you if you're working for me. I don't want to kill you, and I won't if we can make a new deal."

"Okay, I'm listening," Sibal said.

"I still want you to do what I said, but you can no longer be my second in command. You blew that. Any position of authority that I give you will only come after you have proven yourself to be trustworthy. Now, you've got to prove yourself. You think you can do that?"

"Yes ma'am. I sorry. I made a bad decision."

"Yes, you made a very bad decision, and it has cost you a lot. Don't let the next decision cost you everything," Pam said. "I can still use your help; therefore, I'm going to give you one last chance.

"Thank you so much, for giving me another chance, I promise to make the best of this new opportunity to serve you," Sibal said apologetically. "I promise you won't regret it."

"That's good. You won't get another one." Pam paused. "One more thing, don't let anything happen to Walt. On Tuesday morning, provide Walt with a black stretch limousine. I will call him and give him my location. He will pick me up and bring me to the ceremony Tuesday night. And, as of right now, Walt is my personal bodyguard. He takes orders from nobody but me. Tell him right now, so I can hear you."

"Walt," Sibal said loudly looking at Walt. "As of right now you are Madame Pam's personal bodyguard, and you don't take orders from anybody but her." Sibal turned her back to Walt. "Okay, anything else, ma'am."

"Yeah, give Walt the phone."

Sibal turned, gave Walt an ominous stare, and handed him the phone.

"I told her, not, to let anything happen to you," Pam said softly. "So, as of right now, you're under my protection. You should be safe as long as I'm alive."

"I appreciate that," Walt said sincerely.

"You know I could have killed you last night," Pam explained.

"That goes both ways, ma'am. I had the opportunity first," Walt said looking at Sibal not wanting to let know what he was talking about.

"Look! Would you rather work for me or run for your life from Sibal? You said she was going to kill you if you failed to kill me, last night."

"Those are not my only options, ma'am. Like I told you last night, I don't like threats," he said frowning.

Sibal had been watching Walt's expressions as he talked, however, now she was watching more intently.

"Okay, you have other options, and I've seen what you do to people who threaten you. You could take option three and kill Sibal before she kills you, however, I would prefer that you didn't, at least, not now. I still need her alive and in charge. Then, you could take option two and run. Or, you can take option one and be my bodyguard and possibly end up second in command of the whole coven." Pam paused. "So, what are you going to do? I need somebody to watch my back. I need somebody with skills like yours. I want you to be my bodyguard. However," She paused again. "Before you decide, I want you to know that there will be a lot of people who will be trying to kill me, including Sibal," Pam said sincerely. "I can't force you to take the job. You may be better off taking option two, running."

"Before I decide, I have one question for you?" Walt asked.

"What's that?"

"Who has your title, now?" he asked.

"You won. You have my title," Pam said reluctantly. "For now. I plan to get it back."

"No ma'am. You could have killed me last night," Walt said. "Instead, you let me live. I give you your title back and I vow never to fight you again. From now on I fight for you. I am honored to be your bodyguard."

"Okay. Good." Pam was unexpectantly glad. "Now, listen carefully. On Tuesday, when the limo is delivered to you. call me at this number. I want you in full body amour, and attack gear with automatic weapons."

"Yes ma'am." Walt smiled at Sibal.

"Remember, you don't take orders from anybody but me. Put the phone on speaker so I can here if she says anything to you," Pam ordered.

Walt lowered the phone and put it on speaker and then holding it away from him toward Sibal, he spoke. "You're on speaker."

"Sibal?" Pam shouted.

"Yes, ma'am."

"If anything happens to my bodyguard, you die, horribly. Are we clear?"

"Yes ma'am, we're clear," Sibal said softly.

"Walt?" Pam said.

"Yes ma'am?" Walt answered.

"Go, right now, and get ready for Tuesday."

"Yes ma'am." Walt lowered the phone and looked ominously at Sibal.

"Call me Tuesday when the limousine is ready, please," they both could hear Pam politely say.

"I will call you as soon as I inspected the limo, ma'am," he said as he turned and walked out.

Sibal waited until the door was closed, then she picked up her phone and dialed.

"Howard, there's a new threat, Walt. He turned against us. She made him, her bodyguard. When we kill her, we will have to take him out, too. So be ready. How is the trap coming?"

"We will be putting the curtain over the spikes tomorrow. On Tuesday, I'll give you a remote control that operates the trap door release. All you will have to do is push the button, and she's history, or should I say, herstory." Howard laughed.

"We can't make any mistakes. She is very dangerous."

"Don't worry, boss. Everything will go as planned." Howard said.

"It better. We're dead if it doesn't," she warned. She pressed 'end' on her cellphone and rubbed the worry wrinkles from her new brow.

Chapter 20
Billy Returns

(Monday morning 8:00 AM)

Pam put Manny's phone in her pocket. Then she heard Jason.

Jason walked out of the kitchen, coffee cup in hand. "Hey!" he yelled. "Let's go. We've got a lot to do."

"I'm waiting on you," Dave said as he raised his head from the sofa where he had been lying.

"Coming," Pam said walking into the living room. "Are you sure you know where the ceremony is going to be?"

"Well, I'm not sure, but I think it's north of here, off highway 19. It's not that far from here," Jason said looking at an old, discolored map. "There is one thing I'm sure of."

"What's that?" Pam asked.

"I'll know it when I see it."

"That's not very assuring," Pam said.

"Okay, how about this. You and Dave can go and get the gasoline and the explosives, while I go and check this place out. We can meet back here at noon."

"That sounds good," Pam said. "While we're out, we can ask around, someone just might tell us where the ceremony is going to be."

"Whatever," Jason said closing the door behind him.

"Are you ready to go?" Dave said standing up.

"No. Can we sit and talk for a minute?" Pam asked.

"Sure. What's on your mind?"

"I was thinking about what you said last night about caring for me," Pam said sweetly

"Well, you know I haven't expressed any of my true feelings toward you, but that was because I was married. I took marriage very seriously, so I couldn't say anything. I couldn't even let myself feel anything, even though I did feel so much affection and desire for you, from the moment I first saw you," he said.

"Dave, you're still married."

He took her hand in his. "I know, but my lawyer will be serving my wife papers as soon as I get back."

"Are you saying that you love me, and that you want us to be together? You want us to get married?" Pam said moving her face closer to his.

"Married? Well, hopefully, if things work out between us," Dave said nervously. "Now, you know that I probably won't have a job or a place to live when I get back home. And, for a while I won't have anything to offer. I don't have any savings. She took all the money from my accounts but a few thousand dollars I had in cash." Dave released her hand. "When I told you that I cared about you, I wasn't thinking about how bad off I am. I don't have anything to offer but my feelings, and with all that has been happening, I'm not even sure of them. I think maybe, I really ought to let things get back to normal in my life before I make any new commitments."

"Yeah! In the meantime, you ought to keep your big mouth shut until you know what you want. Anyway, what makes you think I would want a man who would get down on his knees and," Pam stopped.

"And what?" Dave said confused.

"Oh, forget it."

They faced each other. She looked angry. He looked stupid.

"Are you ready to go," he asked.

"Yeah! Let's go!" Pam stood and walked out quickly. Dave followed.

When Dave got to the door, Pam was standing motionless on the porch. He walked outside and pulled the door closed behind him.

"Don't move," a man's hick sounding voice said.

Dave turned around and saw a shotgun pointed at him. The man holding it was pushing another man toward them. The other man was duct taped from his waist up. Over his head, there was a plastic grocery bag which expanded and contracted as he breathed. The front of his pants was wet with urine and he walked as if he had something uncomfortable in the seat of his pants.

"I came to get my little lady in the glass ball back. You know, the one that you stole from me," he said.

"We don't have it. We threw it back in the river," Pam said.

"Well, you better go get it."

"It's gone Billy! We will never be able to find it, now," Pam explained.

"If you don't", Billy said as he pointed the shotgun at the covered head of man next to him. "He's dead." Billy pulled the bag off, revealing a very dejected Rev. Zackery. He had duct tape over his mouth.

"You'll just have to kill him. The crystal is gone. It's in the river," Pam argued.

"Fine then." Billy kicked Rev. Zackery behind his knee and pushed. Rev. Zackery fell to ground, face first. Billy put his foot on Rev. Zackery's back as the reverend looked up at Pam and Dave. "Last chance."

"We would never be able to find it, not in a million years," Pam said trying to reason with him.

"Rev. Zackery? Say goodbye, I mean mumble goodbye to your friends," Billy said as he positioned the barrel of the shotgun to the base of Rev. Zackery's head and moved back away from the head as far as possible.

"Wait," Dave yelled. "It's in the house."

"What are you doing?" Pam said looking at Dave.

"I'm saving Rev. Zackery's life," Dave replied angrily.

"Okay, go get it," Billy said.

"I'll trade you. I'll give you the crystal and you give me Rev. Zackery and then you leave us alone. Do we have a deal?" Dave said.

"All right, go get it."

Pam tried to get into Billy's head. 'I need to put the barrel of the gun to my chin and pull the trigger,' she thought. Her thought had no effect on him. 'Something must be blocking me,' she thought. 'It can't be Tamela, she's in the safe. It must be the demons in him,' she thought. Dave backed toward the door.

"You can't trust him. He's full of demons. Dave don't do this," Pam begged.

"It's not him I'm worried about trusting," Dave said without looking at Pam. "I'm going to get it now. Don't try any tricks," Dave said to Billy.

"Don't you try any tricks," Billy replied.

Dave backed to the door, opened it, and without turning backed inside and out of sight.

"Put the gun on the ground and back away from it, Billy," Pam said rhythmically.

"What did you say?"

"Put the gun on the ground, and back away from it, now." This time she said it more forcefully.

"Girly, you must have fell down and bumped your little head, if you think I'm gone do that," Billy said angrily. He pointed the shotgun at her. "Why don't you just shut up fore I shoot you in your big mouth. You ain't part of this deal."

Just at that moment Dave appeared in the door with the safe. "I got it," he yelled holding it up over his head, one hand on top and the other beneath. "I'm going to walk out. Now, you put the gun in your other hand and hold it by the barrel." Billy complied. "Okay when I walk toward Rev. Zackery you walk back away from him," Dave yelled.

"Then what," Billy said.

"Then when I get to Rev. Zackery, I will put the case on the ground. You will let Rev. Zackery and Pam go back in the house. Once they are inside, I will open the case and let you see the crystal. Then you can come and get it. I will stand right here until you leave. Okay?" Dave said.

"What was that first part again," Billy said scratching his head.

"When I move forward you move back."

"Okay, come on!"

Dave started walking toward Rev. Zackery. Billy started walking back. When Dave was halfway to Rev. Zackery Billy stopped and aimed the gun at Dave.

"You ain't as smart as you think you is, city boy," Billy said smiling. "What's to stop me from dropping you right where you stand."

"How do you know if the crystal is in the safe? I told you that I would open the safe and let you see the crystal once you let them go in the house. Billy! We have a deal."

Billy put the shotgun in his other hand again and continued backing up.

"I was just messing with you. We got a deal."

When Dave reached Rev. Zackery, he put the safe on the ground and helped the preacher to his feet. "Go in the house Reverend," Dave whispered. He then kneeled to open the safe. "Once they are in the house, I will open the safe to let you see the crystal."

"No!" Billy shouted. "They have to stay where I can see them. They need to stop on the porch."

"All right," Dave shouted back. "They will stay on the porch until you get the safe and leave.

Rev. Zackery walked wide legged to the porch and Pam helped him up the steps of the porch. Rev. Zackery didn't stop. He went into the house and slammed the door behind him. After watching Rev. Zackery, Pam and Dave turned and waited to see what Billy was going to do.

"What you waiting for? Open it!" Billy shouted.

Dave opened the safe. It was empty.

"You are dead," Billy screamed, pointing the gun at Dave.

"Wait! I have it, here," Dave said reaching inside his jacket and pulling out the crystal. He held it up so Billy could see Tamera. He put the crystal in the safe and closed it. Then he stood up. "It's yours, Billy. Take it and leave us alone."

Billy walked forward pointing the shotgun at Dave. When he was three feet away, Billy stop. "Open it back up."

Dave raised the top. The strange light appeared. Billy became mesmerized as he gazed at Tamera. "You were trapped in the crystal," Billy said to Dave. "The little lady said you know how to get her out. Get up! You're coming with me."

Dave closed the safe and picked it up with both hands. "Are you sure you want to do this. If you let her out, she's going to kill both of us."

"She promised to give me money and powers to get any woman I want," Billy smiled.

"She's evil Billy. Why would you believe her?"

"Why would I believe you?"

"I'm going to give you one more chance to change your mind," Dave said confidently.

"And then what?" Billy snarled. His eyes were angry and piercing until he heard a noise close behind him. Billy turn his head quickly and felt the end of Rev. Zackery's long barreled pistol against his forehead. Dave moved forward grabbing the shotgun and pushing the barrel toward the sky.

"Well, are you going let go of the shotgun with or without a hole in your head," Jason asked calmly.

Billy released his grip, and Dave took the shotgun.

"How long have you been here?" Dave asked Jason.

"About fifteen minutes ago. I saw Billy's car parked on the highway, so I knew something was up. So, I came through the trees and I saw Billy and Rev. Zackery with a bag over his head."

"You really took your time," Dave complained. "Why didn't you just shoot him when he was threatening Rev. Zackery?"

"Who do you think I am, Wyatt Earp? I might have missed him and hit you or Rev. Zackery. Anyway, we need him. I couldn't find the building. The place where I thought was it, turned out to be nothing but a little rundown house in the woods. We need the demon in him to show us where it is. You know, where the ceremony is going to be." Dave pushed Billy toward the house.

"Did you hear Pam? She was going to let Billy shoot Rev. Zackery," Dave whispered as they walked side by side.

"Yeah, I heard her. She cares more about her sister than she cares about any of us. I don't trust her. She been protecting Tamera ever since we trapped her," Jason whispered back.

"It does seem that way."

"If you want her, don't worry about me," Jason said. "You can have the witch."

They walked back into the house. Pam was sitting on the sofa.

"Is there any duct tape left?" Jason asked.

"Where is Rev. Zackery?" Dave asked.

"The duct tape is in your bedroom, and Rev. Zackery is in the shower."

Jason pushed Billy toward the bedroom.

"How is he?" Dave asked.

"Physically, he seems to be in good shape, however, psychologically I think he's depressed. Evidently, Billy didn't let him relieve himself. His pants were really messed up."

"Yeah, I could smell it when I helped him up," Dave said.

They sat in silence for several minutes before Dave spoke.

"Were you really going to let Billy blow Rev, Zackery's head off?" Dave said to Pam.

"No!" Pam said emphatically. "I knew he was not going to kill Rev. Zackery. Rev. Zackery was his only bargaining chip."

"I don't know why you would say that. You said Billy had already killed him."

"I thought he was dead. I thought Billy shot him. He fell down the stairs. He wasn't moving," Pam explained.

"So, you left him there. You took your sister and ran," Dave said accusingly.

"I saved Jason." Pam was becoming angry. "I'm going to say it one last time. I thought Rev. Zackery was dead."

"What happened to all your powers?" Dave snapped.

"You'll find out if you keep on messing with me," Pam snarled.

"Fine," Dave said.

"Stop fighting!" Jason said as he pulled the demon headed Billy into the room. "The demon is going to show us where the ceremony is going to take place. Let's go."

"How did you do that?" Pam asked pointing at Billy's head.

"Rev. Zackery did it. He's in his bedroom. He says he needs to spend some time with the Lord because he's very angry. He quoted some scripture about being angry and sinning not" Jason said. "If looks could kill, Billy would be burnt to a crisp now. I have never seen Rev. Zackery look like that before. Let's go while the demon is still present."

Once again Billy was duct taped from the waist up. They all left and headed down the driveway toward the cars parked on the side of the highway.

"Is all this duct tape really necessary," the demon said angrily.

"Yeah," Jason said.

"Well, would you mind scratching my balls for me," the demon said to Dave.

"You're a demon. You don't have no balls, do you?" Jason asked.

"I'm just messing with him," the demon replied to Jason. "I don't, but Billy is a little uncomfortable down there."

"Don't worry about Billy," Pam interrupted. "If it was up to me, he wouldn't have any balls left to scratch."

"You know, you are going to make a great demon one day," the demon said looking at Pam.

"Stop it! Just show us where the where the ceremony is going to be," Dave whispered to the demon as he opened the door and helped Billy's body into the front seat of Jason's rental car.

"Okay, Mr. Dave. Go down to the highway and turn right and go about twenty-five miles until you pass Turner's service station. You'll take the next right, the second left and the building is at the end of that road."

"Jason is driving, just tell him when to turn, demon," Dave said. He closed the door and got in the back seat with Pam.

Chapter 21
The Break In

(Monday morning 9:30 AM)

Rev. Zackery laid in his bed looking up at the ceiling, a frown frozen to his brow. He had chewed up a sleeping pill, and he was waiting impatiently for it to work. His anger, that Billy had forced him to relieve himself in his clothes, had not diminished. He wanted to hurt Billy. Actually, what he wanted to do to Billy, was downright evil. He forced himself to pray to forgive Billy, even though he didn't want to.

"Lord," he said aloud. "You know how I'm feeling right now. I want to kill Billy, after, I cut off all of his appendages." He took a deep breath. "I know that You said vengeance is Yours. I know that You said that, if I don't forgive others, You won't forgive me. I know You said, love those who despitefully use me. I know that I should know that I wrestle not against flesh and blood, but against principalities, and I know that Billy is being controlled by demons and possibly even principalities. But Lord, please, just let me hit him in the mouth one good lick." He balled up his fist and gritted his teeth. "I know that I should bring every thought under subjection. I know that You love Billy just as much as You love me. I know that I have a calling on my life. You have called me to preach deliverance to the captives and to cast out demons." He began to get into a rhythm. "You have given me authority, over all the works of the enemy. You said all I had to do, is resist the devil, and he will flee. I am the righteousness of God. I can do all things through Christ. Greater is He that's in me than he that is in the world."

He stopped. His frown was gone. His anger was gone. A smile appeared on his face, and he raised his arms toward the ceiling. "Thank You Lord God Almighty for having mercy on me. Thank You for Your Grace. Thank You for Your word. Thank You for Your power. Most of all thank You for loving me." He paused and he began to speak softly again. "Lord, lead me in the way that you would have me to go. Give me the right words to say, not just to Billy but also to Pam, Dave, and Jason. I don't know what to do or say. I'm depending on You. I trust You. I'm waiting on You. In Jesus name I pray. Amen." He closed his eyes and within minutes, went into a deep sleep. It was so deep that he didn't hear his bedroom lock being jimmied open.

The two men who came in were surprised to find a sleeping man in the bed. Both were dressed in dark blue slacks, matching blue shirts, and matching toolboxes. One was thin and wore black framed glasses. He moved quickly to the bed. Against Rev. Zackery's neck, he pressed the knife he had used to open the door. Rev. Zackery didn't move.

"Who is this? Didn't Sibal say there were only four, one woman and three men."

"Yeah, but don't kill him! He's out," he said pointing to the bottle of sleeping pills on the nightstand. "Sibal said not to let anyone know that we were here. We're supposed to place the charges and wait until tonight when they are all in the house sleep."

"I know that, but if I kill him now, that's not going to stop them from coming back in the house. When they come in and find him dead, we'll blow the house then and they will still all be dead. If we do it that way, we won't have to wait until tonight."

"Suppose they don't all come back in the house at the same time? Just put the charge under the bed and let's get out of here."

"All right, but if he wakes up, he's dead," the man with glasses said as he taped the explosives to the bottom of the bed. "Done. Is this the last one?"

"I got the kitchen, the dining room, and the living room. Did you get the other bedroom?"

"Yeah, I got it."

"Okay that's it. Let's get out of here before he wakes up or the others come back." They didn't notice that a pair of eyes were watching their every move. They locked the bedroom door and returned to their position in the woods.

Chapter 22
The Big Barn

(Monday afternoon 12:30 pm)

As they rode through the trees, down a narrow winding dirt road, Jason had to slow to five miles per hour to drive over holes and ditches in the road. Jason stopped when he saw a fallen tree blocking the road that now seemed more like a path.

"Something is wrong with this picture," Pam said.

"Looks like a trap to me," Dave said nervously looking around.

Jason turned to the demon, "Where have you taken us. You said hundreds of witches would be at this ceremony. There's no way anybody could get down this road."

"I say we cut his demon head off and leave him right here in the woods. We can find this place on our own," Pam snarled.

"This is not the way they are going to come. This is the back way." The demon said looking back at Pam unafraid. "We walk from here. The building is through those trees." He nodded toward the trees ahead and to the left. There was a small path. "You need to have a get-a-way plan, in case something goes wrong, don't you?"

"Yeah, we definitely need that," Dave said loudly as they got out of the car.

"Nothing's going to go wrong. Our plan is going to work," Jason said just as loudly.

"Lead the way demon," Pam said pushing the demon in the back. "But, understand this, if this is a trap, you're going to be looking for another body to possess." She pushed him harder. He turned his head back toward her as he went through bushes. A limb from one of the bushes sprang back, appearing to come straight through the demon head and was about to hit Pam in the face. Instantly, the demon's arm reached out and caught the limb with a charred black hand with claw-like long nails. The demon's body had suddenly now covered Billy's body down to his waist. The demon was wearing a black sweatshirt. The demon lowered the limb and moved his face close to hers.

"You don't scare me," the demon said ominously. They all froze in amazement as the demon's body and arms disappeared leaving Billy's duct taped body again. Only his demon head remained. "We're here."

Pam held the limb as they all walked pass the bushes. They looked through the trees and saw a big, old, wooden barn in the middle of a large field. Near the front of the barn, there was a large gravel road leading up to the front of the barn on the other side of the field. Four pickup trucks and two cars were parked at the front of the in a large parking area where the grass was had been recently cut very low. Inside the barn, hammering and talking could be heard. There were no windows on the side of the barn facing them. There was, however, one set of relatively new, black metal double doors in the middle of the side wall. On the back, there was a big sliding barn door which was closed. The high rusty tin roof sloped at an angle of forty-five degrees, straight down on both sides which were about fifteen feet high from the ground to the bottom of the roof. The wood looked old and brittle.

"This is perfect," Jason said. "I've got to get a closer look." Before anyone could object, Jason ran quickly toward the side of the barn. He got halfway and dropped lay flat on the ground. The grass was higher on the side of the barn, however, it wasn't high enough to completely cover him. A few seconds later he was up and running again. He waved when he reached the wall of the barn. They watched as he made his way to the back of the barn by the big sliding door.

Jason looked through a crack between the door and the wall. He could see men working on a platform. He checked out the back door. It appeared that it had not been opened in years. He then went to the other side of the barn, out of the sight of his cohorts. He carefully made his way to the front of the building. Then he crawled to the open front door. He pulled up grass and weeds, laid down, covered his head with the weeds and slid his head over just enough for him to look inside. The place was filled with at least five hundred chairs on a dirt floor covered with straw. The double doors on both sides, had push bars and the doors opened to the outside. What the demon had shown them was very accurate. Two pieces of chain and two padlocks would be all that's needed to secure these doors. There was a large platform about ten feet off the ground with blue drapes on both sides. There were two rows of chair on both sides, one row higher than the other. They were positioned so the persons sitting in them could see everything on the platform. The middle of the platform came out like a stage, the drapes covering its sides were white. There was a podium in the middle of the stage at the front. Behind the podium was a large table. To the left of the podium was a big burlap bag, about five feet tall, with pieces of carpeting sticking out of the top. One of the men on the floor yelled to a man on the back of the platform.

"Are you ready for the test?"

"Yeah. Hit it," the man on the floor yelled back.

A second later the white drapes fell from around the stage, and a trap door on the stage under bag open, causing the bag to fall through it. It landed on a bed of pointed long metal needles, some longer than others. The bag was pierced completely through by the longer needles but only partially by the shorter ones.

"It's ready for our special guest. Good work," the man on the floor said. "I'll let Sibal know right now," he said. He took his cellphone from his pocket, turned, and began walking toward the door. Jason crawled back, got up quickly, and began running full speed around to the side of the barn toward the back. The man, talking on his cellphone, walked out of the door toward his car. While running, Jason looked back and saw him when he reached his car. Jason kept running because he had nowhere to hide. The grass on this side of the barn had been recently cut. When the man got to his car, he noticed something in his peripheral vision on the side of the barn. Jason was still ten feet from the back of the barn. The man quickly turned his head. As he did Jason dived to the ground behind the barn. The man stood there looking for a few seconds trying to figure out what he had seen, then getting into his car, he drove off. Jason made his way back to the woods and his anxious conspirators.

"How did everything look?" Pam asked.

"Everything looks good," Jason said staring into her eyes. "They were doing the final touches on a new stage."

"Is anything wrong," Pam frowned. "You look strange."

"I'm good. I was just wondering if the chain we bought was thick enough for those doors." Jason turned to Dave. We won't be able to set up now. We'll have to wait until tomorrow night when all of them are inside. Then we will spring out final trap."

"Are you sure you want to do this? "Dave said. "Hundreds of people are going to die."

"Hundreds of witches are going to die," Jason said angrily. "They killed my grandmother, they have attempted to kill all of us, several times, and they will never stop unless we kill them first."

"You need to watch him," the demon said. "He's going to mess everything up. He's not dependable."

"Shut up demon," Pam snapped.

"Look at him. He's gone wimp out on you when the time comes," the demon argued.

"I'm warning you, demon. Shut your evil mouth," Pam yelled

"Let me do what he was supposed to you," the demon said walking up to Jason. "I can make Billy do whatever I want him to do."

Suddenly, the demon head disappeared. Billy's head appeared just before he collapsed to the ground. Behind him, holding a big rock was Pam.

"I told him to shut up," Pam said.

"Now we have to carry him back to the car," Jason said shaking his head.

"Not really, I can just bust his head in now, and we can just leave him right here," Pam said calmly.

"No! I'll carry him," Dave interrupted. "Just help me get him on my back."

"Leave him there until we unload the car. We can leave everything here until tomorrow night," Jason said.

It took two trips for them to get the plastic gas cans, and other accessories from the car. Once done Jason motioned for them to come to the edge of the trees so they could all look at the barn.

"Let me tell you what I saw," Jason said. "It looks pretty much like the diagram I drew, when the demon showed it to us, but it's better than we could have imagined. From the outside the barn looks like it could cave in at any moment, however, the inside is just the opposite. The beams are old, but they look strong and sturdy. The wood on the walls is worn and brittle on one side, the outside, but on the other side, on the inside, the wood is strong and looks good. In fact, on the inside, its looks like they have recently stained the walls, which means it's more flammable. There's no electricity. They have these candelabras and they use real candles to light the room. They raise and lower them with theses ropes that are tied to side of the four main roof beams on both sides. I also saw several large torches on the stage they were working on. All that is perfect for us. When those candelabras and torches fall and hit the straw on the floor, the whole place will go up in flames." He paused. "We have the six, five-gallon plastic gas cans we need to douse the sides and back wall, but we will need at more gasoline at the entrance and something to block the door."

"I saw some large barrels at Billy's house," Pam interrupted. We could put lean them up against the front door so that when they open the door gasoline will pour out covering the entrance and everything around it. Then when we lite it they will all be trapped."

"Yeah, but those would be too heavy to carry," Jason said.

"Then we could put them in Billy's old pickup truck and then back it up to the door," she said.

"Great idea," Jason said joyfully. "Billy, you don't mind if we borrow your truck, do you?"

"How many people are we planning on killing," Dave asked rubbing the wrinkles from his troubled brow.

"No people, just witches," Jason snapped as he frowned at Dave. "Anyway, we need to figure out how we are going to pull this whole thing off," Jason said turning toward Billy who was still lying still on the ground. He reached down and shock him roughly. "Demon! Stop playing possum. I know you're listening. Get up before I bible slap you."

The demon head appeared on Billy's body again. He stood up looking angrily at Pam. Pam reached down and picked up the same rock she had hit him with before and walked toward him. Jason quickly walked between them. With his back against Pam, he pushed Billy's body back as he spoke to the demon.

"What's going to happen at the ceremony. I mean, how do they usually go?" Jason asked.

"Keep her away from Billy," the demon shouted angrily. "She's gone kill him and then where would you get your information from?"

"Okay, Mr. Gon," Jason patronized. "I'll keep her away from you. Now, tell us the details about the ceremony."

"All right," the demon said backing further away from Pam. "The ceremony should start promptly at midnight. So, the doors will be closed by eleven forty-five. No one will be able to get in or out after that time. Everybody there will be important persons, medium and upper-level hierarchy of the coven, everybody except the ones who will be serving." The demon turned toward Dave. "Everybody inside will be what you call witches." He turned his back and continued. "The witch head council will then be seated on the platform. Then the virgin who has been chosen to be the mother of the head witch is brought to the stage. She will be placed on a large table. She will be seriously drugged. The warlock, the man witch, chosen to father the child will then come out. He will impregnate her."

"Impregnate!" Pam interrupted. "You mean rape her, don't you demon!"

"Rape, impregnate, semantics," the demon said looking at Pam. "Anyway, if I can continue," the demon said now looking at Jason. Jason nodded. "Then, after the impregnation, a person from the high council will cut the former virgin's wrist. This person will take a large cup of her blood and pour it into a large vat of wine. The wine is then stirred and passed out to everyone. Everybody, including the 'impregnantee,' will drink and swear alliance to the child that will be born. Then there will be a big celebration."

"What will they do in the celebration," Jason asked.

"The usual stuff. They will get drunk, take their clothes off and have orgies all night long. Then the ceremony will end, just before dawn, and the doors will be opened."

"Are you seriously going to believe a demon?" Dave asked.

"I'll believe him as far as I can throw him," Jason replied. "If things go as he says we will follow plan A, if not, will follow plan B."

"So, what is plan A," Pam smirked.

"Pam, you and me will go in as servers. When it's time to serve the wine, we will go to the side doors on the other side of the barn where Dave will be waiting. I'll open one of the doors and then you, Dave, will give me the chains, the locks, and two sticks of dynamite, if we are able to get some. Then, I'll put a chain and lock on those side doors on the inside. If there is somebody guarding the door, Pam, you may have to put them in a trance. Dave, you put a crowbar between the handles on the outside of those doors and tape them in place. Then while we're going to the side doors on the other side, Dave, you will pour gas from the gas cans on the walls on both sides and the back of the barn. Just before we go out, I'll throw a stick of dynamite, if possible, up on the stage where the head council will be sitting. By that time, Dave, you should be in the pickup truck. When you hear the explosion that's when you should back the truck through the front doors. When you stop, the barrels of gas should fall over, pouring gas all over the floor. Then pull the truck out of the front doors just far enough for you to open the truck door and get out. Then, all you need to do is throw a Malakoff cocktail over the truck into the barn." He paused took a deep breath and said definitively, "And that will be the end of all our witch problems, forever."

"Your plan will never work. You have one big problem," the demon said.

"Shut up, demon," Pam snarled.

"No! I want to hear what this big problem is. What is this big problem, demon," Jason asked, feeling that his plan was foolproof.

"It's him," the demon said pointing toward Dave with arms and fingers he didn't have seconds ago.

Everybody looked at Dave. His expression indicated that the demon might be right.

"What about it Dave, can you do it?" Jason asked.

"You said there was not going to be anybody but witches there. What about the virgin? She an innocent victim. She doesn't deserve to die. What about her," Dave pleaded. "Pam's mother was in the same situation. They used her and killed her. That the same thing we're going to be doing to this little girl."

"Told you," the demon said.

"Shut up, demon!" Pam and Jason shouted together. "Even if the killing of the witches, is justifiable homicide, as you say, killing this child is without a doubt cold blooded murder," Dave scolded.

"He's right, whether he really means it or not. We have got to get her out," Pam said.

"How do we know that she's not a willing participant?" Jason argued.

"I knew you would say something hateful like that," Pam snapped.

"Okay, then you go up on the stage and get her when truck comes in and the fire starts," Jason said

"We need to get her before they rape her. We're going to plan B," Pam said angrily. "We can keep some of your plan, but if we are going to do this, we need to do it my way."

"So, what you saying? It's your way or the highway?" Jason asked sarcastically.

"No! What I'm saying is it's my way or you gone die way." Pam stared at Jason for a long time. There was complete silence until the demon spoke.

"So, what's plan B?"

"Demon, one thing you can be sure of, plan B does not include you." Pam turned and started walking toward the car. "Let's go! I need to set up a few things."

"With your friend Sibal?" the demon said slyly.

Pam stopped. She turned and walked up the demon, who was now just a head on Billy's body. She grabbed both of Billy's shoulders and pulled the demon head close to hers'. "We don't need you anymore, demon," she said kneeing him forcefully in the groins. The demon head disappeared, and Billy's returned. He immediately folded over and started groining through his duct taped mouth. Pam turned and continued toward the car. Dave helped Billy to straighten up.

"Sorry about that Billy, that demon of yours doesn't know when to shut up. You need to get rid of him."

"Mmmmmm mmmmmm," Billy mumbled.

Dave pulled the tape pass his lips and let it hang from his cheek.

"You think Rev. Zackery can do it?" Billy moaned.

"Rev. Zackery? Maybe, after he calms down. He's pretty mad with you right now."

"Yeah, I know."

"Dave," Jason whispered as he beckoned him to come closer. "We need to listen very carefully to Pam's plan to see if it involves releasing you know who."

Dave shook his head affirmatively while covering Billy's mouth with the tape again.

Minutes later they were in the car. Jason and Dave were in the front. Jason was driving. Pam was sitting behind Dave and Billy was curled up in the corner as far from Pam as possible. Jason backed the car up a small hill into some bushes and turned around. Then they started back to the house in silence.

Chapter 23

The Fish of Gold

(Monday afternoon 2:00 PM)

The continuous ringing of the house telephone woke Rev. Zackery up from his deep sleep. He almost knocked the phone off the nightstand as he picked up the receiver. He caught it before it fell over, however, when he pushed it back, he didn't notice it was only halfway on the nightstand.

"Hello," he said angrily.

"Hello, is this Rev. Zackery?" the voice asked.

"Yes, this is he," he said with a more refined tone.

"Hiya doing reverend, this is J. Jones, the contractor. I'm just calling to let you know that we have replaced that damaged section of the floor at the church. The pulpit was not damaged. Tomorrow, we will start sanding and staining the floor we replaced. Now, the insurance won't pay for sanding and staining the rest of the floor, however, if we don't sand and stain the rest of the floor, it's going to look very different. Do you want us to stain the rest of the floor, so it won't look so bad?" He waited for a response that never came, so he continued. "For us to sand and stain the rest of the floor, it would normally cost one hundred and fifty dollars, but since I have some stain left over from another job, I won't charge you for the stain. Your cost would be, let me see, one ten. How does that sound, reverend?"

"I thank you so much for your kindness, Mr. Jones. How much stain is it going to take for the rest on the floor?"

"Three gallons, reverend."

"And you are willing to give the church these cans of stain that were left over from another job, you say?"

"That's right reverend. I'll do that just to show you that I appreciate you choosing my company to do the work."

"Thank you again sir. Just leave the three gallons on the pulpit, and I'll have some of the men in the church to sand and stain the rest of the church. Goodbye, Mr. Jones." Rev. Zackery hung up the phone before Jones could reply. However, when he put the receiver on the phone, the phone which was already on the edge fell over. When it hit the floor, there was a loud noise.

"Good grief!" Rev. Zackery shouted in disgust.

Rev. Zackery rolled over and looked down. The phone was lying there but the cord for the receiver went underneath the bed. He reached down, picked up the phone, and attempted to put it back on the nightstand. The cord to the receiver was caught on something under the bed.

"What in the heck is going on?" His frustration growing. He rolled off the bed to his knees. "Sometimes the Lord has to let stuff happen to make you get down on your knees. I haven't prayed on my knees in a long time. Well, since I'm down here." He pressed his hands together, leaned against the bed and began to pray. "Lord, I'm down here on my knees. So, many things have been happening, that I forgot that I needed to humble myself and pray. So, I bow, knowing that if I want to get closer to you, I need to get lower, and getting on my knees is a good start. Lord, I have been so consumed about the things that I'm dealing with, that I've haven't taken the time I needed to ask for guidance from you. Forgive me, Jesus. Speak to my heart. Tell me the things I need to hear. Show me the things I need to see. Then give me the power to do the things You want me to do. In Jesus name I pray amen."

Rev. Zackery looked under the bed. The phone receiver was caught on the leg of the bed. He grabbed the receiver and pulled. The cord was freed, and he pulled the receiver from beneath the bed. There was a pain on the back of his hand. He looked at it and saw a scratch. He moved the receiver an laid his head on the floor so he could see what had scratched his hand. Something was taped to the bottom of the bed. He pulled the tape until the object taped to it hit the floor. He continued to pull the tape until he saw what it was.

"Good Lord, dynamite!" He looked at it carefully. It was two sticks of dynamite with a small black box taped to them. The box had a small antenna coming out of one end and two wires lending to the two sticks of dynamite coming out the other. "This must be a remote control, detonator," he whispered to himself. "Lord, guide my feet," he said as he gently placed the dynamite on the floor and quickly got up. He moved quickly toward the door and stopped.

"If there's a remote control, somebody must be waiting outside to set it off." He turned and walked to the dynamite. He casually picked it up and grabbed the two wires going into the dynamite. "The Lord has not given me the spirit of fear," he said as he closed his eyes and pulled the wires from the dynamite. Two seconds later, he opened his eyes. "Thank you, Jesus!"

Rev. Zackery sat back on the bed and look straight ahead as he began to think. There in front of him was the fishbowl. He had expected to see the goldfish floating on its side, however, there it was swimming normally and looking right at him.

"Oh, my goodness! You're back," Rev. Zackery said shaking his head 'no.' To his amazement he watched as the fish tilted up and down as if it was saying 'yes.'

"It figures, whenever you're trying to do the right thing evil is always present." Rev. Zackery looked down at the dynamite, then he looked up at the fish. "Was somebody in my room while I was sleep."

The fish indicated yes.

"I need to check the whole house," Rev. Zackery said to himself as he got up from the bed. He noticed the fish was moving up and down again. He checked the rest of the bedroom and then walked out.

It was thirty minutes, before he returned to the bedroom. When he did, he laid three more detonators and six sticks of dynamite on the bed. He was tired. "I've looked everywhere. That's got to be all," he said as he sat on the bed.

Rev. Zackery noticed the fish was moving again, indicating 'no.'

"What do you mean 'no'? Are there more?"

The fish indicated 'yes.'

"How many more?"

The fish didn't move.

"Okay, five more."

The fish indicated 'no.'

"Are there more than five left?

The fish indicated 'no.'

"Okay, it is one more?

The fish indicated 'yes.'

"Where is, I mean is it in this room?"

The fish indicated 'no.'

"Hmmmm. The only rooms where I didn't find one were the closets, the bathroom, and the dining room."

The fish started moving up and down frantically when he said dining room.

"The dining room?"

The fish indicated 'yes.'

Immediately, Rev. Zackery went into the dining room. Within minutes he was back. He threw the detonator and two more sticks of dynamite on the bed. "Is that all of them?"

The fish indicated 'yes.'

"Lord," Rev. Zackery said looking up. "Thank You for making even the demons obey me. Thank You, Jesus!" He began to wave his hands above his head. When he stopped, he sat down on the bed. "Now Lord, since I know somebody is out there waiting to detonate this dynamite, tell me what to do. Rev. Zackery waited there for five minutes. Then he got up and went out on the front porch, sat in a rocking chair and started rocking as he waited for the return of his friends and Billy whom he still wanted to hurt. Rev. Zackery sat there trying to forgive Billy as he began to scour the landside for any signs of the location of the persons, he knew were out there waiting to blow up him, Dave, Jason, and definitely Pam. He wondered what he needed to do when they came back. "The Lord will provide," he said to himself.

He didn't have to wonder long because the car came down the driveway ten minutes later. Rev. met the car before it got to the house. Jason stopped. As he rolled the window down, he could see something was wrong by the look on Rev. Zackery's face.

"Someone came in the house while I was sleep. They put dynamite with remote control detonators in four rooms in the house," Rev. Zackery said after he stuck his head in the car window.

"How do you know this?" Dave said.

"I found them, disconnected them. This is one of the detonators," Rev. Zackery said holding it inside of the window so they could see. "I put the rest on my bed."

"See, I told you," Jason said looking over at Dave. "They are not going to stop until they kill us, unless we kill them first."

"Did they take the crystal?" Pam shouted anxiously.

"I don't know. Where did you put it?" Rev. Zackery looked confused.

"We're about to be blown up and all you can think about is your sister," Jason said in disgust.

"Now, children, play nicely," the demon head said as it suddenly appeared on Billy's body.

Without looking, Pam back-handed the demon in the mouth. Instantly the demon head disappeared, and blood began to run from the side of Billy's lip where the duct tape had been knocked off.

"Will you please stop beating on Billy?" Dave yelled.

"And y'all say, I have anger issues," Jason said.

"It's got to be Sibal," Pam said ominously, ignoring their comments. "She's dead. I'm going to kill with my own hands."

"Is that part of your plan B," Jason said. "Just let her burn with the rest of the witches. Dead is dead. You are going to mess up everything."

"Hey!" Rev. Zackery shouted. "I think someone is out there in the woods with the control unit for those remotes, and they're probably waiting for all of us to get in the house before they blow it and us up."

"I'll handle this," Pam said pulling Manny's phone from her pocket.

"And just how do you plan to do that?" Jason asked.

Ignoring him, Pam put the phone to her ear. "Tell your men to bring me the control unit for the dynamite, now. No discussion. They have one minute." Pam closed the phone and waited. No one spoke. They all looked back at the driveway toward the highway.

"I don't know what that was about, but it's been more than a minute. Who was that?" Jason said looking at Pam.

"Hey," Dave said. "Look."

They all looked as a black car slowly came down the driveway. Pam got out of the car and held up her hand for them to stop. The car stopped about ten feet behind theirs.

"Get out and bring me the trigger and keep your hands where I can see them," she yelled.

Two men got out of the car and walked toward her with their hands up. Pam met them halfway.

"I assume Sibal called you," Pam said softly.

"Yes ma'am," the one from the driver's side said respectfully. The other one who wore glasses said nothing. He just walked toward her with hate in his eyes. He had the remote-control trigger in his hand.

"Look, I know you guys were just following orders. I don't have, and I don't want to have, any problem with you. My problem is with Sibal. So, I want you to tell me exactly what she told you to do."

"Yes ma'am," the respectful man said. "We were told…"

"Shut up! We don't take orders from her," the man with glasses said angrily. He held the remote trigger out in front of him. "You want this?" he said flipping the trigger guard with his thumb and then placing his thumb on the trigger switch. "You can have it." He pushed the switch expecting the house to exploded. His partner ducked down. Both men were surprised that nothing happened. The man in the glasses pushed the button several times and then threw the trigger at Pam's head. She caught it, one foot from her face and then dropped it at her side.

Jason, Dave, Billy, and Rev. Zackery watched as the man in glasses, slowly walked up to Pam. His expression was confident yet filled with rage. Then he made his move. With his left hand he reached for Pam's throat, with his right, he reached for his pistol, which was tucked in the back of his pants. Pam brought her right arm up, knocking his hand away. At the same time, she raked three fingernails of her left hand, down his face, across both eyelids and down the middle of his face to the tip of his nose. Then with the base of her right hand, she drove the bridge of his nose into his skull. The pistol which was at his side hit the ground before his knees did. He fell back, dead, blood pouring from his nose. While watching the other man, Pam kneeled and wiped the blood off her hand on his black shirt. She then picked up his pistol.

"You were saying?" Pam said softly.

After he had answered her question, she backed away from the dead man and motioned with the pistol for the other man to get him. The other man walked around the car, picked him up, put him in the car, and drove away. Pam turned, walked pass everybody without looking at them, then she went into the house.

"She has gone completely off the deep end. She has been talking to these witches behind our back. We need to watch each other's backs tomorrow night," Jason said to Dave.

"She won't betray us," Dave said assuredly.

"You're forgetting something."

"What?"

"She's one of them," Jason replied. "She is a witch. She's probably in there right now, making sure her dear witch sister is safe."

"What are y'all planning on doing?" Rev. Zackery asked.

"The less you know, the less they will be able to beat out of you," Jason snapped.

"Jason, you need to be very careful about how you're thinking right now, 'so a man thinkest, so is he,'" Rev. Zackery warned.

"My thinking is crystal clear, reverend. I'm not going to get down on my knees and wait for those witches to come to kill me. I'm going to go after them. I'm going to fight. You want to know what I'm going to do? That's what I'm going to do, fight." Jason paused to let himself calm down. "Reverend, why don't you take your little demon possessed prisoner in the house and torture him some more."

Rev. Zackery opened the back door and Billy got out. Rev. Zackery pulled off the duct tape that was hanging from the side of Billy's mouth.

"I'm sorry about what I did," Billy said looking down at the ground.

"I forgive you Billy," Rev. Zackery said sincerely.

"Do you think you can help me get rid of these demons?" Billy asked.

"I can't," Rev. Zackery replied. "But, Jesus can, and He will help you, Billy. But first, let's go in the house and get something to eat. You should be pretty hungry. I know I am."

"Yes sir, I am," Billy smiled, "but I need to go to the bathroom first."

Jason drove pass the two men as they walked to the house. Dave just looked out of the window wishing he had stayed at home.

"She is changing," Jason said pulling Dave's arm. "Every day, she is looking and acting more and more like that crazy sister of hers. She has been talking to Sibal and the rest of those witches behind our backs. She's planning something. They're planning something that we don't know about."

"What are you really saying," Dave said sarcastically.

"I'm saying if she betrays us, and sides with them, if they try to kill us and she goes along with them, then she has to die with them." Jason paused and waited for Dave's reaction.

"I'm not going to kill her, and she's not going to betray us."

"I hope she doesn't, but you'd better be ready if or when she does," Jason said cutting off the engine and opening the door.

When they walked into the house, they saw her sitting on the sofa with the safe in her lap and four sticks of dynamite lying beside her. There was a frown on her face as she spoke. "Listen up guys. I need to talk to you for a minute about tomorrow night."

They both gave her their attention.

"Jason, I like your plan. We can do it just like you said, with one little change," she said.

"What's the change?" Jason asked.

"Well, you and Dave do exactly as you planned. I won't be going with you when you go. I'll meet you there. I'll make my entrance after the virgin is brought out," she looked at Dave, "before anything is done to her." She looked at Jason. "When I come to the stage and say, 'you killed my mother', that will be the signal. Jason, you will open the door and get the chains and locks from Dave. You'll chain the first set of doors and move into position at the doors on the other side. When you see me grab the virgin and duck down, I want you to light a stick of dynamite, go outside, behind the door and throw it at least ten feet inside the door. Don't blow the wall down. The blast should clear a path for me and the virgin to get to the door." She looks at Dave again. "When you hear the explosion, that's when you should back the truck through the front door and light the fire. By that time, we, the girl and I, should be at the side door. Once we're outside Jason will throw a bucket of gas inside the door and chain the doors from the outside. We'll light the gas from the outside. Then we'll light the walls on the outside. Oh yeah, before I leave the stage and right before I give you the signal, I'm going to kill Sibal, on the stage, in front of everybody, then after you throw your stick of dynamite and clear a path, I'll light a stick of dynamite and blown up the head council."

"How are you going to do all that? Just get the girl and get out. The fire will take care of everybody else." Jason said, his voice becoming loud.

"You don't need to worry about how I'm going to do anything. If you want to get out alive, you need to do what you're supposed to do, when you're supposed to do it, just like I said for you to do it," she warned, standing. "Since I'm not going with you, I need to get a ride to that car dealership where Jason rented his car. Dave, will you take me?"

"Yeah, sure," Dave said

"Any more questions?" She waited for a moment and then began walking down the hall with the taped up safe hanging from its handle, swinging from one of her hands, and the pistol in the other.

"Where do you think you're going with that safe?" Jason yelled.

She turned with piercing cold angry eyes. "I'm keeping it with me, it will be safer that way." She turned, took another step, and then turned back toward them, again. "Unless, one of you wants to come and try to take it from me," she said ominously and waited for a response. They just stood there, not wanting the confrontation to turn violent. It may have only been seconds, but the stare down seemed like minutes. Eventually, she turned, walked into her room, closed and locked the door.

"I guess she told you," Dave smirked.

"Yeah, but I know something that she doesn't. And, if her attitude doesn't change, I'll let her find out the hard way. That's if she doesn't betray us," Jason said.

"She didn't sound like she was going to betray us."

"We don't know what's going on in that room right now. All we know is Pam and her sister are in there together, and, more and more, Pam and her sister are looking like two peas in the same pod. Watch your back, tomorrow!"

Something in the hall caught their attention. They both looked at the same time. There was a blue light shining from beneath the door of Pam's room.

"She has opened the safe. Come on!" Dave said as he rushed to Pam's door.

"Where are you going?"

"Whenever that blue light comes on, that mean danger. Pam's sister is trying to take control of Pam like she took control of you," Dave said.

"What are you talking about. That witch didn't take control of me."

Dave walked up to Pam's bedroom door and yelled. "Pam! Are you all right?" The blue light went off.

"I'm fine. I'm going to get a nap. I'll talk to you when I wake up," she yelled back.

"Okay," Dave said and then returned to the living room where Jason was waiting.

"What did you mean when you said Tamera took control of me?" Jason asked.

"When I got here you were standing over the crystal ball with a hammer in one hand and that cross, I gave you, in the other. You were going to try to get in the crystal with Tamera so you could kill her, weren't you? Or, do you even know?"

"I knew what I was doing. I was going to get in there with her, stab her in her heart with that cross, and watch her die," Jason said.

"Yeah, but you were in some kind of a trance, cause when we stopped you, you came at us."

"I didn't know who was grabbing me. I was just defending myself. I don't remember how I got here, cause I was sleep. When I woke up and saw that I was not tied up anymore and I saw the safe, I just wanted so badly to kill her. That's the only trance I was in."

"If you had killed her, then you would have still been trapped in the crystal."

"I figured that eventually Pam or you would have gotten me out. However, if not, she would be dead and that's all I cared about at the time." Jason said.

"Like I said, you were in a trance," Dave said.

Just then, Rev. Zackery and an untapped Billy walked out of Rev. Zackey's room. They walk into the living room.

"I'm going to fix something to eat. Are you hungry?" Rev. Zackery said.

"Starving," Dave said.

"Yes," Jason said.

Turning to Billy, Rev. Zackery spoke. "Billy, why don't you stay in here with them while I fix us some food."

"Yes sir." Billy said as he sat in one of the chairs.

Pam came out of her room with the safe.

"Pam," Rev. Zackery said. "I'm about to cook some of my famous spaghetti. Are you hungry?"

"No. I'm going to get a rental car, reverend, and I won't be back tonight," she said with the safe by her side. "Are you ready Dave?" she said.

"Yeah, I'm ready."

"Okay, let's go. I'll see you guys tomorrow night," she said.

"I'll be right back, Rev. Zackery," Dave said. "Save some food for me."

"Will do. Be careful, Pam" Rev. Zackery said as she walked out of the house.

Chapter 24
A New Ally

(Tuesday morning 7:30 AM)

Pam was on the balcony of her motel room, sitting in a plastic chair that was propped on its back legs against the wall near the two sliding glass doors outside of her room. She was kicking her feet up in the air as she thought about the events of the upcoming evening. She took Manny's cell phone from her pocket and dialed.

"Yes ma'am, this is Walt?" the voice said.

"Did you take care of everything I told you to do," she said.

"Yes ma'am."

"Are you in route?"

"No ma'am. I'm at a gas station on highway 121, about five or ten miles from Tipton. I've been here about fifteen minutes waiting for you to call."

"Is there a place on the highway nearby where you can see at least a half mile behind you."

"Yes ma'am. About five miles north of here the highway is pretty straight.

"Wait there until you don't see any cars on the highway. Then, I want you to drive north on highway 121. Check your rearview mirror as you go to see if anyone is following you."

"The road appears to be clear now, ma'am," Walt said as he started the car. "I'm pulling out now," he said as he turned and drove down the highway.

"Do you see any cars following you?" Pam said

"No ma'am. Wait, a car just pulled out of the gas station."

"What color is it, and how many people are in it."

"It's a dark blue Ford, Crown Vic. Looks like four people inside," Walt said looking carefully.

"Drive fifty miles per hour and see if they match your speed."

"I don't see them, ma'am. They must have turned off."

"Slow down." Pam waited a minute. "Do you see anything now?"

"No ma'am."

"Okay, speed up and let me know when you get to that straight away in the road."

"It's coming up in about two minutes, ma'am."

"When you get there, I want you to floor it. Then, after you go around the next curve, pull over to the side of the road. Did you bring your rifle with the scope?"

"Yes ma'am, I did. I'm coming to a curve now. I'm pulling off the road."

"After you stop, I want you to run back to where you can see down the road, look in your scope and tell me what you see."

When Walt got to where he could see, Walt aimed his weapon down the highway. About a quarter of a mile back he saw the Crown Victoria. It had stopped on the side of the road.

"I see them. They pulled off the road about a quarter mile back."

"They probably stopped when you stopped, so it looks like they have a bug in your car. Can you see their faces?" Pam asked.

"Yes ma'am. I don't know the two in the back, but the two in the front are Sibal's top security officers."

"Can you kill them from this range?" Pam asked.

"Not all of them," Walt said disappointedly. "If I cut the distance in half, and if use my M16, I could."

"You shot me, and I was deep in the woods," Pam said in disbelief. "Why can't you kill them?"

"I shot you with my long-range rifle. It's single shot. I could kill one, maybe two, but by the time I chambered the third round, they would either be gone or they would have taken cover," he explained. "I brought my M16. It's semi-automatic and the scope is not as accurate on this weapon, so I would need to be closer."

"Do you have any incendiary ammunition?"

"No ma'am. The only special ammo that I have is tracer rounds. I have two clips, fifteen rounds per clip, that have tracers every third round."

"Okay, this is what I want you to do," Pam laid out her plan.

Three minutes later, Walt was driving the limo full speed back down the highway toward the car. He noticed the people who were inside had all ducked down below the window level, so they could not be seen. Walt slowed down as he approached the car. He opened his window, pulled his pistol, and shot the two tires on his side as he passed. When reach his desired shooting range, he turned the limo ninety degrees to the right off the road and stopped. He got out with his M16, ran to the back of the Limo, and propping it over the trunk, he fired two shots. The shots went into the lower back of the car. There were two flashes of light but no fire. He looked beneath the car. He could see gasoline flowing beneath the car. The car began to pull on the road with the two flat tires. Walt put the crosshairs on the driver's head and fired. The driver's head went forward, and the car continued to move forward very slowly. Walt quickly aimed at the puddle of gasoline under the car. He fired several shots until he saw a flame beneath the car. The flames grew, there was an explosion, and the car became completely engulfed in flames. The two men in the back seat were killed in the explosion, however, the man in the front seat emerged running from the car. His clothes were on fire. Walt shot. The man grabbed his neck and fell to the ground. He watched for any movement, then he got back in the car and grabbed his cell phone off the seat and spoke.

"It's done. They're all dead, ma'am," Walt said nonchalantly.

"Make sure they are all dead," Pam shouted. "Check their phones. See if any of them was able to make a call to Sibal in the last few minutes."

"All of them except one was in the car when it exploded, and the other one, I shot him as soon as he got out. He couldn't have made any calls." There was silence as he waited for a response.

"I don't like it, when I have to repeat myself," she paused, "but, I do like you. You're really good at what you do." She paused again. "In the future, I will try to take time to listen to what you say to me, however, I'm not always going to have time to explain why I want you to do, what I tell you to do. This is one of those times. Okay?"

"Okay ma'am, I'll do what you say, but I need to get outta here."

"I know, but right now, I want you to go back and check the bodies. See if the one you shot had a cell phone, please?" she asked politely. "And then get out of there before anyone comes, if you can."

"Okay, ma'am, right away."

Walt drove the Limo twenty feet pass the burning car. Three men inside the car were still burning. He ran up to the man lying beside the road. His clothes were no longer on fire. There was a pistol lying beside him, there was something in his hand. It looked like a remote control. He carefully took it from his hand. Then he quick searched the man's pockets, taking his cell phone. As soon as he put it in his pocket, it began to vibrate. Before he could pull it out again, shots begin to be fired from the car. Walt ran as fast as he could toward the limo. Then he realized that the ammunition in the car was beginning to go off. When he got to the limo, he stumped the accelerator and sped down the highway.

"I got the phone, ma'am," he said examining the remote control.

"What was all that shooting I heard."

"The ammunition in the burning car was exploding, ma'am."

"Oh! Are you, all right? You didn't get hit did you?"

"No ma'am, I'm good."

"I didn't realize I was putting you in danger. I'm sorry about that."

"No problem, ma'am."

"I'd hate for anything bad to happen to you. I need somebody I can trust right now."

"You can trust me, ma'am. I'm not going to let anything happen to you. If you live, I live. If you die, I die."

"I guess you're right. The people I thought I could trust, I have my doubts about. Your people positively want to kill you now. Looks like we're in this together. My life depends on you and your life depends on me, even though you did try to kill me twice."

"That will never happen again, ma'am. From now on, I will give my life, if necessary, to protect you. You should never put yourself at risk for me. You spared my life, when you should have killed me, and then you kept Sibal from having me killed. I appreciate that. There is no one I would rather fight beside than you. You have my loyalty. I will never desert you, ma'am."

There was a long silence.

"Call me Pam. My friends call me Pam"

"Okay, Miss Pam."

"Okay," Pam breathed an emotional sigh. "Did you check to cell phone for any recent calls?"

"I'm checking it now", he said picking up the cell phone. "There is a call about fifteen minutes ago to 'Boss' and yeah that's Sibal's number. So, he didn't make any call after I started shooting."

"Good! Now, go to the Sahara motel in Tipton. When you get there, park the car, go into the office, and wait for me there. Oh yeah, don't hang up the phone. I need to stay in constant contact with you till then."

"Okay Miss Pam, I'm on my way," Walt said driving down the road. He put the remote control in his chest pocket of his black swat jacket.

Chapter 25
The Betrayal

(Tuesday morning 9:30 AM)

Dave walked slowly toward the kitchen. His hair was still wet from the hot shower he had just taken. When he walked in, Jason and Rev. Zackery were sitting at the table. They had just begun to eat.

"Good morning sleepy head," Rev. Zackery said cheerfully.

"Hey," Jason said without looking up.

"Want something to eat?" Rev. Zackery said with a big smile.

"Yes sir. I sure do," Dave replied. "You seem mighty cheerful. It's good to see you back to normal, reverend. In fact, you're a lot more cheerful than usual. What did you do to Billy, I mean, where is Billy?"

Rev. Zackery's smile became even bigger. "I'm happy to report that Billy is not with us today at breakfast, because he is fasting and praying. Today, is a very important day in his life. Billy wants to be exorcised. I'm going to do it."

"What!" Dave said.

"So, when you exorcise him, are you going to throw in some push-ups and some side straddle hops," Jason said shaking his head as he continued to feed his face.

"That's great, reverend. How are you going to know if it works?" Dave said as he put eggs and bacon on his plate.

"I can only do my part. The Lord is the one who does the cleansing. I'll cast the demons out in the mighty name of Jesus, then I'll lead him in the prayer of salvation, and finally we will ask the Holy Spirit to come into his soul, because that is the only way to keep the demons from coming back."

"Sounds like a plan," Dave said smiling.

"Well, I hope you send him away from here when you're done," Jason said looking up at Rev. Zackery. "Cause, I won't be here to watch your back, after tonight. You know I will be leaving town, and since I decided on a closed casket, I won't be back till the funeral on Saturday."

"I'll be fine, Jason. Once the exorcism is over, Billy will be free to go. However, he will be welcome to come and visit whenever he chooses," Rev. Zackery said confidently. "Are you leaving tomorrow, too," he said looking at Dave.

"Yes sir. Things around here may be a little intense for a while. Plus, I need to sign my divorce papers and get on with my life." Dave paused. "I want to thank you reverend. All my anger is gone. Being here with you, has been so good for me emotionally. I realize now more than ever before, we all mess up, and make bad decisions. I'm no better than Carol. I forgive her, cause, I am going to really need the Lord to forgive me."

"And he will forgive you, Dave. Just pray, right now, and repent for the wrong you have done. Ask him to forgive you."

"I think I'll wait till tomorrow, reverend."

"The bible says in 2nd Corinthians 6:2,

'In an acceptable time I have heard you,

And in the day of salvation, I have helped you.'

Behold, now is the accepted time; behold, now is the day of salvation.

"Don't wait, Dave. Tomorrow is not promised."

"How well I know, reverend. I still have a little unforgiveness in me. I'd rather do it tomorrow"

"Why is everybody talking about tomorrow." A frown appeared on Rev. Zackery's face. "What are y'all planning to do tonight?"

"It's nothing that concerns you, Rev. Zackery. It's personal," Jason said pushing back from the table.

"Dave?" Rev Zackery said looking at Dave.

"We have a meeting. That's all I can say. I got to go pack. Oh yeah, I might not be able to make it back for the funeral." Leaving half his food, Dave got up quickly and walked out of the room.

"You need to think very seriously about what you are about to do," Rev. Zackery said pointing his finger at Jason. "What you do is not just going to affect your life, but it's going to affect Dave's and Pam's, too. This hate thing in you, you've got to get it under control."

"I remember a scripture that you read once," Jason said looking sternly into Rev. Zackery's eyes. "You said, 'no greater love than this, that a man would lay down his life for a friend.' It's not just a hate thing that I have in me, it's also love thing. I love Dave and Pam. And, I love you," Jason said and then walked out.

Rev. Zackery watched as Jason went into the room with Dave, then he looked up to the ceiling and prayed aloud. "Lord, I know I supposed to cast the demon out of Billy, but I really need to know what they are going to do. Just let me use the demons in Billy one more time." He hurriedly walked down the hall to his room.

Billy was sitting in a folding chair next to the dresser reading the bible when Rev. Zackery walked in.

"Is it time?" Billy asked excitedly.

"Well, not quite. I really need to ask you to do something for me."

"Okay, Rev. Zackery, whatever you want. What is it?"

"I want to talk to the demon in you one more time."

"What do you want to do that for?" Billy said confused. "I want to get rid of them, not let them take control of me, again. That don't make no sense."

"I know it doesn't, but Pam, Dave, and Jason, are about to do something that may cost them their lives. I need to know what it is. They won't tell me. The demons know. This is the only way for me to find out. Do I have your permission, please? After I find out, then we'll do the exorcism. The demons will be cast out of you forever. How about it?"

Billy thought for a minute. "No, I'm sorry. I don't want to do it. I been fasting and praying, I'm ready for the exorcism. Let's do it, now, reverend."

Rev. Zackery shook his head 'yes,' then taking the bible from Billy, turned his back to him. A whole minute passed as Rev. Zackery prepared himself. Then, turning around facing Billy, he placed the bible on Billy's head. "In the name of Jesus, demon, reveal yourself."

The demon head appeared. "Reverend, reverend, reverend, you little sneak. How could you deceive Billy like that?"

"You can't talk about anybody. You're the sneakiest sneak of all time," Rev. Zackery said guiltily.

"I don't call myself a preacher, a man of God. You hypocrite!"

"Shut up!" Rev. Zackery said, slapping the bible across the demon's face. Billy's face appeared momentarily as his face was knocked to the left. Rev. Zackery could see his anguish as their eyes met. Then, when his head straightened back forward the demon head reappeared. "Don't say anything unless I ask you to." He pushed the bible roughly into his face. "You understand me?"

The bible was covering the demon's mouth, so he just shook his head up and down.

"What are Jason, Pam and Dave planning to do tonight. Answer me now!" Rev. Zackery said louder than he meant to.

"I ain't telling you nothing. What are you going to do if I don't, exorcise me?"

Rev. Zackery stood there, not knowing how to reply to the demon. After several minutes of just staring at each other, Rev. Zackery sat on the foot of the bed. "Well, I guess we'll just have to have a little church. I'll read the bible, pray, sing some hymns, and praise the Lord while I figure it out."

A frown appeared on the demon's face as Rev. Zackery began to read the bible very loudly.

In the nearby bedroom Dave and Jason could hear the reverend's voice.

"I guess the exorcism has started," Dave said, tying his shoes.

"He'd stand a better chance of beating the devil out of Billy than he will with this exorcism stuff. He's taking a big chance. I hope Billy doesn't turn on him again. Billy can be vicious."

"What do you mean?" Dave asked.

"When he had me tied up in his barn, he was going to nail my hands to a chair. He wasn't under the influence of a demon, then. It was him, his evilness. The dude is evil. Believe me."

"Did you tell Rev. Zackery?"

"Rev. Zackery knows. I don't know why he's acting like this. He's seen Billy in action. Billy has tried to kill him more than once. How many attempts is it going to take before he learns. I tried to warn him. He won't listen, so he's on his own. I wish him luck. Anyway, we need to get out of here, and get ready for tonight. We need to get Billy's pickup truck, put a couple of those big barrels in his barn on it, and fill them up with gas."

"Did you tell Billy we were going to barrow his truck?" Dave smiled.

"No. He was going to kill me; the truck is the least thing I ought to take from him. I ought to burn his house down and kill his cat."

"He has a cat?" Dave asked.

"I don't know. However, if he does, I could kill it and his dog and anything else he has, and not feel bad about it."

"I get the message."

The unpleasant sounds of Rev. Zackery singing "Amazing Grace" could now be heard.

"Good lord! Rev. Zackery must be trying to exorcise everything, the demons, the rats, the roaches, and us," Dave said covering his ears.

When "Amazing Grace" stopped, a worse sounding song started.

"Jesus keep me near the cross. There's a precious…" Rev. Zackery sang.

"Let's go. I can't take it." Jason walked out of the room and up to Rev. Zackery's door knocking loudly. "We're leaving Rev. Zackery. We might not be able to get back before you go to sleep, so hopefully we'll see you in the morning before we pull out."

The singing stopped, "Okay," Rev. Zackery yelled back, then the singing continued louder and worse than before. Dave and Jason hurried out of the house and on their way.

Chapter 26
The Body Count

(Tuesday afternoon 12:30 PM)

"We're passing by police cars, a fire truck and an ambulance, all with flashing lights on highway 121 now," the voice said as he described the view through the windshield of his car. "Looks like a completely burnt Crown Vic that's barely on the road, and there is a body covered with a white sheet lying on the ground about ten feet from the car." The voice paused. "No, I can't read the license plate, but it looks like our car. There are also forensic officers looking inside the car. I thought I saw bodies inside." He paused again. "All right, we're coming back now." He hung up the phone.

The person on the other end of the call, ended the call. It was Sibal. She and her assistant Howard were in her office.

"She killed them all," she groaned holding her head with her hands as she walked back and forth. "She's going to kill me for sure, now. She'll never trust me again."

"Not unless you speak to her first," Howard said.

"And say what?"

"Ask her why she killed the men you sent to protect her. Tell her, they were sent to follow her so that nothing would happen to her. Tell her they were there for her safety, that they were told to stay far away from her, out of sight, so that they wouldn't even appear to be any kind of a threat."

"That just might work. Call Manny's number." Howard called the number and handed her the phone.

"Sibal," Pam answered.

"Why did you kill the men I sent to protect you?"

"Protect me?" Pam said suspiciously.

"Yes! They were told to follow you, not to get to close, but if you needed them, they were to offer any assistance necessary. Why did you kill them? What did they do wrong?"

"They didn't do anything wrong. You did, when you told them to follow me. You don't make decisions on your own. I make the decisions. You follow my orders." Pam said sternly. "Do I make myself perfectly clear?"

"Yes, perfectly."

"I won't repeat this to you ever again, understood?"

"I understand. It will never happen again," Sibal replied. "You've got to believe me. I was only trying to protect you. There are other people in the coven who want you dead. Those men who tried to bomb your house, they weren't working for me. They were working for members of the head council. When you called me, I found out who they were and ordered them to give you the remote control for the detonators. I know they brought it to you because, I saw your mark on the face of the one you killed. I also know that they probably told you that I sent them. That's not true either. The members of the head council that sent them, told them to say that. I didn't have anything to do with that. You've got a lot of enemies. That's why I sent those men to protect you. Please, forgive me. I will never do anything else without your approval," Sibal pleaded.

"When I get there tonight at eleven forty-five, I want six of you best guards to escort me to the platform where the head council will be. Have a special seat for me. I will address the assembly before the virgin is brought out, understood?"

"Yes, but what if the council overrules me?" Sibal asked.

"Then, I will overrule the council. I'll arrive at eleven forty-five. Be ready!"

Sibal heard the phone go silent and she handed it back to Howard. "I think she bought it," Sibal said with a sigh of relief.

"Did she indicate that she knew anything about the bomb in the limousine."

"No. In fact, she indicated that she was in the limousine when she, and I'm guessing Walt, killed my team. I don't know why the bomb was not detonated," Sibal said.

"Well, there's no way they wouldn't have detonated the bomb if they were under attack. They must have found the bomb. If she found it then she knows we tried to kill her. That means she will try to kill you."

"Yeah, she said she's going to kill me in front of everybody." She paused. "But the truth is, if she does make it to the ceremony, I'm going to kill her in front of everybody."

"I don't think you should take any chances. Setup up an ambush on the barn road. After she turns off the highway, and goes pass the gate, we will close and lock the gate behind her, then we can have a car block her way and when she stops, we will open fire on the limousine from both sides and kill her that way. Just give me the 'okay' and I'll set it up."

"Okay, but don't mess this up, Howard. I want her dead."

"Leave her to me." Howard walked out quickly.

CHAPTER 27
BODY GUARD

(Tuesday afternoon 2:00 PM)

Pam walked out on the balcony of her motel room. It had been hours since Walt had arrived. He was still in the motel office waiting for her. For some reason she was nervous about meeting him again. By now, she was sure, no one had followed him to the motel, and it was getting late. She needed to talk to him. She needed to know how much she could trust him. She remembered when they fought, how he almost killed her, how he should have killed her, the little flattering remarks he made, and how he hesitated before delivering what would have been the death blow. Why did he hesitate? Why hadn't he killed her? For that matter, why hadn't he killed her when he shot her in the woods. Why a shoulder shot and not a head shot? Two times her life was in his hands, two times he let her live. She shook herself out of her day-dreaming state.

"Okay, girl, let's get on with this. You know what needs to be done," she said to herself. She called him on Manny's phone. "Meet me on the first floor by the washing machines around the corner from the office."

"I'm on my way," he said getting up immediately and walking out of the door.

Pam watched as he walked down the front of the building and then though a corridor leading to the washers and driers. She got her key and went out the door. She went halfway down some stairs and saw him. He wore loose fitting jeans and a dark blue long sleeve cotton pull-over shirt. It fit loose, too. It didn't show the muscles that she knew he had. His hair was cut short but not too short, and he had a neatly trimmed beard. His strong cheekbones and confident stare made him look like a super model. She could see him much better than she had when they fought in the dark night.

"Hey, up here." Their eyes met. She thought she saw the hint of a smile form on the corners of his lips. It made her frown. She didn't want to get attached to him, cause he could be dead before the night was over. In fact, he probably would be dead before the night was over. "Follow me, but stay back thirty feet," she said turning and walking away. She took an extended walk to her room. Finally, he walked in and shut the door behind him. They faced each other saying nothing. Her stare was cold and mean. His was calm and confident. He took one step closer to her, his eyes scanning her body from head to toe. Her new black stretch pants were hugging her thighs. The open black light weight leather jacket exposed a form fitting black V-neck shirt. The jacket and the shirt were new, too. Everything she had on was new, including her lace black panties, her small black pearl earrings, her black lip stick, and the enchanting fragrance she was wearing on her neck, her navel, and on her thighs. He took two more steps. She swung her right leg back, shook both arms and balled up her fists and positioned herself to fight.

"You smell really good. Is that for me?" he said sniffing the air and smiling slightly.

She relaxed her hands, turned away, and walking to the sofa she said, "I didn't want to stink. With so many attempts on my life recently, I haven't had time to take a real bath in a long time. I guess I wanted to feel like a woman for a change," she said turning back toward him. "I finally got a chance to soak in the water for an hour. I only wish I could have taken a bath in one of those old fashion deep tubs. You know the ones with the feet. Then, my whole body could have been under the water." She couldn't believe she was smiling and speaking to him so comfortably.

"I like those, too."

"You like what, too?"

"Those old, deep tubs with feet," he said smiling back at her. "I saw one recently at a building supply store. They are nice."

"Oh yeah, thank you for the compliment. You smell good yourself."

"It's called 'Desire.' The salesperson at the store said all it takes is one whiff and the ladies would be under my spell. Is it working?" His smile was wider.

"Sit down," she said sitting and point to the empty space on the sofa next to her. She had become serious again "You do know that this a suicide mission, don't you? The odds of you living through this are, zero."

"Well, I'm going to die sooner or later, but I wouldn't be so quick to count me out. I've had those odds before, and I'm still here."

"Look, other than the fact that you shot me in the back and tried to stab me in the throat, you seem like a really nice person. Maybe, you should forget about helping me and just leave the state or the country; and start a new life."

"I remember the first time I saw you. You were standing outside your car ordering three hardcore killers to get off your property. You had no fear. As little as you are, you faced down three mean men. I was impressed. Then, when you started running toward the woods, I saw how fine you, are, especially your behind."

"So, what are you saying? You were looking at my behind, that's why you missed me?"

"No," he said. "I was looking at your behind, so, I shot the trees to make you run faster. I wanted you to get away."

"What about when you shot me?"

"I didn't have a choice. You were about to kill Steve. I didn't want to kill you, so, I positioned my scope on your right shoulder above your lungs. But, you moved when I pulled the trigger and I hit your lung. Sorry about that."

"You're saying you could have killed me at least three times that day. You missed me on purpose? Instead of shooting me in my head, you shot me in the shoulder. Is that what you're saying?"

"Yeah, pretty much," he said shaking his head.

"Why?"

"I was hoping that you would survive, but that's not all."

"What else?"

"When Manny and I came to kill you at the house. I saw you when you cracked the door. My scope was on your eye."

"I remember. You shot Manny. Did you do that to save me?"

"No. He had threatened to kill me if I interfered with him killing you."

"So, you killed him to keep him from killing me?"

"No. I killed him cause he threatened to kill me. Like I told you, I don't let people threaten me and live, if I get an opportunity to take them out. Well, nobody but you."

"When did I threatened you?"

"The night we fought. You said you were going to beat me in the ground. That was a threat to me." He paused. "Anyway, I had the knife to your throat, but I couldn't kill you."

"I know you couldn't, because you were hit by a car."

"I had time to kill you. I tried, but I couldn't do it."

"Why?"

"So that maybe this would happen."

"This! What is this?"

"We would end up somewhere, together, so I could tell you how I feel about you."

"How do you feel about me?"

"I don't know how to put it into words."

"I've heard that before," she said standing up and walking across the room.

"Okay, you want to know how I feel? Then, I'll tell you."

He turned around and faced him. "All right, tell me."

"I feel like I need to protect you from anything and everything that would harm you. I feel that I want to do everything in my power to please you, and nothing to disappoint you. I want to keep you safe. I want to make you feel that you are cared for. And I want you to know I will be here with you, as long as you want me to be, as long as I live. In other words, I guess, I love you. I never loved anybody or anything in my life, so this is new for me. I know you don't love me, but maybe some time in the future, you may grow to love me. If not or if you already have someone else, it doesn't matter, cause I like this feeling."

"How do I know that you aren't lying to me, now."

"You don't know if I'm lying, but there is one thing that you do know."

"What is that?"

"You know I'm here, ready to prove to you that you can depend on me. I'm here ready to do whatever you want me to do, whenever you want me to you it, however you want it done. I'll do it, not because I have to do it, I'll do it because I have given myself to you. Why? Maybe, because you spared my life even though I was sent to kill you. Maybe, because you chose me to be your second in command even before we fought. Maybe because you chose me to be your bodyguard and gave me protection from Sibal." He stood up and walked over to her. "So, now and forever, I choose you. I'll be your bodyguard, your servant, and if you want, your lover, whatever you need me to be. I will protect you with my life."

She turned her back to him to hide her sexual excitement. "Did you bring any equipment?"

"Yeah, it's in the trunk." He could see her shoulders rise and fall with each heavy breath she took.

"Go get it. When you get back, I'll go over the plan with you," she said after taking a deep breath.

"Okay," he said touching her shoulder before turning to leave.

She closed her eyes and caught her breath when he touched her. She stood still until she heard the door close. She bent over, putting her hands on her thighs and took several deep breaths. Her skin was tingling and warm. Tiny beads of sweat began to form on her forehead. Then she sensed something in the room. In the corner of her eye, she saw something. She quickly turned and saw Walt standing against the door, looking lustfully at her.

"I thought I told you to go and get your gear," she said angrily as she walked toward him.

"You did, Miss Pam, but something inside me told me that you wanted me to wait. Something inside me told me to me you wanted this." He took her right wrist and turning her hand upward placed his small knife in her hand. She clutched the handle, the blade extending an inch beyond her hand and her thumb pressing against the end of the handle. He then pulled her knife holding hand up to his neck, and he laid her hand on his shoulder. "My life is yours," he said looking deeply into her eyes. Then putting both hands on her waist and lifting her up, he turned and pinned her body against the door with his own. He could feel the tip of the razor-sharp blade penetrating the skin on the side of his neck as he moved his face closer to hers. Suddenly, beyond her control, her anger turned to sorrow, as tears began to flow down her face. She sighed as their lips met. Her lips parted as she allowed him to suck her tongue into his mouth. The knife fell to the floor as she wrapped her legs around him. As they kissed, he walked them over to the sofa, and carefully laid down with her beneath him. They kissed several times and then just lay there holding each other. When the tear tracks had dried on her face, he lifted his head over hers and looked into her eyes. He no longer saw a confident dangerous tigress, he saw a fragile, venerable little girl.

"I'll go get my gear, now," he said as he attempted to get up.

"No! You started this, now you're going to finish it," she said refusing to release him.

"I want to, but something inside me is telling me that you want to wait. Can't you feel it? Don't worry, I'll be here whenever you are truly ready. I want you now. But I know you are not sure. You don't feel completely safe. I don't want you to have any regrets. Do you understand?"

Releasing him and putting her hands over her face she whispered, "Yes." A slight frown appeared on her brow. "Go get your gear." As he walked out the door, she wondered how she was going to feel when he dies tonight. 'Should I tell him of my plan, that practically guarantees his death,' she thought. 'He said he was willing to die for me, and he is one of them. Anyway, he shot me, he tried to kill me twice. I don't believe all that stuff he said. He didn't miss me on purpose, and he would have killed me if Dave hadn't hit him with the car.' She stood and began pacing back and forth.

"But why is he here?" she said aloud. "Why did he give me his knife before he kissed me? Why did I kiss him back? Why did it feel so good when he was lying on top of me?"

There was a knock on the door. There was a rhythm to it. It was, one two, one, one two three. She walked up to the side of the door, deciding not to look out the peephole." Yes!" she said.

"It's me," Walt said.

She opened the door.

"I will always knock like that if everything is okay," he said as he walked in with a duffle bag held on his shoulder with one hand and a long bag held by his other one. He sat them down and began to open them up. He pulled out four bulletproof vests and laid them on the floor. Then, he noticed her expression. "Is something bothering you?"

"I did tell you that this was a suicide mission, didn't I?" she said sadly.

"You did, but it's not my first," he said calmly. "Maybe, if we put our heads together, we can both come out of this alive. If I don't make it, it's okay, just as long as you do, and if neither one of us makes it, let's go down in style. I'm not afraid of dying."

"Look! I know that they are going to ambush us. Sibal won't allow me to reach the ceremony. She's expecting me to arrive in the limousine. She's going to stop it from getting there. My plan is to drive another my car and you drive the limousine. By the time they find out that I'm not in the limo, I will be inside the building, but you will be dead."

"I see. It doesn't look to good for the home team," he said raising his eyebrows and giving her a half smile. "I knew this day was coming. It had to happen sooner or later."

"How can you think about dying so nonchalantly."

"Easy. I should have died many times, many years ago," he said.

"What do you mean?"

"I was told that my mother tried to have me aborted, but the guy that did it ending up cutting her internally. She bled to death, but I lived. I was put in this orphanage. The couple that ran it were very mean. When I was about ten, this bully at the orphanage stole a pie. The man who ran it, asked all the kids who stole the pie. There were about ten boys there. Nobody said anything. He took me in the back room first, and said someone had told him, I stole the pie. He told me if I would admit that I stole it and I if I said I was sorry, he wouldn't beat me. I told him I didn't do it. He beat me anyway. Then he took the next boy in the back room. He was the bully who stole the pie. I guess the man told him the same thing that he had told me. When he was told that someone had accused him, he admitted that he stole it. The man beat him badly. Anyway, the bully thought I had told on him. I had seen him eating something that day, and I was pretty sure he had done it, but I didn't say anything. Anyway, about three weeks later, he decided he was going to run away. However, before he did, he tricked me into going into the cellar. He locked me in, then he set the orphanage on fire and left. I'm thinking he thought everybody but me would be able to get out. It didn't work out that way. While the whole building was burning down, I found some tools in the cellar and was able to make a hole in the wall and I got out. Everybody else died. Since I was the only one who got out, they thought I set the fire, so they put me in reform school till I was eighteen."

"How did you handle that?" Pam asked.

"What? Reform school?"

"Yeah, that too, but I was really asking about how you handled being put in jail for something you didn't do."

"I didn't like thinking about it, so I stopped. Anyway, I was happier there. The food was great. It was the best I had ever had."

"What about the other conditions."

"Well, I had to fight almost every day for about three months when I first got there. Then I found out that this one guy, who was the head of the worse gang there, was telling his gang members to fight me. So, I challenged him to a fight in front of everybody. He didn't fight me. Instead, he had some of his gang member to hold me while he hit me. Afterwards, he said that if I told anybody that he beat me, he would kill me. I was in the infirmary for two weeks and I never told on him. One day, when I got out, we were all in the cafeteria. I walked up behind him and hit him in the back of his head with the edge of my tray. His head fell over in his food. I kept walking like nothing had happened. Some of his gang members saw me but they didn't say anything. The guards thought he had a stroke or a seizure. He was taken to the hospital. He never came back. I didn't have any more problems with anybody else there. He never should have threatened me."

"So, then what happened," Pam asked excitedly.

"Do you really want to know?"

"Yeah, I want to know. You're the only man who ever said that he would die for me, or that he guessed he loves me, and you say that you're mine, so I guess that makes you my boyfriend."

"Okay girlfriend," Walt said smiling very brightly. "I was in reform school until I turned eighteen. That's when I was drafted into the Army. I went to Viet Nam. I saw a lot of action, saw a lot of men die around me, and I killed men, women, and children with no regrets. I did whatever they said to do, killed whoever they said to kill, and anyone who threatened to kill me. One day we were on patrol, we were going to engage the enemy that had been reported about five clicks north of our position. We were going down this path and my bunkmate step on a land mine. I heard him yell 'mine.' I dove to the ground and rolled into a ditch. Everyone in my squad was hit including me. Most of them died. I was hit in the chest. I still have shrapnel in my lungs now. I got out on a medical. I should have been killed then, too. I was standing next to the person who stepped on the mine. See, I have been cheating death all my life. Now, I can choose to die the way I want to, protecting the woman I know I love. It may be the shortest love affair of all time, but, believe me, I'm going to fight for my woman. I won't go down easy, and I will take more than a few with me."

"It doesn't seem like you've had much happiness or love in your life," Pam said.

"I hadn't thought about it that much. They say, 'you don't miss what you never had.' I've never really felt happiness or love, until now. It's about time God did something for me, even if it's just for a day."

"You believe in God?" she asked surprised that he had mentioned God. "I didn't think witches believed in God."

"Miss Pam, men are not witches, they are warlocks and wizards. I'm neither. I just worked for them. But, that's not what you asked. Yes. I believe in God. They do, too. How can you believe in the devil and not believe in God? They most definitely believe in God, but they don't fear him. They fear the devil. Me, I believe in God. He is God, he can do what he wants to do. He put me in the womb of a woman who didn't want me, in an orphanage that didn't treat me right, in a detention center where I didn't deserve to be, and in a war where I killed people I didn't want to kill. I remember one time while I was in the reform school, I asked a preacher, why I should be thankful to God? He said to me that I should thank God for giving me life. I asked him 'why?' I told him, 'if God had just let my mother abort me, then I would have gotten a free pass into heaven, now, I am right outside the doors of hell. I didn't put myself here.' He just shook his head and said I should repent for burning up all those people in the orphanage, and then he walked away." Walt paused.

"I wish I could explain why this happened to you," Pam said sympathetically. "I have no idea why God let's all these bad things happen. My life started out bad, too. My homeless mother was taken in by witches. She thought they were being kind to her. They drugged her. She was raped and impregnated by some demon filled warlock, so they could have a queen leader. Then, when they found out she was going to have twins, they decided that the second child, me, should be killed. However, before they could kill me, my mother secretly gave me to another woman to raise me. Fortunately for me, this woman loved me. She raised me and took care of me. Then a week ago, these same witches found out that I was alive. They sent people to kill me. While looking for me, they killed her. She was the only person, other than my mother, who ever loved me. Now, they are planning to do it all over again. They have tricked another virgin and are going to use her to fulfill their plan. They are going to use her just like they used my mother. I can't let them do it. I've got to stop them. If I kill the head council and take over the coven, maybe then I will be able to shut it down and disband them. The only other alternative is to kill them all."

"You are Queen Tamera's twin sister," Walt said.

"Yeah. Do you know her?"

"No, only a few people get to be around her. We only see her at big meetings. She's guarded twenty-four-seven, at least she was. You must be very powerful. You captured the most powerful witch in southeast."

"I didn't. Jason, the man who was driving the car when I first saw you, trapped her."

"What are you going to do with her?" Walt asked.

"I don't know. We tried putting her in a safe and dropping her in the river, but that didn't work. I guess, burying her in a deep hole somewhere in the desert or dropping her over into an active volcano might work." She paused. "Anyway, first things first. Let's see what you got here."

"Okay, I brought three extra bulletproof vests for you, cause I didn't know your size. I have my long-range rifle, my semi-automatic M16, and four of everything else. There's four nine-millimeter Glocks, with shoulder hoisters, four snub-nose thirty eights with ankle hoisters. I also have two ammo clip belts containing four fifteen-round clips each, and a couple of smoke bombs. I brought as much ammo as we can carry, but we don't have enough ammunition to kill everybody there. Sorry about that."

"No problem. I have that part covered. If I decide, all of them will die together."

"How?"

"My friends and I are going to trap all of them inside the building and then burn it down. Hopefully, I will be able to get out with the virgin before it all goes up in smoke." She looks and sees something black in the duffle bag. "What's that?"

"That's your robe? Everybody there will be wearing one." He pulls it out. "And, I bought you a set on camouflage fatigues, size small, to wear underneath, if you so choose. We will be matching." He smiled brightly pulling out a second set.

"It's so much fun having a boyfriend," she said as she happily moved up to him and gave him a smack on the lips. Looking down in the bag she saw a pair of combat boots. "You have boots, where are mine?"

"What size do you wear?"

"Seven and a half, in ladies, which will probably be a seven in mens."

"Why don't you try on the bullet-proof vest and see which one fits you best, while run down to the army surplus down the street and get you some combat boots."

"Okay honey. Don't be long. Our time is running out, and I'm missing you already," she said giggling.

"I be back soon, beautiful." He smiled back at her and walked out.

She stood immersed in the emotion of feeling adored and being beautiful. No one had ever called her beautiful before.

Chapter 28
Hang-em High

(Tuesday afternoon 4:00 PM)

"Okay, stop it, for satan's sake, stop it!" the demon screamed after listening to the "Jesus Keep Me Near the Cross" song over and over for at least thirty minutes as he sat on the side of the bed in Rev. Zackery's room. "Whoever told you, you could sing, they lied. You sound like shhh…" The demon's words were stopped abruptly when Rev. Zackery's bible was shoved into his lips.

"Hey, don't you dare," Rev. Zackery ordered as he stood over the demon headed Billy. "I'm not having any foul language in this house."

When Rev. Zackery pulled the bible back, the demon now, only covered half of Billy's head. From the lips down, it was Billy.

"Billy is really going to feel that in the morning," the demon said with Billy's mouth and Billy's voice.

"Let's get this over with. Tell me what Jason and Dave are planning tonight."

"Well, let's see. I think they's planning to go to the hoe house in Thompsonville. Do you want to know all the nasty details?" the demon said with Billy's lips and voice.

"Stop that! You're freaking me out. Put your whole head back, demon."

The demon's whole head returned. "My whole head," the demon shouted. "Why not my whole body." Suddenly, the whole body of the demon appeared. A long fin appeared. It extended from the top of his head to the bottom of his spine. His mouth protruded. His body was like a large hairy wolf. He stood and reached out toward Rev. Zackery with hands that had long, dark, hairy fingers with long pointed claws. As the claws closed in on Rev. Zackery's head. Rev. Zackery charged forward, driving the bible into the heart of the demon. The demon howled as it fell back on the bed. The demon headed Billy returned.

"Demon, you don't scare me."

"Why don't you put that bible down, then we'll see if I scare you or not."

"I'll put it down, but first tell me what Dave and Jason are up to. Don't lie this time."

"You're going to put the bible down if I tell you?"

"Yes, demon. If you tell me, I'm going to put the bible down."

"Okay. They are going to a big witch and wizard ceremony tonight. Now, put the bible down."

"Why? What are they going to do there, as if I didn't already know?"

"If you already know then why are you asking me?"

"Tell me all the details, demon. What are they planning to do?"

"They are going to trap all the witches and wizards in the building and burn them up. Is that all you need?"

"No. When are they going to do it?"

"Some time after midnight when the ceremony starts. Anything else?"

"Where is the ceremony going to be and how do I get there?"

"Are you planning to go? What are you going for?"

"I'm going to stop them from murdering all those people," Rev. Zackery said angrily. "I can't let them ruin their lives like that. How do I get to the ceremony?"

"It's at the big barn. You go up highway 121 and after you pass Pinehurst Road, you will come to a gravel road about a half mile down on the left. Turn on that road. It leads directly to the barn." The demon paused. "Now, is there anything else?"

"No demon. You have been very helpful."

"Okay, put the bible down."

Rev. Zackery laid the bible on the bed. "It's down."

"No, put it down on the dresser over there and then come back over here."

Rev. Zackery picked up the bible turned and walked toward the dresser. When he was halfway, he said, "In the name of Jesus, demon, conceal yourself. Instantly, Billy was back. He started rubbing his bottom lip and his stomach.

"You did it anyway," Billy said in disgust. "How could you deceive me like that?"

"I had to find out what Jason, Dave, and Pam are doing. Their lives are in danger. I know I violated the trust you put in me. I hope you can understand and forgive me."

"I don't know Rev. Zackery. You lied and tricked me, and you probably hit me in my mouth, too," Billy said holding his bottom lip again. "Can we just do the exorcism now?"

"Well, Billy, I think you need to pray, and ask God to help you to forgive me. The bible says, if you don't forgive others, the lord won't forgive you. I don't think the exorcism would work under those conditions. I'll give you a minute." Rev. Zackery laid his bible on the dresser and walked out of the room.

Billy sat on the bed with his head down in his hand. He thought about some of his recent actions. "I've done some bad stuff, here lately, and I never asked him to forgive me. Plus, he only did what he did to help his friends," he said aloud to himself. "I'll forgive him. Not!" A devilish look appeared on his face. "That man has kidnapped me, held me against my will, beat me, tied me up, left me in his trunk, and made me pee on myself. On top of all that, he made me turn control of my body over to demons. He needs to suffer for that."

Billy immediately walked to the dresser and picked up the bible. He went to the bed and put it on the floor in front of the nightstand. Then he began to talk loudly, pretending to pray. Rev. Zackery was listening in the hall.

"Oh Lordy," Billy said loudly. "You know that I wants to get these devilish demons outta my body. They is reeking all kinds of bad stuff in my life. Now You know Rev. Zackery did me wrong. He never shouldda done the evil thing he did. It was downright disgusting and he ought to pay for it, that lying, sneaking rascal. But, I'm not going to do anything to him, it's up to You to decide what should be done to him. I'm going to forgive him because You said to forgive, and if I don't, I won't be able to get my exercising done. So, I'm asking You, help me to forgive him, please. Amen." He opened the door slightly. "Okay Rev. Zackery, I guess I'm ready."

Rev. Zackery walked in. He didn't appreciate being called a lying, sneaking rascal, but he knew he was wrong, so he adjusted his attitude and consciously removed the frown from his face and walked into the room.

"Well Billy, I want to say, I was wrong and I'm sorry I had to do what I did."

"Yeah! You 'dern tutten,' you was wrong. Letting them demon take over my body," Billy complained.

"Okay, Billy. Do you forgive me or not?"

"Yeah. I forgive you," Billy snapped.

"Let's get this over with as quick as possible, I've got to get ready for tonight," Rev. Zackery said looking around the room.

"This exercising, ain't the kind of thing you rush through, is it?" Billy asked.

"I don't know. I never did one before," Rev. Zackery replied.

"Well, if you gone do it, I want you to do it right the first time. Don't start, get halfway through, and then stop cause you got to go somewhere to help your friends. What are they doing that's so important?"

"I need to stop them from making a big mistake. If I don't stop them then, they could kill a lot of people, or they could be killed themselves."

"This doesn't have anything to do with that lady in the crystal ball, does it?" Billy asked. "That is the reason why I'm in this mess, today."

"I wish it didn't, but Pam has taken it to this witch ceremony and only the Lord knows what she is going to do."

"Where is the ceremony?"

"At this big barn in the woods." Rev. Zackery looked on the table where the fishbowl was sitting. The fish was staring at Rev. Zackery.

"Oh yeah! I know. Every now and then, I see a whole lotta cars headed up in the woods. They have a big meeting every two or three months."

"Where did I put my bible? I thought I left it on the dresser."

"I thought it was on the bed. Maybe it fell on the floor," Billy said looking suspiciously.

Rev. Zackery walked past Billy and saw the bible on the floor. "If you knew it was on the floor, why didn't you pick it up," Rev. Zackery said reaching down to get it. The fish in the fishbowl was smiling. Billy, who had followed Rev. Zackery around the bed grabbed the fishbowl with both hands, raised it over his head, and brought it down against the back of Rev. Zackery's head. The bowl cracked but didn't break. The water splashed on the everything around them, the fish was flopping in a wet spot on the bed, and Rev. Zackery, lying on the floor, was barely conscious. Billy quickly got the duct tape from the dresser and taped Rev. Zackery's hands together behind his back. He also taped Rev. Zackery's mouth and covered his head with a pillowcase. Billy looked around the room. He saw an extension cord coming from behind the nightstand. He unplugged it, tied a small loop in it and then he pulled the other end of the wire through the loop, making a noose. He put the noose over Rev. Zackery's head and pulled it tight around his neck. Billy pushed the bed over against the wall and then rushed from the room. Moments later he returned with the coffee table from the living room. He sat it in the middle of the room under the ceiling fan. He pulled the wire out of the lamp on the nightstand, stood on the coffee table, and tied the cord around the extension rod from the fan.

"Come on here, preacher man," Billy said as he pulled Rev. Zackery first to his knees, then to his feet. "Now step up, about two feet." Billy lifted Rev. Zackery's leg and positioned his foot on the table. Then he pushed him up on the table. "That's real good. Don't move. I don't want you to fall down."

Billy carefully got on the table, too. He tied the extension cord on Rev. Zackery's neck to the cord hanging down from the ceiling fan. He then pulled the pillowcase from Rev. Zackery's head and stepped down to the floor.

"Now, Zackery, my time has finally come, and your time has finally come to an end."

Rev. Zackery mumbled excitedly.

"What you trying to say? Are you saying you're sorry for letting the demons take over my body when I told you not to. I know I said I forgive you. Guess what? I lied. You are a mean man, and your mean days are over. Now, shake your head yes or no. Do you know where my little lady in the glass ball is now?" Billy waited for an answer. A minute passed with the two men just staring at each other. Finally, Rev. Zackery shook his head 'no.' "That's all right. I know where she will be tonight."

Rev. Zackery began to mumble.

"Keep quiet!" Billy pushed Rev. Zackery causing the wire to tighten around his neck so much the Rev. Zackery gaged. "Where is your God now, reverend? Is He going to save you now?"

Rev. Zackery shook his head 'yes.'

Billy rubbed his swollen lip. "You hit me in mouth again, didn't you?" He turned and picked up the bible. "Hit me with this, didn't you?" Billy said, putting the bible up to Rev. Zackery's nose. Billy turned to walk away, but he quickly turned back slapping Rev. Zackery hard across his mouth with the bible. "How do you like being bible slapped?" Billy threw the bible on the bed. When it landed, he noticed the goldfish on the bed. It had stopped flopping. It's gills and mouth were barely moving now.

"What?" Billy said moving his head closer to the fish. "I'm very hungry. You taste good."

Billy felt as if the fish was talking to him in his mind.

"So, you want me to eat you?" Billy said picking up the goldfish, 'yes,' the thought came to Billy. "Okay," Billy said putting the fish in his mouth. Before he could chew, the fish swam down his throat. Billy, folding over grabbed his chest and stomach and moaned for a few seconds. When he stood up straight again his head was now the head of a demon.

"I'm back, and it feels so good," he said smiling. It was the demon who called himself Bob. He stretched Billy arms and hands up in relief. Suddenly his smile was replaced with a scowl. "Take your positions, I'm taking command," he said sternly as he turned to face Rev. Zackery. "Let's make sure your mouth is covered." He pressed the tape that covered Rev. Zackery's mouth. "A little more tape won't hurt," he said getting the tape from the dresser. He tore a long piece of tape from the roll and taped Rev. Zackery's mouth from ear to ear. "That should be enough."

Rev. Zackery started humming "Jesus keep me near the cross."

"I'd love to stay around and listen to you 'murderalize' another hymn, but I've got to get to the ceremony." He kicked in one of the legs of the coffee table. Rev. Zackery shifted his body to keep the table from falling over. The demon head disappeared, and Billy's head reappeared, as he walked to the opposite leg of the table. "I would put you out of your misery quickly, however, I want you to have a little time to think about how the God who said He would never leave you or forsake you, has forsaken you." Billy was speaking but it was the demon's voice. A look of shock appeared on Rev. Zackery's face as he mumbled something very loudly.

Billy recognized Rev. Zackery's surprise. "Did you think you were reaching Billy, and that you two were going to be buddies." Billy laughed hideously. "You are too dumb for words, Z. I, or should I say, we, control this body." He waved his hand down over Billy's body. "Gotta run. I have an appointment with a little lady in a glass ball. I'll see you in hell." He kicked in another leg of the coffee table, the one on the opposite side and opposite end.

Now, Rev. Zackery had to balance himself on a two-legged table. Every time the table went over too far the wire would tighten around his neck cutting off the blood flow. However, when he regained his balance the noose would loosen slightly, and he could feel the blood flowing again.

"I just thought of something, Z. A great communicator like yourself, wouldn't leave this world without some kind of an explanation, telling why you killed yourself." The Billy demon got a piece of paper and a pen from the dresser and began to speak as he wrote. "I decided to hang myself like Judas did, cause I don't believe in God, and He don't believe in me. Signed, Z." Billy smiled. "Short, sweet, and to the point. Well said Z, I couldn't have put it better myself." The Billy demon put the note and pen on the dresser and walked out. Moments later, Rev. Zackery heard a car speed down the driveway.

Rev. Zackery was getting tired. Balancing on the table was getting more difficult. He knew he had only one chance. He moved his head and shoulders vigorously until the noose was very loose. He murmured 'help me, Jesus,' then he tucked his chin into his chest putting as much pressure against the wire as possible. Then he jumped as high as he could. When he came down, the wire slipped past his chin and was pulled tight around Rev. Zackery's neck cutting off his air and his blood. As he hung in midair, he knew his plan had failed. He moved his head back slowly. There above him, he could see that the fan was being held up by only one screw. He lifted his feet and kicked downward as hard as he could. The fan was pulled from the ceiling. It and Rev. Zackery came crashing down to the floor.

Chapter 29
Final Preparations

(Tuesday afternoon 5:15 PM)

Dave and Jason had just finished unloading the car. The eight full five-gallon gas cans to burn the outside walls of the barn were lined up neatly in the bushes just inside the tree line. Behind them were two homemade torches, two chains, and two huge padlocks. Billy's old truck, loaded with two twenty-gallon drums of gas, was parked and hidden in the trees off the road, near the main entrance to the barn. Everything was in place. They sat in the car in silence as they contemplated what was going to happen in about six hours.

"Are you going to be able to go through with this? If you can't do it, then let me know, now," Jason said earnestly.

"I'm pretty sure."

"Pretty sure. You need to know, if we get caught, we're dead, and if any of them escape, we're dead," Jason warned.

"And, if the barn doesn't burn all the way to the ground, we're dead. If Pam double-crosses us, we're dead. If the police find out what we did, we're dead. Our chances of being dead are pretty good, no, their great." Dave laid his head back on the seat and closed his eyes. "Would you tell me again, why we are doing this?"

"We're doing it because, if we don't stop them now, they are going to keep coming after us until we and possibly everyone close to us are dead. Just think about it, if they can't find you, they are going to find your family members. They will make them tell everything they know, to get to you. Your mother is still alive, isn't she?"

"Yeah."

"Do you want to be responsible for her death?"

"No," Dave said in a heavy breath.

"Either we kill them or die trying. Either way, it's over."

There was a short silence.

"I can't believe how this all started. I took a shortcut, and look at all that I've been through, where I am now." Sadness began to engulf Dave.

"Life can be pretty messy, but it's better than dying."

"What?"

"One day, when I was in the war, three enemy soldiers were after me. I hid in some boulders on this small hill. When I saw them coming up the hill, I rolled two gernades down the hill. When they went off, I was covered with blood and guts. All I'm saying is, it was messy, but I'm glad I'm still here. Sometimes you have to do some things that you don't want to do, just to stay alive."

"Yeah, that's true."

"I've been through a lot, but I never been though nothing like what you been through," Jason said tactfully.

"What I've been through, what are you talking about?"

"I never been in prison, and I never had to go through what some prisoners have to go through. I don't know if I could handle that."

"I wasn't in there but a day."

"But your one day, would have been the worst day of my life."

"What do you know about my day in jail?" Dave asked.

"The demon showed us, when you were in the cell with that big dude, when he made you unzip his jumpsuit."

"Yeah, I zipped it the down to his waist, but when I saw him put his hands on his hips, that's when I made my move. How did you like that?"

"Well, Rev. Zackery made him stop showing it when you got the zipper down to his," Jason stopped.

"So, you thought," Dave said shaking his head. "I didn't do that."

"Really," Jason said doubtfully. "You looked really scared, like you were gone do it."

"I was scared," Dave said.

"So, what happened.

"What happened? I grabbed him by his balls. I stuck my thumb into one of them. I felt it split in two. He was in so much pain that he couldn't even scream. He had to go to the jail hospital. I felt really, bad about it. He was crying like a baby."

"So, you didn't do it. Man, I am so glad to hear that," Jason said with a little laugh.

"Hey, I was just hoping that I wouldn't have to bite it off."

"I thought he had turned you. Hey, I was worried, but I'm good now. No worries, no doubts, we gone get this thing done." Jason balled his fist and grimaced.

"Did Pam think what you thought?"

"Yeah, pretty much. But she was very understanding. You know, she felt like you didn't have a choice." Jason's expression changed. "Are you seriously into Pam?"

"What are you really asking?"

"Dave, do you want to marry her, or do you just want to lay and play?"

"You tell me first. How do you really feel about her?"

"Well," Jason said rubbing his chin. "She ain't got enough butt for me. She needs a little more junk in the trunk, if you know what I mean."

They both laughed.

"So, you're not really interested in her romantically," Dave said.

"Dude, half the time when I look at her fine body, I think what a great lover she would be. Then, the other half the time I feel like she's my cousin. Then, the other half the time, I think my mama would freak completely out if I came home with a white girl. Then the other half."

"How many halves are you going to get out of one Pam," Dave interrupted.

"Then, like I was saying, the other half the time, when I see her fight, I get 'show nuff' scared. She can be treacherous. Can you imagine getting in an argument with her over who's turn it is to wash the dishes?"

"Yeah, it doesn't take much for her to snap," Dave said.

"So? How do you feel about her?"

"Well," Dave said with eyebrows raised and a silly smile. "I'm very attracted to her physically, and I'm pretty sure she's attracted to me, at least she used to be, but I think I still love my wife. Can you believe that? She's a real bitch, and an adulterous whore, but I still want to be with her. Am I crazy or what?"

"You are crazy and what, whatever you want to add to crazy." Jason paused. "Now, if Rev. Zackery were to hear you say that, his response would be, 'Praise the Lord, Dave! Forgiveness is exactly what the Lord requires'", Jason said trying to imitate Rev. Zackery.

"Forgiveness?" Dave asked. "Maybe I could forgive her, if I could just stop seeing her cheating on me with the insurance man."

"You've got a lot more forgiving to do than that. Didn't she accuse you of beating her? Didn't she have you put in jail? Didn't she have you put out of your house? Didn't she take all your money?"

"I know it's crazy," Dave said putting both hands on the back of his head. "But, you know what the craziest thing is? When I saw my wife and the insurance man having sex, it made me horny. I got excited, and now, I want her and me to have sex like they did."

"You need help. A psychiatrist won't do it, not a preacher, not even the pope himself. You need the Lord," Jason said laughing

"I know," Dave said shaking his head. "Maybe killing a few witches is just what I need to get me thinking straight again."

"Yeah, maybe so," Jason said as he realized how much the truth of that statement applied to him. "Either way, it's going down tonight. Let's try to get a little rest." They both reclined their seats and closed their eyes. A frown appeared on Jason's face as he opened his eyes. "Speaking of killing a few witches, we need to be prepared, just in case Pam has let her sister out of the crystal ball. I know you don't believe she is going to betray us, but we need to be ready for anything," Jason explained.

"Okay, just in case, what is your plan C?"

"I figure, if Pam is going to betray us, she would have to do it sometime before we set the fire. In fact, the best time to stop it would be" Jason stopped speaking for five seconds. "Now. And the best place for her to betray us would be right here. Here and now, would be the best time to either kill us or capture us."

They both sat up and began to look around. Jason open the car door and began to look around.

"Do you see anything?" Dave said anxiously.

"No. Let's find somewhere else to put our supplies, just in case."

"What about the car?"

"If nobody comes before the ceremony, we should be okay," Jason said calmly. "If they come before the ceremony, we'll know that we have been betrayed. If that happens, I'll use my dynamite on them, we'll make a run for Billy truck, and we'll push the cans of gasoline on the road going back to the highway and start a fire, so they can't follow us."

"Then what?" Dave said frowning.

"We leave. You go home, I go home, and we'll wait to see if they come for us, unless you have a better idea."

"I would rather die right here than to possibly endanger my family," Dave said angrily.

"Okay, what's your plan?"

"We move the supplies like you said. Down there," Dave said pointing toward some trees. Up there we will be able to see if anyone comes down here looking for us. We can take the car and hide it closer to the highway. That way if they come here and don't find a car or the gasoline, they will think we didn't come. Then we will go through with the plan."

"Sounds good to me," Jason said.

"One thing though," Dave said.

"If nobody comes, then we will assume that Pam is not going to betray us, okay?"

"All right," Jason said. "I'll give her the benefit of the doubt. Either way, the plan will go forward no matter what she does."

"If we die, so be it. I am not going to involve my family," Dave said emphatically.

"That's cool. Let's get started."

Chapter 30

Bubbles

(Tuesday evening 6:30 PM)

Pam sat on the bed wearing nothing but a long white fluffy cotton robe and house shoes. She was frowning. She was frustrated and anxious. "What is taking him so long." She stood up and looked at the bed she had prepared for them. The covers and sheets had been turned down neatly. She had even sprayed the sheets lightly with her cologne. She walked to the balcony door, looked out, and didn't see the limousine. "It shouldn't take this long," she huffed. Then she heard a knock at the door in rhythm, one two, one, one two three. She quickly walked to the door, without looking of out the peep hole, and without asking who it was, she opened the door angrily. "Where have you been?"

He stood in front of her smiling as handed her a bouquet of roses. "I had to make a couple of extra stops. I'm sorry it took me so long."

Her anger faded as she smelled the roses. She had never received roses from a man before. When she looked back up into his eyes she was smiling tenderly. "They're beautiful, thank you."

"Am I still you boyfriend?"

"Yes!" she said as her frown was transformed into a tender smile.

"Come with me. I want to show you something."

"I need to put on some clothes?"

"The limo is right here at the bottom of the steps," he said pulling her hand.

She grabbed the room key as she went out the door. When they got to the limo, he opened the door. She was shocked when she stepped in. There in the limo was an old fashion tub with feet. It was filled with bubbles and hot water.

"How did you do this?"

"You said you wanted this. I wanted you to have it, and it's big enough for two. We may only have this one evening. Let's make it the most wonderful evening that ever was, if you feel safe."

"The water is nice and hot," she said as she put her hand through the bubbles into the water. In seconds she had stepped out of her house shoes, had let her robe drop to the floor, and had slid down into the water. "What's taking you so long? Get in. I don't want to waste a minute of the time we have together."

She watched him undress, her eyes dancing delightfully all over his muscular body. Soon he was in the tub and she slid her back up against him. He wrapped his arms around her. She had never been so excited, never felt so adored, never been so happy. They stayed that way for at least fifteen minutes as the excitement and anticipation continued to build. Then when the moment was right, she raised up turned around facing him, and slowly sat on his legs. He pulled her hips close to him, and slowly slid his hands up her back. Then taking hold of her shoulders, he pulled her face toward his. She closed her eyes for a kiss, but instead she felt his cheek against hers. Then he whispered.

"I love you."

Chapter 31
What Do I Do

(Tuesday night 8:00 PM)

Rev. Zackery opened his eyes. There was a throbbing pain in his knees, a stiffness in his back, his neck was burning, and he had a headache. He tugged at the tape binding his hands as he looked around the room from the floor view. He saw the coffee table lying on its side, the bottom of the dresser, and other things that had been knocked to the floor. Several times, he attempted to stand up, but each time he failed. He needed the use of his hands which were taped tightly behind his back. The end of the tape that covered his mouth was hanging down from his left ear. He slid the side of his face against the floor until the sticky side of the tape began to adhere to the floor. Slowly he was able to peel the tape from his mouth.

"Thank you, Lord. I'm still alive. You made a way out of no way, again," he said in relief. He looked around the floor again. This time he noticed the fishbowl lying in front of the nightstand. It had a long crack in it. He rolled and squirmed until he had the bowl between his feet. He raised it and brought it down as hard as he could against the nightstand. It didn't break. He tried again and again. It didn't break. His stomach muscle became so tired, he was barely able to lift the bowl. When he was about to bring it down, it slipped from between his feet. It fell to the floor and broke into four big pieces. "I like little miracles, too Lord. Thank You." He rolled, lowering his legs away from the broken glass. Then, scooting back, he got a piece of glass and began cutting the tape on his hands. It was much harder to cut than he had expected.

"Lord, I know you didn't spare my life just for me to spend it all trying to cut this tape. I know you have a plan," he said aloud as he continued to cut the tape. "I know Lord, that you order my steps, so this must be your plan," he said as if he had just received this revelation. "You wanted to delay me, or maybe you don't want me to go at all. Which is it? You need to tell me." He waited for ten seconds. "Okay if I get out of this tape in the next five minutes, I'll take that to mean that I should go, but if it takes longer then I should not go."

Rev. Zackery looked at the clock on the nightstand. It was seventeen minutes after eight. He continued cutting as fast as he could, watching the clock as he cut. The clock reached eight twenty-two, he dropped the piece of glass and pulled as hard as he could. He heard a tearing sound, so he paused, took three deep breaths, and then gave it all he had. The tape did not break.

"Augh," he shouted. "My time is up, Lord. I gave it my best. I just about cut off the circulation to my hands. That really hurt," he said twisting his sore wrist and rubbing them together as much as possible in the tape. "Oh, that feels so much better, Lord. Okay, I won't go, but what do you want to do?"

As he continued to rub his wrist against each other, he felt his hand slide under the tape. He wristed a little more and it slid out. His hands were free. He got up and walked to the bed and got on his knees.

"Okay, Lord, I know that I said that I would not go if it took me more than five minutes to get free, but it was just a couple of extra minutes, and they really need me to stop them from making a terrible mistake. If I don't at least try to help them, I know I'll regret it for the rest of my life." Rev. Zackery stopped and looked up at the ceiling. "Okay, Lord, if You don't say 'no,' I'll take that to mean it's okay to go." Rev. Zackery waited again. Then he stood up, walked out of the room to the front door. He stopped. "Lord, I still don't know what to do when I get there." He opened the door and saw that his car was gone.

He walked back into his room, up to the bed, and got down on his knees again. "Lord, I bow before You, coming in the name of Jesus. I don't know what to do, I don't even know if I should do anything at all. All I know is, I want to serve You, and please you in all I do and say. I need your guidance. Speak to me. Tell me what I should do, how I should do it, and when I should do it. I love You, I need You, and I trust You. In Jesus name I pray. Amen."

Rev. Zackery got up, pushed the bed back in its place and sat down on it, avoiding the wet spot. He looked at the phone. Then, picking up the receiver, he dialed.

Chapter 32
The Unforeseen

(Tuesday night 9:10 PM)

Jason had picked a good position in the tree line. It was closer to the front of the barn. If anyone came down the back road looking for them at their old location, they would be able to see them when they passed by. They felt safer, now. Earlier, just after the sun began to set, four men with hooded black robes had come out and placed oil lamps on tall stands which had been hammered in the ground, two at the barn entrance and four in the parking area. Now, Jason and Dave could see the people when they went into the building, they could see the area where Billy's truck was hidden in the trees, and they could see the two security guards at the barn entrance and the four in the parking area. Everybody who entered the building was wearing a black hooded robe, everybody except the guards. They were wearing black fatigues with flax jackets. They were accessorized with semi-automatic rifles strapped over their shoulders, semi-automatic pistols on their sides, and on their heads were black baseball caps with the word security written in small yellow letters.

"We didn't plan for armed security guards," Dave said disappointedly.

"The demon said that everyone would be inside once the ceremony starts," Jason said.

"Suppose they don't go inside. What are we going to do then?" Dave asked.

"We improvise."

"Okay, tell me this. Did your invitation specify black robe attire," Dave said peering through the bushes.

"Yeah! Looks like I'll need a black robe to get inside," Jason said sadly.

"Maybe, it's a sign that we should abort the mission," Dave replied.

As they stood there wondering how Jason was going to get inside, a small bus drove up to the front entrance. Eight guards with rifles and sidearms exited first. They line up in two columns from the door of the bus to the door of the barn. The columns were about four feet apart and each guard was about four feet behind the other. Then on command, they all turned so that one column had its back to the other. The several persons in red hooded robes exited the bus. Once the last person dressed in red had entered the building, the guard all turned together and moved inside.

"That must have been the head council," Dave said.

"Yelp, I believe you are right," Jason said with a sinister smile. "It was very nice of them to make it easy for me to identify them."

"We still need to figure out how you are going to get inside the building," Dave said closing his eyes and rubbing his head as he thought of the futility of their quest. Before he could express his thoughts, two black sedans pulled through the parking area near the entrance of the barn. The first car parked. The second car stopped beside it in the driveway. Four men, armed with semi-automatic rifles, and pistols, and dressed in black military fatigues and flax jackets, got out of the second car. They immediately formed a ten-foot perimeter around the first car, each facing away from the car. They all raised the weapons and began scanning the grounds in front of them.

"Get down!" Jason warned, as he dropped to the ground. "I think they have night vision in their sights."

Dave got down and laid beside Jason watching the men closely. After about two minutes, one of the men made a hand signal toward the first car. The driver of that car rolled down his window.

"All clear," the man who had made signaled said loudly.

Immediately, all four doors of the first car opened. Four more persons got out. This group was dressed in black hooded robes. Their heads were covered. The four closed their doors. Then they all gathered around the one who had been in the back seat, passenger side, the side closest to Dave and Jason.

As Jason and Dave watched, that person uncover their head and began giving orders, loudly. To Jason's and Dave's surprise, it was a woman's voice. They could hear her clearly.

"Get back down there and make sure everything is ready for the ambush," the woman shouted pulling her hood back. "When that limousine comes, sometime around eleven forty-five, stop it. Don't let it get past you. I want them dead. Don't give them a chance to get out of the car. I want bullet holes in every square inch of that vehicle. Then I want you to set it on fire. Burn it up. Do you understand me?" She waited for an acknowledgement, but nobody said anything. "I don't want to hear any excuses, and I want proof. Bring me their burnt heads." She looked at the driver of the first car and said, "Pop the trunk."

The driver walked around the car, reached through the window, pulled the truck lever, and the trunk opened.

"You two, go with them", she said pointing at two of the other men in black robes. "Make sure everything goes as planned.

When the trunk opened, the two designated men, each took a semi-automatic rifle from the trunk. Then, propping their rifles against the car, they removed their robes and put them in the trunk. They were dressed exactly like the other guards, except they did not have caps. The woman pulled the hood over her head and started moving toward the barn entrance. The last man in a black robe, the driver, followed closely behind her. The men forming the perimeter all return to their car and the trunk popped open. The men who had removed the robes sat in the trunk as it headed slowly out of the parking area, their rifles bracing the trunk open.

"Did you hear what I just heard," Jason said in disbelief.

"Yeah. I'm pretty sure I heard her tell them to ambush a limousine."

"Yeah, but I'm not talking about that. I'm talking about that voice. I'd know that voice anywhere. That was Sibal!" Jason said.

"That woman didn't look anything like Sibal. Sibal is a lot older than that."

"Maybe she got plastic surgery. Maybe it's a mask. I don't know." Jason paused. "I do know this, that was Sibal's voice. She was in command, so it must be Sibal."

"That means Pam is going to be in that limousine. We've got to stop her before she gets ambushed," Dave said frantically.

"How are we going to get pass them? They'll catch us and then the plan will fail."

"What are we going to do, then."

"I'm going to get a couple of robes out of that trunk, then we are going to finish this ourselves," Jason said resolutely.

"What about Pam?"

"She left us. We didn't leave her. Anyway, she can take care of herself. We got to complete the plan." Jason was getting louder than he intended. He got quieter. "Look, we all knew what we were getting ourselves into when we started. We all knew that one of us, or even all of us might not make it through this alive. She's on her own, and so are we. Come on! Let's go. If we get those robes, we won't have to hide."

They ran carefully to the trunk of the car, ducking behind cars as they went.

"What now. How are we going to get in the trunk?" Dave said.

"You're saved, aren't you? Why don't you ask Jesus to help us?"

"You're serious, aren't you?" Dave asked.

"Yeah. Either you have faith, or you don't."

"Okay, close your eyes." Dave paused. "Lord, in the name of Jesus, we need your help. I don't know if you approve of what we're doing but please let us get in this trunk."

The sound of the trunk latch interrupted his prayer. The trunk opened and the truck light shone brightly. From the side where he was standing, Jason quickly pushed the truck down far enough to block most of the light. Then he quickly reached in and got two robes and closed the trunk. He gave one to Dave and put the other one on.

"What are you waiting for? Put it on."

"Wait a minute," Dave snapped. "Thank you, Jesus for opening that trunk."

To Dave's surprise, the trunk latch clicked again and the truck door spring up again. Dave looked as Jason removed his arm from the open window of the car, after pulling up the trunk release.

"You opened the trunk."

"Yeah, I saw they left the window down," Jason said smiling.

Dave looked up, "Thank you, Jesus, for leaving a window open and pouring out a couple of robes," Dave prayed.

"My mama would always say, 'you know the bible says, the Lord helps those who help themselves,'" Jason said in a woman's voice as he closed the trunk again.

"Well, there's something else the bible says," Dave said solemnly.

"What's that?"

"It says, 'Do unto others as you would have them do unto you.' I know Pam would not let anyone ambush me if she could stop it, so I am not going to wait here, knowing that those men are going to ambush Pam. I've got to warn her. I've got almost two hours to get past them and stop the limo. This is my plan. I'll circle around them, stop Pam, and bring her down the back road."

"Look," Jason said pulling Dave's arm and leaning his mouth near Dave's ear. "When the next crowd goes in, I'm going in with them. At the designated time, I'll be at the side door to get the locks and chains from you. If you are not there, I'm going to take my two sticks of dynamite and blow up that group in red and as many of those witches as I can before they kill me. I hope you'll be at the door. The lives of your family members and mine may be on the line."

"I'm sorry, I've got to help her," Dave replied.

"Okay. I wish you luck, partner," Jason said as he gave Dave a tight hug. "It's been awesome knowing you." The men separate. "I hope you make it. I hope you save Pam and then you both get back here in time to give me the chains."

"I can do that," Dave said. Dave saw a car coming down the road. "Hey, isn't that Rev. Zackery's car.

Jason turned around and to his dismay he saw Rev. Zackery's car pull up and park at the front of the entrance to the barn. "What is the world is he doing?"

"He's trying to stop us from murdering all these people," Dave said.

"How did he know about this place?"

"That demon, Billy, probably told him," Dave said

They watch as the driver of the car got out and walked toward the entrance. He did not have on a robe. The two security guards at the door rushed toward the man with their weapons aimed at him. They frisked him and zip tied his hand.

"That him all right. He's as good as dead, if we don't save him," Jason explained.

The other four guards from the parking area, came up and followed Rev. Zackery as the first two pulled him into the barn. Now there was nobody guarding the door or the parking lot. Another car pulled into the parking arear and parked. Four people in black robes got out and walked toward the door.

"I'm going in. I'll be at the door at ten minutes after midnight. When I get a chance, I'll knock twice. You knock back, three times, and then I'll open the door just enough to get the chains, okay?"

"Okay, I'll be there," Dave said. Jason turned and quickly followed the four people into the barn. Dave hurried down the road in the direction that the ambushers had taken. He stopped just long enough to push the robe, Jason had given him, under the back of a car parked on the road.

Chapter 33
One Last Time

(Tuesday night 10:00 PM)

Pam and Walt laid in the hotel bed looking up at the ceiling. They both were resting and attempting to regain their composure, but they couldn't. They were so happy.

"Today was your first time, ever?" he said, still looking at the ceiling.

"Yes, you are my first and only."

"You know what they say, don't you?" he asked.

"What do they say?" she said looking at him.

He turned and looked into her eyes. "They say that a woman will always love the first man that she makes love with."

"Really? Who are they?'

"They're the people in the know. They know everything." He smiled.

"I'm sure this was not your first time, making love."

"It wasn't my first time, having sex, but it was my first time ever, making love. I never imagined that loving someone could make such a difference. It was overwhelming and awesome the way you made me feel. It was better than anything that I have ever experienced. You are the greatest lover of all time."

"Really? Have you had many sexual partners?" she asked frowning.

"No. I've only had three. I've only had sex about ten or so times in my whole life, and I paid for at least six of those."

"Why is that? You're a fine, good-looking man, and you definitely know how to please a woman."

"My first time was with a prostitute in Viet Nam," he explained. "My company had come back from the field for some r and r. Some of my squad members decided to sneak out of the compound and go to 'Mamasan's, that was a Vietnamese whorehouse. The lady who owned and ran it, they called her Mamasan. When we got there, while the other guys were getting their freak on, I was drinking at one of the tables. Mamasan came up to me and asked me why I didn't want to have sex with any of her girls. I told her that I wasn't going to put my penis in something where any and everybody has been. She said she liked that about me. She said she had protection and if I would have sex only with her, she would teach me how to completely satisfy any woman. I thought that knowledge might come in handy one day, so I did it, six times.

"You paid prostitutes to teach you how to satisfy a woman."

"Yelp, but it was just one prostitute, Mamasan."

"I can't believe that they had condoms in a Vietnamese whorehouse?"

"She didn't have any condoms. She gave me a sandwich bag and a rubber band."

"You're kidding right?" she asked.

"It worked. She taught me everything I know."

"Well, you must have been a good student."

"I try to be the best at whatever I do." He paused. "I want to be the best lover you will ever have. I may only have this time with you. I want you to remember me and how wonderful we were together, how wonderful we are together."

"I will never forget you. I will never forget our bath together, or our time in bed together, or the way you hold me, and look at me. You make me feel so special, so amazing, so loved." She moved her lips up to his and she kissed him tenderly and then smiled. "I love you."

"I love you, too," he said. He raised his arm and looked at his watch. "It's getting late. We'd better start getting ready."

"What would you say if I said that I had changed my mind, and that I just wanted to leave this place, right now, and never come back."

"Are you talking about leaving with me or without me?" he asked.

"With you! You are the only reason I'd ever consider just leaving," she said emphatically. "If I don't go to the ceremony, my friends will definitely be killed. If I do go, you will more than likely be killed."

"If you said that you wanted us to leave, I'd say, let's go. I would love to go anywhere with you," he said. "I would love for us to be like normal people, to get married, and have babies. I would love it. However, I believe you would be haunted with regret about your friends being killed. Plus, Sibal will never stop searching for us. It may take years, but she wouldn't stop. She would have someone kill us and our children if we had any. I don't want that. We need to end this now, no matter what happens."

"I don't want to lose you. I want a life. I want to be happy."

"So, do I," he said. "Whatever you decide, I'm with you. If you decide to leave, I'll leave. If you decide to fight, I'll fight, but you can't have any doubts. You say I may die, but the truth is we all may die." He paused. "There's one thing I do know, and that is this, if they hurt or kill you, I will die, killing as many of them as I can." He paused again. "So, what's it gonna be?"

"They killed my auntie, burned her up alive. They are not going to kill our children. We are going to fight." That angry look appeared on her face again. "Let's get ready." She started to roll away from him, but he caught her with his arm. She stopped and looked at him frowning.

"Before we get ready, can we make love one more time, please?" he asked.

Her frown turned into a bright smile. "Just as long as you get me psyched up to fight again after we're done."

"No problem, I got a speech already ready," he said as he rolled over on top of her. They looked lovingly into each other's eyes with excited expectation.

Chapter 34
Caught in the Act

(Tuesday night 10:30PM)

Dave could see the flashlights on both sides of the street as the men set up for the ambush. It had taken him longer than expected to reach their location. Now, he had no idea how he was going to get pass them to warn Pam. "Lord have mercy," he whispered aloud as he saw how wide an area the lights covered.

"Hey!" one of guards shouted, loudly. "I want everybody down here, right now. Let's go over the plan one last time."

Immediately, the light began to move. All the men from both sides of the road went down toward the freshly graveled road. Suddenly to his surprise, Dave had an easy opportunity to get pass them. He quickly moved beyond the ambush location where all the lights had gathered. The light of the full moon provided enough light for Dave to see cans of gasoline near the road. He found a spot behind a big tree where he could listen to their plan. Without any warning, he felt a very strong urge to pee. He wanted to wait but he felt that he would pee in his pants if he didn't do it right away. He zipped down his pants and almost before he was ready, a heavy stream began to flow down the base of the tree, as he listened.

"Listen carefully, I don't want any mistakes. We cannot allow that limousine to get through. Leo is at the gate. He has it closed now, so we can get everything in place. He will open it when I give him the word. When the limo goes through the gate, he will notify me, close the gate, and follow the limo in his car. At that time, Lee, Trevon, Mitch, and Alvin we will block the road here with that log and then get back in position. When the limo driver sees the log, they will know it's an ambush and will try to back up. By that time, it will be too late because Leo will have already blocked the road behind them with his car. I don't want them to leave this spot. At my command, the flares will be fired. When we see the flares go up, we will open fire. Lee, you target the gas tank. I want the tires to go out with your first shots. Lee and Mitch, take out the tires on the left side. Trevon and Alvin, take out the tires on the right. I will take out the driver with my first shot. After that I want that limo cut into pieces. Don't stop shooting until you hear my command to cease fire. Then when I say, 'burn it', Atkins and Bird, throw those cans of gasoline on both side of the limo. If it's not already burning by then, Rico will fire a flare into the gasoline. And, we will let it burn." He paused. "Rico!" How many flares do you have?" Cap said looking around. There was no answer. "Rico, front and center." There was no movement.

Dave was listening intently, wondering what was happening, as his stream became a trickle.

"I'm here. We have an intruder," Rico shouted loudly from behind Dave. "Put your pecker in your pants, get down on your knees, and lace your fingers behind your head," he said calmly to Dave.

"Wait a minute, mister," Dave said in his best hillbilly accent. "Let me finish up here. I'm bout done. Ah, what do you want me to do with my fingers?"

"Show your location," Cap shouted from the road.

Rico turned his flashlight on and waved it toward them.

"Stay where you are. I'll come to you," Cap shouted. Then turning to the other men, he said, "Get in your positions, no lights, no loud noises. Turn you radios to channel nine, but don't use them unless it's absolutely, necessary. I'll check this out."

Dave zipped up his pants and slowly turned his head toward the voice.

"Don't turn around. If you want to breathe another breath, get down on your knees and put, your hands behind your head," the voice said angrily this time.

"Yes sir, I'll do what you want me to do. Just don't shoot me. What did I do?"

"Stop talking. Don't speak until you're spoken to, not another word."

Dave stopped the words he was about to speak and rested on his ankles. A minute later Cap was there behind him.

"Who is he and what is he doing here?" Cap asked.

"I saw him coming through the woods with my night scope. He came up here and he stopped by that tree. He was peeing and he seemed to be listening to you. You want me to do him, right here, now," Rico replied.

"What's your name?" Cap whispered in Dave's ear.

"My name is Ty, Tyron Summers, sir," Dave said.

"Well Ty, I want you to take off your sweatshirt and hand it back to me."

"Yes sir, but why do you," Dave stopped talking when he felt the end of a rifle barrel hit his back.

"Do it," Rico said.

Dave quickly removed his shirt and handed I back to the men behind him without looking.

"Tie his hands and cover his head with his shirt," Cap said.

"Mister, I didn't do nothing," Dave said as his hands were zip-tied behind his back.

"What are you doing here, Ty?" Cap asked.

"My daddy said he had a meeting at the big barn. He had put on this fancy red robe. I just wanted to see what he was doing, so, I followed him."

"Red robe? Well, Ty, I'm going to need to keep you here for a while, until we finish some business. You will need to be very quiet. After this is over, I will check out your story. If it checks out, then we'll let you go. On the other hand, if you make any noise, you will be killed. Okay?" Cap said convincingly.

"Yes, sir," Dave said as his sweatshirt was push over his head and tied around his neck with its arms. Then his legs were zip tied and his pockets were searched. He was glad Jason had told him to leave all his ID at the house. He laid there knowing that he had blown the whole mission. Jason would not get the chains and without him the fire would never be set and because of him, Jason, Pam, Rev. Zackery and he would all die. He was totally dejected as he lay there in the cold darkness.

"Leo, come in," Cap said in his radio.

"Yes sir, go ahead," was the radio's response.

"Open the gate and lets the vehicles through."

"That's good news. There's a line going down the highway."

"Leo, make sure you close the gate after the limousine goes pass. Then you are to follow it and block it in at the ambush point. We're going to open fire as soon as the limo stops so you need to get out of the car as quickly as possible. We're not going to wait, so, get out of there." Cap waited for a response, but he didn't get one. "Do you copy," Cap said finally.

"Yes sir. Copy that. Out."

"Leave him there. Walk with me. I want to talk to you for a minute about our little friend," Cap said to Rico.

Dave could hear their voices fade as they walked further away. He took this opportunity to pray.

"Lord," he whispered. "I know I just asked you to help me get pass these men, and you did, but then I decided to wait around to hear their plan, and I got caught. I blew it Lord. Now, I have made matters that much worse. I don't know what to do. I don't even know if anything can be done. Maybe this is your way of telling me that you don't want us to murder all those people. Okay, I already knew you didn't want us to murder them. I was just trying to protect my family. You know, they will keep coming after us until they kill us," Dave was getting louder than he had intended. He lowered his voice and continued. "I guess I don't have to worry about them coming after us now. They are going to kill all of us tonight. That is unless you do some about it. Lord, You are the only one that can save us."

"Hey, who are you talking to," Rico said. "Do you have a radio or a cell phone. I know I searched you, very well."

"Hey, Rico," Dave said in his natural voice. "Did Cap leave?"

"So, the voice was fake," Rico surmised. "What else is fake about you? Is your name Tyrone, or is that fake, too."

"Listen! All you need to know is that I work for Sibal," Dave commanded. "She sent me to make sure that you stopped Pam from getting to the ceremony. I couldn't say anything while Cap was here, because he is suspected of serious crimes against the coven."

"Who is Pam, and what crimes did Cap commit?" Rico asked.

"Uncover my head!" Dave ordered and waited.

Ten seconds later Dave felt the sweatshirt being pulled from his head.

"Now, tell me who you are and what's going on."

"Like I said I work in Sibal's office, I helped plan this ambush," Dave said. "You asked about Pam. Pam is a powerful witch, who is coming here tonight to take over our coven. We need to stop her. That's why Sibal sent me. She wants a full report of what happens here. If Pam gets to the ceremony, then Sibal and the head council will be in danger. Pam plans to eliminate all of them and then take over."

"Why can't I tell Cap about this."

"You heard the orders Sibal gave your group. That's all Cap needs to know," Dave said. "I was sent by Sibal to report what happens here tonight. If you interfere with me in any way, you will answer to her."

"Okay, I won't interfere with your ability to see what happens, sir. I will allow you to witness what happens. I won't cover your head and when it starts, I'll untie your legs, but I won't untie your hands until it's all over. Then, after you verify that the ambush was a success, I will have to tie your legs and cover your head again, so Cap won't know what I did." Rico paused. "If that's not acceptable, I'll just cover your head back now, and you'll have to explain to Miss Sibal why you failed to do what you were supposed to do."

"That's fine. However, if something goes wrong and this witch, Pam, get away, you need to untie me so I can get back and warn Sibal and the head council," Dave explained.

"Okay, sir. I can do that, but I need for you to sit down, and I need to cover your head again, just in case Cap comes back."

Chapter 35
Keep a Low Profile

(Tuesday night 11:15 PM)

Back at the barn, Jason was walking around trying not to draw any attention to himself. When he had come inside, the guards who had apprehended Rev. Zackery, had taken him to front of the platform where a group of men in red hooded robes were standing. Those men had taken him behind a red curtain on the right side of the platform. Although fearful of what could be happening to Rev. Zackery, Jason couldn't help but marvel at how the barn had been transform into place of mysterious beauty and elegance.

From the back of the building to the front of the building, each wall was draped with white linen that was topped with red linen. From the base of each roof support beam, the white linen swooped down to the floor. The red linen, which was on top of the white, only swooped down halfway to the floor. Also, there was linen hanging from the ceiling midway between each support beam. The colors alternated from red to white. They were draped from the high center of the ceiling, down to the top of the walls on both sides. All the seats on the floor were covered with red linen seat covers, while the much taller seats on the platform were covered with white velvet seat covers. The floor of the platform was cover with red carpet and the walls on both sides were covered with red drapes. Finally, there were two very tall black satin curtains at the back of the platform that hung from the ceiling. There was a large gold ring that held the two curtains together about halfway down. There were four more large gold rings attached to the curtains about three fourths of the way down on each side of the curtains. There were ropes for opening the curtains going around each curtain and through both rings on each side. The ropes then went down to the hands of two men in white hooded robes, who seem ready to pull the ropes as soon as the signal was given.

Jason got a glass of wine, from the wine bar at the back near the entrance. Everyone else was drinking it. Jason pretended to drink it. He knew this was no ordinary wine. He could see the changes in the demeanor the everyone drinking it. He attempted to copy their movements and facial expressions, especially, when someone tried to engage him in conversation. He made his way down the aisle next to the wall, looking for the side door where he hoped Dave was going to be later. He couldn't see it. The drapes completely covered the side doors on both sides. He began to push against the drapes until he found it. He cunningly poured a little wine on the bottom of the white drape in front of the door. He then moved to the other wall and marked his escape door.

More and more people were coming in, and the building was filling up fast. Jason quickly went back to the other side and sat next to the door where his wine mark was. Soon, all the seats in front of him were filled and most of the seats five rows behind him on both sides were taken as well, however, the seat next to him was still empty. Jason began to worry that he had given himself away. He began to feel like everyone was looking at him. It wasn't long before he heard someone yell out.

"Last call, for alcohol, before the ceremony begins," one of the men serving wine said loudly. Many people already seated, including the couple in front of him, rushed back to get another drink. Jason felt a sigh of relief. Now, he no longer felt that everyone was watching him. He convinced himself that nobody had been paying him any attention and that he was just being paranoid. He sat there calming himself down when the two people who had been in front of him came back to their seats. Something was different. They had on black hooded robes, but it was not the same couple. The man before was at least a foot taller than the woman. This couple were about the same height. Jason wanted to tell them that someone had been sitting in those seats, however he just sat there with his head bowed. However, seconds later he regretted it, because the other couple had returned and was standing next to him. Each of them had plastic cups of wine in both hands. Jason could see their shoes and the bottom of their robes.

"Hey buddy, you're in our seats," the tall man said sternly.

Jason slowly raised his head. "No sir, those people are in your seat," Jason said calmly, pointing to the couple sitting in front of him. "I was already here when you sat down the first time, before you went to get wine."

Before the tall man could respond, the woman in front of Jason turned and looked at the tall man and disputed Jason. "That's not true, we were already here when he sat down," the short woman snapped. The man sitting next to her said nothing.

"You need to get up, man. You're in my seat. We were sitting here," he said louder this time. The man quickly drank both cups of wine he had been holding and then he dropped the cups at Jason's feet. Then he grabbed Jason's arm with his left hand and pulled back a balled fist with his right. Jason allowed the man to pull him up and toward the side aisle as the couple in front of them watched. Without warning, Jason pulled back and ducked down, facing the tall man. Jason's face was level with and in front of the face of the woman sitting in front of him; the one who had lied. Jason waited for the tall man to drive his fist forward, then Jason ducted down to the floor turned and squirmed pass four the people now standing in his row. Then he looked back to see if the tall man was following him. He wasn't. The tall man had missed Jason and hit the woman in her mouth. Her lip was bleeding. When she rubbed her lip and saw blood on her hand, she went crazy. She charged the man. Her claw-like hands shot out of the sleeves of her robe as she went for his face. He blocked her hands by raising his robe sleeve in front of his face, however this kept him from seeing her kick that hit him in his groins. Before he could retaliate, two men, one from the front and one from the back came running down the aisle. They dropped their robes to the floor as they approached, revealing police riot attire, complete with flack-jackets and batons.

Jason was expecting them to swing the batons, instead they pressed them into the backs of the fighters causing each to fall immediately to the ground in convulsions. That's when Jason realized the guards had cattle prods. The guards continued to press the cattle prods against each of them for several seconds after they were on the ground causing the convulsion to continue. When the guards knew that there would be no more resistance, they pulled back the prods. When the convulsions stopped, the officers zipped-tied each of their hands behind their backs. Then, the two peace breakers were escorted to the right side of the platform behind the red curtain where they had taken Rev. Zackery. After they had disappeared behind the side curtains, Jason made his way back to his seat. The lady who came with the tall man stood beside Jason for a moment. Then she turned to find a seat in the back. The man who had sat in the tall man's seat, just looked straight ahead, drinking his wine, trying not to draw any more attention to himself. Jason did the same.

Chapter 36
Spotted

(Tuesday night 11:25 PM)

Pam drove down the freshly graveled road. There were two cars in front of her and one behind her. She watched the area carefully as she drove through the woods. It was dark and she saw nothing peculiar. "Maybe, she is not going to try to stop me. Maybe, she's going to cooperate, now," Pam said to herself. A few minutes later, she pulled into the parking area and stopped. She allowed the car behind her to pass. Then she turned around in the road and parked on the bank of the road just beyond the parking area. She turned off her lights, lowered her window, and dialed her phone.

"Hey," the voice whispered.

"I'm in the parking area, but I'll be going in with the next group of people. Three cars came in when I did."

"Did you see anything on the road that looked suspicious," he asked.

"No. Everything looked clear. Maybe she has learned not to mess with me."

"Not likely. She's going to do something, so don't turn your back. I'll wait here on the highway until eleven forty-five, then I'll come," he said.

"When you get to the barn, Sibal is supposed to have some guards to escort me in. When they come to the car tell them that I am already inside, then turn the limo around, move it away from the door, and then find a good firing position outside the barn in case I need you when I come out," she said smiling. "Looks like we just might get through this, baby"

"Together, there is nothing we can't do, baby," he said with extra affection on the baby. "You know, I could protect you better if I were inside."

"Just trust me, baby. Stay outside. You do not want to be in the building when the stuff hits the fan. Find yourself a tree that you can shoot from, you're good at that."

"You make one mistake, and people will never let you live it down," he replied. "I love you."

"I got to go, babe. I love you, back. Be careful." She hung up and hurried to the barn entrance so she could mix in with the large group going in.

As the group she merged with passed through the door, they were separated into two lines about five feet apart. Two persons in blue security uniforms, one on each side were using handheld metal detecting wards to scan the people in each line. When Pam approached the man scanning her line, she pushed the thought, 'turn off the scanner.' She stopped five feet from him. He waved for her to come forward. She didn't move until she saw his finger push the on/off button. He scanned her and as soon as he motioned her to go forward, she walked toward the right side and down the aisle next to the wall. She figured Jason would be somewhere close to the side door on the other side. She wanted to locate him without him seeing her. She brushed against the drapes along the wall till she hit the side door push bar, then she looked straight down the aisle toward the other side of the building where the other side doors would be. Most of the people were talking among themselves, but there was one, who was sitting very still and straight in his seat. She walked down further to the front to see if she could see his face clearer. She was almost at the first row, when the side curtains were suddenly pushed open and held apart as a woman in a red hooded robe came out. She was followed by six tall, armed, physically fix men in security attire. They turned and walked toward the center aisle. Once there, they walked toward the entrance. They got the attention of everybody, including the man who Pam had been trying to see. Now, as he watched the security team go down the aisle, Pam could see his darker skin. It was Jason.

Now, Pam turned her attention to the woman in the red robe. There was something familiar about her. It was her frown and her eyes. Pam knew them, especially the eyes. "Sibal," she said aloud. Even though Sibal was halfway down the aisle, she stopped and looked in Pam's direction. When Sibal looked so did Jason. He knew it was Pam. Pam quickly turned her body away from Sibal. Sibal waited and then continued toward the entrance. Pam turned and moved down the side aisle, toward the entrance where Sibal and her guards were. Jason also got up and moved toward the back. Two persons with white hooded robes, carrying long handled torches, began lighting the eight very long torches on the platform. Pam stopped and looked back, as everyone got quiet and focused their attention ahead. When the torches had been lit, the two men in white robes walked to the black curtain at the back of the platform and parted them, allowing a procession of persons, robed in red to inter. They filed to their white velvet covered seats. These persons were the members of the head council. Anger began to fill Pam's head, as she thought about how this group chased her mother off a rooftop.

Pam continued walking. When Pam reached the last row of seats, she sat down and listened. Jason, who was watching her, sat down on the other side. The voice of the woman in the red robe was unmistakable. Pam frowned as she realized that Sibal had a new face.

"In about fifteen minutes a black limousine may be coming," Sibal said looking at one of her guards. "I have a team out there to stop it, however, I'm not going to take any chances. Get a rifle with a silencer and get up there in the loft. When we go out to meet it, if it comes, I will go up to the limo and open the door. Then I'll step back. When the person in the limo gets out, put a bullet in her head. Don't miss!"

"Yes ma'am," the guard said and then immediately left.

"You," Sibal said to another guard. "Go outside and radio Cap. Tell him to let me know when the limo comes through the gate. Tell him, I said to leave all radios on after that. I want to hear everything that happens." Sibal commanded. The guard waiting for further orders, did not move. "Go!"

"Yes ma'am," he replied and then he left, hurriedly.

Pam took her phone out of her pocket and saw 'no service available.' Tears began to flow down Pam's face as she thought about her worse fear about to be realized. Neither her tears or her sorrowful expression lasted very long, because when she looked up and saw Sibal with her new face, her tears dried up, and her sorrow turned to rage.

"You witch, bitch. I know I said I was going kill you in front of everybody. I don't care about that, anymore. I'm killing you, now." she whispered to herself. "But, before I do, I'm going to rip off that new face clean off your head." Pam reached down and pulled the pistol from her ankle holster and move back behind Sibal. When she was in position and was about to come up to Sibal, she saw a familiar face.

It was Rev. Zackery. He had just come from behind the curtains on the left side of the platform. He was standing with two security guards. Pam could see him pointing toward where she had seen Jason sitting. Then he pointed to the other side of the building where the side door was. Then, he made a circular motion with his finger and finally waved his hand across the front of his body from his right to his left.

Pam moved back in the corner. "He told them about our plan," She said. "Why would he do that? Why is he even here?"

"You need to go to your seat, ma'am," the guard said as he blocked her path to Sibal.

"Okay, where is the Ladies Room?"

"Over there under that big sign that says restrooms," the guard said frowning.

Pam walked behind a curtain on the side that said 'Ladies." Behind it, there were four port-a-potties. When she opened the door, a battery powered motion sensor light came on. She closed the door and went back to the curtain and peeped out, waiting for her opportunity.

Jason, who had not seen Rev. Zackery come out, made his way back to his seat.

CHAPTER 37
THE AMBUSH

(Tuesday night 11:30 PM)

Dave sat on the ground with his back against the tree he had earlier marked with his scent. His sweatshirt covering his head. Then he heard a voice coming through a radio.

"Rico, come in."

"Yes, sir," Rico replied.

"Take the gasoline down to the road, fill the buckets, and then get back to your location and be ready with the flare gun. It's almost time. Over."

"Right away, Cap. Over and out," Rico said.

Dave could hear the gas cans hit together as Rico picked them up and started down the hill to the road. Remembering that there was a bush next to the tree, Dave leaned over and touched a limb of the bush with his face. He found a limb with his mouth and bit into it. Turning his head, he partially broke it. With his teeth he pushed his sweatshirt through the pointed end of the broken limb. Then he gradually worked his head out of the sweatshirt. He looked up.

"Lord, please help me. If I can't help Pam, at least let me help Jason and Rev. Zackery," Dave prayed softly. He tried to pull his hand out of the ties several times until he felt pain in his wrists. "I guess you're saying, 'How can I come to You and ask for anything, when I'm planning on killing all those people. I know you don't condone what we are planning. I know you don't want us to murder all those people, cause we don't know what they have done." Dave paused. "Lord, if you just let me get back there, I will stop the plan. I won't give Jason the chains. I won't block the doors. Lord, if you let me get back to the barn, I'll set the fire on the outside and when they see that the building is on fire, everybody will run out. Nobody will die. They will all get out alive. Then me and Jason will be able somehow to free Rev. Zackery and the virgin. How about that Lord? Is that something that You can bless?" Dave said looking up through the trees.

"The limousine is coming through the gate now, Cap," the voice in the distant radio said. Rico was coming back.

"Lock the gate after it goes through. Then, follow it and block it in. Get out of car immediately. We are not going to wait on you." There was a short silence. "Miss Sibal!" Cap said.

"Miss Sibal in inside," a voice said.

"Well, it's starting," Cap said disgustedly.

"I'll let her know. She said to keep the radios on this channel."

"Right"

"Okay, Cap. I'm locking the gate now," Dave heard different voice say.

With a flare gun in both hands, Rico walked over to Dave. "I see your uncovered you head."

"It's starting. I need to see. You said you were going to untie my legs so I can see," Dave pleaded.

"All right! But you can't go any closer than you are right now." Rico cut the plastic ties on Dave's legs and then he pulled Dave to his feet.

Dave could see the bright lights of a black limousine passing through the trees below them. Another car was closing in on the limo fast. The limo slowed and stopped ten feet from the large log blocking the road. The car behind the limo came up and blocked the road ten feet behind it. The driver jumped out of the car and ran into the woods.

"Open fire," was sounded on the radio.

Immediately, Rico fired a flare into the air above the car and the sound of gunfire began. The tires exploded first, then the sound of the impact of bullets hitting the limo's glass and body rang out. The gunfire lasted at least five minutes.

"Hold your fire," Cap's voice rang out. The shooting ceased. Rico shot another flare. "It's bulletproof. I want everybody to change your ammo. Use the amour piercing rounds and target the glass. Fire!"

For five minutes, the bullets rained down on the windshield and the side windows of the limo. Little by little, holes began to appear in the glass. Then after a minute, half of the windshield fell in.

"Hold your fire." The shooting ceased again. "Move our car back and douse the limo with the gas."

The driver of the second car got in and backed the car a hundred feet and shined his bright lights on the limo. Two other men came up from behind the limo with buckets of gasoline. Each threw gasoline on it and disappeared back into the woods.

"Rico. Lite it," Cap's voice shouted.

Rico fired a flare directly at the limo. It became completely engulfed in flames. Tears began to fill Dave's eyes. He lowered his head so that the tears would fall from his eyes straight down to the ground.

"Tyrone," Cap said loudly. "You are free to go and make your report. Over and out."

"You told him?" Dave asked Rico.

"I take my orders from Cap, not Miss Sibal," Rico answered. Rico cut the plastic cuffs from Dave's hands and Dave left quickly without saying a word.

The fire became more and more intense. The burning tires began to squeal, as they warned that an explosion was about to occur. They didn't lie. The sound of the exploding gas tank could be heard clearly, even at the big barn. Everyone there reacted to the sound for two seconds and then went back to their conversations. Outside the barn, Sibal and her guards could see the light of the fire. Dave, who had been running, stopped, and dropped to one knee, when he heard it. He put his face in his hand, sighed for a moment, got himself together, and then started running again. When Pam heard the explosion, she closed her eyes and became stoic. The ceremony was about to start. She sat on the last row waiting for Sibal to come back in.

"Miss Sibal, are you there?" Cap called out as he watched the limo burn.

"Yeah, is she dead?" Sibal snapped.

"We stopped the limo. We have done as you requested, ma'am," Cap said calmly to conceal his disdain. "It's burning as we speak."

"Well then, if they're dead, I want their heads. When you bring me their heads, that's when you will have done what I requested. Over and out."

"All right, you heard her," Cap said angrily into the radio. "Put out the fire. The woman wants their heads. Put it out!"

The ambush team surrounded the car with CO2 fire extinguishers. They sprayed the car until almost all signs of fire were gone.

"Okay, get that back door open," Cap ordered. "There should be two bodies."

Four men took hold of the door, not knowing that a flack-jacket covered head was emerging from the water in tub inside the limo. Walt unwrapped the plastic from the stick of dynamite he had gotten from Pam. He blew the wet top of his cigarette lighter and then clicked it until it lit. He saw a large hole in the top of the limo where the sunroof had been. He lit the dynamite fuse two inches from the dynamite and threw it through the hole in the direction of the men. Then he ducked back down in the tub of water. As they pulled the door open, most of the men didn't see the lighted dynamite when it flew over their head and hit the ground behind them. Cap did, but he didn't realize what it was until it was too late. The explosion blew all the men and the limo off the road into the woods. The limo flipped over on its side, dumping Walt, his favorite rifle, and the water from the tub. Walt slowly emerged from a cloud of steam, that had formed inside the limo when the water hit the hot metal. His helmeted head rose up and back down quickly into the steamy mist just above the opened door. He came up again to eye level and turned slowly, first looking one hundred and eighty degrees back to his left and then three hundred and sixty degrees to the right. The road had been blown clean. There was only one thing to be concerned about. That thing was the car, a hundred feet down the road with its lights shining directly at him. At first, Walt didn't see anyone. However, when the man standing near the front of the car, saw Walt's head, he scrambled to get back to the car door.

Walt pulled his rifle out of the door window and took aim just above the steering wheel where he expected the man's head to be when he shot. He knew that he may have a chance for only one clear shot. He had to make it count. He watched as the door opened and the inside light came on. The man quickly got in and slammed the door shut. The light went out as Walt pulled the trigger. He cocked and fired five more times. The last two shot knocked out the headlights. Walt waited for his eyes to adjust. He didn't see any movement. Walt climbed out of the window, jumped to the ground, and began walking toward the car, his rifle aimed at the windshield. Then he stopped, realizing that he needed to get to Pam, he turned and ran down the road toward the big barn. When he jumped over the log that had been used to block the road, saw the rope the had been used to pull it across the road. Thinking it might be needed to climb a tree, he untied it, wrapped it around his shoulder, and started running again.

CHAPTER 38
THE CEREMONY

(Tuesday 12:00 midnight)

Four men, spaced apart equally, came to the front of the platform. They all carried identical ram horns. In synchronized motions, they raised the horns and brew a disharmonic cord that brought the audience to their feet, cheering. The cheers turned to jumping and arm waving. When the sound of the horns stopped, everyone began to chant in a language that sounded to Jason like Latin. As the chanting continued the crowd began to go into a trace. The chant turned into mourning, waling, and screaming. Jason, unsuccessfully, tried to imitate the people beside him. However, since no one was paying him any attention, he moved closer to the side door. He hit it twice and tried to listen for Dave's knock. He knew it would be impossible for him to hear anybody knocking, so he felt through the curtain for the bar of the door and pushed the side door open, slightly. Then he pushed some of the curtain out of the door, causing it to stay ajar. Now, when Dave came, he could just slide the chains through the door to Jason, Jason hoped. The horns sounded again, and everyone stopped. There was complete silence in the room. One of the men robed in red stood and walked to the podium. He spoke into the microphone. "We have come to celebrate the conception of our new queen, Queen Dora."

"Dora! Dora! Dora!", the audience chanted.

The man at the podium silenced the audience by holding up his hands. "Bring on the virgin receptacle," he said turning as he pointed to the back of the platform. The horns were sounded again. This time it was a series of disharmonic cords. The black curtains were split apart as a large, wooden table was rolled out to the middle of the platform. It stopped directly between the two elevated sections where the head council members were seated. On the table was a mattress, covered by a white satin sheet. The horns sounded again, and the black curtain split again as four very slender men appeared, carrying a woman high above their heads. The men were covered from head to toe by black skin-tight elastic. The woman they were carrying wore a white sheer spaghetti strap gown that fanned down at the bottom. The men carried her petit body as high over their heads as possible. The two in front, walked together, each holding her up with one hand on one of her thighs and the other holding one of her ankles, which they held slightly apart. The two behind, each held her up with one hand under one of her shoulders and the other hand holding one of her wrists out away from her body. As they moved slowly past the table toward the front of the podium, the gown flowed straight down between the front two men. The woman's head lay back motionless as her long black hair flowed straight down toward the floor.

When the men arrived at the front of the platform, they spun her around and around, faster and faster, then slower and slower until they stopped. The two men in front lowered her feet together as they went to one knee. The men behind pushed her shoulder's forward. As they did the men lowered her arms. Suddenly her head began to fall forward. However, because the two men behind were holding her hair, her head remained straight up. The light from the spotlight zoomed in on her face. Her mouth and her eyes slowly opening, revealing her drugged state of semi-consciousness.

The men in the front lifted her legs again, this time to shoulder level. Then they slowly spread her legs apart. The gown fanned out further and further until her legs were perpendicular to her body. The men then turned and walked to the back of the table. For a moment neither the men nor the girl could be seen. Then, slowly the men began to rise from behind the table. This time they were not holding her above their heads. The two men holding her wrists were followed by the other two holding her ankles. As they marched forward up the ramp onto the table, the girl's body, being pulled in four directions, hung limp between them below their waist. When they were in position, they gently lowered the girl's body onto the body shaped pillow on the mattress. It became clear that this was not a regular pillow because as she lay on it, her hips and legs were higher than the rest of her body. The pillow slanted down from her hips to her shoulders so much that the audience could see her clearly from her hips to her head. The pillow was slanted down again at her neck, so that her face could be seen clearly as well. The two men in the front carefully arranged her hair so that it spread out in a circle around her face. The two men in the back carefully adjusted her legs which were spread apart just as the pillow legs were spread apart. When the men had positioned her body just right for viewing, they left. The spotlight tightened its circle from covering the entire table down to covering just the girls face. Then it moved down the center of the platform to the podium. Once the light stopped, the announcer in the red robe walked into the light. He was just about to speak when the spotlight left the podium and went to the side wall where Jason was. Everyone turned their attention to Jason.

Guards from three sides closed in on Jason, one from the front, one from the back, and one from the center aisle. Jason quickly ducked under the drape, pushed the bar to the side door, and was gone. The two guards that had gone down the side aisle, raised the drapes against the wall, exposing the open side door. They all went out the doors after him. The first one went straight, the next one went to the right, and the last one went to the left. The curtain fell back into place and the door slammed shut behind them. The people began murmuring as they watched the spotlight which remained mysteriously on the curtain where Jason and the guards had disappeared.

Sibal, standing near the entrance, turned to her personal security team, pointing. "You, and you, go left. You two go right. Find him and bring him to me," Sibal yelled.

Immediately, the four guards ran out the door. This left Sibal with only two guards.

"Um, um" the man at the podium said clearing his throat. The spotlight returned to him. "I don't know what that was about, however, let's get back to the ceremony. I'm very happy to welcome everyone here tonight. We haven't had a crowd this big since the last baby sacrifice. How many of you were here for that?"

There was applause and shouts from the audience.

"Yeah, that's right, three mothers sacrificed their babies to the dark lord, Lucifer. That night, we drank their blood in the wine. It was magical," he said smiling. "We had a little blood left, so as a special treat for the ones who got here early, we mixed it with the first batch of wine we served you tonight."

The people began to cheer. At that moment, all the guards who had gone out looking for Jason came through the entrance door.

"What happened?" Sibal said softly. "Where is he?"

"He got away. He must have made it to the woods, so we came back," the lead guard said. "Do you want us to go back out there?"

"No! Forget about him," Sibal said. "If he knows what's good for him, he'll keep running. Go to your posts." As all but two of the guards began to leave, Sibal caught one by the arm. "Have you heard anything from Cap? I haven't gotten my heads yet."

"No ma'am, I haven't seen anybody, or heard anything since they set the car on fire."

"Go and find out why I don't have my heads," Sibal said, her words ringing out throughout the building. She looked back and noticed that everyone in the building was quiet, and many of them were looking back in her direction, including the person at the podium.

"Now, if I can have everybody's attention," the speaker said and waited to see if Sibal was going to stop talking. She said nothing. She pointed to the door and the guard left. When the door closed the speaker continued.

"It is now time to call into the darkness, and ask our master, Lucifer, to inhabit the seed of our donor." The announcer turned toward the black curtain and shouted, "Let the seed donor come forward."

While the audience cheered, as they watched the spotlight move from the announcer straight back, passed the girl on the table until it stopped above her on the black curtain, something else happened that no one noticed. Near the entrance, someone crawled from behind the drapes on the wall. It was Jason. He quickly sat in an empty seat on the last row.

Pam, looking from the restroom curtain, decided to make her move. She still had the pistol in her hand that was covered by the sleeve of her robe. Everyone, including Sibal and her two guards, was intently watching the spotlight on the platform. Pam walked behind Sibal and was about to walk between her guards when the head of a figure appeared at the base of the spotlight. The head was crowned with a ram's horn headdress. More and more of the man's head was revealed as he walked up the ramp behind the bed. His bare chest and stomach came into view as the spotlight narrowed in on him. He had on a short skirt covering his groin area.

"What in the… It can't be. It's that preacher," Sibal said.

Pam was about to put the revolver up to Sibal's head when she heard Sibal. Pam looked around Sibal's head and for a moment forgot about Sibal and her plan to kill Sibal. All she could think about was what she saw on the platform. Pam didn't want to believe it. It was Rev. Zackery.

Jason was so shaken that he stood up.

Rev. Zackery continued to walk forward until his entire body was revealed. His oiled, shiny body was bare, except for the headdress, the short skirt, and a white preacher's collar. He crawled onto the mattress just below the girl's open legs. Then he raised his arms and looked up. Immediately, everyone except Pam raised their arm and began to chant, "Come, lord of darkness, inhabit the donor. Come lord of darkness, inhabit the seed." They kept repeating the words over and over, each time louder than before.

"Sibal," Pam shouted.

"What?" Sibal shouted back angrily as she turned around frowning. Her frown turned to shock when she saw the revolver and the face above its sights.

"Tell your guards to put their weapon on the floor," Pam yelled.

"Do it!" Sibal said to the guards standing beside her, who, after hearing Pam and seeing her pistol, had already started to reach for their nine-millimeter Glocks. The men slowly put their pistols on the straw floor and stood up straight again.

"All of them!" Pam commanded. Her voice was muffled by the chanting crowd. "Take off the belts, and any other weapons you have." The guards dropped everything to the floor, including the knives they had in leg sheaves. "Get your hands up," Pam said to Sibal. Sibal complied. Then Pam pointed to the guard on the Sibal's right. "Take off her robe." He grabbed Sibal's robe by the waist and quickly pulled it up. When the robe went over Sibal's head, Pam stepped back and pulled the other guard in front of her and stepped behind him. As Pam had anticipated when the robe was being pulled over Sibal's head, she made her move. Her hand dropped below the robe and shot forward. A switchblade popped open just before going into the stomach of the guard. It didn't penetrate the flax jacket. She instantly pulled it back and drove it up toward the guard's throat as the robe came over her eyes. The guard caught her wrist before the knife reached his throat. Sibal was distraught, discovering it wasn't Pam standing before her. She tried to pull the knife back, but the guard would not release her wrist.

"Put the knife under her chin and push it into her brain," Pam said calmly in the guard's ear.

The guard grabbed the back of Sibal's head, pushed Sibal's wrist back so that the knife was under her chin, and then, forcefully he and pushed her wrist up to her chin. They all expected Sibal's body to fall to the floor, but it didn't.

"Wait," Sibal said as the sound of the knife could be heard hitting the guard's boot. Sibal had switched the blade back inside the handle before it could penetrate her chin. Then she released the knife from her hand as the guard pushed her head back. "You wanted me to introduce you. I'll introduce you as our new queen. Don't kill me! You need me!"

"I don't need you for," Pam said and stopped mid-sentence. The chant had changed. The people were saying something different now.

"The lord is here," could be heard by some and "inhabit the seed," by others. Pam looked up at the man on the table. His face had changed. His skin was red, his chin pointed, and his smile evil. His head was much bigger, and his body had changed into some type of grotesque monster version of Rev. Zackery. He began to lower his body onto the girl. As his six-inch forked tongue protruded from his mouth, he glared at the audience

"Call your guard in the loft. Tell him to shoot that thing in the head," Pam ordered.

"What? I can't do that?"

"Do it or die," Pam ordered pointing the revolver in Sibal's face again.

"Joe!" Sibal stepped out so she could see in the loft.

"Yes, ma'am," the guard in the loft looked out and replied.

"Shoot the seed donor in the head, now!" Sibal screamed.

"What?"

"Shoot him!

Without hesitation the guard raised the rifle, aimed, and fired. The flesh tore into the monster's shoulder and he raised up in anger. Then dark dense smoke rose up out of his mouth. The smoke flowed down, covering the monster, the girl, and the bed. Then, just as quickly as the smoke had appeared, the smoke went down through the floor of the platform. Instantly the monster body transformed back into a normal human state. It was Rev. Zackery again. He looked lost and confused.

"What are you waiting for," Sibal shouted. "Kill him!"

"No!" Jason yelled. "Don't shoot him!"

The second shot knocked off the headdress and tore off the top half of his skull as he fell back and rolled off the side of the table. The audience was in shock. They all turned and looked back at the guard in the loft.

"He killed the donor," someone shouted. At the same time the spotlight operator, who was also in the loft, turned the spotlight on the guard

The guard, blocking the light from his eyes, pointed at Sibal. "Sibal, she ordered me to…" he shouted.

There were several shots fired from two different locations near the platform and the guard fell from the loft to the ground at Sibal's feet. Pam walked around the dead guard and whispered in Sibal's ear.

"Yell out, for them to stop the ceremony, then lead me down to the platform."

"What?" Sibal replied.

"Do it now or die now," Pam snarled as she put her pistol under Sibal chin with one hand, and with the other grabbing the cheek of Sibal's new face. Pam pulled until the stitches were pulled a loose near her ear.

"Okay!" Sibal screamed. Pam released her. Sibal walk forward a few steps. Then, holding her face in place, she yelled at the top of her voice. "Stop the ceremony!"

"Get that man," Pam whispered to the guards, "the one on the last row on the end."

The two guards quickly apprehended Jason and brought him to Pam.

"You had them shoot Rev. Zackery. You killed him," Jason cried out as he watched the men in tights hand Rev. Zackery's body down to four hooded men on the floor.

"Tie his hands around that post," Pam said bending down and picking up the switchblade.

After the guard had tied his hands together around the post, Pam walked up to him, held the switchblade out in front of his face. She pressed the button and the two-edged blade out shot straight out. The side of the blade slightly cutting the side of his right nostril causing Jason to pull away.

"If you say another word, I'm going to send this guard back here to cut out your tongue," Pam said switching the blade back in and tossing the switchblade to the guard. "You two, lead the way," Pam said to the guards.

They moved in front of Sibal and made their way straight down the aisle, followed closely by Sibal, and then by Pam. When they got halfway the spotlight followed them. Once the guards reached, the platform they turned.

"Put us on the stage," Pam said.

Both guards, kneeled on one knee, and cupped the base of their hands together for Sibal and Pam to step in. Pam went first. She placed one foot in the cupped hands, and then stepped up on the guard's shoulder. Sibal did the same. Both guards stood slowly lifting them up. Then they lifted the feet in their cupped hands over their heads. Pam shifted her weight from the shoulder to the cupped hand and then stepped onto the platform floor. Sibal was about to lose her balance when Pam reached out, grabbed her hand, and pulled her to the platform.

"Thanks," Sibal said.

"Introduce me as their queen. Make it good," Pam whispered in Sibal's ear as she led her to the podium.

"Sibal!" one of the men in red stood and shouted. "What do you think you are doing?"

Pam raised her robed arm and pointing at him, she said, "Sit down and shut up."

The man fell back in his chair holding his heart as if someone had hit him. Several others of the head council also had stood, however, when they saw him fall back in his seat, they immediately sat down, in fear. They couldn't see Pam's face well, but they could see her eyes glaring beneath the hood. "Go ahead," she said turning to Sibal.

Sibal pulled the microphone attached to the podium toward her. However, seeing the four men in hooded robes bring the dead guard's body down the center aisle, she waited until they had passed.

"My brothers and sisters, sorcerers of the highest caliber, we know the law. There can only be one supreme leader of this coven" she said reaching into the shelf of the podium trying to locate the trapdoor remote. "It is for that reason that I was forced to stop the seeding portion of the ceremony. We can't seed a new virgin when we already have a supreme leader. That would cause a split and a war in our coven."

The murmuring in the audience began to get loud.

"Listen to me," Sibal shouted. "The last time we had this ceremony, the virgin conceived and bore a girl child, our former supreme leader Tamera. Tamera is dead now. That's why we're here. However, what the head council did not tell you, was that after Tamera was born and they took her to be circumcised, unknown to them at the time, the virgin delivered another baby girl. When the midwife told them that a second baby girl, an identical twin, had been born, they went to kill the second child, which by law should be done. However, the virgin had run away with the baby. Days later, the head council caught the virgin on the roof of a tall building. She did not have the baby with her. She jumped from the building before they could find out where this baby was." Sibal hit the remote with her hand and looked back at Pam for a moment and then she continued.

"They were unable to find the baby. Without her mother, everyone assumed the other baby had died. For twenty-one years, there was nothing, until about six months ago. Tamera began sensing that something or someone was taking her powers. Eventually, we discovered that it was this other child, Tamera's twin sister, who was taking Tamera's powers. Therefore, we started searching for her and we found her. We sent assassins out to kill her. The first was Doug. You all remember him. As assassins go, he was the best of the best. He almost had her. In the end she burned his head up so bad that Tamera had to put him down like a lame horse. Then we sent Jake. He had over a hundred kills. He failed, too. She plucked out one of his eyes. When we recovered his body, he had been burned to a crisp, and his head had been detached. We don't know if the head had been pulled off before or after being burned." Sibal grabbed the trapdoor remote and took a long breath.

"Finally, we all went after her. By all I mean, Tamera, Dutchman, and me. We had her trapped in a church in Tipton. Dutchman and Tamera were killed, and I was blown up. I barely survived. Now at this point, you would think that we would just leave her alone. But no, certain members of the head council decided to send me and several others to kill her. They are all dead except me. I'm alive only because she allowed me to live. I'm alive only because she wanted me to introduce her to you, tonight. I don't know the extent of her powers, however, I do not recommend that she be challenged by anyone here tonight, when the challenging time comes." Sibal paused. "At this time, I would like to present to you, the person who is asserting her legal claim as our Supreme Leader, queen Pamela," Sibal said looking to her right and holding her right hand out hoping the Pam would come to her right and step on the trap door. Pam remained still, so Sibal continued.

"According to our law, anyone desiring to challenge her, will have an opportunity to do so. All challengers will have the opportunity to demonstrate their supernatural powers in a fight to the death. The person exhibiting the greatest powers, or to say it more precisely, the person who is still alive, will become our supreme leader. Do I have anyone who desires to challenge. If so, come now." Sibal stopped for exactly three seconds. "If there are no challengers, we will all, now declare allegiance to our new leader," Sibal said beckoning Pam to come forward to her right side, where the trapdoor was. As Pam moved forward, Sibal stepped back to the side of Pam. "I present to you our new Supreme Leader." Sibal pulled the hood back from Pam's head and then with her hand on Pam's back guided her toward the trap door.

The audience was amazed. The ones who had known or seen Tamera could tell no difference. They thought it was Tamera standing before them. Pam stepped one foot on the trap door as Sibal prepared to push the remote.

"I challenge her," a man's voice shouted out from the audience. "It's time for a man to lead this coven."

Pam stepped back, pushing through the force of Sibal's arm. Pam walked around Sibal to the other side of the podium to get a better look at her challenger.

"Come forward," Sibal said after moving back to the podium.

The spotlight circled the only man standing. It followed him as he moved to the center aisle, walked down the aisle and then to the side of the platform. It followed him as he walked up to and through the curtains red curtains on the side of the platform, where he disappeared, then the spotlight moved to the curtains at the back of the platform, where he reappeared, and finally the spotlight widened as he moved to the front of the platform next to Pam. Pam didn't even look at him as he approach. She stood still with her head bowed. He, on the other hand, continuously glared at her. As he walked up behind her. He saw Sibal mouth something. It seemed like she was mouthing, 'she has a gun.' Sibal looked down at Pam's right sleeve. Sure enough, he could see the tip of a pistol barrel at the bottom of her sleeve. Quickly grabbing her arm, he twisted it behind her back, took the gun from her hand and then he lowered his head next to the side of her face.

"Get off the stage now, while you have a chance, little girl," he growled. His intimidation tactics should have ended there, but he pushed it too far. While he held her arm with one hand, he hit her in the back of the head with the side of the pistol while also clutching some of her hair at the back of her head. Then, he pulled it back hard, and licked her cheek. That was a big mistake. When his tongue touched her cheek, her shoulder shot up, knocking his chin up causing his teeth cut deeply into his tongue. Jerking her hair, he pulled her back and jumped away from her holding his bloody mouth. The pistol and strands of her hair fell from his hand to the floor. He quickly pulled his robe over his head and throwing it on the stage, he charged her. He kicked up at her head with his left foot, but she pivoted and spun completely around facing him, still standing with her hands her at her side. He quickly followed the kick with a hard, right-hand punch at her face. She moved her head just enough for him to miss, however, the power of his punch brought him well within her reach. She brought her three fingers up like a claw and ranked them down his face. Her nails cut deep. The center fingernail cut down the center of his face from his forehead down to the tip of his nose. The outside fingernails cut from above his eyebrows, down across his eyelids, to the middle of his cheeks. With all his strength he brought his elbow back toward her face as blood filled his eyes. She didn't duck. Instead, she knocked his elbow up over her head. Then, when his momentum brought his body around, she hit him in the throat with her pointed knuckles. Holding his throat with both hands, he staggered back a few steps toward the edge of the platform. Pam followed. Behind Pam, Sibal picked up the hair and the pistol that fallen from the challenger's hand. When the man had reached the edge of the platform, he took a defensive stance. Pam stepped forward with her right foot. She pulled up the front of her robe with her hand, and then kicked her left foot toward his groins. He crossed his arms, just below his groins to block her kick, however, her kick never reached them. Instead, she used her first kick to elevate her body for the second kick, which landed forcefully under his chin. He was immediately knocked unconscious and fell like a tree off the platform. The man hit the floor headfirst, the weight of his body pushing his head back snapping his neck. The spotlight, capturing it all, stayed focused of the body which seemed more like an abstract sculpture. His head could not be seen. His arms were out in front. His body was protruding forward, and his legs back with his feet against the wall of the platform. The body appeared to stay that way for minutes, however, it was only seconds. Then it fell over. The audience moaned. Immediately, the same four hooded men, that had taken Rev. Zackery's body, went up to the body, and carried it behind the red curtains to the right of the platform.

As the spotlight moved from the body, up the platform wall, to where Pam was standing looking down at the body, Sibal, handed Pam's hair to one of the men dressed in red. Pam turned, walked slowly to the podium, lowered the microphone, and scanned the audience. Some expressions were awe, some fear, but some to her dismay were anger. Then she spoke.

"Know this," Pam said ominously," anyone who comes against me, defies me, or disobeys my orders will be killed, without hesitation. I claim leadership of this coven. I am the rightful heir. Just like Tamera, I was seeded by the dark master. It was the head council that disregarded my blood. They killed my mother and would have killed me if they had been able to find me. However, because they thought they were following the law, I will be merciful. Still, the head council will have to pay for their crimes." Pam turned and faced the persons in red robes, most of whom were waiting to see the response of the head councilman sitting on the end of the bottom row on the left side. His expression was one of rage. She turned back to the audience. "My sister, my own blood, came after me. I did not come after her. I didn't even know about her. Still, she came after me to kill me. We fought, and I prevailed. I could have killed her, but I did not. I imprisoned her. She will be locked away in a crystal prison for the rest of her life. Tonight, you will have to decide to either swear allegiance to me or die. You will." Pam stopped and held her hands over her chest in pain.

Behind her, the man in the red robe that had been given Pam's hair stood and walked forward. The ends of the sleeves of his robe were pushed together in front of him so that his hands could not be seen. Under one sleeve, he was holding a clay figure of a person. The figure he held had Pam's hair pushed into its head. This man, who was the leader of the head council, also had a long pin in the hand under the other sleeve, that he had stuck into the chest area of the figure. He concealed his hands under the sleeves of his robe as he walked up beside Pam. Pam turned her head toward him and raised her hand toward him. When she did, the figure turned its head and raised his arm in the same direction. The leader of the head council released the pin sticking in the figure's chest and grabbed the figures arm, pushed it down, pinning its arm to its side with his thumb. Pam's arms simultaneously went down and became stuck to her side. Then he pinned the figure's other arm against its side with his fingers. Pam's other arm became stuck to her other side. Then he grabbed the head of the figure and turned it back toward the audience. As the figure's head turned, Pam's head turned. He had control of her. He pulled the needle out of the figure and his sleeves parted. Pam reacted as her pain was relieved.

Nobody could see the figure under his sleeve, except one person. That person was in a tree about five hundred yards away. It was Walt. He had positioned himself where he had a partial view of the platform. There were tree limbs blocking some of his view, and because of the angle of the tree he was in, and the loft opening, he could only see the podium and the left side of the platform. The man in red was only halfway within his view. Fortunately, his right arm and Pam, who was on his right, could be seen clearly. Walt positioned the sights of his rifle on the red sleeve and zoomed in. He saw the figure. It was a voodoo doll. He had seen the witches use them before. Knowing that the man was controlling Pam, Walt raised the sights to the man's head and was about to take his shot, when he saw something move beside the building. He scanned the side of the barn through his sights. Somebody had a gas can walking along the side of the barn pouring what he assumed was gas against the outside walls. When Walt moved the sights of his rifle back to the platform. The leader had moved to the podium. Now, his arm was behind the podium. Walt zoomed back so he could see Pam, too. The man must have pushed the needle into the figure again because Pam was winching in pain. Walt's chance for a shot was gone. If he shot him now the pin may accidentally be pushed so deep into the figure that Pam may be killed. Walt could only wait and hope.

The man at the podium waited for all the murmuring to stop, then he spoke. "Have no fear of this intruder. She comes in here making demands of us, threatening to kill us. Well, I have control of her now. No one, I mean no one challenges the head council, not even the queen supreme leader. We, the head council, and we alone, are charged with maintaining the laws and the continuance of our society. For centuries it has been the head council that ensured our survival. We have endured every force that has come against us. Our traditions are sacred and must be maintained. We will not swear allegiance to her or any other queen. Allegiance to the dark lord, and to our coven, is our ultimate and primary duty, and therefore, following the directives of the head council is imperative."

He stopped and looked at Pam. "Get down on your knees intruder," he demanded. Inside his sleeve, he bent the legs of the figure and as he did Pam went to her knees. Then he faced the audience again.

"It is true that this one was born of the same seed as our queen, Tamera. She is Tamera's twin. However, the law says clearly, that there can only be one queen. By law, only the first-born girl child should be allowed to live. Therefore, when we found out that another girl child had been born secretly, and that this child had been taken out into the world and hidden from us, we acted to recover her and kill her. It took years, but we finally found her. We sent some of our best to take her out, and we lost some good men." He paused. "Anyway, all that doesn't matter, we have her now."

"Kill her! Kill her! Kill her!" the audience began to chant. Pam slowly raised her head.

"We can't kill her yet. She says that she has Tamera imprisoned," the head council leader said as he tried unsuccessfully to push the figure's head down with his forefinger. "We must force her to show us where Tamera is. Then when Tamera has been released, we will sacrifice this one to the dark lord," he said, the strain of trying to push the figure's head. He stopped trying to push the head down. Instead, he tried to push the needle deeper into the figure and looked over at Pam to see her response.

"Sacrifice her to the dark lord! Sacrifice her to the dark lord!" they all began to shout.

The council leader could see the muscles in Pam's neck tightening. He could not push the needle deeper into the figure. It seemed to be getting harder by the minute, and the needle was coming out. He looked down and extended his hand out from his robe sleeves. What he saw terrified him. The figure was more defined. It now had fingers, toes, and a face with dark eyes, a nose, and a mouth with teeth. The figure was holding the needle with both hands, and it was pushing the needle out of its chest. The leader knew that Pam was getting stronger. He had to kill her, now. He believed if he could drive the needle through the figure's heart, he would kill Pam. He decided to give it one last try. He pulled the needle out and held it about a foot away for three seconds. Instantly, Pam's eyes opened, her pain was gone. She reached in her hand through the cut Walt had made in her robe pocket. She tried to reach the pistol in the shoulder holster above her hand, but her arm from the elbow up was still clamped to her side. She tried but couldn't reach the knife in her leg strap. The only thing she could reach was the crystal in her fatigue pocket. Maybe, she could throw it and hit him in the head. She pulled the crystal out of the cloth, out of her pocket, and through the slit in the robe, just as the council leader pushed with all his might, driving the needle forward. Seeing his motion, Pam twisted her body. As she did, the figure in the leader's hand also twisted. The needle missed the figure's heart. However, it did go completely though it's chest on its right side. It also went completely through the leader's hand.

"Ahhhh," the leader moaned. The needle had gone so deep into the figure that the head councilman could not get hold of it. Instead, he pulled the figure and the needle came out of his hand. With the needle still in its chest, the figure was dropped to the floor behind the podium. Pam also crumbled to the floor, her body partially over the trap door. Sibal's eyes widened as she put her thumb on the trap door trigger. The council leader looked at Pam. He was surprised that she was still alive. She was looking up at him. He also noticed there was a blue light coming from something she was holding in her hand. As he watched, Pam turned her hand over, exposing most of the crystal. He saw a woman in the crystal who was frantically pointing toward his feet. He looked down just in time to see the figure stab him in the ankle with the needle. He quickly moved his injured foot back, he stepped on the figure with the other foot. He had its legs and body pinned down to the floor. Only its head and arms were free. He raised his injured foot over the figure's head and as he stomped down, he saw the figure pull the hairs from its head throwing them away from itself. The power of the stomp, completely mashed the figure's head, separating it from the body. With a look of gratification, the leader continued to twist his foot, grinding the now soft clay into the floor. His gratification ceased when he saw Pam slowly get up from the floor.

Pam looked piercingly into the council leader's eyes as she put the crystal back into her pocket and walked quickly, toward him. He moved back just as quickly. When she reached the place where the figure had been crushed, she stopped and looked down. There on both sides of the figure's crushed head were the strands of Pam's hair that her challenger had pulled from her head during their fight. Pam quickly and carefully picked up each strand.

While Pam was squatting, the leader of the council waved for the two guards at the back of the platform to come to him. When Pam had the last strand in her hand, she held her hand out in front of her face and looked up at Sibal. With a half-smile on her face, Sibal raised her eyebrows, looked at, and pointed at the guards, who were pointing their rifles at Pam. Pam looked around in time the see half of the nearest guard's head being blown away, and his body crumble to the floor. The second guard jumped in shock as he turned and watched the first guard collapse to the floor.

"Shoot her!" the council leader yelled.

Then, fearfully he raised his weapon and retrained his sights on Pam's head. However, before he could squeeze the trigger, the second guard's head exploded, and he went down.

The council leader, Sibal, and everyone in the building could hardly believe their eyes. Everyone was on their feet, as a loud moan was heard from the audience. The crowd noise was so loud that it muffled out the sound of the gun shots that had been fired a second earlier from the trees about fifteen hundred feet away. Everyone, except Sibal, believed that Pam had caused the heads to explode just by looking at him. Everyone, except Sibal, was terrified of her power. Sibal knew someone had shot the guards, and she had a very good idea who it was. She looked through the loft opening and could see the trees beyond the parking area.

Pam still squatting, picked the headless clay figure and saw the needle that had been lying beside it. She noticed that there was blood still on the tip of the needle. She pulled a portion of the clay from the figure's body, rolled it and made another head and stuck it on the figure. Then she quickly picked up the needle and pushed the bloody tip slightly into the figure. The blood immediately soaked into the clay. Instantly, the figure wiggled in her hand, as did the council leader. Pam turned and faced the council leader. With her back to the audience, she held up her hand so only he could see the figure.

"Proclaim me the legal supreme leader of the coven, now," Pam said softly.

"Right away, my queen," the council leader said bowing as he moved up to the microphone on the podium. "Let there be quiet in this building," the leader yelled. All the murmuring and whispering stopped immediately. "I declare that Pamela, the powerful, is the sister of our former queen, Tamera. She has the blood of the dark master. She has defeated all challengers, including our former queen Tamela. Therefore, she is the legal and rightful supreme leader of our coven." He bowed and moved back from the podium.

Sibal quickly moved to the podium. "Now, we will all declare our allegiance to our new queen." Sibal held out her arm for Pam to stand next to her on right on the trap door.

"No!" Pam shouted. She walked to the podium, pushing Sibal to her right over the trap door. Sibal quickly moved back. "I am now, going to give everyone a choice. You can either stay or leave. If you stay, you must declare your unwavering, undying allegiance to me. You must follow my orders, without question or hesitation." She paused. "If you leave, you must swear that you will never engage in witchcraft again, and never reveal anything about the coven." She paused again. "Let me be perfectly clear. I'm giving you an opportunity to leave. However, if you leave, you must swear never to engage in witchcraft again. If you leave and are caught doing any act that could be considered witchcraft, or if you stay and fail to follow me in any and everything I command, this is what will happen to you," she said turning toward the leader of the head council.

He looked first at Pam and then at everybody else, hoping that someone would ask her to have mercy on him. There were no cries for mercy, and none was given. Inside her sleeve Pam grabbed the head of the figure, bent it straight back and pulled it off and dropped it and the body to the floor. Likewise, the council leader's head fell to the floor behind him and two seconds later his body fell to the side.

Pam looked back at the audience. She allowed them a few minutes to fully comprehend what had just happened. Then she spoke. "Is there anyone who desires to leave, who will renounce witchcraft, and who swears never to engage in witchcraft, ever again. If so, stand up now!" she commanded.

Nobody moved. She waited as she scanned the room. A whole minute passed and then one person in the back stood up. She was pregnant with her first child. Then a young couple in the middle of the right side stood. It was easy to see the woman was pregnant, too. Then two more very pregnant women stood with their partners. Nobody else stood.

"Everybody standing come down front," Pam commanded. "Untie that man from the post and bring him down here, too. Also, get those bodies out of sight." Pam turned to Sibal. "Get the virgin and have her stand down front, too."

Immediately Sibal directed the guards to get the virgin, who was now conscious but still groggy. When the guard lowered the virgin down off the platform into the group of persons who had been nervously standing there for several minutes, Pam spoke again. "Those of you who are standing here, one at a time, swear that you renounce witchcraft, and swear that you will never engage in, or practice witchcraft ever again, and then leave and take the virgin back to her home or at least wherever it was that they stole her from."

Pam walked in front of the first person to her left and pointed at her. "You first."

"I renounce witchcraft and I swear on my life, I will never engage in it ever again," the first woman said.

Pam stepped in front of the next person and that person swore. As they swore, she moved closer and closer to the trap door. Sibal flipped the trigger guard off the remote control to the trap door and put her thumb on the trigger. Jason, who was standing in front of the trap door, was the last person. Pam stepped one foot on the trap door as she moved to get in front of Jason. Sibal began to push slightly on the trigger. Jason realizing where he was, quickly moved back to his right behind the group. Pam immediately pivoted and followed him to her left.

"You! Stop!" Pam commanded as she pointed. "If you don't swear, you don't leave."

"I swear, I mean, I renounce witchcraft, and swear never to do it anymore."

Sibal, recognizing his voice, stepped forward trying to see under his hood. Jason could tell she was trying to see his face, so he looked at her. There was so much hate in their eyes that it caught Pam's attention.

"Guards, escort them out and lock the doors," Pam said. "And you," Pam said to Jason, "take the virgin back to her home, or at least where they found her." Then she looked at them all. "You have five minutes to leave the parking area. I will know if you don't leave." Pam turned and moved back to the podium.

Sibal got to the podium first. "Now we will declare our allegiance to our Supreme Leader, Queen Pamela. Sibal pulled Pam's arm leading her toward the trap door. The audience began to chant. "Queen Pamela, the powerful, Queen Pamela, the terrible, Queen Pamela, the great," they chanted.

"Close and lock the door," Sibal ordered as she gently pushed Pam onto the trap door Pam watched as Jason was being pushed out the door. She saw him push against the guards, waving for her to move and shouting something to her. She strained to hear his voice through the chants. It sounded like "door," she whispered to herself. "Door, door, door trap, door trap," she said whispered. She looked down and saw the lines splits in the wood on the floor.

"Trap door," she said aloud as she looked up at Sibal who was pushing the trigger on the remote to the trap door.

As the loft door was closing, Walt watched as long as he could. As the entrance door was being closed Jason watched. The trap door and the curtains around the platform fell, exposing the sharp steel spikes. Everyone had focused on the spikes waiting for Pam to fall on them. They looked up. There on the platform was Pam with her feet on both sides of the platform, holding on by her toes, and balancing her body over the spikes. The audience stood and took one loud gasp. Pam instinctively, reached out her hand for Sibal to help. Sibal slowly walked up to the edge of the opening extending her hand. When Pam hand was almost within reach, Sibal snatched her hand back and shouted.

"This is for my face," Sibal said as she kicked Pam's toe. As Pam's toe slid off the edge of the platform floor, she threw her robe above her head, rotated her body, and fell head-first onto the spikes. The robe followed her. There was a flash of lights as the spotlight hit sharp spikes, then the doors of the loft and the entrance doors were closed.

The last thing that Walt saw before the loft door closed was Pam's black robe permeated with the needles and blades. The people standing, blocked him from seeing anything else. Horror struck his heart, and he began to cry in agony. Three cars drove below him as he tried to contain his sorry.

Jason had seen Pam fall just before the door was pushed shut. He fell in shock to his knees outside the door.

Dave seeing some people going to cars and driving away came to the front of the barn and saw Jason kneeling and crying.

Dave ran up to Jason, "What's wrong? What happened," Dave asked putting his arm around him.

"I should have warned her about the trap door. She's dead. Rev. Zackery is dead. Sibal killed her," Jason cried.

"What trap door?"

With tears rolling down his face, Jason looked up at Dave. "Sibal had a trap door built on the stage and I saw them test it the other day when we were here. I didn't tell her about it," Dave sighed.

"Why didn't you?"

"She told the guards where I was, she told them to tie me to a post, and she had one of the guard shoot Rev. Zackery."

"She had Rev. Zackery killed?"

"It wasn't really Rev. Zackery. Well, at first it was Rev. Zackery, but then he turned into this devilish creature, and he was going to rape the virgin. That's when she had him shot."

"She killed Rev. Zackery." Dave began walking back and forth.

"The first shot didn't kill him, it hit him in the shoulder," Dave said and grabbed Dave's arm. "That's when he turned back into Rev. Zackery. She could have stopped them then, but she made them shoot him again. The second shot hit him in the head."

"I heard her. I heard what she said to those witches. She made her choice, she chose them," Dave said frowning. "She chose them, and they killed her."

"But she let me go."

"Who were those people leaving?" Dave asked.

"Pam let them go, too, after they swore never to practice witchcraft again," Jason said.

"Pam let them go?"

"She took over the coven and she gave anybody, who wanted to quit doing witchcraft, a chance to leave. Then she let them, the virgin, and me go." Jason broke down again. "And then Sibal killed her. This is all my fault. If I had only told her about the trap, she would still be alive."

"Some of the fault may be yours, but it's not all your fault. There's a lot of fault on everybody's part. All that doesn't matter now. If there is one thing Rev. Zackery has taught me, it is this. No matter what happens, it is the Lord's doing. The Lord put us here, now, we need to do what He wants us to do," Dave said.

"And what is that?" Jason said.

"At first I thought I was supposed to let those witches go. Now, I believe they should all be put to death. They are evil. They belong to the devil."

"Yeah, that's right, and they were doing all kind of evil stuff, including sacrificing babies to the devil, and drinking their blood," Jason said.

"That's as evil as you can get. Let's do it," Dave said. "Let's kill them all."

"Okay. I'll go get the truck," Jason said.

"I'm going to chain the side doors," Dave said. "Signal me when you get back."

Jason ran toward Billy's truck and Dave went to chain the side doors of the barn.

Nearby, between two cars Walt was listening. He had heard their plan. Walt slung his rifle over his shoulder and ran back toward the tree. He wanted to be ready, if needed, to protect the friends of his dead lover.

CHAPTER 39
THE BURNING

(Wednesday morning 2:45 AM)

The eyes of everyone inside the barn were glued to the spikes under the trap door. All the men in red robes on the platform were gathered around the trap door opening, trying to see the body. Nobody saw the gasoline flow under the side doors into the building. Dave was on one side. Jason was on the other. They both propped two gas cans against the door so they would empty into and around the door. Since they could not chain the door bars on the inside, they chained the outside handles, even though they knew the handles would be easily broken if several persons hit against them. They figured the fire would keep everyone away from the doors at least for a while.

While Dave was pouring gas on the back wall, Jason blocked the entrance door with Billy's truck. He got on the truck bed and slid one of the large containers of gasoline about a foot from the door. He removed top and carefully leaned it against the door. Then, Jason climbed on top of the cab. He uncovered the other large cans of gasoline and kicked it over. The gas gushed out of the can, flowed swiftly down and out of the truck bed, splashed against the entrance door of the barn, and flowed under it, saturating the straw floor around it. Jumping from the cab, Jason ran to the side of the barn and signaled Dave, who was waiting to start the fire in the back. Dave lit a hand full of straw and threw in toward the barn. Instantly, the flame climbed the back wall of the barn. Simultaneously, two flames ran down both sides of the barn. When they reached the side doors, there were two loud whoosh sounds as the flame exploded outside and inside the doors. The whoosh call of the flames was answered by the screams of the persons inside near the doors who were instantly ignited. Other stood motionless for seconds mesmerized by the fiery spectacle of people running frantically around trying remove their burning robes. By this time smoke could be seen coming from the back of the platform. When the head council started running, everybody else did, too. They headed for the entrance door, not noticing the straw under their feet was wet with gasoline.

Jason watched as the flames stopped at the front corners of the building. He lit a handful of straw and waited. He thought that the door would fly open quickly, however, so many people were pushing, trying to get out, that the people at the door couldn't pull the door open. Finally, in a coordinated effort the crowd moved back, and the door opened. When it did, the unfortunate persons at the door were drenched with gasoline as the large can fell through the door. Jason tossed the burning straw to the ground and backed away from the door where Dave was now standing. The flame engulfed everyone near the door, which started a stampede back toward the platform. By now the flame had ignited the drapes on the walls and were climbing up the ropes that held the chandeliers. Like synchronized swimmers the chandeliers dove to the floor smashing the screaming people below and dousing them with raining fire.

As they stood near the parked cars in front of the barn, Dave and Jason looked on as the flames cover the entire wall of the building in the front and the back. However, on the sides near the doors the fire appeared to be going out. Then they heard a loud noise. Something hit against the side doors. They ran toward the side door. They could see a cloudy fog coming from beneath the side doors.

"They have fire extinguishers. They are going to get out," Dave yelled. "What are we going to do?"

"Let's try to push this car against the door," Jason said opening the door of the nearest car.

Jason put the car in neutral started pushing. Seconds later Dave joined him. As they push the car along the side of the building toward the doors, there was very loud noise. It was the sound of the door handles being stopped by the chains locked to them. The chains held initially, however, on the third try, one of the handles was pulled partially out of the door.

"Hurry up!" Dave screamed. "The handle is breaking."

They pushed with all their might. Then, just as they were able get the side of the front bumper in front of the doors, the doors came out, breaking the handle completely off. The doors hit the car and were stopped. Arms appeared through the opening in the doors as Jason and Dave continued to push. Once the middle of the car was in front of the door, a head appeared as a man attempted to squeeze through the opening. When the man saw Dave, he raised his hand through the door. There was a pistol in it. He immediately started firing. Dave ducked down beside the back tire. The man continued firing until he was out of bullets. While he was changing ammo clips, Dave ran into the parked cars and hid. When the man had reloaded, he began shooting into the cars where Dave had gone. He didn't see Jason remove the car's gas cap, and put a piece of torn upholstery down in the hole. Jason waited as watched the pistol being lower, then he lit the cloth, darted into the parked cars toward the front of the barn, and waited. A few minutes later the gas tank exploded. The man's head and arm were instantly ignited as the fire climbed up the wall again

"Good job," Dave said walking up to Jason.

"We'd better do the other side," Jason said immediately moving toward the other side.

This time it took longer to get the car in place to block the other side doors, however they did not stop there. They pushed two other cars close to the building and set them on fire. By the time the job can been completed they were exhausted. By now, the screams of the people had long since been replaced by the eerie screams of the flames. Dave and Jason were filled with conflicting emotions.

"That should it," Dave said as they walked back toward the front of the barn.

"Yeah nobody is going to get out of there," Jason said. "We did it!" Jason held up his hand for a high five, but Dave did not respond.

"I just wish Pam and Rev. Zackery were here with us," Dave said sorrowfully.

"I think Pam sacrificed herself for us. If Sibal hadn't tricked her, she probably would have escaped because she knew we were going to burn the barn down." Jason paused. "I have no explanation what happened to Rev. Zackery. Maybe one of Billy's demons jumped on him and took possession of him."

"No matter what happened to him in the end, I will always remember him as my friend and spiritual teacher. He changed my life. He introduced me to Jesus. Thank you, Jesus," Dave said looking up. "We never could have survived this without You being with us."

"That's right," Jason said shaking his head. "We didn't just get lucky. God had to be on our side."

"Too many things fell into place at just the right time," Dave said. "Miracle after miracle happened tonight. We can't take the Lord for granted. We need to pray and thank the Lord for what he has done."

"I agree, Dave. Soon as we get back to the house, we can both get down on our knees and pray."

"No!" Dave shouted. "We need to pray now! We need to thank Jesus for sparing our lives, but there something else we need to pray for." Dave paused. "Rev. Zackery and Pam are in that fire. We also, need to pray over them!"

"Okay," Jason said. "Let's do it, but if you don't mind, can you keep it short. It's starting to get light. The sun will be up soon."

Dave turned to Jason and held out his hands. Jason held his hand and they both closed their eyes. Jason peeped to make sure Dave's eyes were closed, then he opened his completely and began to look around.

"Lord Jesus, we come to You now, with our heart full of gratitude to You for being with us and blessing us to come out of this alive. Lord, our hearts are also full of sorrow because Pam and Rev. Zackery did not survive," Dave prayed. "We don't know why You do the things You do, but we know that You are good, and Your ways are always right and just. We lift-up Pam and

Rev. Zackery to You right now, accept them into Your eternal care, Lord Jesus."

Jason took a deep breath and breathed it out loudly.

"We need You, Jesus," Dave continued, his annoyance revealed in his voice. "We love You, and we trust You. We will always give You the honor and the praise. In Jesus name we pray amen."

Jason closed his eyes before Dave opened his. "Amen," Jason said. Then, opening his eyes again, he released Dave's hands. "That was a good prayer. You sounded a lot like Rev. Zackery. He would have been very proud of you."

"Was that short enough for you," Dave remarked.

"Actually, it was a lot shorter than I expected."

"You're right," Dave said looking up. "It is beginning to get a little light out here. Maybe we should leave, now?"

"Let's give it a few more minutes."

"I thought you wanted me to keep the pray short so we could leave."

"I did, but I want to see the roof fall in," Jason said. "Then, I'll know that they are all dead."

They walked over and sat on the hood of a 1985 vintage, Pontiac GTO, and watched as the barn burned.

Chapter 40
The Introduction

(Wednesday morning 4:50 AM)

Walt had finally come down from the tree, after watching Pam's friends set the barn on fire. Since they hadn't needed his protection, he decided to take a minute to think. He was sitting in Pam's rental car with the seat reclined all the way back. When she arrived, she had parked on the road just beyond the parking area. The car was turned away from the barn, however he had adjusted the rearview mirror so he could see the fire. In his lap, he gripped his Glock. He began to think about a significant moment that changed life.

He thought about the girl at the orphanage that he liked when he was seven. The scene changes as he sees the past from a bird's eye view.

He is walking up to her. She is standing with her girlfriends. Behind his back, he is holding a bouquet of red roses that he bought with the money he had saved from doing extra work at the orphanage. When he stops beside her, she turns and frowns at him.

"What do you want?" she snaps.

"This is for you," he says holding the roses out to her.

"What are you giving this to me for," she says indignantly.

"He likes you," her friend says laughing. "He wants you to be his girlfriend."

"Well, I don't like him, and I wouldn't be his girlfriend in a thousand years," she scolded.

"No, it's not from me," the young Walt said. "Someone told me to give this to you. You have a secret admirer." Walt handed them to her, quickly turned, and walked away as tears began to well in his eyes.

"Who is he?" Walk heard her say. He didn't respond, he didn't look back, he just walked away.

"That hurt me more than I thought it had," Walt said aloud to himself. "But at least, I learned, and the pain went away." He thought for a minute. "Learned what? Not to give my heart. Well, guess what, it took twenty years, but I did it again and now look at me. My heart is completely broken. This time the pain won't ever go away. Why didn't I talk her into leaving with me? For the first time I loved someone so much that I was willing to die for her, and she loved me. I was the one who was supposed to die, not her." He raised the pistol and put it under his chin. Then he smiled as he looked up to see the dawning of a new day, his last day.

"She changed me," he said. "I used to be a cold heartless killer." He thought about a time when he was is Vietnam. He was on a hill with his sniper rifle protecting a squad of soldiers who were going through a village looking for Vietcong troops. The scene is changes as he remembers.

Walt, the soldier, is looking through the sights of his weapon as his squad enters the village. They are approached by a seemingly friendly Vietnamese family of four. The leader of his squad takes out some chocolate to give to the Vietnamese boy and girl. Walt notices that the boy is holding something behind his back. Walt sees that it is a grenade in his hand. As his squad leader get on one knee holding out the chocolate, Walt fires. The boy falls. Walt then kills the father, the mother, and the sister. Every member of his squad looks up in his direction. His squad leader grabs his radio.

"What in the name of god did you do that for, Walt," the squad leader screamed as he walked toward the boy who was still moving.

"Get back!" Walt shouted as he fired a shot that hit two feet in front of the squad leader.

The squad leader and his men quickly moved back and took cover as Walt fired two more shots, both hitting the boy lying on the ground. The boy stopped moving.

"Cease firing," the squad leader shouted. "That's an order."

Walt fired once more. The body of the boy was rocked by the impact.

"Look in the boy's hand," Walt replied, "but, you better be careful. He has a grenade."

"What are you talking about? That boy didn't have a grenade," the squad leader screamed. "I'll make sure you get court marshalled for this. You just killed a whole family for no reason," the squad leader said as he kneeled and turned the boy over. When the boy was rolled over on his back, the lever on the grenade sprung off and the grenade rolled off the boys back onto the ground and stopped at the squad leader's knee.

"Grenade!" the squad leader shouted. He picked the grenade up, tossed it into a nearby rice paddy, and dived to the ground. There was a loud explosion. Moments later, the squad leader got up checking himself for blood. He raised the radio to his mouth and looked in Walt's direction.

"Okay. You were right about the grenade, but you still didn't have to kill the whole family."

"Did you just say you were going to have me court marshalled?" Walt said into his radio while putting the crosshairs of the sights of his rifle a few inches above the squad leader's head. He squeezed the trigger. The rifle fired and the bullet hit the hut behind the squad leader.

"What are you doing," the squad leader said ducking.

"I thought I saw something moving behind you," Walt said. "So, are you going to press charges against me?" Walt lowered the sight directly on the squad leader's head.

"No! You had to do, what you had to do. You saved our lives," the squad leader said. "Disregard that statement. We're good."

The memory fades and Walt, now back in the car, wipes the tears rolling down his face.

"I used to be a cold heartless killer," Walt said to himself. "She loved me, and gave me my heart back," he said lowering the pistol. "Even though we only had one day, it was the best day of my life. Nothing could have been better. No one will ever be more perfect for me than she was. I will cherish the time we had together for the rest of my life," he paused, "which should be about five more minutes." He holds up the pistol again. "I can't go back to the way things used to be. If there is a life after death, I want to be with her, now. Either way, I don't want to live without her." He puts the pistol under his chin again, closes his eyes, and pulls the trigger. There was a loud noise, but not the kind Walt had expected. Walt opened his eyes, looked in the rearview mirror and saw part the roof of the barn missing. The noise was part of the roof falling in. He looked at his pistol. It had not fired. He had forgotten to cock it. He quickly cocked the pistol and put it under his chin. He heard a different noise this time. It was the noise of a car going past him. He raised up and saw a black sedan pull up and stop fifty yards from the barn just as the rest of the roof fell in.

Twenty feet in all directions around the building, thousands of pieces of flaming shards were blown into the air. Jason and Dave jumped off the car hood and ran into the field a few yards away from the cars to get out of the burning shower. Seeing them, four men jumped out of the black sedan and began moving in Dave's and Jason's direction. Jason brushed Dave off, and then Jason turned around so Dave could check him for any burning debris. Then as Jason was checking Dave, several gunshots rang out. Jason spun and fell to the ground in the tall grass. As he fell, he reached out and pulled Dave down with him. Dave and Jason looked in the direction of the gunshots and saw four men running between the cars toward them.

"Are you shot?" Dave asked.

"I don't think so. Stay down and don't move. I'll go that way. You wait here for a minute. Maybe they will think you are dead, and they will all come after me. If they split up and come at both of us, you go that way, and we'll meet at the car," Jason said and then immediately jumped up and started running between the cars toward the back of the barn away from their getaway car.

The men began firing shots at him. Dave laid there watching to see which way the men would go. Three of them went after Jason. The last one came toward Dave. Dave was about to start running when he saw the last man following Jason fall. He had been shot in his head. Dave looked back toward the road and saw a man with a rifle jump off a car and disappear. Dave ran back into the cars and crawled under a pickup truck and waited. The sun hadn't come up yet, but Dave could see if anyone was standing close to the truck. He looked to his right and saw nothing. He slowly moved his head to look to the front. He saw nothing. He moved his head to the left and saw nothing. He looked down in the direction of his feet and saw nothing, however, he could not see completely. His legs were in the way. While moving his legs over, his heel hit the gas tank. Then he heard something to his right. He turned his head around toward the other side of the car. There in front of him, two cars down, was a man's head. He was on his hands and knees, looking in Dave's direction. His pistol was lying on the ground in front of him. Immediately, Dave began to crawl from beneath the truck as he continued to watch in the man's direction. He saw the man's head disappear, his knees disappear, and the pistol disappear. Then the man's feet moved quickly toward the front of the pickup trunk where Dave was. Dave had slid from beneath the truck and had pushed himself up to his knees, when he saw the man come around the front of the truck. Dave raised his hands to surrender. He saw no mercy, only rage in the man's face. Dave watched as the man turned the pistol toward him. Then suddenly, he saw the man's body go back hard against the truck and then immediately heard a gunshot. Dave watched as the man bounced off the truck and turned his pistol and face away from Dave in the direction of the gunshot. Dave wanted to run but he froze when he saw the back of the man's head disappear. He heard another gunshot as the man fell to the ground in front of him. Even though Dave knew that someone had just save his life, he stayed low, between the vehicles, too afraid to move.

Further down in the parking area, the man closest to Jason fired several shots at Jason. Jason dove to the ground in between two cars. When he peeped through the window of one of the cars, he saw them coming down the two lanes on both sides of him.

"We got him!" one of the men said. "Behind that Ford."

Jason was trapped. He watched, through the car window as the first man slowly circled to the front of the car Jason was hiding behind. Jason could also see where the other man was. He had stopped on the back end, one car down. Jason could see that the man was kneeling on one knee. Jason knew he was waiting with his pistol aimed in Jason's direction for Jason to make a run for it. Everything went silent in Jason's mind as Jason turned his back and slid down the side of the car to the ground. He sat against the car, and accepted death as the only option.

Without saying anything, the man ducked his head and pistol around the front of the car. Seeing Jason sitting there, the man stood up.

"I got him," the man said.

"Hey," Jason heard a familiar voice say.

The man turned and looked down in front of himself.

To Jason's utter disbelief, the man took two shots to his head, and he crumbled to the ground next to Jason. Then Dave ducked around the bumper of the car.

"There's another one over there," Dave said smiling.

Jason quickly grabbed the pistol of the dead man. Without looking, Dave stuck his pistol over the hood of the car and started firing. Jason did likewise.

The other man, seeing his comrade fall dead in front of him, and then being fired at, turned and ran back toward his car.

Dave and Jason watched as the last attacker made his way carefully toward the front of the barn where his car was.

"Let's go," Jason said. "We can't let him get away."

Dave stood up calmly. "I don't think he's going get very far."

"Why is that?" Jason asked as they both watch the man run to his car. "It's too late now, anyway."

"Wait for it. Wait for it." Dave said expectantly.

"What are we waiting," Jason stopped mid-sentence as they heard a gunshot and watched the man fall beside the car.

"What just happened," Jason asked ducking back down.

"I would say somebody just finished our unfinished business," Dave said. "And, I think we should go and meet him."

"What makes you think he's not going to kill us?"

"Why would he kill us?" Dave said. "He just saved our lives."

Jason peeped over the car waiting for someone to either come out into the open or shoot at him. He saw nobody.

"Give me your pistol, Marshall Dillon," Jason said taking the pistol from Dave's hand.

He ejected the clip, wiped the pistol off carefully with his sweatshirt and dropped it to the ground. Jason then took the pistol he had, filled the clip with the bullets from Dave's pistol. Then he tucked the pistol in the back of his pants. Finally, he stood up slowly, held his hand up high, and walked out into the open looking toward the front of the barn where the shooter had to be. He stood there a few feet from the cars and waited. After several seconds, he lowered his hands and began walking toward the woods.

"Come on! We need to get out of here," Jason said. "He evidentially does not want to meet us, and I am fine with that."

With his hands held up, Jason started walking toward the woods where the getaway car was. When he had gone a third of the way, he started jogging. When he got two-thirds of the way he started running full speed until he disappeared into the woods. When he looked behind him, Dave was not there.

Walt had returned to Pam's car. He leaned his rifle against the seat on the passenger side. Then he picked up his pistol which he had left on the seat.

"Well, baby. I couldn't save you, but I did safe your friends," Walt said looking up at the sky. "Your mission is now complete. The coven is destroyed, and now, you and I can be together again. He put the pistol underneath his chin. When he began to squeeze the trigger, he heard another sound. He looked to his left. Someone, one of Pam's friends, was knocking on the window. Walt lowered the pistol, then aiming it at Dave, he rolled the window down.

"I just wanted to say thank you for saving our lives," Dave said.

"Not a problem," Walt replied.

"I'm Dave, a friend of Pam."

"I'm Walt, Pam's bodyguard and," Walt paused, "her boyfriend."

"I remember you," Dave said with a look of shock on his face. "You're the one I hit with my car. You were going to kill Pam." Dave looked at the pistol in Walt's hand. It was aimed at his nose.

"It's strange how things change," Walt said laying the pistol on the seat. "One day you're trying to kill somebody, the next day you're making passionate love to them. You may not believe this, but I was helping Pam with her mission to destroy the coven. That's why I helped you. I actually did it for her."

"I couldn't help but notice when I came up, that you had your pistol under your chin," Dave said cautiously.

"It was my job to protect her. I failed. I told her I would die for her. If I can't be with her in life, I'll be with her in death."

"Well," Dave said, "we are planning a home-going service for Pam, her aunt, and now Rev. Zackery on Saturday. I don't have all the details yet, but I would like to invite you to come and pay you final respects to her. I believe it would mean a lot to her. I'm sure she will be there looking down on us. I'm also sure she would want you to be there. It sounds like you loved her."

"I did very much," Walt said softly.

"Well, if she loved you, I'm sure she wouldn't want you to die for her, not now. If she loved you, she would be glad that you survived. She would want you to live for her, to live your life doing good because of your love for her."

"Actually, if there is an afterlife, I'd rather be with her now. If not, I really don't want to live, not without her."

"You said, since you can't be with Pam in life, you wanted to be with her in death?" Dave asked.

"Yeah. That's right."

"Well, I don't know if Pam told you or not, but she was saved," Dave said.

"What do you mean?"

"I mean she had accepted Jesus as her Lord and Savior," Dave said. "It means that she is going to spend eternity with Him in heaven. It also means, if you want to be with her again, you need to accept Jesus as your Lord and Savior. Jesus was the son of God. He is God. If you don't accept Him, you will never see her again. You do know about Jesus, don't you?"

"Yeah. He's the Jew, who was crucified on the cross by the Romans. He was a Jew, but the Jews don't even believe the He is God. Why should I?'

"I don't know what to say about that. All I know is, when Rev. Zackery told me about Jesus, something happened inside me, and I just believed. I can't really explain it. Either you believe or you don't. I guess, Jesus gives you the desire to believe."

"That's not very convincing," Walt said.

"Tell me this. Did you believe in Pam. Did you believe that she loved you?"

"Yes, I did. I do and I love her even though she is dead," Walt said confidently.

"Well, that's how it is. When you hear of Jesus' sacrifice, it makes you want to believe in His love for you. It makes you want to love Him back," Dave said. "I can't explain it any better than that."

"You say the service is Saturday," Walt said. "Okay, give me your phone number. I'll think about what you said and maybe I'll call you tomorrow to get all the details about the funeral."

"That would be great, Walt," Dave said excitedly.

Walt gave Dave a pen and a piece of paper from the dash of the car. While Dave was writing his phone number, Jason drove down the road. He saw Dave standing beside a car talking to a man. He pulled up beside Dave.

"Hey! What happened to you? I thought you were behind me. I waited for thirty minutes for you to come," Jason shouted. "I thought something bad had happened to you.,"

"Jason, this is Walt a close friend of Pam," Dave said. "He's the one who saved our lives."

"Thank you, sir," Jason said trying to calm himself down. "I don't mean to be impolite, however, we need to get out of here, now."

"Okay, Walt," Dave said. "I'll look for your call."

Dave rushed around the car and got in. Then, Jason turned the car around and drove away. They were passing burned up limousine when they heard a gunshot. Dave closed his eyes and said a silent prayer. Jason looked over at him and saw a tear roll down the side of his face.

Chapter 41
The Surprise

(Wednesday morning 7:15 AM)

Dave and Jason rode in silent for several minutes. Dave was constantly looking over his shoulder to see if they were being followed. Jason was looking in the rearview mirror just as often. They reached a straight portion of the highway. They could see behind them for at least a mile. The intersection for their turn was just ahead.

"Is that a car?" Dave said looking in the side mirror.

"Yeah! I'm going to go down to the highway and turn right." Jason said.

"Rev, Zackery's brother's house is to the left. You think we're being followed?" Dave said.

"I don't know. I don't want to take any chances."

"Now what?" Dave said as Jason turned the car to the right.

"I'm going to pull off the road. Let's see what happens," Jason said taking the pistol out of the dash and checking the clip for bullets.

Jason opened the door, hid behind a nearby tree, and waited. Dave watched through the trees, to see which way the car would go. It went straight ahead. Dave expected Jason to come back to the car immediately, but he didn't. He appeared to be wiping tears from his eyes. Eventually, Jason came back to the car.

"I guess it's safe to go now," Jason said, still emotionally shaken.

"Are you all right? I mean as much as can be expected."

"No. I don't think I'll ever be all right," Jason explained. "I've killed a group of enemy soldiers before one time, with a grenade launcher, but today I just killed hundreds of people. I burned them alive. I know they were evil witches and all, but I murdered three, maybe four hundred of them. The police are going to track us down and those very same relatives that I was trying to protect are going to be condemning me. Then, to make matters worse, I've lost Pam and Rev. Zackery. Why? Because I had to get revenge on those witches for killing my grandmother." Jason stopped and looked up. "And, I'm gonna burn in hell."

"I know how you are feeling, at least some of it," Dave explained. "First of all, that coven of witches had to be destroyed. They were Satan worshipers who sacrificed babies, committed murder, kidnapping, rape, and who knows what else. I know that God wanted them destroyed. We wouldn't have been able to do it without God's help."

"What about the police," Jason's voice got louder. "If they determine that it was Billy's truck that blocked the barn door, then they are going to find him. Then he is going to tell them about us and then we'll fry in the electric chair."

"Billy's truck exploded," Dave argued. "There's no way for them to find out anything," his words slowed, "unless they talk to Billy."

"Yeah, Billy or Billy's demon knew everything," Jason frowned. "He is the only link connecting us to the crime."

"Maybe Rev. Zackery got rid Billy's demon before he came to the ceremony," Dave said hopefully.

"You wouldn't say that if you had seen Rev. Zackery on that platform," Jason said.

"What did he look like?" Dave asked.

"I told you. He turned into a monster, a devil. The witches called out for the dark lord, Satan, to inhabit the seed, him. Then Rev. Zackery walked out. He was the rapist who had the seed they wanted Satan to inhabit. As they chanted, he was transformed into a giant, red, hideous, devil." Jason paused. "The chances are slim to none that that Rev. Zackery casted any demons out of Billy. It was more likely, that Rev. Zackery was reason Billy was possessed by demons in the first place."

"How can you talk about Rev. Zackery that way?" Dave said holding his head.

"It doesn't matter what I say about him now, he's dead," Jason shouted. "The problem we need to eliminate is not Rev. Zackery, it's Billy."

"What are you saying?"

"Nothing," Jason said softly putting the pistol back in the dash. "Let's go."

Jason started the car, made a U-turn, and drove toward Rev. Zackery's brother's house.

"What are you going to do about your grandmother's funeral," Dave said finally.

"Maybe we can find another preacher and have it at the funeral home," Jason said more cheerfully. "It won't be as special without Rev. Zackery, the old Rev. Zackery. What happened to him to make him change so drastically."

"It could have been drugs, demonic influence, or heavens knows what else. I don't know. But I do know this, I loved Rev. Zackery and I will always remember all the good things he did in my life and yours. I don't know what happened to him, but he was a good man, a Godly man, and he was a saved man."

"Yeah, you're right," Jason said shaking his head up and down. "He was my friend. I told them not to shot him, but Pam told them to kill him. She wasn't drugged. She just wanted power."

"I thought you said he had turned into a devil, and he was about to rape the virgin."

"Yeah, I know," Jason said apologetically. "She still wanted power."

"The desire for power is one of the most powerful psychological drugs," Dave said. "However, you need to remember she, too, was our friend. How many times did she save our lives? No matter what she became, we should forgive her. Didn't she let the virgin go, like we planned. You said she even released the witches who swore not to engage in witchcraft ever again. Then, she let you go, knowing that you were going to set the barn on fire."

"Are you saying she wanted us to burn her up with the rest of the witches?"

"No Jason," Dave declared. "She was following plan C, her plan. She was going to escape, too, but she was killed before she could. We all knew we might not live through this. She sacrificed her life for our mission. We should be honoring her, not castigating her."

"You're right again," Jason smiled for the first time in a while. "You're on a roll." His smile went away. "So, what are we going to do about Billy?"

Dave didn't respond. He didn't have an answer. He turned into the driveway, knowing that they had reached their destination.

The house looked unfazed by all the violence and evil it had seen. It sat there with its door waiting like a hungry mouth to consume anyone that entered.

"Do you think he's still here?" Dave asked hoping that he wasn't.

Jason took the pistol from the dash. "I tell you one thing, if Billy comes at me with a knife, a bat, a toothpick, or anything else I think can do me harm, I'm going to blow his brains out."

"Why didn't that come as a surprise to me?" Dave said. "Let's talk to him first. Then you can shoot his brains out."

They got out of the car and walked up the blood-stained steps.

"I'll go in first," Jason said crouching down and slowly turning the doorknob.

"Billy!", Dave yelled. "Are you in there. It's Dave and Jason."

"What the heck are you doing," Jason said looking back at him.

"I'm stopping you for killing him, hopefully,"

Suddenly, Jason felt the doorknob being pulled from his grip, and the door flew open.

"Welcome back," the familiar voice said.

Jason fell back on his behind, and Dave just stood there with his mouth open in disbelief.

"You two look like you have just seen a ghost."

"You're supposed to be dead," Dave said.

"I saw you die," Jason said pointing the pistol at the figure in the doorway.

"I am so glad to see you," Dave said as he walked up and hugged the man tenderly, and then quickly stepping back. "It is you, isn't it?"

"It's good to see you, Dave, and you, too, Jason," Rev. Zackery said smiling. "I've been praying hard. Where is Pam?"

"How did you survive that blast to your head?" Jason asked vehemently.

"Yeah, how did you get out of there. We both saw you when you went in the barn," Dave said.

"That wasn't me," Rev Zackery stated. "That was Billy. The demon in him was much stronger than I thought. He fooled me into thinking that I could control Billy, that I could cast him out of Billy, that I was more powerful than he was. I was prideful. He almost killed me, but the Lord came to my rescue." Rev. Zackery said, backing away from Dave and looking suspiciously at Jason. "Anyway, Billy must have taken some of my clothes when he left. The person you saw wasn't me. It was Billy."

"Praise the Lord! Hallelujah! Hallelujah! Hallelujah!" Dave shouted and did a little dance.

"Thank You Lord, Rev. Zackery is alive, and Billy is dead. Amen," a relieved Jason said, lowering the pistol.

"Amen is right. The Lord looks beyond our faults and sees our needs", Dave said looking condemningly at Jason.

"Where's Pam?" Rev. Zackery asked again.

"She didn't make it, reverend," Dave said sadly.

"The witch, Sibal, killed her," Jason said angrily.

"And what happened to Sibal," Rev. Zackery said frowning.

"She's dead," Jason and Dave said together.

"And who has Pam's body," Rev. Zackery asked.

"It was burned up. The place where the witches were, caught fire and they and Pam, all the bodies were burned up," Jason explained. "Her body is gone."

Rev. Zackery turned and walked back into the house. Dave and Jason followed. After they had all sat down, Rev. Zackery spoke again.

"She was a wonderful little girl. I guess Miss Mammie raised her the best she could. Sometimes, how you come into this world, there's no rhyme or reason to it. But the Lord knows, and He has a plan. There is a thing called eternal justice. For those who start out in a bad situation, God's eternal justice has a way of making things just and right in the end." Rev. Zackery looked at Jason. "If you don't mind, can we say goodbye to Pam and Miss Mammie at the homegoing celebration."

"Yes sir. We can have a double service. I'd prefer that," Jason said.

"Okay that what we'll do," Rev. Zackery said smiling.

"Reverend, do you think Pam will go to heaven?" Dave asked.

"Only the Lord knows. I believe she had a good heart. If she truly believed and trusted in Jesus in the end, we'll see her again in heaven."

"I doubt that you will see me," Jason said. "I don't know if the Lord can forgive me for what I've done?" Jason asked.

"If you're sorry for what you've done, and you ask the Lord to forgive you, He can and He will," Rev. Zackery explained.

"I want to be forgiven and I wish I hadn't done it, but they killed my gramma and I'm not sorry," Jason replied.

"Just trust in Jesus, continue to develop a relationship with Him, and pray. He brought you this far. He will do the rest."

Suddenly there was a loud knock on the door. Dave and Jason jumped in their seat in fear.

"I'll get it," Rev. Zackery said as he got up. He walked to the door and opened it partially. Dave and Jason stood up and waited anxiously. Jason cocked the pistol and held it behind his leg.

"Hello, sir," a voice said. "I'm looking for Dave. I don't know his last name, but he was in that car earlier today."

"Okay, he's here," Rev Zackery said. "Who should I say is calling."

"My name is Walt."

The End

Printed by Libri Plureos GmbH in Hamburg, Germany